THE SKY IS YOURS

A Novel

CHANDLER KLANG SMITH

Hogarth
London / New York

Copyright © 2018 by Chandler Klang Smith.

All rights reserved.

Published in the United States by Hogarth, an imprint of the Crown Publishing Group, a division of Penguin Random House LLC, New York.

crownpublishing.com

HOGARTH is a trademark of the Random House Group Limited, and the H colophon is a trademark of Penguin Random House LLC.

Library of Congress Cataloging-in-Publication Data is available upon request.

ISBN 978-0-451-49626-3
eISBN 978-0-451-49628-7

Printed in the United States of America

Book design by Elizabeth Rendfleisch
Illustration by Danny Evarts
Jacket design and illustration by Michael Morris

10 9 8 7 6 5 4 3 2 1

First Edition

For Eric Taxier,
who never stopped believing in the dragons

PART ONE

PRINCESS IN A TOWER

~~~~~

Anyone with any sense had already left town.
—BOB DYLAN

THE FALL

This is a story of what it is to be young in a very old world.

Even before the dragons came, our city was crumbling. It was as though this place was a dream we'd dreamed together, a dream gone to tatters in the morning light. Dull-eyed humans drifted past boarded storefronts, walking all kinds of animals on leashes. Vultures perched on sick trees in the park. A man clad in garbage bags sang his song in the middle of a bleak avenue as a single taxi sputtered past. Young girls dressed as if for the grave in Sunday dresses and secondhand shoes. Couches appeared on the curbs, were joined there by beds and rugs and tables; whole rooms assembled piece by piece, and the shadows of people occupied these rooms. It became the fashion to speak of oneself in the past tense. Wine flowed from dusty casks into dusty glasses. Chaw regained its popularity; dream-candy, some called it, mutant psychotropic moss mashed up with molasses and additives whose names we'd never know. We chewed it up and spat it out. Neon words went dark, leaving orphaned letters behind. Sometimes we heard laughter in our unfinished apartment complexes, though no one else was renting the units on our floor. We lived in a ruin.

The dragons were old when they were born, or else always had been. In the fall of 301970 AF,* they rose out of the waters at Nereid Bay.* The first to see them was a little girl who sat in a clanking basket at the top of the Wonder Wheel. The motor had stalled, and

---

* AF, meaning the current era—after the human discovery of fire.

she, the only rider, waited patiently for the firemen to raise their ladder. The sky, gray with thunderheads, hung low as a blanket over the world. Out past where old men with metal detectors prowled the shore, an island breached the sea's frothy waters. An island with a pair of eyes. She pointed, but no one turned to look.

There are two dragons, the yellow and the green. One would be an aberration, a hundred would be a proliferation, but two: two is a species, either dying off or just getting started. Two is a threat. Some think they hatched from moon rocks or nuclear waste the government dumped into Nereid Bay, or that the hands of God shaped them from the bountiful putty of our sins. These explanations are as good as any. The fact is, we know little more about them now than that day, fifty years ago, when they rose from the silver waves with dripping wings. Here is what scientists have learned:

1. The dragons never land.
2. The dragons never eat.
3. The dragons never sleep.
4. Ballistics, rockets, stun guns, paratroopers, lassos, toxic sprays, nets, high-pitched sounds, mass hysteria, and prayer do nothing to deter the dragons.
5. The dragons will not let us be.

We cannot name them. We cannot grow accustomed to them. Even those who cannot remember a time before they filled our skies cannot look at them with anything like calm. They are very large and very wild. When they pass overhead, they cast our skyscraper canyons into dusk. Eclipses confuse animals, and the animals of the city are deeply confused. Most of those animals are us.

Sometimes the dragons quarrel with each other. At those times, they seem like a single creature, a snake biting its tail, the helix of DNA. They twist together in a mass, tooth and eye and claw. At other times, they work together, moving over the city in parallel lines, a destruction patrol. They've torched the billboard that said KEEP SHOPPING. They've torched the building shaped like a lip-gloss tube. They've torched every bridge at least once, and Torchtown, the prison colony in the hardest-hit reaches of the lower city, has been en flambé in one place or another fifty years solid, to the day. Dragon fires start at the roof and work their way down. Often they fizzle out of their own accord. Sometimes they catch and spread. But for the most part, the fires are little love bites on the city's face, not too big to extinguish but too frequent, too persistent, to ignore. We've developed slang for all the different kinds: a sparkler, a smoker, a powder keg, a belch—that's when the gas tank blows. We make light when we can. It's not in us to think the worst. Even that little girl said the island winked.

~~~

Empire Island is a winking island too, an island full of eyes. We used to watch one another through its windows, to catch glimpses of ourselves in the mirrored windows as we strolled past. Those windows, cracked or hollow, watch us now, slogging through the cinders on the streets. They watch the skies for more bad news.

It's late afternoon in the death of summer. The dragons are flying low today, churning the air over Torchtown. A cloud front's rolling in, gray and muddlesome. High in the vacant blue stretches a thin white line, a crack in the dome over everything: a teenager in a HowFly, trailing out exhaust.

Duncan Humphrey Ripple V. Heir to the Ripple fortune. The dying city's final prince, in everything but name: his grandcestors never bothered to pony up for a title. But Ripple's got princely looks anyhow, even tousle-haired today in a hooded sweatshirt, pinkened from a deep-pore acne scrub. It's something around the eyes, too long-lashed and dopey for a boy's. Something dreamy, destined. *Late Capitalism's Royalty*, that was the name of his Toob series, printed in bling at the start of each episode. The recappers thought it was all scripted, but nope: Ripple played himself, enacting the most intimate details of his own life, from ages six to eighteen, for an omnipresent camera crew he called the Fourth Wall and spoke straight at on occasion during shooting. It was like imaginary friends. They couldn't talk back or else they'd have to join the actors' union.

Then, three months ago, Ripple flunked underschool and his dad had to contribute the place into graduating him. It was then Ripple's parents decided he didn't get to be a celebrity anymore. In fact, his whole life changed, and not so much for the better. Ripple was pretty fucking jarred. He doesn't understand delayed gratification or compromise, he's never seen the point. He doesn't want to want; he's never wanted for anything. It's not in his nature. He's been spoiled to perfection. He has foie gras for brains.

Ripple rubs condensation from the driver's-side window with his sleeve and squints down at the dragons. The two creatures move in tandem. The green one spews out unending ropes of cursive flame, the yellow one shorter blasts, as if punctuating. *Printed in bling.* Down there in the streets, the fires seem random—unnatural disasters, crap luck. But from way up here, the fires look like graffiti.

Ripple cranes his neck, moves his lips to sound out the words. Who do these poon loogies think they are anyway? They can't even spell. He twists the knob of the HowFly's stereo. Thrumming bass fills the cabin of the air car. He'll show them how a man leaves his mark.

> *BOOM. BOOM.* Wicca wicca whoo. *BOOM. BOOM. Wicca wicca whoo.*

Ripple pumps his fist. His knuckles graze the HowFly's padded roof as his song pounds out of the speakers.

> *The name is Ripple—fuck with me, I'll fuck you up triple*
> *Any torchy lookin' twice end up cripple*
> *Think I don't own you?—Yo' girlfriend showed me her nipples*
> *Nasty-ass slag that she is with her pimples*
> *Cock pocket, you think I'm just drunk*
> *Drunk, yeah with power—that's why they call me the Dunk*

Fuck with me, you end up in the trunk, punk
This city is mine, that's one test you can't flunk

When the female vocalists come in for the chorus, he sings along.

Ohh I'll lick you up and down
Cuz I'm the Dunk
Ohh I'll lick you up and down
Cuz I'm the Dunk
Ohh . . .

His parents commissioned it from his favorite artist, DJ S-Carggo, almost three years ago for his sixteenth birthday, and he's never gotten tired of it. Now he pulls up on the throttle. The music is giving him an idea. He toggles the steering, presses the gas. A bag of bacon crisps tips over onto the HowFly's floor mat; his LookyGlass slides off the dashboard. Ripple ignores it, checks the rearview scope, the pale exhaust streaming in his wake. Nobody can stop him from being famous. He'll write his own name in the sky.

Ohh I'll lick you up and down
Cuz I'm the Dunk
Ohh . . . AAAH!

Ripple shrieks, still in falsetto. He desperately slaps at the various levers surrounding the steering column as first one pigeon, then another, then a third, splatter against his windscreen: a red, feathery Rorschach blot he can barely see past. He finally flips a switch marked VIB, and the glass rumbles, shaking the bigger chunks loose. Ripple peers through the bloodstained glass, the light in the HowFly strangely rosy now. The left engine gulps and belches black clouds, tail feathers.

"Rut-row," Ripple wheezes. The cabin fills with the fumes: it's a smell somewhere between burnt hair and roast turkey. He paws at the ignition switches, finds the knob, and kicks the left engine off. It blows a prolonged metallic raspberry. The HowFly lists to the right, but stays in the air. Next time he takes this rattletrap up, he's bringing the manual.

The HowFly is a recent purchase, an early wedding present from his parents, and maybe a consolation prize of sorts. Ripple is still working out the kinks. One thing for sure: the commercials get it wrong. Since he was a kid, he's been watching the gleaming images of candy-colored HowFlys zooming up, past the deserted cranes, the sooty streets, the cracked and blackened windows of skyscrapers, and then into a clear blue, oddly dragonless sky. As the ad-world HowFly emits its trail of exhaust in a clean white line, CGI clouds shape a heavenly city around the vehicle, one with intact bridges and a puffy amusement park in the place of Torchtown. The view cuts to a close-up of the windscreen: "Rise above," whispers a throaty blonde, her head sliding down into the lap of the contented driver, a handsome youth about the age Ripple is now. He's seen it all a million times on the Toob, enough times to make it seem as real as his own heavily edited life.

But what the ads don't say, and what Ripple now knows, is that a HowFly can go only so far in taking him away from it all. There's nobody up here to come pounding on his door, demanding that he turn down the woofers, but there's also bug guts on the windscreen and crunched-up Carbon8 cans on the floor and the constant bleeps and whirs of the control system where something's always flashing EMPTY. And worst of all there's a notable lack of anybody to blow him; he's probably even farther from the nearest damsel here than back in his room. It's a sweet ride, but he'd rather be parking.

What the commercials also don't say, but what everyone knows, is that only the very rich even bother with HowFlys anymore. Their slogan—"The Sky Is Yours"—got outdated at least two decades ago, when it became apparent that the dragons actually owned the shit out of the available airspace. Since then the brand has acquired an air of willful disregard, of proprietary eccentricity, as during the celestial registry boom a few years back, when it became chic to buy up the stars. Ripple usually takes his wealth and privilege for granted—he saves the bragging for his fame. But taking off in his HowFly from the mansion's sixth-floor battlements, his parents below waving goodbye, he felt, for the first time, something suspiciously like family pride. It occurred to him then that everything—the city, the sky—belonged to the rich, not just because they were born powerful but because they'd die before they'd give it up.

Of course, technically the Ripples don't stake a claim on the city itself. They live to the north of Empire Island, just out of the danger zone, on a cliff overlooking the city's trashed splendor. The best views, Ripple learned early on, are from the greatest Heights.

He pulls up on the throttle again, feels his ears pop as the How-Fly zooms above the clouds. When he's gained altitude, he shifts to HOV and gropes around on the cabin floor, tossing aside empty Voltage bottles, a muscle pump, and a pair of Hotfoot thermal protection sneakers before he finds it: his LookyGlass. He tilts it against the steering column impatiently as the images scroll past: Hooligan, his German apehound, napping on the treadwheel; twelve pictures of doorknobs from the first night he smoked loam with his uncle; an action shot of his friend Kelvin taking a lance to the teeth at the Power Jousting tournament. And then, the Pic, with its box of text over to the side:

Dear Monsieur & Madame Ripple:

I hope this won't seem too forward at this stage of our negotiations, but I've taken the liberty of attaching here a pertinent "Skin Pic," taken by my mother on the occasion of my Legal Endowment to the rights and privileges of my title (18 yrs). I humbly urge you to see the merits of our offer, and to execute the contracts with the due haste I know you know they require.

    At your service always,
    The Baroness Swan Lenore Dahlberg

She's a little chunky, there's no getting around that, and the out-fit she chose—black bustier, ruffled half-apron, white knee socks, black patent-leather shoes, feather duster—brings to mind a corseted penguin more than a chambermaid, sexy or otherwise. But she's half-naked, and the contracts are signed. What choice does he have? Ripple slides a hand down his pants—he still has on his pajama bottoms—and gives himself a tug.

"Rise above," he mutters.

~~~

Just beyond the splintered skyline of Empire Island, the sprawling outer burghs of Kings and Crookbridge, there lies another place, a land of twisted oaks and wild rabbits and haunted sounds in the raf-ters. Wonland County. The Baroness Swan Lenore Dahlberg, now betrothed to the heir to the Ripple fortune, spent her girlhood here, lying on her shingled roof, blowing the fluffy seeds off dandeli-ons that had grown in the gutters, and snagging her petticoats on nails. Her roof was a ship in a green ocean of treetops. There were no other houses for miles. Sometimes she sat on the chimney and watched the dragons through her spyglass. Their leathery wings, their roiling claws, spoke to her of city lights, glamour, and com-munion with like souls.

"They're flying low today, Cyril," she would intone, warming an imaginary snifter of brandy in one hand. "Love me while you can." She'd never seen another child.

In those days, Swanny lived with her mother in a house of thirty rooms. In wintertime, they warmed the space in phases, followed the rattle of the radiators from parlor to hall. Some rooms stayed locked for insulation. They had two hireds, the dentist and the maid. The dentist was for Swanny, mostly. His job largely consisted of tying long threads to certain of her teeth and then attaching those threads to the manor's various doors, which he gleefully slammed. Over the years, as her tooth roots gripped deeper, he moved on to pliers. For the longest time, Swanny saw nothing odd about this.

The maid, Corona, was a sad-eyed muttering woman who called Swanny's mother *"La Diabla"* and skinned rabbits in the kitchen. She carried a rolling pin at all times. Swanny had, on more than one occasion, seen her unscrew the handle of this rolling pin and take a hearty swig, but she said nothing to her mother about it. When Swanny took ill, Corona always came to her room to sew and read stories and sometimes to cry about her son, whose incinerated remains she kept in a ceramic cookie jar in her little room under the eaves.

"The sickness devoured his body, but his eyes—his eyes were still alive. *Esos ojos, esos ojos* . . . It is a mother's duty to remember, a duty and a curse," she would whisper to Swanny, furtively wiping her mouth as she lowered the rolling pin. "Our sins are visited upon our children. Your mother knows this. This is why she turns away."

"Corona, get me a fresh Carbon8." Swanny would tap her glass with a swizzle stick. "This one's gone flat."

It was true that Pippi Dahlberg, Swanny's mother, never even came upstairs when Swanny was sick. She said she could not bear it. To Swanny, this was understandable. Swanny could still vaguely remember the days when her father was dying: the dim, furry light that crept past the velvet curtains in the master bedroom, the bags of fluid, red and yellow and yellow-green, that seeped into his body and then seeped back out. "Your father is not himself," Pippi had told her, as the twisted figure amid those pillows contorted itself unnaturally, like a hand shaping shadows. Pippi had tended him through his sickness, and now she had no nursing left for Swanny. Besides, they were together the rest of the time.

The first time Swanny saw her mother without makeup, she did not recognize her. Pippi was a petite woman, trim and active but not slender, with the grasping look of someone who has always strained against the natural tides of metabolism and hair color. Her fingers tapered to lacquered talons; a stenciled mole marked a spot just above her upper lip. Her skin pressed too tightly against the bones of her cheeks, as if her inner self longed to break through the thin barrier of flesh and at last breathe air. Her shoulders, always padded beneath her rainbow of suits, were square and hunched forward slightly. She seemed as though she might pounce.

Pippi was an Old Mom and an active member of the Old Mom Movement. When Swanny was small, Pippi chaired the local chapter of the organization. The Gray Ladies of Wonland County, as the members called themselves, met each month in the house's ballroom, around a massive mahogany table still battered and gouged from the days of the Siege. The other Gray Ladies, like Pippi, were anything but gray. Their hair came in shades of Burnt Umber, Sienna, Hayseed, Ebony, Dusty Rose, even Robin's Egg—Swanny named the colors from the fan deck of paint samples in her Junior Decorator's Kit. The Gray Ladies wore ostrich plumes and leopard print, patterned tights and fractal hats. Their high heels rang against the ballroom tiles. Though they were Old Moms, not one of them would tell Swanny her age.

According to Pippi, Old Moms were the target of discrimination by prejudiced individuals who believed women should not bear children after menopause. Corona was one of those prejudiced individuals, though she tenderized meat for their luncheons just the same. Swanny didn't know what the dentist thought of them; sometimes she noticed him leering through the ballroom French doors, or leaving his business cards on the table for them to find.

Little Swanny found their meetings dull. She sat beneath the mahogany table, staring at the pointy toes of lizard-skin shoes, and snacked on pinwheels of rabbit prosciutto and cream cheese that Corona had assembled. The other Old Moms did not bring their children. They spoke about the perils of inbreeding (though "Who could blame a person for wanting to keep good genetics in the family?"), thieving servants, seepage, and the declining condition of their various estates, where vines choked hand-quarried stone, and copper monuments crumbled to green dust. Sometimes in their excitement they dropped pamphlets to the floor, with titles like "A Childless Life, Then a Childish Life: Priorities, Motherhood, and the Federal Constitution" or "You Can Have It All, Just Not All at the Same Time." Sometimes their faces were bandaged; soft neck wattles vanished, noses changed.

As the years passed, one by one the Gray Ladies stopped coming. First it was Vidalia, with her antique wigs and her eternal scent of apricots, which lingered for days after the meetings she attended. Her disappearance was the source of endless, hushed consternation in the group, which Swanny strained to hear because she sensed she was not supposed to. But all she could decipher were a handful of troubling phrases: "listened to the rumors," "no time to sell," and "soil testing here—imagine." The next to go was Nanette, who according to Pippi had not worn the same pair of earrings twice in twenty years; later, Swanny would struggle to recall her face, but only an unbroken parade of pearl clusters, teardrop diamonds, and tasteful emerald studs would present themselves. Her departure was met with more sympathy, and with speculation about whether it would be appropriate for the group to attend her son's funeral. It was around this time that Pippi and Swanny began bathing in bottled spring water, heated by Corona in enormous kettles on the stove, rather than in the faintly metallic well water that poured from the house's taps.

By Swanny's ninth birthday, there were no more meetings of the Gray Ladies of Wonland County. There was only Pippi, paying stacks of bills at the immense mahogany table, and Swanny taking tea with her dolls beneath it. Once, Swanny asked why the other Old Moms had gone.

"I wouldn't hazard a guess. They sold in a buyers' market." Pippi rapped more numbers into her adding machine. "Do you know what estates like ours once cost? To buy outright, then restore? One doesn't simply abandon such investments in a panic. The market has a way of correcting itself, you know."

The dentist tuned up Pippi's face from time to time: he used that phrase, "tune up," because the fixes were minor. She'd had her Major Work done the year before Swanny was born, the year she'd retired, the year that she and "Chet" (as she called Swanny's father) had moved out here to "the boonies." Once, and only once, with an air of decided confidentiality, she told Swanny that this had all happened the year she turned fifty-five. Because of this secrecy, the number took on talismanic significance for Swanny. She often wrote it in the soot on the chimney ledge while she watched the dragons. It seemed unlikely to her, at age six or nine or eleven, that anyone could ever be so old. It seemed even more incredible, however, that her mother had once been young.

Before she relocated to Wonland, Pippi Dahlberg had been Prime Mover of McGuffin-Stork, one of the city's leading content firms. Sometimes she told Swanny stories of those days: the time one messenger, scorched and roughed-up but still alive, had glided up to her window on his HowScoot with the necessary contracts, just barely in time for an important meeting; the afternoon she recalibrated the projection settings on a competitor's LookyGlass so that all the models in the other woman's presentation appeared to have sickly green skin and gowns the hue of toxic waste; the diamond brooch her mentor had made for her when she was finally promoted above him that spelled out the words EAT SHIT & DIE.

"The city was glam in those days, glam and dangerous. The dragons separated out the wheat from the chaff. Either you were in it to win it, or poof, off you went! I was just an assistant then: what a time to be starting out. But now I'm dating myself." Pippi, scrutinizing the mirror, deftly swabbed lipstick off her teeth with a handkerchief. "I remember the Strike Ums account. Selling lighters to a city on fire, can you imagine? But we did it. We had content for any product, any day—and subliminals every night. Always onward, always 'What's next?' Powdered Zip to keep you going—I never ate. Well, you're only young once, darling. Besides, the world has changed."

Pippi's stories made little or no sense, but Swanny just liked to hear her mother talk. It was far better than going through the old purse of foreign coins, or sketching pictures by herself. Pippi's voice echoed through the empty house in a kind of song.

"What career will I have, Mother?" Swanny asked one afternoon, obediently holding out her nails for Pippi to paint. Pippi frowned at the cerise polish she'd just applied to her daughter's pudgy fingers.

"Go, go, go, it's no life for a little girl," she said at last. "Now, don't blow on them, that makes ripples."

"But I won't always be a little girl. I'll be a Prime Mover and then an Old Mom like you."

Pippi shook her head slightly. Swanny looked at the little seam by her mother's ear, where the dentist sewed the skin back during "tune-ups."

"The better firms have all shut down, dear," Pippi said. "Too many people have gotten burnt, in every sense of the word. Now it's all shilling on the streets. Tawdry."

"So I won't have a career?"

"Stop crying."

"I'm not crying."

"Well, you mustn't, because there's no reason to. There's investing in your future, and that's nearly the same thing as a career."

"Can I wear the diamond brooch?"

"Yes. When I'm dead."

~~~~

Now, a decade later, the baroness, age eighteen, is packing her hope chest, pausing, every now and then, to visit her vanity mirror and fret about her chins. This morning, over brunch, Pippi commented on those chins, on their plurality, and though Swanny's usual response would involve the defiant consumption of bon bons, today she feels apprehensive. It's begun to occur to her that her meeting with her fiancé, in the flesh (oh the troubling carnal frisson of that phrase!), is no longer a distant hypothetical, but a reckoning soon due. And though she hardly doubts her own beauty, the thought of her body so near his fills her with uncertainties.

Meanwhile, up in the sky above Empire Island, Duncan Ripple might as well be a world away. He wipes jizz from the steering wheel with the elbow of his hoodie. He yawns. Stroking off reminds him of deleting the junk folder on his ThinkTank. It clears the memory, sure, but you have to reboot right after. Otherwise you crash.

Ripple zips up, shifts back into DESC, eases the HowFly down a few hundred feet. He wishes he'd thought to bring a few brewskis. The camera crew used to keep a cooler of them under the craft service table and looked the other way when he and his friends helped themselves. It made for better footage. Now, having a brewski at home usually requires chugging it in the walk-in fridge so his parents don't notice, and he fucking hates shivering. Of course, he could always take the elevator up to the library to see his uncle, who keeps his old-timey icebox full of Bog Peat Stout or Lantern Oil Bock or some other bitter sludge in jugs he calls growlers. But that means having to deal with his uncle, who re-learned English as a second language so he could talk with a British accent whenever he wanted, and who's lately taken to wearing caftans with tassels that snag in the gears of his wheelchair. Ripple really just needs to get a glove compartment chill bin installed, like his friend Kelvin did.

Ripple flips on the left engine, just to try it. More grinding, a hint of fumes—he shuts it down in a hurry. To the shop it goes. He's hungry. He wonders what Hooligan's been up to, if he's eaten any more of that unicorn hide rug Ripple's mom just put down in the third-floor den. Probably did, little stink goblin. Next time the pooch stays in his cage.

It's gotten kind of foggy, Ripple's noticing now; he squints, shifts from DESC to FLY and clicks on the beams. Outside, it's almost like that commercial, only instead of forming a city, these clouds are more like a cave—a gray one, closing him in. He's going to be late to dinner. He hates having to eat with the kitchen staff. The beams are showing him nothing but dense vapor. Ditto the brights.

The first time Ripple took his new HowFly up, his father rode along. Ripple had already taken driving lessons from his impulse-control coach, a squirrelly little guy with an annoying habit of wresting the glide-thrust lever out of his hands, but this was worse. The smell of Humphrey Ripple's toupee glue filled the air car as he pointedly strapped himself in. What kind of butt nugget doesn't trust his own son?

"Dad, I got this," Ripple said, bringing it up nice and easy, just like he'd learned.

"This isn't one of your immersive simulations." Humphrey depressed a phantom brake pedal with his shoe. "You have to take into account variables that run counter to your expectations. There's no foreshadowing in reality."

"I understand reality. I star in reality."

"Starred, past tense. And you don't understand it, Duncan. You understand narrative constructs, virtual realms. I'm talking about cause and effect here, harsh and brutal. The kind without a laugh track."

Ripple wished his dad would stop bringing up laugh tracks; the Toob series hadn't used one since Ripple was in the fifth grade. Which Humphrey would know if he ever watched it at all.

"Why did you even buy me a dragon wagon if you don't want me to drive it?"

"I want you to drive it *cautiously*. And referring to the vehicle in those terms doesn't do much to set my mind at ease. If I ever get an inkling you've been using it to taunt these monstrosities, or—"

"Relax, I'm not stupid."

"Wiser men than you have made worse mistakes." Humphrey's LookyGlass pinged with a stock update; to Ripple's surprise, he ignored it. "Listen, Duncan. I was sixteen once too."

"I'm *eighteen*."

"I'm speaking developmentally here. I know you feel invincible, especially behind the wheel. But you're not. None of us are. Even if you're not seeking out the dragons, you aren't completely safe. Stay attuned. It's best to keep them in your sight. You may find it hard to believe, huge as they are, but they can have a way of sneaking up on you."

But now, Ripple isn't attuned. And that's why he's fiddling with the buttons on the dash when he glances up to see the dragon tail whipping toward him in the fog. He has time to notice the spikes protruding from it—knobby, bone-colored, like exposed vertebrae—the puffy scars amid the dull green scales, the dried starfish and anemones that cling on still, despite the many years that have passed since the creature rose from the seas. It's as though he's never seen anything so clearly in his life. It blocks out all view of the sky, and it's still swinging nearer.

It'll stop.

It'll stop.

It smashes through the windscreen.

Ripple closes his eyes. Pellets of glass hail into his face and hair; the wind gusts around him. He has a sudden sensation, not of falling but of weightlessness, suspension, as though he's been thrown loose of gravity's pull. The breath leaves his lungs; he lets it go. He doesn't need it anymore. A new city, beyond the sky, opens its gate and bathes him in radiance.

Warm radiance.

The HowFly is on fire.

And falling fast.

Every light on the dash is flashing. The hood's popped up, the engine's blazing, and the heat of it pours in through the glass-fanged hole where the windscreen used to be. Ripple slaps every button, twists every dial, yanks up and down on the throttle to no avail. Alarms sound. A cheerful female voice chirps, "Flyby assistance has been contacted. Please be patient. Flyby assistance . . ."

Ripple wheezes. The world's rushing up to meet him. He gropes the floor mats for his inhaler. He feels Sin Bun wrappers, currency, a pebble beneath his hand. He knocks a lever with his wrist. A new light starts flashing.

"Flyby assistance has been contacted. Please be . . ."

Ripple coughs. Dark, gritty smoke tears his eyes. He can't breathe. He sees the light flashing EJEC, EJEC, EJEC, sees the moon roof pop up. Then he passes out.

2

CASTAWAY

The Lady brought the Girl to the Island in a big green tub. The Girl bailed out the bottom with a small pink cup. The Girl does not remember this, but the Lady once told her, so it must be true. What the Girl does remember is the water all around and the sky that drizzled into it. Their world was just a rift for water to pass through. No amount of bailing could keep it at bay.

The Island was a Human Nature Preserve, beyond the dragons' reach. Mountains of garbage formed a new horizon there. Shiny black trash bags, tire towers, a piano with a gappy smile. Rusty machine parts. A fridge with magnets still on it. Dead flowers wrapped in plastic. A mannequin's outstretched hand. A kitchen sink, part of a couch, broken bottles, an iron lamppost. There was no interruption, no bare place for the eye to rest. The litter was the land. The Lady stood at the water's edge with the Girl on her hip, looking in.

The Lady did not bother tying up their tub. She let it bob away. The first house she built was made of rotten crates. The second one was a smashed HowFly with the seats torn out and pink insulation for sleeping. The third house she never built because by then most of her had been eaten by the vultures and the gulls. The Girl couldn't keep them away, but she didn't try too hard either. She needed the company. She liked the vultures best. Their faces were haggard and creased, like the Lady's had been.

The Girl lived on the Island alone after that. She learned to cast the Lady's pantyhose nets to catch the mossy fish. She scraped out the insides of unlabeled cans. When the barges came, tooting, to pile more trash on the shore, she hid, as the Lady had taught her. In time, her memories of the Lady became vague, crowded out by the cries of the gulls. In time, the barges stopped coming.

There were still things she couldn't forget, though. The Lady had told her the Truth about the city, a Truth that God had told to her. This was a Truth that only God, the Lady, and the Girl knew, and now that God and the Lady were gone, the Girl would not forget it.

"That city is the land of the dead," the Lady had told her. It had been in the early times on the Island, when they still lived in the crate house. The night was full of thunder, and the wood so wet that the Girl could press marks into it with her fingernails. "Don't let nobody tell you different. The only people left there is the People Machines."

"People Machines?"

"Unholiest thing there is, People Machines. It's what comes of an unholy union."

"What's that?"

"When a skin-and-bone woman gives in to her lust for a machine, the Devil lets form a terrible thing. A People Machine. All wires inside, no breath of life, no heart and soul. They don't want nothing more than to be the only people on the face of this Earth. You can see them coming a mile away. Their eyes burn up the night. They ride in Contraptions powered on hellfire." The Lady cast her crafty gaze through a chink in the boards. "They won't find us out here in nature. They fear it. They need electricity to survive."

The Girl licked a candy wrapper. "What's a lectricity?"

"It's the juice they feed on. It's what they used to build the dragons." Another bolt of lightning cracked the sky. The Lady nodded. "That's it. Right there. They're looking for us." Thunder boomed back. "And that's God saying we can't be found."

Even now, the Girl sometimes dreams of the city. She runs down cavernous streets, eternally dim in the shadows of the buildings, and the People Machines roll after her, beams shining from their searchlight eyes. Trails of lightning glisten in their wake, like the slime snails leave behind. The People Machines let loose an awful wail, louder than the tooting of the barge horns, louder than anything the Girl has ever heard. She can't even hear herself screaming until she wakes up. But at least these dreams leave her feeling relieved, grateful, even, to awaken in her nest of pink insulation and rags. Sometimes the Girl dreams of impossible things, and then she almost can't bear to open her eyes. She dreams of another pair of arms looped around her, lifting her up; of another hand holding hers, as the Lady's did long ago; of the heavy warmth of another person sleeping nearby; of the smell of another neck, the sound of a laugh answering hers across the rolling dunes of garbage. Once she even dreamt of a face.

The Girl watches the dragons while she scavenges. She stands atop a heap of broken dishes and stares at them dipping through the far-off sky. They remind her of the vultures, of the flopping fish whose heads she smashes on the shore. They are too distant to see clearly, but they mesmerize her. It is hard for her to believe that the People Machines could create something so beautiful.

Not too long before the Lady lay down on that jangly, tattered mattress for the last time, sweating and clutching her forearm and grumbling about shooting stars only she could see—not long before that, the Lady gave the Girl a name. The morning of this naming, the Girl woke up alone in the HowFly to see the Lady tromping her way alone amongst the garbage hills. The Lady was bent forward, yammering, shaking her head, sometimes pausing to gesture at the sky or wipe her nose down the length of her sleeve. She only moved this way when she had been Called on a Mission. The Girl wrapped a checkered tablecloth around her shoulders, pulled on her too-big galoshes, and followed.

The Lady made her way down to the shore, twisting her head left and right, as if to shake water from her ear. The waves were strong for spring; some of the junk had gotten pulled out by the tide, and the Lady began marking the naked sand at the water's edge with a stick. It took the Girl a minute to realize she was writing something there. The Lady had taught the Girl to read a little, really just to recognize words like POISON and DANGER and TOXIC. But the Girl had never seen a word like this. It unfurled upon the Island's lip, a single breath. The Girl stood on an oil drum, frozen, as the word moved through the Lady's arm into the stick into the dark wet sand. The Lady talked to herself, to God, in a low grumble all this while, with patches of humming here and there. Finally she threw her stick into the bay. She glanced up and saw the Girl watching her.

"God told me your name this morning," the Lady hollered. "He said sorry for the holdup. Time ain't the same up there."

"What does it say?" the Girl asked.

"What do you think it says?"

The Girl's mouth moved soundlessly. She tried to take in the whole word at a glance. It was impossible.

"Abracadabra?" she finally guessed. It was the longest word she knew.

The Lady jerked her head. "Close enough."

Nowadays, the Girl tries to put the Lady back together in her mind. She remembers the Lady's feet, the cracked black toes, the bristle on her chin, the tomatoey way she smelled. She remembers the tattoos: the skull and snakes, the wilted rose, the pillars of cloud and fire. The Girl still wears the puffy green coat with the flag sewn on one pocket, the coat the Lady never took off, even in summer. Little feathers poke out of the holes. The coat hides her knees, the sleeves her arms, even though she is a lady herself now, as much as she will ever be. She's passed countless winters alone so far, countless sunburnt summers, and the Lady's old, terrible prophecies of moon blood and brain aches have all come true scores of miserable times, and still the coat is too big. It will always be too big. Sometimes it makes her cry. The Girl is the last human in the world, and she has stopped growing.

~~~~

The Girl floats on her back to watch the sky, that map of weather and time. Her ears are underwater. Her knees and breasts are four little islands just above the waves. She likes to look up on evenings like this, when the dusk is furred with gray. She feels like she's inside of something, that space isn't infinite but woolly and snug, intended just for her. She moves her arms through the water; it isn't warm or cold, just there, a liquid as familiar as her own blood.

And then, in the sky, she sees it: a ballooning dome of white that she first takes for a plastic bag. But as it billows down, it's much too big. It's a sheet, but like no sheet she's ever seen, unstained and filled with air—a cloud touched by gravity. A cloud with something attached.

The Girl flips over in the water and begins to swim to shore.

~~~

A strange girl is straddling Ripple. Her eyes are so blue it hurts to look at them; strands of blond hair halo her face in the pale gold of dawn. Not bad, but Ripple's had dreams like this before. He smiles vaguely, lets his eyelids drift shut—and she presses the dull edge of a rusty pair of scissors against his throat. When she speaks, her voice is uncertain, with an uncanny accent like nothing he's ever heard: "Human? Human? Say your name."

"Don't," he groans. His skull feels swollen on the inside and he can't move his left arm. Or rather, he probably could, but it doesn't feel like it would be a good idea.

"Speak human-speak." She presses the scissors harder against his voice box. "Talk like they do."

"Fuuuck." This is real, and he can't breathe.

It takes all the energy he can muster to grab her bony wrist and wrench the scissors out of her hand. Ripple sits up woozily as the girl scrambles out of stabbing range. She's about his age, eighteen or so—he can tell from her pointy, wild little face—but weirdly scrawny: less than five feet tall, in an enormous army jacket and not much else. She looks like a mouse magically transformed to human. Her big ears stick up through the uncombed strands of her stringy waist-length hair; her front teeth gnaw her lower lip.

"What am I doing here?"

"I *saved* you." She sounds like she can't believe it either.

Ripple is on a saggy mattress, outside. It smells awful, and he's noticing now that in addition to the stabbing pain, something warm is trickling down his arm, warm and sort of viscous, but she's still staring at him, not smiling, not blinking, afraid but respectful—like he's some kind of god. *Cuz I'm the Dunk*, comes the thought, unbidden. Ripple's eyes linger on hers. Who . . . how . . . why . . . Then he glances to his right. Lying beside him is a human skeleton.

"Corpsefucker! Gaah!" Ripple jumps up, somehow dropping the scissors in the process, but before he can pick them up again, a volt of mind-erasing *Ow!* shoots through his left arm. He clutches it to his chest. His sleeve is wet and kind of sticky. He doesn't want to think about what's underneath. "What the—"

"I brought you to the Lady. I *saved* you."

"—the snuff is going on?" Ripple glances dizzily left and right. Flies zigzag through the air; his foot's stuck in a coffee can. Flocks of gulls circle above, weeping. Dunes of garbage cover the ground in all directions and stretch, undulating, to the distant shore: a literal wasteland.

It's barely light outside—early morning?—but Ripple can see the terrain well enough to recognize where he is: Quick Kills, on Hoover Island, the city's now-defunct landfill. It was all in the edutainment special they had to watch for his Desperate Activism course: *Something Really Should Be Done*. Dumping stopped here like forty years ago, when the Enviro Czar complained the whole place was going to sink. Maybe it would have been better if it had. They said it was the biggest mess people ever made.

The mattress is the ghost of a mattress really, not much more than springs. On top of it is the picked-clean skeleton, half covered in a Ladonian flag. Meanwhile, the girl has scrabbled away, crouches behind a nearby splintered crate marked FRAGILE. She peeks out at him furtively above the slats.

"How did I get here?" Ripple kicks the coffee can off his foot; she lets out an "eep!" and ducks back into hiding. "What kind of sick game is this, anyway?"

"Did God send you? From the sky?"

"What?"

She tilts her head. Some yards away, he sees the white deflated folds of his parachute, snagged on trash, blowing in the wind.

"It deployed," he murmurs in wonderment. The HowFly chutes don't have a good reputation. Usually they don't open at all, or if they do, it happens inside the vehicle, causing the crash. He feels nothing but grateful for a second—until he looks back and sees her scrutinizing him with new suspicion.

"Are you . . . human?" she asks. The words dislodge from her throat like foreign objects. She doesn't get a lot of visitors, he's guessing.

"Am I what?"

"Are you a man of flesh?"

That sounds like the sort of question a cannibal would ask. Ripple glances back at the bones. They're old and dry, no meat left on them at all. "I'm not answering till I know what happened to this guy."

"She's the Lady. She's good to sleep near when you're sick."

"How did she die?"

The girl frowns.

"I couldn't save *her*," she admits.

Ripple would feel sorry for asking, but hey, he's not the one who left a skeleton lying around. He changes tack: "How long was I out for?"

"All night. Morning now."

Ripple glances east. Sure enough, the sun is rising, slowly, above the glass towers of the city. The dragons hang almost motionless against the orange sky, twined together like two insects trapped in amber. They seem so far away.

"They don't torch you? Out here on the landfill?"

The girl shakes her head. "Their cords don't stretch that far."

Ripple's arm is still dripping and he's pretty sure it's not motor oil. Plus a few vultures have joined the gulls above, and one of them seems particularly interested in him. "Listen, is there anywhere we can go? Like, I dunno, a building or something? A shelter? Maybe with a first-aid kit and some flares?" No flicker of comprehension from the girl. "You know, someplace less fucked? Anywhere?"

"What is fucked?"

"This place—this whole place—is fucked."

The girl looks around her. "Fucked," she says with approval.

"Where do you live?" The girl hesitates. He adds: "Could we— go there?"

"Are you human?" she repeats.

"Why do you keep asking me that? What else would I be?"

"I need to know," she pleads.

Ripple pats his pockets. His LookyGlass, his expired dormitory ID/keycard, his organ-recipient VIP med badge are all still in the flying car he crashed. And somehow he doesn't think they would help much anyway.

"I have a heartbeat," he offers.

"You do?"

"Want to check?"

The girl emerges from behind the crate, her forehead warily scrunched. She's barefoot, he notices, and there's a strip of duct tape in her hair.

"In there?" she asks, pointing at his chest. He nods, wonders what the alternative would be. She presses her ear against his shirt and they stand that way for several moments while above them the birds scream and swirl. Ba-bum. Ba-bum. Ripple should be scared, but weirdly, he finds himself thinking of that one time his mom tried to teach him to slow dance ("This is a life skill," she told him at the time). He isn't sure what to do with his arms.

"I guess technically, all animals have hearts," he realizes out loud, but the girl shushes him. When she finally pulls away, tears are streaking lines of clean down her dirty face.

"I prayed and I prayed and you came," she whispers.

Huh.

Ripple follows her across the Island. She scrambles over compacted bundles of yellowed newspaper, their headlines smeared—ALL IS NOT WELL—and the charred body of a busted HowScoot. The way she moves is kind of incredible—ducking and scampering, pulling herself over debris by her hands. She's almost four-legged. And she's definitely not dressed underneath that coat, not even a miniskirt. Maybe not anything at all. Ripple is so focused on the shadowy place where those spindly legs disappear under the army jacket that he doesn't see the vulture swooping down until it's too late.

"Hey. Hey—fem! Fem! Watch out!"

The girl turns. The vulture—it's a big one too—descends almost lazily, its heavy black wings sending shivers through the air. Ripple clutches his bad arm, glances to and fro for a weapon—a telephone receiver? A soiled rug? When he looks back, the vulture is perched on the girl's shoulder. He gapes as she strokes its wrinkled head. The vulture pecks her ear, and she giggles affectionately, as though it just whispered an inside joke.

"The hell?" murmurs Ripple.

"This is Cuyahoga." The girl reaches into one pocket of her army jacket and removes from it the gray swinging tassel of a dead mouse. The vulture snaps its jaws, leaving only the tip of the tail. "She remembers you from my dream."

~~~~

The last day of taping, after the film crew packed up their cameras and spotlamps, the boom mic and the craft table, and left Ripple just the way they'd found him twelve years earlier—alone in his room, surrounded with his electronic and proactive toys, his bubbling wraparound Brine Shrimp Experience® and patented pain-response punching bag—he felt emptier than a soul-sucked husk. The room looked dimmer, grayer, not bright enough for shooting: they'd taken the light out with them. Defiant, he socked the punching bag ("Ow, my loins!") and then, in the silence that followed, confronted the showless set with the same glare he'd use to face down an enemy. He was still an icon, even without anyone there to see it.

"Today," he vowed, "the adventure begins."

Now the adventure has definitely begun, and Ripple is less than stoked. The girl lives in a former horse trailer, it turns out, one she has bespangled with rusty wind chimes and what appear to be strings of burnt-out holiday lights shaped like chili peppers. Ripple can't be too sure, because right now he's keeping his eye on the bird. Cuyahoga is perched on the bald pate of a cracked phrenology head, staring at him and occasionally ruffling her feathers. Ripple, uneasily shirtless, shifts his weight on the girl's saddle-blanket-and-foam-pad mattress, and takes another look at his arm. It's tight in the greasy bandanna she used to wrap it. The blood's stopped seeping through, but he doesn't want to think about the nasty gash under-neath, or the long shard of windshield glass the girl pulled out of it with her nimble fingers. On the outside of the bandage, the wound has left a pattern of brown misshapen blots like an archipelago of is-lands. Islands—islands of blood—islands like this one. Oh fuck, he's never getting out of here.

"Hungry?"

The girl stands on the drawn-down ramp of the trailer, backlit by her campfire outside. She holds a steaming cauldron. On her hands, she wears two soiled panda slippers in lieu of oven mitts. Ripple shudders.

"I'm good, thanks."

"OK." She joins him on the mattress. The cauldron thunks down on the metal floor before them; stew slops over the sides. At least, it looks like stew. It smells like fish and burned ketchup. The girl pulls the pandas off her hands and shoves the long sleeves of the army jacket up above her elbows. She digs a linty spork out of her hip pocket and tucks in.

"You sure you don't have any communication with the city?" Ripple asks again, though he knows it's hopeless. "No ThinkTank?

No LookyGlass? No telegraph, no hog radio? We can't tie a message to your vulture's leg or something? There's no way?"

The girl pats his knee. They've gone over this once already.

"I'm so screwed." Ripple slumps back on the bed. "I never even joined swim team back in underschool. All us legacies went out for Power Jousting."

The girl scoops up another sporkful of steaming dinner and pokes at his mouth with it. "Yum, yum."

"Why not." Ripple opens wide. The food is surprisingly good: baked beans, trout, what he really hopes is a noodle. "Mmm." She feeds him another sporkful, then another, then another. "Hey, that's your dinner. Save some for yourself."

"You matter more." She beams.

Ripple sizes her up. In the dim light of the campfire, her tangled, filthy hair almost looks high fashion, the result of a particularly intense encounter with a wind machine. And her face is cute in a feral sort of way; he noticed that before. She's practically hot. With some bodywash and a makeover, she could be Toob-worthy—well, almost, considering her tendency to wipe her nose on her sleeve, which she's doing right now.

"What did you mean, earlier?" he asks. "When you said you prayed for me?"

"The Lady said I was the last one. But I always hoped."

"You thought you were the last person? On Earth?"

"The last *human*. At first I was scared you were one of the . . . others." She wants to say more, maybe, but she trails off and licks the spork instead. "I should have practiced talking-out-loud. It's hard to say everything."

"You're doing great," he reassures her. She picks her teeth with a fishbone in lieu of a reply. "What's your name?" he asks when the silence becomes unbearable.

The girl shrugs. "Dunno."

"You don't know your name?"

"Uh-uh. The waves washed it away."

"Huh. Well, you have—a nickname, or something like that?" She tilts her head, perplexed. "Something people call you?" Wrong question. "Something *close* to your name?"

"Oh! Abracadabra."

"Abracadabra?"

"Abracadabra!"

"Abracadabra."

"Abracadabra!"

Ripple wonders if this is really happening, or if he's getting the landfill equivalent of jungle madness. "How about I call you Abby? For short."

"OK!" She bumps her hip into his. He's still sore from the crash landing, but he manages a wan smile.

"I'm Duncan Ripple. Only fans call me by my whole name, though. They don't know the real me."

In fact, Ripple has never met any of his fans; he's actually never met anybody who wasn't part of his family, his staff, or his under-school. One time a blind beggar lady came to the door of his parents' mansion with a message for him, but he only saw her later, on the security footage, after the guards turned her away.

His fans are out there, though. At the height of his popularity (ages fourteen to sixteen), his Toob series reportedly reached millions of unique viewers, though very few in the metropolitan area. Sure, some were the Empire Island unevacuated, the Survivors still waiting perilously in their flammable apartments or toting their portable electronic devices through the burnt-out streets, tilting them skyward for whatever faint rays of infotainment the battered monopoles could provide. A few were even like him, the city's owners, sticking around to protect their properties and their turf, their presence a symbol to ward off urban decay: the Tangs and the Liddells and the Lowries, each with a full staff, commercial real estate holdings, a mansion the size of a city block. Even with the decades-long exodus provoked by the dragons, their city was still among the most populous in the country during the run of his show. So the local market wasn't one Ripple could ignore. That might be different if the show were airing today—in the last six months, with the fire department's mutiny and the shutdown of public transportation, the local max cume has taken a major dive.

But even in those better times a couple of years ago, Ripple's core audience was out there in the hinterlands, farther away than even Upstate or Wonland County, dwelling in unaffected areas as if no giant monsters had ever risen up out of the seas. Having never seen the rest of the country, Ripple learned his geography from viewership regions, ratings, and demographics. Turned out he was big in the Sprawl, that expanse of asphalt, mini-malls, corporate farms and their subsidiaries that stretches from the Huckleberry River to the Inhospitable West. Sometimes in his heyday, when he was having trouble sleeping, he would contemplate those likely recappers and tuners-in, snug in their single-family dwellings, tooling around via ground transportation, purchasing items in their unlooted stores, and wonder why they would spend their evenings chilling to the Very Special Episode when he had his first wet dream:

```
             RIPPLE (age 12)
It's like I just became a man. A desperate man.
```

Ripple never did figure it out, but his uncle Osmond, who considered himself an expert on the genre of reality, was eager to explain. He said that the dragons had hollowed out the city's center, its stabilizing core, and now all that was left were the high and the low, the opulent and the destitute, the chosen and the damned, those incarcerated by misfortune or the state—and those trapped in gilded cages of their own making. Against such a backdrop, according to Osmond, even the misadventures of a prurient youth such as Ripple seemed of mythic consequence. Ripple thought about the Sprawl and agreed that it did sound super boring where those people lived. By comparison.

"Fems usually just call me the Dunk," Ripple tells Abby now.

Of course, Ripple doesn't really know any girls his own age either, unless you count his fiancée, and he's pretty sure her mom has been writing those letters for her. They have a lot of references to his "boyish good looks" and the need to get documents notarized pronto.

"Dunk?"

"Yeah."

The girl giggles. "Dunk."

In the awkward pause that follows, Ripple goes for another sporkful of stew, but half misses his mouth. The girl licks the drips from his stubbly neckbeard. Ripple grabs his hoodie from where it lies crumpled on the floor and casually arranges it in his lap.

Back in the dorm at underschool, when he and Kelvin used to look through Skin Pics together, they always picked out their favorite damsels, and the nasty-ass slags. Of the nasty-ass slags, they always said, "I'd never do her. Well, maybe on a desert island." Sometimes Ripple has even daydreamed about this nasty-ass slag island scenario, about how the nasty-ass slag would be crying in her shark-bitten tube top, and he'd say, real offhandedly, "This can be our little secret, my videographers drowned," and then he'd bang her in the sand and afterward she'd be all grateful and dance for him in a coconut bra and serve him mai tais and stuff. Now Ripple's on a desert island with a near damsel in *real life*, zero cameras present, and he's shunning her worse than a nasty-ass slag. Of course, it smells like a diaper pail, and his arm is probably infected, and there's no hope of rescue, and a bird of prey is giving him the evil eye, but how often do chances like this come along? Hey, she even tended his wounds. That's basically foreplay. He takes a deep breath and tries the yawn move with his good arm. The girl sniffs his armpit and smiles.

"Time to feed Cuyahoga!" she says.

"Oh boy," says Ripple. He feels himself blush.

The girl crosses the trailer and the vulture flaps once, hopping from the phrenology head up onto the girl's shoulder.

"Pretty, pretty," the girl coos. She reaches into her pocket and pulls out another dead mouse. Ripple balances the spork on the rim of the cauldron. He's lost his appetite.

"You like Cuyahoga," the girl announces. It's not a question.

"Uhh . . . sure."

The girl holds out the mouse by its tail. "Your turn."

Ripple gets up and edges toward the vulture. Cuyahoga's black eyes gaze unblinking at the blood spots on his bandage.

"Easy girl," he says. He takes the mouse; between his fingers, the tail feels rubbery, boneless. "Here you—aah!" Cuyahoga snaps her jaws quick, nearly taking off the tip of his thumb.

The girl smooths the vulture's breast feathers. The vulture pecks her scalp. "Friends."

"I dig." Ripple notices the phrenology head is balanced on a stack of ancient VD cassettes. The one on top shows a buxom blonde with a sputter gun, straddling a cannon amidst blowing sands. Pre-dragons, definitely—probably not a ThinkTank left in the world could read that data. "You must get really lonely around here, huh?"

The girl twists a finger in her ear. "Not anymore."

Ripple grins. This is the opening he's been looking for. Awkwardly, he cups his hand around her shoulder, knobby even beneath that puffy coat. "And what do you do when you get lonely? At night?" His voice sounds low and sexy, like that narrator from the cat-food commercials ("Feeling Feisty™?"). "When you just can't stand it anymore? Huh, fem?"

"Sleep?"

"Oh . . . OK . . ."

"Time for bed!"

So they go to bed. The girl starts snoring right away, and wiggling her butt around and making little whimpering noises, and Ripple lies on his back, willing his laceration to heal faster and cursing himself for the many, many mistakes he's made since the previous afternoon. He hears rodents scuttling on the dunes outside. He hears the ultrasonic cries of bats and the buzzing of insects. He wonders if anyone is looking for him. He wonders if his parents think he's dead. He wonders how long you can stay a virgin before it gives you ball cancer. He dozes lightly, sitting bolt upright half a dozen times when nightmares—of a giant rat gnawing on his arm, of a skeleton with bright blue eyes, of his name spelled out in orange flame—startle him awake.

Finally, he falls into a deep, dreamless sleep. When he wakes up, the girl is straddling him again, slapping him in the face. This time he knows what to do. He doesn't hesitate. He pulls her down on top of him and howls when she crashes into his bad arm.

3

THE DRAGONS' NEST

Torchtown is a hell of a place.

It didn't start out that way. It started with our best intentions. Long ago, before the dragons came, we used to export our criminals. We sent them to faraway concrete compounds, to think about what they'd done. Upon release, the ones who'd thought the hardest came back with a plan to do it all again. Why not teach them to live in a city instead, we asked ourselves. Why not build a city within our city that could teach them to be good?

We nicknamed our plan the Nest. We chose a section downtown where buildings stood empty and derelict and we walled it off, an irregular hexagon. We decorated the iron gates with birds in flight. The Metropolitan Police Department provided guards, but we also hired rehabilitators, men and women who could teach a trade—carpentry, masonry, rooftop farming, first aid—to the most jaded of pupils. We went ahead and made the Nest co-ed. That was our first mistake.

The early inmates took to their new home in the prison colony. Carefully selected among available offenders, their crimes were serious, but never damning, and for some, the Nest was their first, best chance at redemption. They set up shops in the storefronts; they set up house in the apartments. They worked alongside rehabilitators until they learned the trades, and then the inmates taught these trades to one another. Guards strode through the Nest's twilit streets with no more fear than the police strode through any part of our city. For the first few years, the experiment was a success.

That all changed when the dragons came.

We could not have predicted that the dragons would attack, much less that they would attack the Nest with a vehemence unparalleled even in the rest of the city: it would become, in short order, the burningest locale per square mile that statistics have ever recorded, ten times more likely to flare than anywhere else in the metro area. What drew the dragons there? What draws them still? Is it the strange boundary formed by the concrete walls, a jagged shape like a character from an unknown alphabet?

Or is it our hubris, our notion that the city, in this measured dose, could be an inoculation against all future harm?

We should have evacuated the prison colony at once, but in the early days of the dragon attacks, we made a lot of big mistakes. We were distracted, just trying to survive. We were stretched to our limits. HowDouses swooped in to extinguish the prison colony's first few fires, but soon were needed elsewhere. We promised the prisoners relief and left them to their own devices for a time, a few days, a week at most. We did not forget them. But they felt forgotten.

First they rioted. Then they killed their guards.

We could have reacted differently. But it was a moment when retaliation, swift and brutal, drew cheers and votes, in the sky or on land, it made no difference.

We sentenced the prisoners to life, unilaterally, without the benefit of trial. We no longer sent guards into their zone. Instead, we topped their walls with electrified barbed wire, automatic sniper rifles, observation platforms with hourly patrols. And Torchtown, as it was now called, became the destination for cold-blooded murderers, rapists, the perpetrator of a zillion-dollar Match King scheme—the worst of the worst, irredeemable. We threw them all in together and dropped crates of supplies over the wall: canned goods, bottled water, live chickens, mass-market paperbacks. We released no one. We figured it was just a matter of time before they killed one another off.

But the inmates didn't kill one another off, at least not entirely.

They made some kind of society in there, amid the abandoned buildings we deprived of city gas for fear of explosions—amid the daily jets of dragon flame that burned the roofs above their heads. Under the shadow of those wings. They certainly made some babies. Even now, with our own streets nearly empty, we hear their new babies crying in the night. These are the Torchtown natives, born into the original sin of their ancestors' convictions. In the last fifty years, who knows how many have lived and died behind the walls? Nowadays, none of the originally incarcerated remain; "inmates" have taken on the aura of legend. The only inhabitants are their children, their children's children, their children's children's children, generation upon generation, fast to breed, fast to die, born into a nest of violence with no knowledge of the world outside.

We should knock down the walls. We should let them all out. But we cannot, for fear they might deal us the justice we deserve.

The prison colony is a special kind of damage to the city: a collaboration between the dragons and ourselves. A hell we built together.

But in all the years of destruction, all the blasts and combustion, one corner of Torchtown has remained untorched. It's a small building, three stories with a basement, unassuming dark red brick. SHARKEY'S CHAW SHOP reads the sign. The letters are made of solid gold. No broken windows. No lock on the door. There's an alligator chained to the fire hydrant outside—the only working fire hydrant in Torchtown.

Sharkey is IN.

Eisenhower Sharkey is the oldest man in Torchtown. He's forty-three years old: a native, yes, but with firsthand memories of those inmates of yore, the fabled ancient dead. Sharkey's lost most of the hair on his head, but none of it on his chest. Or back. He shaves twice a day. He had a mustache for a week twenty years ago. One of his swillers made the mistake of asking if it was ironic. He shot the swiller twice in the chest, dumped his body onto the roof of a burning building, and looted his apartment. Then he shaved the mustache. He's been clean-shaven ever since.

Sharkey is six feet tall with his hat on. He's five foot two without it. He wears high-heeled boots with silver taps on the soles and wife-beater undershirts beneath the jackets of his zoot suits. He has eleven gold chains and one gold medallion shaped like a dragon tooth. The knuckles of his right hand read FUCK. The knuckles of his left hand read FIRE. Sometimes he carries a backpack full of explosives. Most of them are fireworks. Some of them pack a little more punch. He uses a pince-nez when he reads. He likes the classics: *The Governor of Illinois*, *They Call It Criminal*, *Richard III*. He calls himself a "cultivated man." He never forgets a face. He can rattle off the name of every man he's killed to the tune of "I Am the Very Model of a Modern Major-General." Of the women, he says, "Aw, let 'em rest in pieces."

It's been a while since Sharkey killed a woman. It's been longer since he's had one. He's picky. A connoisseur. And the women in Torchtown are too young for him. Not too young in years, though he does like 'em on the older side. But too young in attitude. With no culture, no respect for what came before.

Eisenhower Sharkey steps outside the Chaw Shop, chewing. He's wearing the pin-striped slacks of his zoot suit with the suspenders down and dangling in loops around his hips. His undershirt is white. His gold gun glints in its holster. No jacket. No hat. He paces on the stoop and chews some more. It's a beautiful morning in Torchtown. The sky is blue. No fireballs. Two club rats, laughing, round the corner to his block. They're still dressed from the night before in flashy mesh tops and latex pants; one of them carries a fire extinguisher. They see him out on the stoop; they duck their heads, they cross the street. One glances over his shoulder, his eyes curious beneath singed-off eyebrows. Sharkey spits emphatically down the concrete stoop stairs. The club rats quicken their pace.

Sharkey's got no family and won't say more on the subject. But rumor has it his mother died in a fire, his father died in a fire, his uncle and brother and sister and cousin died in a fire. There sure aren't any of them left, and wherever they've gone, Sharkey's not telling. People sometimes say that Sharkey knows where the fires will be because the ghosts tell him in his dreams. Sharkey says, "I'm alive. They ain't. Maybe they should take some pointers from me."

Sharkey scrapes the tap of his high-heeled boot against the stoop, looks at the pale line it leaves on the concrete. Nobody knows how he knows where the fires will be. But he does. If Sharkey's in a place, it won't burn. Sometimes at night, when Sharkey bothers going out, packs of natives follow him from club to club. Sometimes Sharkey'll lead them to a club, order himself a drink, then drop an unlit fire-cracker and slip out the door. When the place explodes behind him, the firecracker goes up like a warning. Don't follow too close.

Sharkey used to lead raids out of Torchtown. The last one he led was thirteen years ago. He's through with all that. It's a young man's game. These natives are too soft, anyway. Brought up to duck and run. Out on an expedition, one fuck-up and it's curtains for everybody. The inmates back in the day, they had discipline. He still thinks fondly back to the Siege, nineteen years ago now. That was an operation with scope. Vision. Five raiding parties, a dozen men to each, working in tandem: it wasn't a jailbreak, it was an up-rising. The kind of thing that gets your name in the history books. Brass knuckles and baseball bats, an oil drum for a battering ram. Chain saws. They marched through tunnels with their dragon-flame torches lighting the way. When they came up to daylight in Empire Island, they hijacked a packboat full of cheap plastic crap off the docks and made their way to Wonland.

Out there, they took over for the better part of a week. Felt like the better part of a life. They lived like pirate kings. Bashed in the doors of houses and pillaged. Some of the places were empty. Some of them weren't. Sharkey saw his first private bowling alley, shot his first horse. He'd been on plenty of raids to Empire Island, but this was different. This was nature, unspoiled. It makes him sad, how it ended in so much bloodshed, a man's head spiked on a fence, but he wouldn't trade those days for the world.

Most everything nice in Torchtown came from raids Sharkey's helped to orchestrate. Like his books. The Chaw Shop electrolier. His rhino-foot trash can. His pinky ring. He still helms expeditions, commands them from afar, but he's lost his old ambition. Today's raiders are small-time, out for a score. They want currency, porn, they want to turn it all over right away. Torchtown's all they know, all their parents and grandparents knew. It's all Sharkey knows too, but these young ones lack imagination. They don't have an interest in the finer things. Most don't even think about staying out there. On the loose.

Sharkey goes down the concrete stoop steps, opens the metal hatch in the sidewalk, descends the concrete basement stairs. He's making chaw today.

Sharkey steps beneath a clothesline hung with undershirts into the concrete cell. He's got a kitchen upstairs where he cooks his dinners, but the basement is where he performs his art. In the middle of it is a hulking gas stove, six burners, covered in blackened grease. On the counter to the left is a cast-iron frying pan, a set of knives in a wood block, a stained wood spoon, and a jar of grain alcohol. To the right is a set of wire mesh shelves, laden with cans, jars, bottles, vials, pouches. A lidded crate fills the bottom shelf. The only window is close to the ceiling, barred up and gray with soot. Sharkey lights the wall sconces. He spits what's left in his mouth into the spittoon. He puts the frying pan on the burner and cranks up the flames. He figured out how to reconnect the gas a long time ago.

Sharkey makes ninety-two varieties of chaw. His recipes are secret. They're not written down. He uses bricks of loam, dried and packed with rice in crates, but no one knows from where. And beyond that his ingredients are a mystery to everyone but him. Today Sharkey starts off with a jug of hard apple cider, boils the liquid away to a glaze, then douses the pan with the contents of a small brown bottle and a pinch of fine red powder from a cup made from an ox's horn. The liquid sizzles. Sharkey adds some yellow dust and a dash of salt from a shaker shaped like a piglet in a chef's hat. He lightly drizzles the hissing pan with maple syrup. Then he upends a jar of molasses. He thumps the bottom a few times; when the glob finally plops out, liquid spills down onto the burner below. Sharkey curses. He's sweating. The gray strands in his chest hair sparkle in the dim light. He's making variety number twenty-nine, Forbidden Fruit Jam.

When the mixture on the stove is stirred and bubbling, Sharkey tastes it, mutters, salts it some more, adds a few slices of dried apple that fall into the brew as white and spongy as human ears. Then he flips off the heat, takes a new brick of loam from the crate, and carves off a hefty slice with his biggest knife. It's dull greenish-brown and fragrant, like musk and fresh-turned earth. Sharkey crumbles it into the goo on the stovetop and folds it in with the wooden spoon.

Once it's cool, he'll come back down and shape it into ropes: penny width, two-penny width. He'll wrap them in rags and twine and hang them over the clothesline to dry, in heavy twisted coils like nooses. Then he'll douse the pan with grain alcohol and light it on fire, to burn away the traces. He's not sloppy with his chaw. A new batch is never tainted with the aftertaste of the last one.

Sharkey peels off his undershirt, dunks it in the bucket on the floor, and pats his face with it. Then he takes a new undershirt from the clothesline and walks up the basement stairs. No one's on the street. The gator snaps at him. He kicks it in the teeth.

4

ELECTRICITY

Duncan Ripple is writing his name on the inside of her body. The Girl holds him close while he grunts and puffs, breathing in the woolly dust of the saddle blanket beneath them. His face is hot and near, but she doesn't notice the greasiness of his unwashed hair, the clogged pores on his forehead, his morning breath, or his chapped lips, which occasionally scrape her neck. When he mumbles, "Hey, fem? Hey, Abby, is this technique too hardcore for you?" she doesn't respond in words-out-loud. Instead, she shapes her mouth around each letter of this foreign alphabet, spelled out in flesh and ache and heat, reverse tattoos on the inside of her skin. The *R* is two pairs of legs, hers looped around the top of his. The *I* is a blue-green vein pulsing in his temple. The *PPLE* is the beginning of *please*, the beginning of *pleasure*. Ripple moves clumsily, persistently, in his one-handed push-ups. A mouse skitters across the floor. In the corner of the ceiling glows a patch of morning sun. Who is he? Who is she? Answers beyond language fill her heart. The Girl breathes in the Island, this fragrant museum of a dying world, then breathes it out. The horse trailer contracts around them, her bird lets out a cry, and the shapeless, nameless thing within her vanishes in the new light.

Later that morning, Ripple lies stunned, stark naked except for his bandage, on a sagging trampoline near the water's edge. The Girl adorns his hair with bows of dental floss. Gulls tug at fish entrails amid the busted rocks.

"Whoa," he murmurs. His eyes are shut. "I can't believe it. We just fucked."

The girl ties a bow around a lock of his chest hair.

"Yes, fucked," she says with approval.

Ripple coughs noisily, wheezes. A few yards away, a gull squawks in answer. "I mean, *I* can believe it, but for you, it must be like discovering fire or something. Well, you've already got fire, I guess, but you know what I mean. It's like an alien came down from Mars and ate your planet's face. Only, you know, in a good way, obviously."

The girl adds another bow to his sideburn. She tries to tie his neckbeard, but the stubble there is too short.

"And I mean, not just once, even. That was three times in under two hours. I was like, 'Let's go, wench,' and you were like, 'Bring it, son.' That was hot. That was so hot I didn't care about the bird watching us. This is the best day of my life."

The girl admires her handiwork. "You're pretty."

"I bet I hit your G-spot. I'm pretty sure. I struck oil the first time I drilled."

The girl winds what's left of the dental floss around the metal trampoline frame. "Dunk?"

"Yeah?"

"Go fishing now?"

He yawns. "Do what you gotta do. I'm pretty comfortable right here."

"OK!" The girl springs up and bounces off the elastic mat. Ripple raises himself up on his good elbow.

"Hey. Hey, Abby?"

She's zipping on her coat. "Uh-huh?"

"You don't happen to have a few brewskis lying around, do you?"

She rubs her nose with the back of her hand, perplexed.

"Never mind."

He watches her as she scrambles away, over the exploded macrozap ovens and cracked PVC pipes. Then he looks beyond her, out to where the water is flashing and twinkling with the full light of midday. No barges toot in the distance; no HowFlys roar overhead. So ironic, the coolest thing he ever did, and no one was around to watch. What would his old film crew say about this?

The thought makes him sad for a second, but only a second: he feels too good for regrets. Sure, he could stand some pills to numb his arm, but right now his body's making quite a few chemicals all on its own. Maybe sex works like acupuncture, or massage, or that weird thing with the candles and suction cups. Holistic healing—his mom believes that shit. It needs some time to work, is all.

It might be just as well to stay lost another day.

~~~

Katya Ripple can tell her husband isn't enjoying the lap dance. She tosses her head, platinum hair cascading down her back, and shimmies, moving her shoulders faster and faster until her bangles shake. Her manicured hands cup the delicate fabric of her gold lamé bikini top, then release its central clasp. Out bob two tanned, perfect breasts, naked except for tasseled pasties. Distractedly, Humphrey fingers her ruby-encrusted belly-button ring, plucks the G-string of her thong. She grinds her hips a moment more, then rises and sulkily sashays back to her pole in the center of the room.

"Please call the police," she says, squeezing the polished chrome between two toned thighs. She enunciates her words with the uninflected care of a nonnative speaker. She arches her back, the column of her throat, and the platinum hair sweeps the floor. "It's on your mind too, I know. Three days, Hummer. I'm asking you. If anything, we've waited too long."

"What good will it do to get them involved?" Humphrey sighs. His toupee is askew. He releases the backrest of his leather recliner and reaches for the half-empty bag of BacoCrisps on the nearby end table. "It's a family matter. I grease enough palms as is. Besides, he's a big boy. He'll get found when he wants to get found."

Katya kicks her leg and hugs the pole in a waist-high knee hold. She licks the daggerish spike of her six-inch metallic heel. "And that child the Torchers took, whose electric heart they used to charge the motors of their SkateBlades? He didn't want to be found?"

"Kitty, that's an urban legend. Next you're going to tell me Duncan's been abducted by Leather Lungs."

"He would have texted. He would have called."

"He would've thought twice about worrying his mother."

"Don't tell me you're not worried too."

"I'll get *worried* if I have to contact the Dahlbergs for a postponement. Pippi doesn't miss a trick; she'll make us pay out the nose. Leave it to your son to pull a stunt like this less than two weeks before the wedding."

"He's your son too. Maybe he has cold feet and is too afraid to tell you."

"Good. He should be."

"You don't mean that."

"Honey, you're a beautiful dancer. Don't let this weigh on you so much." Humphrey picks up his copy of insight guru Maxwell Gladfish's *It Feels Like You're Thinking!* and brushes orange crumbs off the expanse of his hand-stitched maroon velour tracksuit. He chews noisily. The conversation is over.

Katya frowns. She swings around the pole one more time, then traipses across the room to switch off the low funk music emanating from the room's surround sound.

"Get me a tallboy while you're up?" Humphrey calls after her as she leaves the room.

Katya Ripple, age thirty-seven, strides down the hallway of her mansion in a T-back and bunny pumps, thinking about her son. She's never lost the model's way of walking, and even now, she holds her shoulders low and her head high, her narrow hips swinging with cool insistence. Her face is the Golden Ratio made flesh; her body is hairless, ageless, and glowing. Generations of Ripple men leer at her from their portraits on the walls to either side. Her placid eyes do not return their gaze. With these shoes on, she's nearly tall enough to see the dust atop the picture frames.

Katya enters the kitchen. Two dishwashers sit at the center island, eating their lunch beneath the elaborate mobile of copper pots and pans suspended from the ceiling rack. They look up, and in their eyes, Katya recognizes the gaze men have cast in her direction since the first stutters of her adolescence. For an instant, she is twelve again, walking the frozen river to school, while the neighbor boys and tradesmen stare down from the banks, halted by the sight of her. Her homeland had given up religion on principle, deposed God like all the rulers before, but on the back roads they still practiced the ways of awe.

"Pardon," she murmurs. She pulls open the steel door of the walk-in fridge; steam pours off her body as she enters.

Katya came from Smoczek, a village in the snowy east of an adjacent continent. In her country, girls entered at birth into the National Attractiveness Registry and underwent development inspections once annually—if their aggregate scores qualified, they were permitted at age fourteen to apply to the National Modeling Bureau, which shipped top candidates overseas for government-sanctioned fashion and prostitution assignments. It was either that or chop work in the National Ice Manufactory. Although her life hasn't turned out exactly as she dreamed, Katya still feels that she chose wisely.

She wasn't so certain her first two years in the city, which she spent on a packboat in the Empire Island harbor, cramped in a hull moist with the breathy hope of a dozen other girls, every surface strewn with lingerie. Always she was bent toward a radiant mirror, eyes wide, mouth an O of surprise, an implement of beauty trembling in her hand. Always was the fear, indistinguishable from the sensation of being awake, that she would gain a pound, an inch, a blemish, a size—that she would take up too much space, and she would be sent back. There were more where she came from, so many more. So many pretty girls. And Empire Island was no longer even a top destination: all but the richest and most eccentric zillionaires had already fled the city.

Why, Katya sometimes wondered, would anyone stay here, least of all these men, who could carry their wealth and privilege with them far away—to the ends of the Earth? It would be a long time before she learned how riches could tether you in place, harness you to a burdensome hoard that made true flight impossible. The remainders, as the city's bachelor holdouts were known, were in one sense already married, to their real estate and their investments in infrastructure, to the institutions their ancestors had founded, the streets in their names. To disavow these assets would cause a panic, a loss; it could wipe them out entirely.

Nevertheless, she and her sisters hunted those remainders with a single-minded desperation. The models were technically competitors, but they banded together as orphans in a strange land do. Katya hardly knew her own body, her own thoughts, from the others'. By day, they piled together in the packboat waterbeds, golden limbs interlaced, makeup smearing the pillowcases. By night, their eyes burned in their starved faces as they designer-stripped on the catwalks of deserted nightspots to the songs of distant and not-so-distant sirens.

Humphrey Ripple, financier, didn't speak to her the first few times she lap danced him, but he kept coming back to her stage. Once he brought a videographer. Once he brought his impotent brother. When at last Humphrey chose her, brought her to his home, he gave her an identity: a name that rendered her visible in his world, collapsing though it was. And when she bore his child, he gave her a vocation too.

Katya peels a grapefruit, delivered here from the balmy tropics, and eats a bitter slice. She knows what Humphrey is worried about. He's worried Duncan is on the chaw, like the Liddell heir was a few years back. Enterprising torchies do smuggle it out to the surface streets sometimes; some say they travel in the sewers, on a network of dinghies for hire, mercenary gondoliers circulating drugs through the city's intestines, down where they're safe from the fires. Katya's no innocent and she'd like less than anyone to see her son carted off for Chemical Re-Education, but privately, she thinks Humphrey's giving their son a bit too much credit. Duncan left the house in a Bot Tot hoodie and a pair of pajama pants with dolphins on them. He uses his inhaler like a pacifier (it's to treat his affluenza, which the pediatrician reassured her "isn't even a real thing") and his sneaker soles light up when he walks. Probably the worst thing a chawmonger would give him would be a bloody nose, or some condescending advice. Besides, even if Duncan was using, that's no reason why he would vanish for three days. If anything, he'd be back to get more cash. Chaw doesn't make you disappear. She should know. She's tried it herself.

No, what worries Katya is the possibility of an accident, up there in the sky. When she first arrived in the city, she didn't know what to make of the dragons. They looked beautiful to her then, the sort of danger, vital and carnal, that spoke in the voice of poetry, nothing like the file-cabinet bureaucracy that reduced her face to the sum of its angles and her waist and hips to their ratio. But death is death is death. Motherhood has taught her there is no poetry in that.

Katya picks up a tallboy and presses the cool aluminum can to her forehead. To her, things are very simple. When your child is missing, you find him and bring him back. She remembers following Dunky's damp footprints through the hallways of their house, when he was small and naked and refusing to wash himself; coaxing him back inside when he went out on the roof to pet the gargoyles. This situation is the same. But Humphrey doesn't think Dunky is a missing child—he doesn't think Dunky's a child at all anymore. He thinks that Dunky is a man, and that it's high time for him to start acting like one. Which means it's up to Dunky to find himself. No matter how lost he gets.

Doesn't Humphrey know that problems like this don't just go away on their own? Sometimes Katya thinks her husband is a little boy too, stubborn and sulky. Maybe no one born into this family ever chooses to grow up.

Katya leaves the fridge, holds the beer out to one of the dishwashers in the kitchen, a wide-eyed youth not much older than her son. His resemblance to the men of her hometown is no accident. All the members of the house's staff are imports from her village, cousins and the offspring of cousins, the stepchildren of former friends, charity cases and bastards sent over by packboat at her request. She once believed that surrounding herself with them would bring her comfort, make her feel that this was at last where she belonged, but nothing could be further from the truth. The servants' quarters make a new village here, a wing of rooms and hallways not so different from the cottages around the ancient square, but she has barred herself from entry. To these maids and underbutlers, she is a lady of this city now; through their eyes she is foreign even to herself. The native words fall leaden from her tongue: "My husband asked for this. See that he gets it." The young man nods mutely, and wipes sandwich grease from his hands onto his apron before reaching for the can.

Katya skips the stairs and takes the elevator to the sixth-floor library: between her pole dancing and the morning's session on the mechanical equicizer, she's gotten her exercise for today. Besides, the elevator is one of her favorite rooms in the house. Lined with gilt-edged mirrors, a sumptuous ruby carpet underfoot, it's modeled after the dressing room at Fiona Tres Belle, where Humphrey took her at the start of their second date, after he explained that her bra top and tramp pants were most likely verboten at the four-star restaurant where he'd made reservations. It was then that Katya truly realized he was serious, not just out for a good time.

Men are always ashamed of the women they love.

The ebony doors part with a pleasant chime, and Katya tentatively steps into Osmond Ripple's domain. She and her brother-in-law are not exactly friends. Back when she and baby Dunky were learning English together from the talking giraffes on the Kinder-Speak, she heard Osmond refer to her as "aphasic," and he sometimes still speaks in Cockney rhyming slang just to exclude her from conversations. She retaliates by spreading rumors among the servants about the unseemly origins of his rosacea and night terrors. Still, they're family.

"Osmond?" she calls, stepping onto an elaborate Oriental rug that depicts a monkey and a bird quarreling amid cherry blossoms. He answers from the upper stacks with a lengthy coughing fit. She scales the spiral stairs two at a time. "Osmond, are you all right?"

When she reaches him, Osmond is waving smoke from in front of his face, an elaborate bronze hookah towering on the floor beside him. One blue-and-gold tube still lies in the crook of his arm. He appears to be rereading *Back There Again*, a book he pressed on Dunky repeatedly throughout childhood.* An ermine throw covers his lap, half hiding the bald tires of his wheelchair. The air reeks of loam.

"Sick again," Katya observes, not unkindly.

"It is a fine disease, and I am its finest symptom." Osmond pounds his chest. He's dressed in a kimono today, the frizzy strands of his gray hair pulled into a messy topknot.

"Osmond, I need your help."

"And I need my privacy, you trespassing strumpet. Put some clothes on. If I want to see you naked, I'll go online."

"Dunky is still missing." Katya pauses as Osmond draws another lengthy, burbling pull from the hookah tube. "I hoped that you could find him."

"I will say this slowly. A genetic predisposition to bewilderment is rarely overcome. As the biologists say, when a penguin makes for the mountains, he can't be stopped." Osmond exhales a floating zero, then an exclamation mark. "All I expect to find today is a brief respite from my suffering. Now, get out of this library before I retrieve my thwacking canes."

"You don't understand. Humphrey won't call the police—"

"Pardon?" Osmond fingers the joystick of his wheelchair, rolls backward several inches. His nostrils flare; his bristly jaw juts for-

---

* This classic epistolary novel is written in the form of a letter from an uncle to his young nephew, recounting the tale of the uncle's long-ago adventures in a mythic land located "halfway between the Realm of Dreams and the Empire of Light." Though the uncle encounters a multitude of beasts and monsters, underground caverns and dark forests, in the end he identifies the ultimate threat to heroes like himself as something much more prosaic: forgetfulness. In the concluding passage, the uncle tells his nephew that, though the boy himself is not a hero, he is faced with an even greater task. "True power lies not with the hero, however quick his sword, for one day he will surely fall," the uncle writes. "True power lies with the one to whom he tells his story, for it is only this Rememberer who can grant immortality. He is the lord of us all."

ward like the underbite of an angered boar. "Could you repeat that immense presumption, please?"

"Humphrey won't—"

"You told me I didn't understand. *You* told *me* I didn't understand. Who are you to tell me what I understand?"

"Osmond, I—"

"Dislodging a Ripple heir from the humid jungle of your loins does not, I am afraid, qualify you to perform psychological examinations."

"I only want—"

"In fact, I understand the situation full well. Your mentally disabled son has wandered off, no doubt to squander his inheritance copulating with machines and submitting to a vast array of brutal muggings. You beseech me to save him from himself. And I ask you, simply, to leave me to whatever chemical tranquility these weak herbs can achieve."

Katya crosses her arms over her pasties. "I will not leave until you promise to help."

"And I will not help until you promise to leave."

"Done."

She extends her hand to shake. He waves her away.

"Spare me the formality, gigolette. Any moisture on those palms is suspect. Now, how do you propose I accomplish this daunting task?"

"Do you remember when we had Dunky microchipped?"

"He howled inconsolably for days, as I recall, dramatically clutching his negligible incision. And then wept when the stitches were removed to reveal no scar. Tell me again, what medical practitioner condoned you bringing the pregnancy to term?"

"All little boys want scars, Osmond. They think it makes them brave. There was a time, I think, when you wanted one yourself."

Osmond snorts. "You're doubtless unaware that the BlackBean is not a tracking device. Its sole use is as an identifier of the amnesiac and the dead. A face tattoo for your boy would have been cheaper and more efficient."

"That isn't true, Osmond. A BlackBean shows up on scans. Remember when the fire department burned, and they scanned the ruins for the fire chief's Bean? They've done it with others too—that Laidly brother, the Tangs' last nanny . . ."

"But that's preposterous. We have no idea where he is. I would have to cruise a low-flying craft over the whole of Empire Island and the outlying environs, touching down to investigate every blip on the viewscreen." In the cloudscape of his drowsy eyes, a spark catches, ignites. "It would be . . . a quest."

So Katya sounds the call once more: "Will you please find my son?"

"Very well. But you must do me a favor in return."

"Anything, Osmond."

"Fetch me a smoked porter from the icebox." He pats the armrest of his wheelchair. "Since you're already up."

Katya's demeaned herself enough for one afternoon, but she smiles placidly just the same. "Bring my son home, and I'll fetch you anything you want."

~~~

A ceiling of electric white. Rats with eyes like blood drops. Tile everywhere, gleaming. The People Machines have caught Abby. They have beamed her up into their Contraption and will never bring her home. They watch her through their one-way glass. They think she cannot see them, but she can: their bleached robes are half-materialized ghosts haunting her reflection.

As Abby gazes into the mirror, she sees too that they've turned her small again. They've taken her back in time to the days before the moon blood came, before her hair grew long enough to tangle, before words even, when she was just a wisp of herself, a soul awaiting a woman's body.

Abby hears footsteps in the hall, shouts, crashes, rodent squeaks. Abby hears, and she feels fear, because this has all happened before. Someone is coming for Abby—more than one Someone. And the Lady is with them.

"Ow! Abby, what the snuff?"

Abby and Ripple are wrapped in the old green coat, zipped up together, and he's grabbing her hands to keep her from punching him. Feathers erupt from a new rip in the jacket's shoulder as she twists and squirms.

"Sorry, sorry," she pants. She snuggles against his chest. Her heart is still jumping.

"You really got my bad arm there." Ripple unzips them, sits up. They're spending the night camped out on the Pier, a stack of busted packing crates near the water's edge; a cool breeze makes the air smell almost clean. Or maybe, after ten days and nights, Ripple is just getting used to it. He gently prods his bandage to gauge the damage. "Fuuuuck."

"Sorry." Abby clumsily drapes the jacket around his shoulders. "I didn't mean it."

"Nah, I know. It's cool. I'll shake it off." He squints at her. "What was up with that anyway? You OK?"

She nods. "Bad dream."

"I figured." He pauses, watches, as Abby scoots to the edge of the pier and dangles her legs off. "I used to have some scary ones when I was a kid. Like I had this one that the dragons burned down our house and Hooligan—he's my dog—was running around with his fur on fire, and everyone was like, 'Dunky, save him, save him, you have to save him!' And I woke up, and my mom was all, 'Pro, you wet the bed,' and I was like, 'Oh yeah? One minute ago you were calling me a hero.'"

Abby gazes off across the waves, at the distant lights of the Electric City. The ripples on the water distort them, mix them with the moon.

"Get it? It's a joke. Because I had to pee on him to put out the fire. I didn't actually wet the bed." Ripple stretches. His recappers out in the Sprawl were always talking about how funny he was, but you'd never know it from this audience. "Stop being so quiet. It bugs me."

"Dunk?"

"Yeah?"

"Will you go back to the city?"

"Uh . . . I hope so. I mean, I guess it just depends."

"Depends?"

"You know, on if I get rescued or not." Ripple picks at an insect bite on his thigh. "Were you having nightmares about how it would be if I left? Because I'd understand if you were. I'm the best thing that's ever happened to you, I get that. With great power comes great responsibility. Like, I *own* you, you know?"

Abby leans her head on his shoulder. "You own me."

"Achievement unlocked." Ripple fondles her breasts. "Mmm. You've got such primo ta-tas. They're, like, exactly the same size."

"Dunk?"

"Yeah?"

"When you get rescued, will you still own me?"

"Sure. I own you forever."

"So you'll come back?"

"Yeah . . . or . . ." He hesitates, glances around. There's Cuyahoga, some yards away, perched sleeping on a hat rack like a huge feathered chapeau; there's a mound of broken bottles, glinting in the moonlight. Amid the trash dunes there is stirring, but nothing human—no sign of visitors from land or sea. No witnesses. "Or maybe I'll take you home with me."

"Home? To the Electric City?"

"Why not? I have a ball pit in my bedroom. You'll like it."

"I don't know . . ."

"Relax, it's never going to happen. Just let me have my fantasy."

"What's a fantasy?"

"Something so sweet and weird, it could never ever happen." Ripple contemplates this. "Like being stranded here with you."

Abby grabs him by the ears and pulls him into a kiss. Ripple pushes her onto the pier and puts a hickey on her collarbone. They're deep into the making out when Ripple hears something—a grumbling in the distance. He freezes.

"What was that?" he whispers. They lie still. Abby gazes past him, wide-eyed. Her lower lip trembles.

"The People Machines," she whispers. "They're coming."

"Who?"

"The People Machines." Abby starts to cry. She smacks her head. "The Lady *warned* me. She sent me the scary dream."

"Fuck that." Ripple rolls off of her, knots the jacket like a loin-cloth around his waist. The grumbling noise is louder now. He squints up into the night sky. "I'm gonna flag them down."

"Dunk, no!"

"Don't daunt me." He grabs a splintery plank with nails stuck in it and brandishes it, caveman-style. "I got this."

Ripple scrambles up over a mountain of disassembled refrigerators and past a leaning tower of truck tires. Abby whimpers. The grumbling noise is overpowering now, more thunderous than the voice of God. Then, descending through the low-hanging violet clouds, it emerges: an enormous, darkly gleaming craft, all curves and chrome and circular headlights. It is shaped like the body of a spider, armored in a carapace of black steel. Smoke pours from it, and Abby can feel the heat of its churning engines from the ground. A yellow beam sweeps the garbage dunes, searching, searching. Abby cowers in the shadows of the pier. She hears Ripple yelling, but his words are consumed by the roar of the Contraption and her own white-hot terror.

Abby shuts her eyes. Her heart is thudding in her ears. Images flash through her mind without sense or reason: the Lady's tattoos of a pillar of cloud and a pillar of fire; the dead, jellied eyes of a killed fish; the endless letters of her name, jumbling together, too fast, one after another after another. *Someone is coming.* Then she sits bolt up-right, gripped with sudden knowledge. The only thing worse than being taken is to be left behind.

Abby is shaking, but she wobbles to her feet and creeps through the garbage dunes. Like a giant crab, the shiny black craft squats on six legs. A creature has emerged from a hatch in its underside. From the waist up, he is a man, gray-haired and grizzled. But from the waist down, he is made of wheels, new rubber and metallic spokes: a People Machine.

Abby half hides behind a drawerless chest of drawers. Ripple and the People Machine are talking to each other. Ripple is explaining quickly, using his hands. Some part of her still wants to run, over the rusted springs and gooey puddles, to a secret place in the Island's rotting heart. But when Ripple glances over his shoulder nervously, her eyes meet his, and she knows what she must do. His face is so beautiful. She steps into the unnatural light and stands there, naked and blinking, offering herself to the electricity like a sacrifice.

5

SNAPDRAGON

Getting teeth pulled never bothered Swanny much. She didn't hate the sting of the Novocain needle, and before she got old enough to drink with her mother in the evenings, nitrous offered the only thrills she got. Sometimes, breathing through the mask, she would squeeze her eyes shut to see points of light that, with only a little effort, she could reshape into the city's dazzling fires.

Swanny kept these pulled-out teeth in a Bakelite jewelry box, which played "The Way You Look Tonight" whenever she opened the lid. Sometimes she would arrange the incisors on the velvet cushion into little smiles. Sometimes she would balance a single molar on one finger, a pearl solitaire. The box began to fill, her mouth was full already, and still new teeth kept coming. She got to know the feeling of teething well, the vampirish taste of her own blood, the perversely pleasant itch of bicuspid breaching gum. And after the dentist did his work, it amused her to poke at her own cheek as though it were a stranger's skin, to feel pins and needles on her tongue, to watch her lip droop like a stroke survivor's, to slur her words. She loved ice cream, and brie, and foie gras, and flan, and the invalid treatment she got after an extraction: dinner brought to her in bed on a domed tray, her mother worrying aloud about dry sockets and her bite. She was almost thirteen before it occurred to her that it had all gone on much too long.

Swanny's own body was a mystery to her. Her late father's study had an extravagant library, but the medical textbooks she had glimpsed on the highest shelf as a child disappeared by the time she was permitted to use the ladder. What little she could perceive down her throat and between her legs indicated only that the inside of her was very dark. Her illnesses were strange and sudden: a sharp jab in her side; an ache in her ribs. They subsided without ever seeming to completely go away. Once, when she dared to ask her mother what caused them, Pippi replied tersely, "Growing pains," and strode briskly from the room. A few minutes later, Swanny heard the furious sounds of Pippi's Contrology workout video echo through the house.

The medical textbooks were off-limits, but the other books weren't, and between her lessons in elocution and tap Swanny liked nothing more than to laze on the gray velvet fainting couch, one finger in her mouth, a book propped up against the cushions before her. She loved descriptions of parties, loved the way a passage of dialogue could sparkle like a flowing river or glitter, cold as frost. She learned that the words "wit" and "intrigue" on a dust jacket signaled the presence of great things. In a single, dizzy night she read the entirety of *Canfield Manor*, anxiously cutting a new tooth on a sterling napkin holder all the while; in the end she wept, not for the drab little heroine, but for the passing of a world. The characters were figures upon the deck of a fabulous cruise ship, laden with stores of crumpets and conversation, receding endlessly into the horizon, and Swanny stood on the dock alone with only a broken Champagne bottle in her hand.

The women in the books sometimes had mysterious ailments, treated with laudanum or heated water; they went mad, drank poison, bungled abortions, and went to the countryside for their health. Sometimes they drowned: seaweed mingled with their hair in thick, dark strands while their eyes gazed on, sightless and knowing; sometimes they wasted away. More than one coughed blood into a handkerchief. More than one owned a pearl-handled revolver. But in none of the books did a woman have thirty-two teeth in her head, seventy-four more in a box, and a new one on the way. In none of the books did a woman have a dentist living in her house.

Swanny convinced herself that she was dying. The idea suited on the wall; a fire roared to life in the fireplace. She peeled the ermine stole from around her neck and draped it over the back of a chair. "Now, tell me, dear. Isn't it glorious to be a woman? Don't slouch."

Swanny slurped gin from the lip of her glass. "I just wish you'd warned me."

"I suppose you'll be moody now, and wanting chocolate. Oh, the things you forget. But it's just like a bicycle. It comes back." Pippi tossed back the rest of her drink and shook herself another. Swanny observed, with some mild surprise, that her mother was already drunk. "Swanny, have I ever told you the difference between a first and second wife?"

"No."

"The difference between a first wife and a second wife is that the first wife has fake jewelry and real orgasms. The second wife has real jewelry and fakes the orgasms!" Pippi let out a little shriek; her laughter rang against the vaulted ceiling. "You'll be a first wife, of course. Nothing tawdry. But don't worry. We'll get you the real jewelry too."

It was that night, for the first time, that Pippi explained what investing in Swanny's future meant.

~~~

Pippi Dahlberg homeschooled her daughter Swan Lenore from the ages of thirteen to eighteen in a battery of courses that she herself designed. Some of the courses lasted a matter of weeks; others were ongoing over the entire five years. Regardless of their duration, the rigor and mental discipline demanded for each was considerably intimidating. Swanny was awakened each day, Monday through Friday, by Corona in the gray, pale hours of dawn and summoned to the "schoolroom," a chilly glass annex at the back of the house that had once been called the solarium. Her mother was always there waiting, alert and bony and bejeweled, with a vial of espresso and an emery board. On wicker chairs, separated by a wicker tea table, her. She thought to ask for a quilted dressing gown for her birthday, but her birthday was three months away. By then, she thought dolefully, it would be too late. It irritated her that her mother, the dentist, and Corona were all keeping the news from her, as if she were an infant. She was no infant; she was a woman, a perishing one.

Gazing into the abyss made her sultry with wisdom. She posed in front of the full-length mirror, dressed in a gauzy slip, practicing for when she would be a ghost. She took sumptuous baths. However, early one morning, when she woke up to find her white monogrammed sheets soaked in blood, she started screaming and wouldn't quit.

"I'm dying, I'm dying," she wailed. "Make it stop."

Pippi pounded on the outside of her door. "Unlock it this instant."

"I can't." Swanny pounded the mattress with her fists. "I'll never rise again."

Over the noise of her own sobs, Swanny heard the sound of the heavy key ring jangling to the floor, her mother's curses, the key clanking in the lock. Then Pippi was in her room. Her shoulders were high; her dark eyes smoldered. She strode across the seal pup rug. In a sudden fit of terror, Swanny clutched the blankets to herself. Pippi wrenched them from her hands and cast them aside. Both looked at the purplish-red stain spreading from the seat of Swanny's silk bloomers to the Egyptian percale.

"Oh, thank God," Pippi sighed. Her face relaxed. She reached into the pocket of her housecoat, took out a jade earring, and clipped it absently to one lobe.

"I'm dying," Swanny repeated with less conviction.

"Not yet, darling." Pippi smiled wryly. "Give it a few years."

That night during cocktail hour, Pippi served her a martini. For thirteen years it had been a Shirley Temple; now it was a martini. Swanny imitated Pippi and ate the olive first.

"I hope Corona showed you how to use the LunaTamps."

"There were instructions on the box."

"I'm not paying her to hand you a box." Pippi flipped the switch the women faced each other in all kinds of weather. Wind howled in the cracks of the skylight panes; sodden leaves on the lawn gave way to muffling snow, and then to the moist buzzing stupor of spring. A chalkboard on wheels tilted near one wall, its green slate never completely erased. Ghosts of names and dates mingled with the vivid silhouettes of fresh verbs and adverbs. At the wicker table, Pippi branded each completed worksheet and test with a red rubber stamp bearing the family seal. The mimeographed papers left ink on Swanny's hands.

The courses Pippi taught included Penmanship, Self-Defense, Table Manners, Nutrition, Reproductive Health, Portfolio Management, Elocution, Ballroom Dancing, Evening Wear, Gemstones of the World, Wills and Trusts, Home Surveillance, Decorating, Voice, The Hostess's Role, Prenuptial Agreements, and Divorce. The lessons of the last two were woven into the fabric of all the others, and could be encapsulated in a single pithy phrase: Not without my signature you don't.

"Say it for me," Pippi instructed, scrutinizing Swanny over the leopard-print frames of her half-moon glasses.

"Not without my signature you don't."

"Oh, darling, no. Say it *sweetly*."

In the beginning, Swanny was petulant and daydreamy, with runs in her stockings from the sharp rattan of the chair. She had a tendency to write test answers on her wrist, though Pippi caught her every time. She ate indiscriminately from the zenith of the food pyramid down to its basement, often while her mother lectured at the board, and she refused to acknowledge a difference between turquoise and lapis lazuli. Still, despite herself, she learned.

For Swanny, the sensation of learning was not unlike the sensation of getting yet another new tooth. It began as a subliminal irritation, the semiconscious knowledge of something in her head both unwanted and unnecessary, and soon began driving her to distraction. Her mother employed what she called the Socratic method, which consisted of coldly interrogating her daughter hour upon tedious hour with a series of enigmatic, hair-splitting, formally indistinguishable, nigh well unanswerable questions that tested her rote memorization and mind-reading abilities simultaneously. More than once, Swanny found her tongue dumb as a thumb in her mouth, or heard herself stuttering (as her mother said, "unattractively") in rage. More than once, she retreated from lessons to join Corona in the kitchen, where she pitched in by thunking the cleaver into the fresh-skinned rabbit shanks.

And yet, far from extinguishing an interest in her studies, this anger kindled it. Swanny hated the diagrams of properly and improperly arranged silverware; she did not care about the eclectic array of newel posts in the Steelworth mansion. But she wanted more than anything to humiliate her mother. At night, in bed, she would kick her legs beneath the monogrammed linens, muttering scalding retorts to Pippi's terse queries and disappointed sighs. Enveloped in the coral porcelain of the bubble bath, she stewed over her improper suppression of unaccented vowels. Depressing the keys of her klangflugel with errorless precision, she strove to sound whatever diabolical chord it would take to lift her mother's eyes from the daily crossword. She and Corona took turns spitting in the espresso machine, and slapped discreet low-fives when Pippi broke a heel. But Swanny wasn't satisfied. Sometimes she wondered if she ever would be.

One evening, after a daunting Language of Flowers exam followed by a wintry, interminable dinner conversation, Swanny slipped out of the house. It was a cloudy night in summer, with heat lightning flickering in the purple clouds like the neon lights of a celestial city. She squinted up into them, and wished, not for the first time, that her mother would send her away to boarding school somewhere cosmopolitan, because here she was so lonely she could scream. She knew all the risks of dormitory life, and she honestly didn't care. She'd keep mousetraps in her jewelry box to ward off thieves. She'd wash her hair in lamp oil to keep the nits away. She finished her amontillado and threw the glass down the outside cellar stairs.

Swanny meandered unsteadily through the overgrown garden,

assembling angry bouquets in her mind. The weeds beneath her feet were no goddamn use. She needed birdfoot deervetch for revenge. Monkshoods to murder the world. White carnations for disdain, lime blossoms to say fuck you. And snapdragons—don't forget those, snapdragons, snapdragons, snapdragons.

She wandered beyond the garden's edge, into the tall grasses that no one ever bothered to mow, and was surprised to see Corona, some distance away, standing on the barren patch where they'd filled the in-ground swimming pool. Corona was holding a lit match and dipping at the waist, and as Swanny got closer she could see she was lighting candles, several of them. Swanny was going to say something snide about witchcraft or exorcism when she noticed Corona was also crying.

Instead Swanny said, in a voice that sounded uncharacteristically meek even to her, "Are those for your son?"

"I didn't see you there, *gordita*. Yes. For my son, and for your father."

"My father?"

"They loved to swim in this pool. Don't you remember?"

"My father wasn't doing much swimming the times I can recall." Swanny remembered almost nothing of her father, but she was loath to admit it. She scratched her toe in the dirt. It was strange how this one patch on their estate never grew much, when all around it the plants were riotous and flourishing.

"Your father treated Ignacio like a son. I come here to pay my respects."

"The sentiment is well meant, I'm sure, but shouldn't Mother be doing that?"

"Your father was smart. He stayed out of her way. Now he's gone, she returns the favor." Corona set down the last candle. The little flames danced in the summer breeze. "You don't remember him. It's sad."

Swanny snorted. "Don't be ridiculous. I am his daughter, after all. I remember how the doctors looked at me the day he died. The intensity of my grief frightened them."

"That wasn't what frightened them. It was your teeth. A little girl so small, with all her teeth come in."

"They thought I was going to bite them?"

Corona dried her eyes on her apron. "No."

"Were Mother and Father first cousins?"

"Why would you ask me that?"

Swanny rubbed her gum with one finger. "Mother says that's why I have so many teeth—from inbreeding. I wondered if perhaps Mother and Father were first cousins, like President and Mrs. Roswell."

"Oh, *La Diabla*," Corona murmured softly.

"Corona, incest is imprudent, I'll grant you, but it's not criminal. You can't blame a woman for seeking someone of her own class. Now, tell me, before they were married, did they have the same last name?"

Tiny raindrops darkened the earth around them. Corona frowned at one sputtering candle. "There are many things a child should not know."

"Sometimes I think you take offense at my becoming an educated woman."

The two of them began making their way back to the house. Corona's step was heavy and slow. Swanny's kitten heels sank into the moist earth.

"What she's teaching you is no education. Where I grew up, we studied math and history, language and poetry. Maps of the world."

"Say what we will about Mother, I hardly think she's skimping on my lessons. By the time she's through, I'll know everything under the sun, twice over, whether I want to or not."

"*El tiempo da buen consejo.*"

"Speak English. You know I can't understand you."

6

HOMECOMING

The HowLux is a fully loaded recreational vehicle: it boasts three sleeping berths, a built-in icebox, a macrozap oven, two Think-Tanks with unlimited connectivity for in-air chat and trading, a fold-down card table/ironing board, a Wash 'n' Dry, a Port-a-John, and in-seat massage functions with three focus areas: Upper Back, Lumbar, and Adult. Customized for Osmond's special needs, this one also features a ramp hatch (most have stairs) and entirely hand-operated steering, enabling him to manipulate the acceleration and brake with a pair of antique gold knobs that bear the likeness of stately gryphons.

"I don't get how I can be in *trouble*," mutters Ripple, sitting shotgun, "when I didn't do anything *wrong*."

Osmond pointedly adjusts the rearview mirror. Behind them, the HowLux's main hold is a U-shaped space, lined with an oxblood leather banquette. The craft's attendants, two janitors borrowed from the mansion's disposal and maintenance staff, sit to one side, exchanging bemused glances. On the other, Abby kneels, naked except for the chamois toga Ripple hastily fashioned for her after boarding the craft. Her hands are pressed flat against the window. Steam clouds the glass between her fingers. The sound she's making is otherworldly—a high-pitched keening emitted between clenched teeth. She's looking back, though there's nothing left to see. Night has swallowed the Island whole.

"What became of your clothes?" Osmond asks.

"I told you, I was hurt. We had to cut them off. Check out my arm. She totally played doctor on me back there, you should thank her."

"I'll do no such thing."

Abby rocks back and forth, clutching at her bony elbows. A foam packing peanut falls from her hair. Her keening stops. Then, all at once, she vomits yellow bile onto the leather seat. She tries to wipe it up with her bare hands, but succeeds only in smearing it. One of the janitors flicks a switch on the wall. With a faint whirring sound, a brass-plated Sorcerer's Apprentice scoots out from a cubby near the floor, diodes flashing. Abby shrieks, scrambling backward as it sweeps up the side of the banquette to shampoo the upholstery. She pulls her chamois toga off over her head and drops it onto the cleaning bot, then smashes at it with her fists, as if attempting to squash a very large, very persistent insect.

"Won't they just be glad I'm alive?" Ripple asks, quieter.

Osmond reaches for the glass of stout in his cup holder. "No."

Ripple stares glumly out the window. Below them, in the dark, the dragons' sleek bodies glide like rayfish over the city's lustrous fires.

"How's Mom?" he asks.

"Cringe-inducing, as always. The other day she was parading through the Great Hall of our ancestors, wearing nothing but a smile." He nods at Ripple's handmade loincloth. "Fashion sense runs in the family, it appears."

"Actually, I'm freezing. Do you have any PJs or anything?"

"None that I'm willing to share."

Meanwhile, Abby has succeeded in disabling the Sorcerer's Apprentice. She flips it over to prod at the casters and the sucto-grips, and to twist the little nozzle, which pitifully fizzes detergent.

"Dunk?" she calls plaintively. "Make it die?"

"Hang on, fem. We're still talking." Ripple lowers his voice. "Pro, you gotta help me out here."

"It would appear that I've already done you a rather large favor, by rescuing you from certain death on that noxious landfill."

"Help me sneak her up to my room."

Osmond sighs and resettles the voluminous folds of his tan-and-black djellaba. "Duncan, if you think you can conceal this feral woman-child in your toy box for deviant sexual purposes, you vastly underestimate the prowess of our resident exterminator."

"C'mon, Uncle Osmond. I thought we were buds."

"I will not be swayed. This behavior is despicable and unsanitary. If your parents weren't so inexplicably eager for your return, I would airlift you to a pediatrician at once to make sure you've had the necessary vaccinations."

"I like her, though."

"That's the infection talking. In my youth, we called syphilitic lunacy 'the beer goggles of the damned.'"

"Well, what am I supposed to do? I've been banging her nonstop for a week plus. I can't just throw her out the window like a Voltage can. Besides, she's got . . . *skills*. It'd be wasteful."

"And what of your upcoming nuptials?"

"Fuck. Is that next week?"

"The day after tomorrow. Your bride arrives tomorrow night."

Osmond adjusts the acceleration knob. Below them, in the Heights to the north of Empire Island, the Ripple estate is coming into view. More fortress than mansion, it stands six stories high and a city block square, with battlements ringing the roof's Astroturf landing pad and the terrace around the fifth floor. Despite the late hour, many of the windows are alight and glowing, with shadows passing by the curtains: night sweepers thumping pillows, dust-sucking the furniture, polishing mirrors for a new day. Osmond taps a panel in the dashboard, radioing in their coordinates. "No, I don't foresee any potential impediments at all to your long-term happiness."

~~~~~

When Ripple arrives home, he finds his mother anxiously waiting for him on the roof in her feathered lingerie with two butlers, a maid, a first-aid kit, and his apehound Hooligan straining on a leash. Ripple hesitates on the ramp, wishing he were dressed, wishing he were showered, wishing he didn't have quite so many of Abby's claw marks on his back. Beneath them, the city's whole skyline darkly slumbers—above it, the dragons blot out the stars. Beside him, his uncle Osmond chortles.

"How good to be home." Osmond raises his arms in a two-handed victory salute. Duncan brushes some coffee grounds off his knee and clears his throat.

There is an art to disappointing one's parents. It helps if one does not disappoint already low expectations. It helps if one does something for which there is a name, because no one likes to be both disappointed and confused. It helps, most of all, if one can explain what one has done, preferably without profanity and while fully clothed. Ripple realizes that he's screwed. Fortunately for him, his father stays downstairs.

Katya doesn't speak as she cleans the gash on his arm with stinging disinfectant, seals it shut with liquid stitches, and rewraps it in a roll of gauze. She puts pressure on the bone and frowns when he winces, then takes his hand and looks closely at his fingers.

"Your nails," she says sadly.

She's right: they're ragged and disgusting, gray-black underneath. For just a moment, Ripple wishes he could transform into another sort of animal, preferably one without hands. Hooligan licks his face.

It takes two hours to coax Abby off the HowLux. It's a Sin Bun, stuffed with Insomnisnacks from the first-aid kit, that finally does it. Ripple feeds it to her, crumb by gelatinous crumb, until her wild blue eyes turn heavy-lidded and drooping and her whimpers grow infrequent and she loosens her grip on the corpse of the Sorcerer's Apprentice, which she's clutching to her bosom like something precious. Then he picks her up, and to his surprise she clings to him, a drugged and flea-bitten marsupial, her sharp chin digging into his shoulder. With his one good arm he carries her back out onto the roof, where his mother and the servants are sitting on deck chairs, casting long shadows in the landing lights.

"Oh my." Katya unplugs the meditation aids from her ears. She smiles the way she used to on the bare nightspot stages: like her entire family has just been killed. "Oh my!" Now she's looking up. The servants follow her gaze; Ripple does too. A piece of the night sky is slowly dropping toward them. With a final fluttering plunge, it perches on one of the battlements. Ripple never thought a bird could glare, but there it is: Cuyahoga.

Under normal circumstances, Abby might resist a bath. But fuzzy-brained and limp-bodied, she sinks compliantly into the Swirlpool with hardly a mew of protest. Later, she will barely remember the numerous pulsing jets, the scented froth, the slick, pearly porcelain that encircles her like the shimmering mouth of a nautilus. What she will remember are Katya's fingers, patient and deft, scrubbing her hair, working out the tangles, trimming the split ends, and finally plaiting it into a single braid that lies as heavy and reassuring as a hand on Abby's back as she falls facefirst into her dreams.

~~~

Though they've been married for nineteen years, Katya Ripple has only on rare occasions had cause to visit her husband's office. The room is wood-paneled, windowless, deep in the fortress of the house. She cannot talk to Humphrey here without feeling outnumbered. Mannequin heads line the shelves behind his desk, each one sporting a different toupee.

"So she's a prostitute?" Humphrey hasn't had his morning coffee yet. He wears a puce velour tracksuit today with a "Ripple Bros" logo embroidered on the sleeve, and is squirting wig glue between the sparse strands on his scalp.

"Hummer, you do not understand. You need to talk to your son."

When Humphrey is annoyed, he looks even more like his brother than usual. *Who are you to tell me what I understand?* "Give me the broad strokes."

"He fell onto Hoover Island. This girl found him and nursed him back to health."

Humphrey squishes today's toupee—a salt-and-pepper thatch with bushy sideburns—down onto his head and combs it in place with his fingers. "Found him? What was she doing out there?"

"It was her home."

He's dubious. "What does she want? Money?"

"You didn't see them together. She was so trusting in his arms. And he—he looked so brave and strong, holding her up. They care for each other."

"For crying out loud, Kitty. Not this again."

"Again?"

"Listen, I know you have your doubts about the Dahlberg match . . ."

"I might have doubts, I might not. How can I know, when I was not CC'd? So many letters, back and forth, back and forth, and you never shared a single one!"

Humphrey digs through a desk drawer, withdraws a large black trash bag. "Kitty, I told you, Pippi and I go a long way back. McGuffin-Stork helped us out of some real scrapes when I was working in Empire. Talking shop, she and I developed a kind of shorthand."

"Anything you say to her, you should say to me."

"There's no reason to have you confusing things you don't know anything about."

"I know my son!"

"You don't know about contracts, or trusts, or the larger holdings of this family. Nor can you possibly, possibly understand the responsibility that comes with carrying on a legacy like ours."

"And Pippi Dahlberg can?"

Humphrey heaves himself up from his wingback swivel chair and opens the secret compartment behind the built-in shelving and watchful heads. The door to the family vault is an enormous steel porthole. He twists the hand wheel several times, and as the walk-in safe unseals, the office smells suddenly of gunpowder and currency, the nasty watermarked sweaty greenbacks you use to pay off a ransom or hush someone up, the kind you give to people you never want to see again, whose names you don't want to know, the kind that doesn't leave anything behind when it burns.

"We could have lost him, Hummer," Katya goes on, lowering her voice. "This girl brought him back to us. This is a second chance for him—for our family. This is a *sign*. How can you not see?"

Humphrey fills the garbage bag with stacks of rubber-banded currency. "I'll see if she'll go willingly. If she won't, there's a Quiet Place in North Statesville that always has an extra bed or two."

Katya's heard of Quiet Places: state-run institutions for citizens afflicted with Too Much. So overcrowded lately, they cram two patients to a sensory deprivation tank and electroshock whole rooms at once. "No. No, no, no. This Abby is just learning to live with people. She grew up all alone. If you send her to a Quiet Place, she will go crazy."

"That's their specialty. Bottom line, I'm not going to let this young woman ruin our son's life."

"Hummer, Dunk and Abby are just like us. Their bodies have told them what to do. And that thing is love. What does all the rest of this matter—contracts, fortunes, names—in the face of love? We are animals, and the only happiness we can know is sweet animal happiness, the pleasure given without thinking that demands nothing in return. Tell him to follow his heart."

"I'm not going to say that, Katya."

"But why? Why would you deny him what you wanted so badly for yourself?"

The words are out before he can hesitate. "Because I don't want him to make the same mistake I did."

He says more words after that—quick, apologetic ones—but though Katya hears the syllables, sees his lips form shapes she knows she's seen before, she can no longer understand his language. She understands even less than she did on her first day in this country. Back then, she did not believe she would always be a stranger here.

She leaves the room and knocks into Duncan on her way out; his ear was pressed against the door, eavesdropping.

Sometimes, when Katya looks back at pictures from her short-lived modeling career, she suspects an eerie thing . . . that some-how, she was not in her body at the moment when the image was snapped . . . that even before the airbrushing and the digital tweaks, the pixels lighting her from within, she had become, for a single instant, that elusive sublime being, an object of pure surface, an un-inhabited woman. Now, for one moment, it happens again. All ten-derizing humanity drains from her; she is impassive and empty and beautiful. Her hand could be plastic when it strikes her son's face.

"Hey! That's, like, child abuse!"

"Your father will see you now."

~~~

Abby wakes to the odd sensation that she is still floating in the enormous tub. She rolls over; the surface beneath her ripples alarm-ingly. She sits up. She's on a gigantic bed, strewn with pillows and a mammal-warm blanket which, she notices to her horror, appears to be attached to the wall via electrical cord. She hits the blanket with her fist. The mattress jiggles irritably. Abby jumps up and scampers across the dim room. She trips over an amorphous obstacle and hits the carpeted floor, panting. All of her calm from last night's drugs and bath has disappeared. She is surrounded.

She raises herself up onto all fours and scuttles to the nearest wall, which is draped in what looks like a billowing sail. She grabs onto it to pull herself up. With a terrible jangling sound, the sail wrenches loose and envelops her like a net. Abby shrieks and flails and kicks, then, once freed, grabs a metal rod—which has suddenly appeared, lying useless on the floor—and whomps the pile of crumpled fabric several times for good measure.

The satin's fall uncovers a bank of windows that span nearly the entire wall. Now nothing but glass separates Abby from the smoggy panorama of the morning city. She uneasily peers out.

Even in better times, our city was never meant to be seen in day-light. In those half-forgotten glory days, the lights of our skyscrap-ers and building complexes and bridges thrust upward, gorgeously, into the endless night like frozen fireworks. Dreamlike, fleeting, they were a spectacle that existed for us and us alone, that promised to vanish by the break of day. They blazed, but without substance, without origin, without threat. They were the fire without a dragon's mouth around it.

Now, by night, our city glows with the heat of what consumes it, spells out in neon orange nothing but a last request. But by day, our true city has no choice but to reveal itself: a heavy thing, the steel anchor that tethers our dreams to the earth. The buildings, those pillars of glass and concrete, cast their monstrous shadows over the land, and the movement of those shadows marks the passage of our time.

Abby stares out the window as the reflections of clouds sweep across the blank faces of towers. What does she see? Before her are all the landmarks we know so well: the Windsor Building, its spire twisting heavenward in a child's dream of infinity; the Gemini, the world's tallest illusion, its two identical 'scrapers each impossibly dwarfing the other; the charred remains of the Lipgloss Building, that once-unassailable temple to global finance, its top ten floors windowless and gutted, tarps blowing from them like flags. She sees the Twolands Bridge, its damaged cables hanging unstrung as broken jewelry, and the barricade walls containing Torchtown bristling with their sniper posts and searchlights and alarms. Yet she sees all of this without words, without history or expectation. She sees a pure play of form, unafflicted by human striving or suffering or triumph. To her, it's not something made or damaged; glorified, gentrified, vilified; corrupted, hallowed, or hollowed out. It simply *is*.

Abby sees the City *itself*: something few of us know how to see anymore, in the midst of this destruction, if we ever did.

And then she sees the dragons.

She's been seeing them all her life, but never so close—never from these Heights. Now she wonders if she's ever really seen them at all. The dragons swim the air over Torchtown, majestic, gluttonous, expansive in their skins. The green one, she sees at once, is the frailer. Its scales are dull, almost mossy, the joints arthritic, swollen, barnacled. It resembles a grandpa lobster she caught once by mistake, a creature grown large beyond its nature by time. Its face has turned melancholy with age, bearded with useless frills, the eyes rheumy and half-seeing. Its wings flap the air in tatters.

The yellow dragon is the stronger, but only just. Puffed up, it's a bully past its prime, a hunk of muscle with the precision gone. It circles through the air in uneven, oval-shaped loops, unable to corner properly. Its square-jawed face bears a look of willful stupidity, its eyes slits, half-hidden beneath a heavy brow. Its brawny tail whips the air, all bulging tendons, but its limbs are as little and vestigial as the arms of the T. rexes who decorate Duncan's underpants.

As they dip and somersault amid the morning haze, they blow their first fire-breaths of the day: the yellow in a steady, unendurable stream, the green one in staccato bursts. Abby backs away from the window. She backs into the footstool—it was a *footstool* she tripped over; the long-forgotten word returns to her now with ease in the face of this wordless terror—and sinks down onto it, still staring. No cords, no wires. The Lady was wrong. These are no tools of the People Machines, no simple weapons to be disarmed. These dragons are *alive*. The world is so big, even God will never find her here.

~~~

The Baroness Swan Lenore Dahlberg is practicing her new signature. Her handwriting ranks among her finest accomplishments. The line is strong, each stroke adorned with minute tassels and curls; her ascenders soar, slender but never pinched, and her descenders hang in orderly bunches, like the fruit of well-tended vines. The space beneath she saves for the flourish, a textless undulation of pure calligraphy, more resplendent than even her title.

The Baroness Swan Lenore Ripple, née Dahlberg

How strange that the name will be hers in a mere matter of hours: after years of waiting, months of negotiations, only a single night lies between her and marriage. But now, as she signs, the hired car jolts and shudders, upsetting the ink, and darkness engulfs the name before she can complete it.

"Damn," Swanny mutters, peeling off a kid glove now spattered black. She places a sheet of blotting paper over the offending page and presses her diary closed, then sets the cedar lap desk on the floor.

The inside of the limousine is red plush, upholstered like a coffin, and it hasn't been recently vacuumed. Motes of dust swim in the late-afternoon light. Swanny settles herself back into the cocoonlike folds of her chinchilla fur coat. She's an ample girl, with chocolate-brunette hair; pendant, sensual lips painted the color of wine—and arms like beluga whale flippers. Her arms do not rank among her finest accomplishments. They are flabby and pale, and have been on her mind since she looked into the mirror this morning. She adjusts the coat around her shoulders and consoles herself thinking of the elegant puffed sleeves of her wedding gown.

"Mother, I don't know why you wouldn't ask my intended to retrieve us in a flying machine."

Beside her, Pippi is bent over a stack of documents; in addition to her reading glasses, she holds a pearl-handled magnifier over the lines of tiny type. In her other hand, she grasps a martini glass, empty except for an olive pit. She grunts noncommittally.

"I would have preferred to ride in a flying machine. To be flung loose from the bonds of Earth, to share the sky with *dragons*—well. Every tragedian knows that the fear of death gives love its meaning and its import." Swanny gazes sorrowfully out the window, fingering her ringlets as they pass the last of the Lionel Roswell Expressway's famous shantytowns. Years ago, when the dragons first came, the highway used to host a thriving subculture of enterprising beggars and thieves, sustaining themselves upon the never-ending caravan of moving vans headed somewhere, anywhere, else. Now, the few remaining squatters dwell in scattered, haphazard assemblages of tarp and plastic resembling broken kites. "My intended would have looked so masculine, piloting our craft with unerring skill, delivering us from all harm, as the city fell away beneath us. I can't imagine a more illuminating first encounter. And the HowFly has a quite romantic reputation, you know. It's said that, at a certain altitude, simply breathing in the air is like sipping Champagne. People become quite giddy. Of course, it would be difficult to speak intimately with one's mother along. But in a flying machine—"

"Swanny, *enough*."

"The least you could do is engage me in conversation. You've reviewed those documents a dozen times, I can't see the urgency in your going over them again."

Pippi looks up sharply. "You are about to enter into a binding legal contract. That is the urgency." She rattles the olive pit in her glass. "And as for the flying machine, the last thing I want is a Ripple vehicle touching down on our estate. Suppose they brought their own appraisers."

"You make it sound like a corporate takeover. If it were up to you, I'd be married via conference call."

"Swanny, I'll remind you that the contracts I've negotiated are not some unimportant side note to marriage. They *are* the marriage. You may have all the expectations in the world, but when it comes to ink on paper, it's either there or it's not. What are you worrying on your gum?"

Swanny removes a finger from her mouth and peers at it fretfully. "I think I need another extraction."

"Darling, I asked you before we left."

"And I said I didn't know but we should bring the dentist just in case."

"And how would that look? Bringing your own dentist to the wedding?"

"Like inbreeding?"

"Like—well, like rather *severe* inbreeding, dear. Here, let me shake you another martini."

"Just a small one. All this jostling makes me queasy."

"You have a point." Pippi rolls down the window and leans out. "Driver, would you please avoid these potholes? My daughter, and our martinis, are *very sensitive to motion!*"

The limousine driver rides on the hood in a seat of his own devising, fashioned from a barber chair with massage beads slung over the back. It's bolted down with rusty screws the size of doorknobs. He absently grips the reins of the two lumbering oxen who pull the vehicle; one glances over its shoulder, snorting through its nose ring at the stridence of Pippi's voice.

"Driver? Did you hear me?"

"Wanna go off-road?"

"What?"

"Want me to drive on the shoulder? Maybe in the ditch?"

"No! I simply asked that you cease and desist this constant bumping!"

"Only way to avoid potholes here is to go off-road."

Pippi sighs. She rolls up the window and fans herself with the heavy cuff of her fox fur coat. "That man is impossible. I'm going to report him to the service."

"Mmm." Swanny relishes having her mother cater to her for a change: "I'll have that martini with two olives."

"Yes, of course. Pass me the ice tray."

The Ripple mansion shimmers at the end of this road, large and bone-colored and terrible, a dreamed thing, abuzz inside with nearly imperceptible tremors of doom. It is an enormous tooth being drilled. It is an enormous tooth in a mouth full of teeth, and that mouth is the city, and as they lurch forward, yard by yard, mile by jarring mile, the Dahlbergs are swallowed whole.

7

WHY WE STAY

A ruin becomes a ruin by degrees. Even a year ago, our decision to stay in the city did not seem like madness. Then, the Center for Global Capital still kept limos in our streets and HowLuxes in our skies. Content firms still sent unpaid interns on risky lunchtime errands to the hot-meat carts, since the majority of restaurants had closed. If we were renters, we dubiously renewed our leases; if we were owners, we fretted over the sharp decline in property values—though some doubled down and bought one apartment, two, an entire building, an entire block.

Entrepreneurs still proposed solutions: dragon-proof glass for windows, thick and tempered and threaded through with wires; dragon-repellant sound emitters, the size of kettle drums, that vibrated at frequencies none of us could hear. The products were sketchy but we bought them anyway. In our secret hearts, we continued to dream of a slayer, a scientist, a whisperer, who would understand what we never could. Even then, after all those years, we still longed for a hero who would cut the ties that bound disaster to this place we had loved too well for too long. We still hoped.

Many had evacuated, to be sure. The streets were quieter than they had ever been. But even on the loneliest night, we were never alone. Always there was someone half a block ahead of us, fedora illuminated under a streetlamp in the mist, walking an outlandish creature on a leash. Always there was another rider on the bus, reading a volume printed in a language of tildes and ampersands. In the city, we have always treasured secrets: the speakeasy entered through the coat-check booth, the unlisted number on the business card. The city itself had become secret, more precious than when it was cherished by many.

The dragons were not the end of us. Or so we made ourselves believe.

It was possible to think this way, a year ago, because back then, the Metropolitan Fire Department was still extinguishing the vast majority of fires. Our fire department had forever been a point of pride. Long before the dragons came, we named our firemen "Empire's Bravest" and sacrificed a building to them each year, immolating it for their practice. We erected a temple in their honor, a Fire Museum, with daytime tours to indoctrinate schoolchildren and midnight sex galas to benefit elite philanthropic institutions. We bestowed crests and medals upon our firemen. We held them in genuine esteem.

Unlike the city's police force, the Metropolitan Fire Department was holy, incorruptible. A fire offers no bribes. No force is excessive in putting it down. So we believed at the time. When the dragons came, it was only natural that we would turn to the fire department and say, "Tell us what you need and we will give it. Take our water. Take our taxes. Take our sons." We did not want to believe they would take too much, that they would risk more than they saved. We told ourselves that conscripting youths into the fire department was *worth* the risk, that we were investing in the city's future. But our nightmares told a different story. In these, we saw a figure, gas-masked like a fireman, tapping at our window, though we lived on the fourteenth floor. We saw him beckoning to us from the other side of the mirror.

Nightmares spread in a city like ours.

Then, six months ago, the Metropolitan Fire Department disbanded after a series of mutinies. Blood was shed. When the fires began to rage unchecked, many reconsidered the decision to linger in this place. Over the years, we had seen many waves of evacuation, but for those of us inextricably bound to the city, this was the worst. The hot-meat carts rolled away. The last of the fluorescent lights flickered off in the conference rooms. The buses, stolen by their drivers, rumbled over the bridges, never to return.

Other places beckoned: Upstate, the Sprawl, the Inhospitable West, even the East, all beset by their own calamities and pollutants, but nothing on the order of this. Some of us idly browsed faraway rental listings, halfheartedly filled out work visa applications, but we knew we didn't intend to go anywhere, despite having lost our jobs, our property values, our illusion of safety, all of our excuses to stay. All excuses except the true one: we do not know how to live anywhere else.

Perhaps we do not know how to live at all.

~~~

Even in the best of times, a city does not love you back. We city-dwellers are a strange breed, lodging in cramped rooms, filling our lungs with smog. Our buildings block the sun; our lights weaken the night. Humans make a city, but a city makes humans tolerate the intolerable. We have always known this in our minds. Now we know it in our broken hearts. Empire Island will kill us in the end. But what would it mean to leave?

We used to believe that the city made nobodies into *somebodies*. Staying here was an expression of fierce individuality—that stubbornness, that drive to carve out a name and own it. Yet one cannot own a city. It is a system we plug into . . . a system that we are. As that system fails, we fail too, by degrees. Abandoning it would mean abandoning ourselves.

So instead, we stay. We wait for buses that never come. We walk the streets at night, but we are never alone. The dragons fly above, unleashed.

8

THE WAY OUT

Sharkey is carving his name into a scrawny kid's back. Three swillers hold the fucker down, wham his head into the table when he thrashes. Sharkey's parlor is no place for heroics—more prayers. The walls are a mottled pattern of bullet holes and cursory attempts at spackling them. Rumor has it the carpet, an intricate pattern of brown and darkish red, used to be just brown.

Sharkey's hand is steady, his eye typesetter-keen, even as each blocked letter oozes itself bloodily illegible.

"I'll sans-serif this, seeing it's a first offense." He strips off his white undershirt to pat the trademark dry, admires his handiwork. The *w* in Eisenhower is a bit aslant, but he doesn't pay that any mind. In his old age, he's learning to ease up on the details. "Kid, you look so pretty, I should hang you up outside. A sorta shingle for the business. Swillers, what do ya say?"

The swillers eagerly hoist the kid back to his feet, make as though to drag him to the egress.

"Mr. S! Swear to shit"—the kid's Mohawk is limp with sweat, his green plastic shutter shades cracked in three places—"next raid we go on, you'll get pick of the litter and then some!"

"Isn't gonna be a next raid unless I get whole haul. No fucking joke."

The kid squirms. The swillers hold him so his heelies barely skim the floor. "Whole haul! Swear to shit!"

"Pocket so much as a watch fob and I'll be making diamonds from your cremains," Sharkey snaps. The swillers let loose the kid and he's out of the parlor, through the shop, and down the steps outside faster than his blood drops can hit the floor. The welcome bell on the shop door jingles as it slams.

Sometimes Sharkey thinks he should start going along on the raids himself again. Keep an eye on things. But he's management now. The legwork is beneath him.

Sharkey started working out an atlas of the tunnels more than twenty years back. Now he has the city's underground drawn down to the manholes, with a key marking what's been plugged up and what's yet to be busted through. He calls it his masterpiece. No one's seen the thing entire, not that they could understand it if they did. The knowledge is his alone. The city has not one but two abandoned subway systems, the Black Line and the Blue, intertwined: city planners didn't dig deep enough the first time, so whole lines had to be filled with limestone and dirt, hasty graves to prop up skyscrapers. But parts of the original are still there, ghost tracks beneath the streets, with cumulous black scorches on the bricks from where red-bellied locomotives used to blow off steam.

Sharkey knows what's fastest for crosstown transit and where the last trains are stalled, blocking up the tracks. He can recognize the platforms by their tile. Deeper down, he knows the routes of the sewer gondoliers, those taxis of the damned—their going rates and medallion numbers, how much you have to tip. (It ain't a bad way to transport product you don't want scorched, though he's lost his patience for the smell.) Beyond all that, he possesses a knowledge so eldritch, it wasn't common even in the city's youth.

He knows what you have to do to *drive*.

His book is leather-bound, stuffed with maps and legends, cross sections and blueprints, more a landscape sketchbook from the pit than a travel guide for the uninitiated. *The Way Out* reads the title page. *By Me.*

What's more, Sharkey knows how to storm just about anyplace worth the time: security systems, panic rooms, bank vault–thick locks just add style to an operation, far as he's concerned. He knows how long it takes to drill up through a concrete basement floor, which name-brand families go hands up at a HowScoot backfiring, and which ones itch to play home-invasion avenger in the name of self-defense.

He knows too that things have changed, these last six months. Money's leaving the city, in the form of the moneyed; nobody's stopping the fires. It used to be you could find a penthouse, a brownstone, within blocks of the Outer Walls—you'd rob it and three weeks later you'd rob it again. Now it's looking like another Siege of Wonland will be in order before too long, not from ambition but from necessity. What happens when there's nowhere left to raid? Sharkey doesn't know. But if lean times are coming, he's stocking up.

Sharkey gives the orders and sends his raiders on their merry way. In return, he gets "pick of the litter": his choice of the schwag, and an option to buy the rest at a discount. Unless of course the raiders hold out on him. Then he can take whatever he wants, merchandise or a life—he went easy on the kid today. It's all in the contracts he drew up years ago, when he went through his law books phase. He has the raiders sign them still. Even if their X's hardly constitute a sig.

Whole haul: Sharkey's got big plans for this next job. Bigger than anybody's tried in a while. He'll send these raiders all the way to the top this time. They can't say no; they owe him. And if they don't make it back alive, he'll just chalk it up to experience.

You never know what's possible unless you reach for the Heights.

Sharkey takes his place back at the head of the table. Duluth, his most trusted swiller, a twentysomething old-timer built like a fridge, tosses him a fresh undershirt. Sharkey puts it on.

"Next order of business," he says. The swillers hustle to their seats.

Sharkey doesn't like having regular employees. He prefers contracting out jobs, like he does with the raids. Employees get to know their boss's habits, things he'd rather keep quiet: how much currency is in the safe, when he's got a broken finger or a flat limo tire. That sometimes he keeps the gator in his own bathtub, nights. Not secrets exactly, but knowledge about Sharkey that, if compiled, could create some sort of picture more nuanced than any he'd care to portray. He knows the power of good PR, both for instilling terror and its kissing cousin, reverence. To some of the natives, Sharkey, the oldest man in Torchtown, is half-sacred, half sci-fi: a suspected time traveler, thrown up from a past splendiferous beyond imagining, whose unhindered passage through their era back to his own guarantees the present existence of the world. Natives can believe whatever they want about him as long as they go by faith alone. Which is to say he don't like snoops.

The swillers he hires are the bare minimum, the skeleton crew he needs to keep operations up and running. Right now, it's just these three. Officially, Sharkey's never had to retire one of his own men, and he tries to keep it that way. Unofficially, Sharkey's sent a few of them out on errands over the years—to buy a jar of hooch at a saucemart, say—that've ended with a different kind of firing. "Accidents happen," is what Sharkey always makes a point of supposing, and his employees never contradict him. The next day's always like Sunday school around the backroom table.

"Lemme see." Sharkey flips open his account ledger. "Keelhaul, you got tributes from the Dolls?"

Keelhaul, his newest recruit, a kid with waist-long dreads and second-degree scars on his forearms, forks over a jingle bag. It's full enough, but Sharkey puts on his pince-nez and counts it right then anyhow: currency, some bangles, two artificial fingernails. He wonders, not for the first time, if Keelhaul's been skimming, then tables the worry for now. He'll know for sure sooner or later, probably sooner. Sometimes a swiller's sly enough to avoid being obvious, for a while, till he gets greedy. Happens every time.

"Bronco, you take care of that thing?" Sharkey asks the buck-toothed hothead sitting farthest from him down the table. Bronco flips shut his gravity knife in mute assent.

"Duluth, what about the Mudpuppies? They pay up?"

Duluth shrugs, a gesture that doesn't signify much: he's all shoulders and no neck anyway. "Said they'd have it tomorrow."

"You squeeze them?"

"Said *tomorrow*, Shark."

Sharkey sets down his pince-nez, and Duluth picks at a scabby face tattoo, like making himself bleed might preempt any inklings Sharkey has in that direction.

"You think they didn't have it?"

"They said that."

"You think they hadn't sold the chaw? You think to ask for it back?"

"Next time I'll squeeze them."

"Smart kid."

He ain't, though, and Sharkey knows it. Duluth may be as reliable as an Outer Wall, but like Keelhaul and Bronco, in fact, like every swiller Sharkey's ever had, he's turned out disappointingly dumb. It's enough to make Sharkey saw a man's legs off at the knees, if only that would do some good. It isn't so much that the swillers are slow, though they can be that too—Sharkey's got some pet theories about the neighborhood gene pool. But it's their flatfooted incuriosity that makes him mad.

At twelve, Sharkey was apprentice to Jawbone Park, a mean old inmate who'd been sentenced to Torchtown for manslaughter, armed robbery, assault with a deadly weapon, and siccing dogs on a police horse, and who'd most recently set about making a name for himself in the growth field of home-cooked psychotropics. Jawbone had spent some years previous working his way through the grislier parts of a prison library, and young Sharkey made it his habit to linger in the evenings, scrubbing molasses and sometimes gore off the floorboards while Jawbone, deep in his evening chew, pontificated on all things applicable, historically, from the final fate of the dinosaurs to lantern-kicking cow-arsonists and where their fires spread.

More important, Jawbone taught Sharkey about the chaw business: how to keep an inventory, how to balance the books, the difference between profits gross and net, and when to bother playing fair. Sharkey's amassed a shelf full of books on management and free-market econ since then, as well as some useful true-crime titles.

But most of what he relies on still comes from those early days with Jawbone. He's always expected that sooner or later one of his own swillers would take a similar interest, but so far, no dice. They're too dumb, or too scared, or maybe they figure life's too short. When he tries to explain anything more complicated than a thumbscrew, they squirm like they need to piss and he's running water by their ears. It wouldn't matter much, except Sharkey's getting old. He needs somebody he can trust, somebody he can talk to, somebody to take the shop over when he's gone. Somebody who doesn't need him to explain every little thing.

The window's propped open behind the blinds. From somewhere outside, Sharkey hears a fire start. The whoosh of wings, and then the crackle, like wind with dead leaves in it. Probably a block away. That rubble lot with all the tents in it. Yeah. Sharkey looks at his swillers. He can tell they can't hear it yet. No one can: it's coming from the future. Ten minutes from now, max. Some days he'd keep the meeting running straight through, watch the worry flicker across their faces while they tried to ID the screamers. But today he's not in the mood. He wants them out of here. He cracks his knuckles, running his thumbs over the letters inked into his skin there—FUCK FIRE—and shuts the ledger.

"All right," he says. "It's break time. Scram."

9

BEGONIAS

MEMO
TO: *Duncan H. Ripple V*
FROM: *D. Humphrey Ripple IV*
CC: *Osmond Strangeboyle Ripple, Katya Ripple*
SUBJECT: *Re: Troubling Developments*

As per our conversation yesterday, I am attaching herewith my Guidelines for Legally Tenable Courtship Practices. These guidelines were drawn from formal written agreements with the Dahlberg household and from informal discussions with those family members copied in here; they have been annotated to address the specific challenges of your current entanglement. Please note that these points are nonnegotiable under the terms of your marriage contract, and that noncompliance may result not only in the termination of that agreement but also in disinheritance, familial estrangement, and repossession of assets from this estate as well. Study this document in full before engaging in any form of communication whatsoever, with your Intended or any other parties not CC'd.

Guidelines for Legally Tenable Courtship Practices:
I. Appearance and manner. The Bride-to-Be (hereafter "B2B") is entitled to a clean, wholesome physical appearance and manner in her Affianced Male (hereafter "AM"), including but not limited to: coordinated business-casual attire; clean-shaven face or evenly trimmed facial hair; pleasant-

smelling skin; proper use of grammar; warm yet respectful use of endearment terms, such as "dear," "beloved," "pet," and "my lark" (a longer list of suggestions available upon request). Use of profanity or terms deemed derogatory to women (such as slang idioms referring to prostitution), especially when describing one's relationship to a Wild Teenaged/Twentyish Female (hereafter "WTF"), is absolutely impermissible.

II. Disclosure of sexual health concerns. The B2B is entitled to an AM with no known sexual health concerns or risk factors, including a history of unprotected sexual intercourse, unprotected fellatio, unprotected cunnilingus, unprotected mutual masturbation, and unprotected anal penetration. I am going to assume there were condoms on that island, Duncan.

III. Disclosure of financial concerns. Fortunately a non-issue. Refer B2B to me or any of our accountants with questions.

IV. Premarital conference. The B2B is entitled to at least one private premarital conference with her AM; acceptable activities include lively discussion, the viewing of educational Toob specials, a garden stroll in the greenhouse, or the consumption of a meal. At no time should a WTF be present during the course of these conferences, nor should a WTF be the subject of the aforementioned "lively discussion."

Duncan, these Courtship Practices should be fairly self-explanatory; as I recall, we went over them in depth six months ago when you originally signed your contracts. But if you have any questions whatsoever, please contact me immediately.

I will remind you that, upon your graduation last year from the Chokely Bradford Underschool with the lowest scores in that institution's history, you chose to engage a partner to share your fiscal and other responsibilities rather than re-taking the economics courses that would enable you to enter the Chokely Bradford Overschool

Finance Program and shoulder the burden alone. The Dahlberg fam-
ily has long had an illustrious reputation for their canny judgments
in business and their role in philanthropic circles, and as you'll recall,
Penelope "Pippi" Dahlberg and I were once professional colleagues.
The Baroness Swan Lenore Dahlberg is, to all appearances, a highly
intelligent, circumspect, and resourceful young woman, one I would be
proud to have as a daughter-in-law or, indeed, as an only child. Your
alliance with her will prove invaluable for the success of this family in
the years to come. I strongly advise you to keep that in mind.

> *Best regards,*
> *Dad*

~~~~~~

"Only child," Ripple, sprawled out for his afternoon nap, scoffs at
the LookyGlass. "Yeah right, Dad. Like you'd want your only child
to be a *girl*."

Even if Ripple's father doesn't understand him at all, at least he
appreciates having a son to buy things for. The proof's everywhere
in Ripple's room, a whole fleet of merchandise modeled on the
stylized-violence-and-weaponry aesthetic, not least of all the berth
where he's currently reclining au naturel. The Slay Bed, as Ripple
calls it, is a twelve-foot, thousand-year-old warrior grave boat with
a king-sized mattress in the hull, where once lay the funeral pyre
of some unwashed pro named Reldnach the Irresponsible. The craft
was sent out to sea in flames, but it didn't stay lit. The Super Bitch
had other ideas. She's the figurehead of this vessel, a snake-haired
lady on the prow screaming to scare off sea monsters. Or, maybe
now, in her new incarnation as furniture, to keep bad dreams away.

Humphrey got the Slay Bed as a surprise for Ripple when Ripple
was eight, the year the Museum of Human History auctioned off
their permanent collection. The price was right. Tourism in the city
was way down and the curators were eager to off-load the treasures
before they went up in smoke. Uncle Osmond called it a "fire sale,"

chuckled ruefully, and passed out at the dinner table. Humphrey called it an "investment." Ripple didn't care, it was awesome. At least he and his dad could agree on that.

Now the only thing that could make the bed more epic would be to have a naked damsel in it—but oh wait, Ripple's got that covered. This afternoon, Abby lies bare across the pillows, chin on palms, head tilted intently, as she watches old episodes of his Toob series on the 3-D projection screen that covers the entire opposite wall, all the way up to the twenty-foot ceilings. They've started on Season 4 and at the moment Ripple's prepubescent likeness is getting hauled off to the headmaster's office for starting a food fight in the cafeteria.

"BLEEP lima beans!" he yells, devil-horning his fists for his cheering classmates as the vegetable-splattered double doors slam shut behind him.

"They were always trying to get me to settle down and pay attention," Ripple explains, absently kneading her ass cheek. "But I was like, 'No. I'm the star. Pay attention to me.'"

She doesn't seem as turned on by this as he would have expected. In fact, the last twenty-four hours have been the most terrifying of Abby's entire existence, and she's currently in a state of shock.

Earlier That Day . . .

Abby's dumbfounded, self-obliterating awe at her first close-up sight of the dragons had an almost religious quality, as if a portal to eternity had opened in that window's shatterproof plexipane. But she didn't have time to linger for long in the knowledge of her own cosmic insignificance, because close to a minute later, she was summoned for an audience with Ripple's father in the Lap Dance Room.

It was not Ripple himself but his mother who materialized to escort her on this unwelcome venture. In the morning light, Katya appeared somewhat faded, platinum-haired in a wispy shift—the mind's eye afterimage of the angel whose nurturing touch had coaxed Abby back from the brink of madness the previous night, diminished now, in the face of brighter horrors.

"It isn't properly called the Lap Dance Room," explained Katya, leading Abby by the hand down the grand stairs to the first-floor hall, "he calls it the Man Cave. But that makes it scary, don't you think? In my village back home, we had a man cave, all darkness with drips of stone like teeth. Animals painted on the walls, running for their lives—how do you call them? Mammoths."

"I don't want to go to the Man Cave."

"Don't worry, it will be over soon. How did you meet my son? Forgive me, I still don't understand."

"God sent him to me."

Katya nodded; she seemed to know what Abby meant.

"You must love him very much," Katya said. "To leave your home behind."

"I have to go where he goes. I'm his."

The Lap Dance Room housed a chrome pole on a raised platform, the spine of a machine displayed like an altar of worship. Above a sunken bar in the room's far corner, a sign blazed with the likeness of an incandescent bottle of lightning juice: EL SEGUNDO LAGER—2ND TO NONE! Nearer to the door, in a tilted box on stilts, a maze of electricity imprisoned tiny metal orbs under a ceiling of glass. The room hummed; Abby could feel the humming through the whole house. But it was strongest here.

Humphrey Ripple sat before her on a throne of tanned animal hide, with a smaller furry pelt slung across the baldness of his head. When he stood, she was relieved to see his legs were legs, not wheels like the other one's. He extended his hand. Abby grasped it in both of hers and gazed up at him imploringly.

"Have mercy on me," she pleaded.

"No need for any formalities." Humphrey glanced at Katya nervously, extracted his hand, and wiped it on his pants. "Annie, is it?"

"No. Abby. Like Abracadabra."

"Your name is Abracadabra?"

"No . . ."

Humphrey cleared his throat. "Well, let's get down to it."

He spoke then, at some length, about the nature of Reality and certain Arrangements that had been made, and about how the nature of Reality, like the terms of those Arrangements, was fundamentally unalterable, no matter what ideas teenagers might have in their heads. Fame, and hormones, and frankly, inflated self-perception, might make a young person think that anything was possible, but his son was not prepared to run his own life successfully and he, Humphrey, was not prepared to watch him run it into the ground. Humphrey didn't care if it made him the Bad Guy to say so, because it was nothing personal; he was simply stating the laws of Reality, which, like the laws of Nature itself, could not be bent or broken simply because of human desire. His son could not fly; he was subject to Gravity just like the dumb rock he frequently resembled, and in the same way, his son could not break the laws of Reality, since such an act, like Gravity, would send him crashing to the ground without a net to break his fall. Humphrey thought past precedent had established as much.

"Do you understand?" he asked her.

"No," said Abby.

At this point, Humphrey sighed and lifted an enormous black plastic garbage bag from behind the chair—garbage, yay!—and Abby embraced it, tears of relief springing to her eyes, before he pulled apart the drawstrings at the top and revealed the contents to be not trash, that glorious variegated amalgam of rot and rinds and coffee grounds, but identical stacks, each bundled smartly with an elastic band, of green-and-white rectangular paper slips that smelled of nothing but ink and linen and, faintly, greed.

"No!" cried Abby.

"Huh." Humphrey squinted at her. "I suppose you want me to believe you're above all that. Well, if you want to take the high road, what do you say to this?"

At that point, he removed a square of black glass from his pocket, tapped its surface, and aimed it at the pole-stage. A whirring orifice on the edge of this mysterious device shot out a beam of light. In it swayed a shimmering emissary from the spirit realm, its substanceless form constantly disrupted with flurries and jolts of electricity. Dimly, Abby realized it had once been a girl, one not so unlike her, though plusher and with a strange, false affectation of manner. Yet Abby could also see *through* her, as through a smog, to the pole and the wall beyond it. The ghost-girl bent over some sort of strange instrument, also translucent, a complicated system of valves and lung-like protrusions, which emitted odd, cloying tones at the prodding of her chubby fingers.

"All the tales of old, all the stories told of a gem both rare and fine," the flickering specter sang. *"No diamond's sweet as when two hearts meet, and call each other mine. A treasure to have and hold: love's a dearer thing than gooooold."*

Humphrey tapped the surface of the black glass again, triumphantly this time, and the stage was dark and silent once more. "Now I'm sure you understand."

"Yes. You're a wizard who steals girls' souls."

This exhausted the remaining store of Humphrey's patience. He shouted that he would not be insulted in his own house, and that Abby should consider herself lucky to get anything at all, since she didn't have so much as his son's signature on a cocktail napkin, let alone Right of First Refusal, which the girl from the Hollow Gram was entitled to under the law. Abby tried to protest or apologize, but the words jumbled together with the sobs that reshaped her language into a dialect of sorrow, until at last Katya stepped from the shadows to insist, "You are frightening her, Hummer!" at which point Abby bolted from the Man Cave back into the hall, where Duncan leaned against the wall under a torchiere, cleaner than she'd ever seen him, waiting for her.

"So how'd it go?"

She was so relieved to find him, she almost fainted.

"I guess you need some breakfast."

Abby clung to him, eyes half shut, as he led her through various corridors, into an echoing chamber made of cold metal and tile. Two men in white smocks stood at a slab of wood, hacking the wings off the plucked carcasses of birds and tossing them into a steel bowl. It was as though she had stepped into a dream. *A ceiling of electric white. Rats with eyes like blood drops.*

"Where have you taken me?" she whispered, digging her fingers into Ripple's arm.

"Uh, it's just a kitchen. Don't let the village idiots bother you. Pros, do you mind?"

The wing cutters glanced at each other; one of them rolled his eyes as they exited through a door marked THE HELP.

"Zero privacy, seriously. What do you want to eat?"

"Um . . ."

"I know how to make toast."

"OK."

Ripple produced a spongy loaf sheathed in a rainbow-colored plastic sleeve. Abby had seen such bags on the Island, but every one of them was filled with a chunky, moldy, vile-smelling gruel that even she considered inedible. She watched with interest as he removed two unblemished slices and placed them in the matching slots of a chrome box in front of him on the counter. "So what exactly did my dad say?"

"He showed me the girl from Hollow Gram."

"Yeah, I probably should've told you about her. Are you mad?"

Abby gazed down into the chrome box. Inside each slot, around each slice of bread, tiny metal coils were glowing orange though untouched by flame. The heat was coming from *somewhere*, it had to be; in some far-off place, the heat had separated from its source and traveled here, lost, on the wires of forgetting. Electricity: it stole life from nature and brought it inside. "Who is she?"

"Some random GEP from Wonland. My dad picked her, not me. I'm trying to get out of it."

"Gep?"

"Genetically engineered princess. You know how an Old Mom gets pregnant, right? A turkey baster and a trait menu. And she definitely ordered Swanny well done."

The slices of bread, so near to the chrome box's nexus of unholy power, had begun to smolder, releasing thin tendrils of smoke as their surfaces browned and cauterized. Yet still the coils warmed. "Swanny? Is that her name?"

"You should see this fem's test scores, it's unnatural. If I was se-lecting for shit, 'looks good naked' would be way higher on the list. Maybe it just wasn't in the genes. You can't express something that's not there."

"She sang to me."

"Yeah, that's one of her 'accomplishments.' My sex life is a talent show, apparently."

The bread was burning, trapped in the torture box of tongueless flame. Abby could see it, could feel it, on her skin and in her core. Where did these machines come from? Who made them? What were they for? The Lady had warned her, but she had not listened; she had left the Island where she was safe, and now she was damned. The wires were all around Abby, pulsing with energy. *She was the bread in the toaster. She was the bread in the toaster.* It was too much to bear, and she felt something inside her on the brink of snap-ping until, instead, the bread leapt up, entirely of its own volition, scorched beyond all recognition, and she screamed, "It's ALIVE!"

~~~

Ripple thought some toast and fucking would calm her down, but nope: Abby's still pretty tense. He can't tell if the fucking made things better or worse. One thing's for sure, she is not a fan of toast.

"Ever watch Toob before?" it now occurs to him to ask. "When you were a little kid or anything?"

Abby shakes her head. "I don't remember anything before the Island."

"Do you like my show?"

"It's OK. Can they see us?"

"Who?"

"The people on the screen."

When Ripple was a kid, he once saw a Toob exposé about these special new hybrid "poochi-poo" dogs that turned out to be sewer rats on steroids. It was creepy, though, because in the video cov-erage they looked so plainly undoglike—their twitchy eyes, their overbites, their warty faces and muscly backs, even their wiggling, hairless tails. Ripple slowly removes his hand from where it rests on Abby's ass and looks her over carefully, trying to reassure himself that she is not a human poochi-poo. Lots of hot girls pretend to be dumb, he knows that.

But what if she's *so* dumb, *so* ignorant, it's impossible for her to understand him? What if she's a different kind of creature than he thought?

"Fem, that's *me* up there," he instructs her, carefully. "Me and my parents and everyone I know."

"How . . ." She trails off.

Is it even legal to date a poochi-poo?

"It's a recording of my life. Like, drawing a picture to remember something. Only with cameras."

"So we're looking into the past?"

Ripple breathes a sigh of relief. "Yeah, you got it."

"When did you come back?"

"From where, underschool?"

"When did you come out of the light and become human again?"

Ripple opens his mouth and just leaves it open while he tries to figure out how to respond. Fortunately, he doesn't have to. With an obtrusive metallic trill, a LookyChat opens at the lower left-hand corner of the projection screen, containing a real-time capture of his friend Kelvin, waving his arms.

"Maximize me, urgent, urgent! We need to parlay!"

"Kelvin, fuck yeah! So good to make contact!"

Ripple met Kelvin Tang the first day of underschool, more than twelve years ago now. At Chokely Bradford, you got to know the other kids' last names before their first ones, on account of the family crests embroidered on the Kevlar vests they wore as part of their uniforms. At six years old, Ripple still didn't read too good, or at all, but he knew to keep an eye out for the phoenix and pandas. According to his dad, the Tangs were the only family in the city richer than the Ripples, and he wanted to size up the competition. It was during the first season of his show, and the videographers edited it like he was spoiling for a fight. "Will Duncan finally . . . meet his match?" the voiceover intoned during the teaser for the next week's episode.

Their first encounter was during recess in the courtyard, a square of lush photosynthetic green that the classrooms and dormitories surrounded like a fortress. Kelvin sat alone on the swing set, urgently mashing the buttons of his Boy Toy handheld, sonically sequestered in a pair of headphones as big as earmuffs. Ripple had to smack him on the shoulder to make him look up.

"I challenge you," Ripple said, like he'd practiced, "to a battle of laser blades." As the camera crew encircled them, he offered Kelvin one of the two light-up fencing swords he'd brought from home.

Much to Ripple's surprise, Kelvin was awesome. He kicked Ripple's ass at laser blades (the motion-sensor hilts kept score) but by the end of the duel both boys were laughing too hard to care. After that, they were best friends. They ate each other's paste during art class, snuck to each other's suites after lights out, and shared all the passwords to their gaming platforms. They were the most popular guys in underschool, hands down, but although the other students clustered around them at mealtimes or Holosnapped their antics for posterity, at heart they were blood brothers and that shit was exclusive. Ripple had met his match, and it ruled.

He made Kelvin famous; Kelvin helped him understand stuff the night before exams. Ripple thought that was a fair deal. But that all changed in season twelve, when the showrunner, tiring of the endless pranks and unfilmable stroke-off sessions, determined it was high time to inject the series with a note of romance. Humphrey, sensing the probable necessity of an arranged marriage for his son in the near future, nixed this as far as Ripple was concerned. So it was Kelvin who chastely dated an "intern" hired by the videographers—really a twenty-nine-year-old YA impersonator named Cheryl—for fourteen weeks, almost a whole season, during which time Ripple had the unpleasant experience of feeling like a subplot in his own episodes. The ratings eventually tapered off and they fired Cheryl, but he and Kelvin weren't quite as solid after that.

Now Kelvin is all like, "I do not need an eyeful of your unsheathed katana, pro." Trying not to seem too interested: "Who's she?"

"You *said* they couldn't see us," Abby cries, diving under the blanket.

"A lot of things have changed around here." Ripple wriggles into his boxers, trying to keep the triumph out of his voice. "I have a scar now too." He flashes the wound wrap like a badge.

"Right. Tell me straight, was this a brand-building exercise? Because a lot of us seriously thought . . ."

"I wouldn't fake my death without warning you."

"Whatever."

"No, I'd make you the prime suspect or something." Ripple feels magnanimous. He's got nothing left to prove. "You're a main character in my life, Tang. You're my best supporting actor."

"Maybe not for too much longer."

"What's that supposed to mean?"

"Not everybody got the man-child stamp of incompetence on graduation day."

"My diploma says 'For Entertainment Purposes Only.' There's nothing on there about incompetence."

"What I'm saying is, my dad wants me to work for him back East. Overseas."

Ripple blinks. He knows Kelvin's been taking Wunderkind-level classes for a while now to proficiency out of overschool. But entering the *workforce*? What, like adults? "That makes no sense. You live here. Your stuff's here. You went to school here."

"I have dual citizenship. I've got family over there, the company's based there. And business works the same everyplace. Except here, where it doesn't."

"Just tell your dad you'll ruin everything."

"He won't believe me." Kelvin looks off-camera sheepishly. "He said I make him *proud*."

Not acceptable: "Uh, *Late Capitalism's Royalty*, remember? Our families own half the city. We're supposed to party on like kings."

"Half of nothing is still nothing."

"No, it's infinity. ∞"—Ripple draws the shape in the air with his finger—"isn't that what you get when you twist a zero around its middle?"

Kelvin isn't buying it: "Nope, Rip, it's nothing."

Ripple doesn't care to take this lying down, but he doesn't feel like getting up either. All of a sudden, he's drained. "It's like you *want* to go."

"There's no future here, Ripple. Empire Island is over. Maybe you forgot, they shut down the fire department *six months* ago. Water and power are probably next. If you knew what was good for you, you'd be bailing too."

As if Ripple could pass an immigration test. Or hold a job. Getting stranded on the Island was one thing, but he can't imagine a life outside his parents' mansion, where he would have to meet anyone else's minimum standards. "No fucking way. I'm sticking around to protect my assets."

"And I want to live somewhere that isn't a total wasteland. No offense."

Ripple asks it nonchalantly: "When do you leave?"

"Tomorrow."

"Tomorrow?!"

"Pro, I sought your input. You were unreachable."

"But you would've gone no matter what."

"Well, yeah."

Ripple doesn't feel like talking anymore. "Clobber Mechs or Skyscreamers?"

"Skyscreamers."

"Team or battle?"

"C'mon. You know I'm always on your team."

～～～

The last leg of the journey to the Ripples' mansion is the steepest. The Heights, a mountainous outcropping at the city's northern tip, was once an exclusive enclave, a promontory from which the then-teeming entirety of Empire Island could be seen and observed, and upon which one's own edifice stood as a monument, dwarfing those below. As the hired car progresses along the Lionel Roswell Expressway, Swanny cranes her neck, but can only glimpse a sheer, vertical sheet of rock, richly embellished with graffiti and the chiseled initials of the long dead. Atop this pedestal, her husband dwells. The hired car takes the next exit, into a tunnel encircled with spray-painted script and watched over by the peeping eyes of a faded leggy snake.*

Here the darkness is complete, the stillness perfect except for the clomping of the oxen's hooves, until the driver flips on his grumbling generator and ignites the buzzing halogen brights he's affixed to the limo's grille. Then the tunnel reveals itself, a concrete cave with burnt-out sconces on the walls. Rats skitter across the pavement; a crumpled bag of BacoCrisps crunches under the wheel. Swanny holds her breath. Beside her in the darkness, Pippi seems to expand, to exert a gravitational pull the way objects do in the cold void of space. The two have never sat together so silently. The road tilts up beneath them. When Swanny speaks, her voice sounds disembodied.

"Mother? What if he doesn't like me?"

"Then he'll get used to you, darling."

When light pours in the windows again, it is as though a night has passed.

Forty-eight high-definition face-recognition security cameras are positioned at various locations on the outside of the Ripples' mansion, courtesy of HomeShield, the private security firm that monitors the property remotely. Some cameras stare out from the mouths of gargoyles, some perch atop the battlements, some crouch

---

*A ubiquitous graffiti tag in the burning metropolis, the two-headed wingless dragon—or leggy snake—pictured Empire Island's nemeses rendered cageable and earthbound, fused to each other as if by a nuclear explosion, weeping tears of blood. It was widely regarded as a symbol of hope.

at ground level, behind the tough iron lattices that line the basement windows. As the hired car pulls up to the barred entrance to the grand inner courtyard, all forty-eight cameras swivel furiously in its direction. And when the Baroness Swan Lenore Dahlberg rolls down her window and presents her round, uneasy visage to the crisp autumn afternoon air, all forty-eight cameras beep and click and whizz and scan in a flurry of electronic desperation until, at last grudgingly satisfied, they confirm the arrival of the family's honored guest to the staff, the Locksure alarm system, and the robotic hinges of the impenetrable metal gates, which regally, deliberately, swing inward. The Dahlbergs park and disembark in the circular drive.

The Ripple mansion is a medieval castle with a spaceship crashed into it. The east wing is gothic, all spires and flamboyant arches, windowpanes the colors of gemstones, flying buttresses ornately carved in bas-relief. The west is Romanesque, fortressy and unadorned, almost surly beneath its battlements. But the central façade and entryway is an angular, crystalline entity: all jutting steel and planes of glass slicing like merciless razors into the stones of the past, mirrored sharply in the courtyard's limpid, silvery reflecting pool. It takes Swanny's breath away. Pippi frowns up at it, putting on her oversized suncheaters to get a better look.

"Generations of bluebloods, and yet they build like this. Money doesn't care whose pocket it's in."

Swanny couldn't disagree more: "It's bold. And modern."

"*Post*-modern, darling." Pippi turns back to the limo for her crocodile briefcase.

"Mother, the driver wants his tip."

Pippi pats the pockets of her fox fur coat for change. But the moment is already past: a stream of butlers is issuing from the spaceship's portal, uniformed and white-gloved, to seize the Dahlbergs' luggage.

"Just charge it!" Pippi calls airily, and then she's hustling Swanny inside.

Once in the lobby of the Ripple mansion, Pippi Dahlberg shrugs off her fox fur and lets it fall unhindered to the floor. She drops the hatbox she has tucked under one arm and strides toward the visitor desk, where she immediately presses the large gold buzzer, despite the fact a butler is already stepping forward to man the station.

"We are the Baroness Swan Lenore Dahlberg," she explains, gesturing vaguely behind her. "We have arrived."

Swanny stands back awkwardly, uncertain if she should be embarrassed or relieved that she apparently won't be doing any of the talking. It's difficult even to think: the entry hall is working its spell on her. The ceiling is so high, she doesn't feel like she's inside of anything. The stone floor rings beneath her feet. Before her, a grand two-sided marble stairway swoops upward, half-encircling an indoor fountain of a naked male colossus, stabbing the belly of a kraken with his trident. Here, as in the reflecting pool outside, the water has a metallic gleam, which Swanny realizes now comes from money: the water shimmers with tossed coins. Spent wishes. But here in the Ripple mansion, what need would one have to wish for anything at all?

Beneath the vertex of the staircase, an elevator chimes open, revealing an unlikely trio: one fat man in an obvious hairpiece and a sweatsuit; a second, fatter man in a wheelchair, guzzling a viscous, night-dark elixir from a tulip glass . . . and the tallest woman Swanny's ever seen, whose sequined minidress does little to conceal the skyward ascent of her endless golden legs.

"Mother," says Swanny, interrupting Pippi's litany of requests to the butler as the strangers make their way toward them across the lobby's vast expanse. Pippi turns and her expression of momentary irritation transforms into a starburst of ecstatic delight.

"*Hum*-phrey!"

And before Swanny can even recoil in horror, her mother and the first fat man are embracing. He swings her through the air in a half-circle; her witchy stilettos punctuate the air with little kicks.

"Pippi," he says, flushed, straightening his skull merkin. "There's a portrait of you rotting in an attic somewhere."

"No, wrong pact: I promised my firstborn instead. Speaking of which—" She grips Swanny's shoulder through the soft gray fur of her coat. "Darling?"

"The pleasure's all mine." Swanny curtseys.

"*Enchanté*," says the second fat man around a burp. He grabs Swanny by the hand and drags her toward his wheelchair to kiss her wetly on the knuckles.

"And this must be *your* daughter," Pippi tells Humphrey. She laughs uproariously; shrill echoes hail from the vaulted ceiling. "Oh, you scandalous rascal, wherever did you *find* her?"

"I first traveled to this city with my modeling company," Katya says stiffly.

"Why, of course you did. I'm absolutely famished. Could we sneak a bite before dinner, something very light, don't trouble yourself."

Katya glances at Humphrey, who makes shooing motions.

"I'll ask the kitchen," she says.

It's Pippi's favorite subject: "You must be firm with your waitstaff or they'll absolutely walk all over you. I remember my first round of firings, when we still lived in the city. It was unpleasant for a day or two, but then you forget what the old ones looked like."

"Where's Duncan?" Swanny asks. Everyone turns in her direction.

"He's upstairs, no doubt, frolicking in the bedroom," grumbles the man in the wheelchair.

"Always a good sleeper," says Katya. Her mouth smiles; her eyes don't. "A restful boy. I'll see about those sandwiches."

"May I take your coat?" Humphrey asks Swanny.

"Oh, thank you, no, I feel a chill." Swanny smiles and resettles the fur around her shoulders. He may be heavier than she is, but he's still not going to see her arms. "I would like to meet Duncan, if he's awake."

"He's awake all right. I'll show you."

"Osmond . . ."

Humphrey's tone is a warning, but the man in the wheelchair zooms away. His engine has surprising pickup for a medical aid. Swanny has to scurry to keep up. He backs into the elevator smoothly, then beckons with a wink: "Going up?"

Swanny resists the urge to glance back toward her mother for reassurance and steps inside the little gilded chamber. The door slides shut.

"You're Duncan's uncle Osmond?" she asks as they glide up into the house.

"Forgive me, yes. My manners have atrophied, along with my withered loins."

"What a horrifying image," Swanny says. She perches on the edge of the small ruby-colored bench. The gray curls of Osmond's topknot look like frayed electrical wires. She has a funny urge to touch them. "Do you speak to all of your nephew's guests so outrageously?"

Osmond regards her in the mirrored wall as he slurps his brew.

"Paralysis of the body is no disadvantage compared to paralysis of the mind," he says. "Sometimes it takes a shock to reinvigorate a dying muscle."

"Perhaps I flatter myself, but I don't believe I'm in need of shocking."

"My nephew seems to think otherwise."

"If the family resemblance extends to repartee, I'm sure I'll be all right."

The elevator doors open. A bamboo cane emerges from beneath the folds of Osmond's cape. He swings it recklessly, giving directions: "End of the hallway, last door on your left. You won't miss it."

Swanny steps into the hall. "Shouldn't you accompany me? As a chaperone?"

Osmond almost spews imperial porter on her. He wipes his mouth with the back of his hand. He's still chortling when the door slides shut again.

The only sound in the hallway is the eternal humming of a fully automated house. There are no windows, only a row of closed-shut doors appearing on either side of a carpet that flows in patterns like calligraphy beneath Swanny's feet.

Ever since she first heard the name of her intended, a picture of Duncan Ripple has been forming in her mind. She has seen all of his Holosnaps (albeit usually in static two-dimensional thumbnails on her mother's obsolescent machine), has memorized them, but in her mind's eye he is not posed, grinning, in the driver's seat of a HowFly, or sporting the Kevlar vest and mortarboard that signify his graduation from underschool. She imagines him instead in the most erotic pose imaginable: propped up in bed, one hand supporting his well-hewn jaw while the other leafs lazily through the pages of a book. He is a scholar in an unbuttoned shirt, with the torrid, brooding gaze of a pirate. She already plans to encourage his growing a beard.

Swanny walks down the hallway, trying to impart, as her mother always urges, some natural grace into her step. She passes an end table, where a celadon vase full of begonias fills the hallway with its scent. She hopes he doesn't read mysteries, or those cheap spy thrillers where black-clad assassins fire stun darts from their cuff links. It would be utterly dull to discuss, hour upon hour, characters who are distinguished only by their motives to kill. Perhaps he prefers poetry—that would be refreshing. The door of his room is labeled clearly enough: ersatz caution tape zigzags across it, instructing the visitor DO NOT ENTER. How droll. She places her hand on the knob, then hesitates, half-frightened, half savoring the moment. She can already feel his caress on her cheek, his hot breath in her ear: "Swan Lenore Dahlberg, you strange, otherworldly thing—let me love you." The years with her mother in the cold schoolroom, learning how to sit, how to speak, how to laugh, what to know, who to be, are now concluded. This is the moment before the test, and she is entirely prepared. With an anticipatory shiver, she twists the knob and enters.

A gust of air-conditioning buffets her, as though she's opened the door onto a windy cliff. The ceiling is much higher than in the hall, and the walls are papered with a minute repeating pattern of blue and red robots shooting each other in the face. The plush blue carpet is strewn all over with toys: nunchucks, a plastic shirtless man with articulated muscles, a crossbow with foam darts, a jetpack, a giant melodica keyboard, model HowFlys with their bellies popped open, revealing empty sockets for battery packs. A vast aquarium blurps and bubbles, seething with minute crustaceans, and a seafaring death pyre somehow appears to be functioning as a sperm-splotched, unmade bed. Explosions detonate on a massive projector screen.

They say the instant before one dies lasts for all eternity. Perhaps the same also applies to the instant before one's heart breaks in two.

A ball pit, almost overflowing with rainbow-colored plastic orbs, sunken into the floor: in it sit Duncan Ripple and a young woman, topless.

Swanny considers resorting to an old comfort. Screaming has not solved many of her problems in the past, but in this case she thinks it best. However, when she opens her mouth, nothing comes out except for a garbled croaking, at which point her betrothed and the young woman turn in her direction.

"Whoa," says Ripple. "You're early."

"I am the Baroness Swan Lenore Dahlberg," Swanny says, as if to remind herself. Her voice sounds foreign, uncharacteristically high and tremulous.

"Shit, pro," says a disembodied communicant, speaking through the projector's sound system—how many strangers are observing Swanny's humiliation? "Is that your *wife*?"

"Gotta log off, Kelvin."

"Fuck that, I need you to pierce this freighter before it deploys its drone hull. I am destroying on defense, back me up here."

Ripple sighs. With a rapid fumbling of buttons, he executes a move that results in a giant fireball annihilating all other images on the projector screen.

"Boom! You're the abuser!"

"Do a save. You should be OK on single player for the rest of the level."

"Eh, I'll start a new game."

"Have a nice trip."

"Have a nice marriage."

"Have a nice career."

"Let me know if you ever need one. I'm a job creator now, I'll find you something cushy."

"Yeah, in the boringest place on Earth. Thanks but no thanks."

The projector screen clicks to black. Without the celestial inferno of its dreamscape, the capacious room seems far too small for three.

"*What* did he just call you?" Swanny asks, icily. She's taken hold of herself again.

"Who? Kelvin?"

"You didn't bother to introduce us."

"Uh, sorry . . ."

"He called you 'the abuser.'" Swanny moves to the lip of the ball pit and stares down at Ripple, as though her gaze could melt and boil the plastic immersing him. He is the same as always—the same face, the same name—but the meaning is entirely different, like a word in a foreign tongue that she has always misunderstood. *La Diabla*. She does her best to ignore the girl.

"Oh, right. Because I tore that freight ship a new one. I was dominating."

"Doesn't the term 'abuse' generally refer to domestic situations?" Swanny removes her fur coat and defiantly drapes it over one arm. I could knock him out with these arms, she thinks. He may be stronger, but I have the element of surprise.

However, Ripple is onto her. "Better dress for dinner," he mumbles, hoisting himself (clad in boxers, thank God) out of the ball pit, leaving the topless young woman half-submerged, anxious and alone. It is now, only now, that Swanny trains her gaze on this competitor—a starved and fragile beauty with luminous, frightened eyes. She has the same look as a half-grown rabbit caught in one of Corona's traps.

"You're the dead girl," she tells Swanny now.

Swanny laughs. The sound is like glass breaking. It feels like shards in her throat. She thinks of Etta from *Canfield Manor*, the scene in which she succumbs to the hysteria that "bubbled up from some deep internal spring," but the thought only makes her laugh harder. "Is that a *threat*?"

"I . . . I saw your ghost on the stage. You sang . . ."

"Are you Duncan's ex-girlfriend?" Swanny inquires.

"Ex?"

"Perhaps you don't know. Duncan and I are to be married to-morrow."

The girl draws her knees protectively to her chest. They emerge, bony islands in the plastic sea.

"Does that make us sisters?" she asks.

"No," Swanny says sweetly. "That makes you dispensable. Redundant. Do you know what those words mean?"

"Um . . ."

"He's going to toss you out with the garbage."

The girl nibbles her lip. Her bite is uncorrected, with protruding central incisors and diastema. Swanny has read that such flaws are a sign of an oral fixation, or poor breeding, or both. Her own mouth itches with its unborn tooth.

"I like it here," the girl murmurs. She doesn't sound too sure.

"How very inconvenient for you."

Back out in the hallway, Swanny closes the door behind her and pauses for a moment, thinking, before starting the long walk back toward the golden elevator. She has met her husband. The house still hums. She passes door after door; her stride quickens; the carpet patterns blur beneath her feet.

The celadon vase doesn't break the first time she smashes it into the end table. But the second time, it does. And then the crunch of ancient china and flower stems is so satisfying as she stomps them into the carpet. In fact, she is so focused on grinding each shard of pottery into absolute dust that she does not even notice the elevator door has pinged open until Osmond Ripple, still aboard, clears his throat.

"Pardon me." Swanny retrieves her fur coat from where she dropped it on the floor. "I seem to have had a little accident."

"I can see that." He closes the book he holds on his lap and beckons. "Well, no matter. The whole house will be yours soon enough. Perhaps you'll do us all a favor, demoiselle, and burn it to the ground."

10

COURTING DISASTER

When Ripple was a kid, he and his pooch Hooligan used to spear-hunt big game in the wilds of the imagination. They were stouthearted slayers with their foam harpoons and shrapnel-grade pith helmets (rare gifts from Uncle Osmond, who bopped them both on the head and warned them—with a wild gleam in his eye—to watch out for snarks). They tromped through the underbrush, sniffing bent branches, measuring rogue footprints in handspans; they tuned their ears to crackles and thuds below the range of ordinary perception. Nothing escaped them. In the darkest jungle, Ripple often thought to himself, the fiercest predator is *me*.

Which was probably true in the darkest jungle where they ever went exploring, because that jungle was the greenhouse in the heart of the mansion, where trees grew up to three stories, straining toward the geodesic glass of the skydome. There, the air hung moist, stinky with leaf breath and aflutter with twelve nonindigenous species of trapped butterflies. Even though it was still, technically, inside, the space felt more outdoors than outdoors, overgrown and maybe even a little bit treacherous: unlike the other rooms in the house, with their Sorcerer's Apprentices and semiholographic Toob screens, which gave up their mysteries at the push of a button, the greenhouse kept its secrets well. It seemed possible for almost *anything* to be lurking there, under the green prehistoric light that filtered through the fronds. But Ripple didn't have any doubt in his mind that when he found the beast in question, he'd vanquish it, uffishly and with maximum flair.

Today, though, knowing the foe he seeks, he isn't so confident of his success. Ripple powers through the groundcover, cursing and swatting away the little monarchs and *Caligula thibeta* that beat the air around his face. On the scent. When he parts the dense vegetation—he's in the area packed with neck-high bulrushes—he reveals his quarry, hulking on a stone bench barely four feet away, all decked out in ruffles and lace, pouting beside the artificial pond.

Like it or not, he has to bring this one back alive.

"Wench, they sent me to find you. Soup's on."

Swanny doesn't turn around to look at him. Her voice is brittle and aggrieved: "How can you think of food at a time like this?"

"Because it's *dinnertime*."

Swanny tosses a pebble at the water. It banks off a lily pad and disappears without a splash. "So. Who is she?"

"Who is who?"

"You know exactly whom I mean."

"She's—" Ripple isn't even sure what the honest answer would be. He doesn't want to explain, and he definitely doesn't want to apologize. "She's just a friend."

"Do you invite all of your friends to your . . . ball pit?"

He does, actually, but it sounds dirty the way she says it. "Listen, I'm not some no-pubes grail boy. I'm a man. I do what a man does."

"Please. You're a *child*."

"And you're *so* mature. You think I don't know about your little tantrum in the hall? I got news for you: that vase was a collectible."

"I haven't the slightest notion what you're talking about."

Her reply is so airy, so assured, that Ripple almost lets it slide. She's no damsel, but her flesh is creamy and inviting, agreeably squished into the boning of her dress. When the dusk light from the skydome hits her curls just so, he remembers why he used to tug it to her Skin Pics. Woman: the most dangerous game. He reminds himself to show no mercy. He aims straight for the heart. "Did you think I was in love with you or something?"

Boom. Swanny's disappointment is so total, it's like the extinction of a species. When she finally spits out a reply, Ripple isn't even sure if her words are directed at him, or at the entire course of her life leading up to the chain of events that summoned her from Wonland County and brought her to this place: "What a waste."

~~~

Pippi and Humphrey stroll down the Hall of Ancestors, now dressed for dinner, shoulder-padded in their suit jackets, chartreuse and navy respectively. Humphrey breaks the companionable silence: "I'm glad we're getting a chance to speak candidly before the ceremony. Without the lawyers present."

Her suspicion is piqued: "Is there something you were reluctant to disclose?"

"No, no, of course not. This position really is a terrific opportunity for the baroness to come into her own and play an integral role in the future of the family."

"In consultation with Duncan, of course."

"Pippi, let's be frank. He's my son. My affection for him goes without saying. But he's not up to the task. The scale of our holdings—it's considerable. The real estate, of course, but also the controlling interests, the shell corporations, the vulture funds, the offshore accounts . . ." Humphrey hesitates, scrutinizes his loafer tassels. "Sometimes I'm afraid he takes after his mother."

Pippi is all condolences: "You mustn't blame yourself for that."

"Marriage is not a decision to make emotionally. I learned that the hard way. Which is why I'm so relieved about nailing down this deal. We were in talks with some other families, but none of them compared, in terms of the total package."

"Swanny *is* a top-drawer candidate, by any objective standard. Of course I'm biased, but the test scores don't lie."

"I don't just mean Swanny. I'm hoping you'll stay on in an advisory capacity." He smiles ruefully. "It's been too long since I've had a sounding board for executive-level decisions."

"I'm flattered."

"If you'd like to take a look at the financials, I'd be happy to show you the books after dinner, over a cognac in my office. There are some exciting new additions to the portfolio."

Pippi grasps his bespoke sleeve. "It's a date."

~~~

Upstairs in the locked guest room, Abby is still watching the Toob. The Lady used to call it "the hypnotist's jukebox," and though Abby still isn't quite sure what those words mean, she's beginning to understand. She's watched four hours now: four solid blocks of content, interrupted briefly by edutainment specials about fire-retardant fashion and an edible rodent charcuterie in South Crookbridge. She thinks of the toaster she met this morning, the Electric City flowing through its cord from an unnamed source. The Toob is a toaster of black-hex enchantment: a toaster full of souls.

A girl looks through the other side of the Toob screen, as if gazing into a window, or a mirror. She looks like Abby: blond hair, tan skin, spectral cheekbones. The only difference is her eyes, jade green instead of dawn blue.

"You are not alone," she tells Abby, close enough to touch. Though the surface of the screen is flat—Abby's checked—she seems to lean a little ways into the room.

"I am not alone," Abby murmurs back. She huddles under the blanket she's unplugged from the wall. Abby wonders if the girl in the Toob knows she's in a Toob. She wonders if she can see out, and if so, what she sees. Maybe when you're inside the Toob, it doesn't seem like you're in a sleek white box at all. Maybe it seems like you're in a locked cell where there's nothing to do but look at a screen flashing rainbow colors and lithe bodies, and through that very screen, others see you.

Maybe Abby is a Girl in the Toob.

"If you're one of the countless women in this city affected by hideous, disfiguring burns, you may feel you can't go on. But now there's hope—with Graftisil."

A different woman appears in place of the first one. "My scabs started sloughing off the first day!" she exclaims. She has a thick chunk of hair covering half her face. RESULTS MAY NOT BE TYPICAL scrolls across the bottom of the screen.

Clack. Clackety-clack.

Abby twists around, startled. The knob turns on the locked door. She imagines Dunk's father, who dragged her here, returning to take "further disciplinary action," like he threatened. Or worse yet, the chortling People Machine, with his wire hair and riddle tongue. But when the door opens, it's Katya, clad in a dress that shimmers like the bay in sunshine, that sparkles like broken glass. Abby takes one look at her and bursts into tears.

"Oh dear," says Katya. She steps inside and deftly strokes the side of the Toob with her hand, as if soothing it. Immediately the people vanish. "Poor little one. You didn't know how to turn it off."

"I want to see Dunk."

"Dunky is at dinner with his wife."

Abby covers her face with both hands. She sees Dunk's body in her mind, every part: the curly hair on his belly, the scar on his knuckle from Power Jousting. The column of his throat bobbing as he chugs. After a moment, she feels the mattress slosh. Katya has sat down beside her.

"You shouldn't worry," Katya says quietly. "He can never love her. A mother knows."

"Really?"

"Yes. She is big and fat and will boss him around. They may have babies, but they'll never make love. They'll have their babies in a tube."

Abby sniffles. "So that's how it works." She glances at the dark-ened Toob. "You're born into it."

"Yes," says Katya. Her sadness makes her face almost old.

"OK."

Katya hesitates. "Abby. We're not so different, you and I."

"We're not?"

"I don't belong here either. Humphrey also found me and brought me back from somewhere else."

"Somewhere trashy?"

"Somewhere trashy."

"Do you ever miss it?"

"Even if I did, I could never go back."

"Why not?"

"I have forgotten how to survive alone. You must be careful that you don't forget." She stands up. "I came to make sure you had your dinner. Did Hummer show you where the dumbwaiter is?"

Abby shakes her head. Katya stands up and presses on a panel in the wall. It retracts, revealing a serving tray under a silver dome.

"Still hot," she says without touching it. "Eat."

~~~

Downstairs in the dining room, the molecular gastronomist has outdone himself. Every course is freeze-dried, liquefied, aerated, cubed, sphered, crystallized, cold-smoked, or on fire. Familiar flavors haunt alien textures like déjà vu: wasabi pop rocks, beet dust, salmon thread, marrow foam, bourbon ice. It's erudite, mocking food, food that laughs at one's attempts to understand it. Swanny savors it. It seems only right that in this place, every form of nourishment is a parody of itself.

"Of course, the long-term effects of the mutiny remain to be seen," says Humphrey. "It hasn't even been a fiscal year since the walkouts. Some of the literature I've been reading suggests that this is the time to invest in private-sector emergency service providers. But that raises the question, without the Metropolitan Fire Department functioning, how is anyone going to keep living in the city at all?"

"I don't understand how these mutineers think they can simply abandon their civic responsibility," Pippi opines. "If they don't want to be conscripted, they should pay for their exemptions like everyone else. And honestly, what are they planning to do instead?

They have no prospects. It isn't as though their educations are going to waste. This city is all they know, and yet they want to let it burn."

"Too bad they shut that shit down, I'd've made a pretty great fireman," Ripple puts in. "The main thing is, no fear. I don't even know what fear is."

"Duncan, the next time this mongrel begs at the table, I'll be feeding him cyanide tablets from the panic room," grumbles Osmond, forcefully shoving a black furry creature away from his wheelchair. "Begone, you barnyard abomination."

"My God," says Pippi, "does that dog have hands?"

"Katya got him a hybrid. Damned if I know why." Humphrey helps himself to another ladleful of liquid foie. "The apehound's since been discontinued, incidentally."

"Dunky had no brother." Katya slides into her seat. "He needed a playmate."

"It seems he has no shortage of those," Swanny murmurs, patting her lips with a napkin. Osmond snorts.

"Low disease resistance, engineering defects, you name it." Humphrey mops his plate with a roll. "It's incredible that thing has lived as long as it has. It takes more heart medications than I do."

"He can't throw for shit, but he can catch a Whamball pretty good." Ripple feeds Hooligan a nugget of Hollandaise, and the dog slaps him a high-five. The fingers are stubby and monkeyish, but with an opposable thumb. "And he's a hella tackle."

"Pets do teach one such life lessons. I remember, when I was a child, I had a *newt*, can you imagine?"

"Funny, Mother, *I* never had a pet."

"You were out there in the countryside, darling." Pippi sinks her knife into a sweetbread. "Don't you remember when we had raccoons under the veranda?"

"Baroness, we're all quite impressed with your musical talents," Humphrey says. "Maybe we could persuade you to perform a few airs after the wedding. We have a klangflugel in the upstairs parlor, just collecting dust."

Osmond begins lifting bourbon cubes from the steaming dry-ice tureen and dropping them directly into his mouth with the tongs.

"Perhaps there's a reason for that." Swanny drains her glass. "I'd think we'd be better off with recordings."

"Nonsense. It can be a delightful instrument in the right hands."

Swanny's in the 98th percentile for note accuracy, with marks of distinction in dynamics and tempo control, but she's in no humor to make her mother proud. "*I* make it sound like a tuned typewriter."

Pippi flashes a warning: "Darling, you're being absurd."

"Perhaps I am. Ours isn't always so well tuned."

"She plays like an angel."

"Mother, you're too kind."

"Dunky plays drums," Katya offers.

"The tintinnabulation of a child's pots and pans. As if any of us could forget." Half-melted cubes roll like marbles in Osmond's mouth. "I credit your son entirely with the ontogenesis of my Exploding Head Syndrome."

The waiter clears Swanny's spotless plate. She leans around him for a better look. "Your head appears intact enough."

"But my mind, *mon cygne*, my cherished mind: that's been rent asunder."

"A pity. You might have made a splendid conversationalist."

"I would have made a splendid lover." Osmond is visibly drooling. He wipes his mouth with a swath of his caftan. "Perhaps like you, I would have been sent for by a faraway kingdom and married to the throne."

"Wonland is hardly 'faraway.' It's less than an hour by flying machine. Though that isn't my preferred form of transportation," Swanny adds darkly.

"They do say it's exhilarating to fly." Pippi lifts her dripping talons from the fingerbowl. "I worked on that campaign, you know. 'The Sky Is Yours.'"

"Rise above," Ripple agrees.

"You'll never get me up in one of those things," counters Swanny. Only this morning, she longed to be swept up and away. But that desire, along with so many others, is foreign to her now. Her arms feel enormous tonight. "All that bumping and jostling, up and down, up and down. The very thought gives me the most terrible nausea."

Osmond lifts his glass unsteadily. "I'd like to propose a toast."

"Osmond-you're-drunk." Humphrey says it so automatically it comes out as one word.

"To love, marriage, and virgin sacrifice. To this saintly girl, this *woman*, whose virtue we hold in our thrall." Osmond folds his hands around the wine stem, saying grace. "Our baroness, who art in Wonland, forgive us for our vampirism, as our ruined family consumes you, forever and ever, amen."

"Baroness, let me apologize for my brother. He can be quite cruel."

"The cruelty is yours, *mon frère*. Perhaps she should marry me instead of your wretched son."

"Fuck yeah! You guys would be *perfect!*" Ripple blasts out a laugh.

Pippi swiftly joins him: "What a charming sense of humor, Duncan. Like the old comedians: 'Take my wife, please!' But I'm dating myself. Humphrey, who did the sponge-painting in here? It's exquisite."

"I'd sooner see this maiden play the harlot to a den of Torchtown brigands than carry *his* slavering imbecility forward another generation." Osmond sloshes in Ripple's general direction. "And I would wager, so would she."

A heat radiates from Swanny's heart outward, a feeling like rage but not as unpleasant. She stares at Osmond, who shatters his now-empty glass on the floor and lunges for the nearest decanter. Impossible. In this house, she never would have expected it: he's outraged on her behalf.

Pippi snaps her fingers. "Wheel him away, waiter," she says, as if he's the dessert cart.

Humphrey nods. "What she said."

The staff scramble to oblige. The sommelier swings open the doors. The fromagier yanks the napkin from Osmond's lap. The crumb scraper kicks loose the brake of his chair.

"Yegor, have the starfruit cobbler sent to my chambers!" Osmond shouts as the waiter steers him haphazardly toward the egress. *"À la mode, s'il te plaît!"*

"I'm Maxim," says the waiter dryly. The doors swing shut again, but they can still hear Osmond shouting in the lobby.

"He will have no ice cream tonight," says Katya. Of course, Katya herself hasn't eaten anything at all.

～～～

After dinner, Humphrey and Pippi disappear in the direction of Humphrey's office, Katya slinks off to bed, complaining of "heartburn," and Ripple takes Hooligan and Swanny on a tour of the house. He doesn't bother hooking Hooligan's leash onto the collar. Swanny coldly regards the dog.

"Shouldn't he take these jaunts outside? In case he needs to relieve himself?"

"Nah, he likes going where it's climate controlled."

"Your dog defecates *inside* the mansion? On the floor?"

"Sure, they're always shampooing these rugs. It's like somebody's full-time job."

They're walking down a hall near the Man Cave, the carpet plushly patterned beneath their feet. Swanny wrinkles her nose.

"That is the most revolting thing I've ever heard."

"You'll get used to the smell."

"No, I assure you, I will not."

Ripple stops in his tracks. "Fem, do not tell my dog where to poop."

"Or you'll do what? Refuse to marry me?"

"Maybe. Maybe not. I haven't really decided yet. This is your audition."

"*My* audition?" Swanny's laugh is an ear-gouging little shriek. "Let's abandon the pretense, Duncan. You're terrified of your father, and of my mother. You'll marry me even if every fiber of your being screams for an eleventh-hour reprieve."

Ripple fakes a yawn. "Break another knickknack, Super Bitch."

Swanny grabs an obliging candelabra from a nearby hall table and hurls it into an enormous gilt-framed mirror on the opposite wall. Glass shatters and rains to the ground.

"Tell them to clean that up!" she wails, and runs down the corridor.

Whoa. She must be stopped. Ripple blinks twice, gives chase. But Hooligan, catching on to the game, runs on ahead. They race past the entrances to the ballroom, the animatronic zoo, the mud baths. As Swanny rounds the corner into the Hall of Ancestors, surprisingly swift in heels, Hooligan vaults into the air and tackles her to the ground.

"Get it away!" She pummels Hooli even as he lands slurp upon slobbery slurp on her face and neck. His preternaturally human hands paw her cleavage.

"Down, boy," says Ripple, yanking the dog back by the collar. "Swanny? You OK?"

Ripple is not accustomed to seeing girls cry. At underschool, they had a class called Gender Differentiation, to make up for the fact there were no wenches in a three-mile radius (except for a couple of postmenopausal teachers, who had apparently taken vows of natural aging). By the end of term, they had learned all about stuff like Feminine Wiles, Estro-Rage, and Breast Tenderness, the illustration for which looms large over Ripple's masturbation sessions to this day.

Still, nothing could prepare him for this.

Swanny does not just have a few tears trickling out of the corners of her eyes. She's given herself over to a possession dark and voluptuous, which seizes her in gasping, heaving tides. Her body strains at its constrictive garments, like all that flesh has turned lycanthropish and is about to bust seams. And yikes, she's got a lot of teeth.

Ripple's scared, he can't lie. Yet another part of him is curious, even a little turned on. He thought Abby was untamed because she doesn't wear shoes or eat with a fork. But this one is wild on the inside.

"Hey—hey, um, don't be sad."

Swanny lunges to her feet; Ripple recoils.

"You're intimidated by my intelligence! Mother warned me this might happen. She warned me, but I didn't believe it. Because I am—so—beautiful!"

"Yeah! Yeah, super hot!" Ripple, backpedaling, can't agree fast enough.

"But what does it matter," she sniffles, "when you don't even love me."

"Look, I just met you. The beauty hasn't had a chance to work on me yet."

"One always falls in *true* love at first sight."

"There's a rule about this?"

"Have you read any of the books I recommended?"

Ripple vaguely remembers a lengthy missive titled "My Most Essential Personal Library," with a numbered list that went well into the hundreds. "I'm a reluctant reader."

She pronounces it as a verdict: "Unforgivable."

"Wait—so you wrote all those letters? Yourself? I just figured they were from your mom. They had so many big words in them and stuff."

"You haven't even read my letters." Swanny turns away, gazing dolefully up at the portraits on the walls. Hooligan shoves his head under Ripple's hand, whimpers, but Ripple shushes him. They're not done here.

The Hall of Ancestors isn't Ripple's favorite room in the house; it isn't even in his top five. Back before reality, the only way to immortalize yourself was art, but executive portraiture doesn't do much to bring a person back to life. The paintings are muddy and heavily shadowed, the Ripple men in them going back seven generations, bluish-pale and stiffly posed, pin-striped and cuff-linked, displayed in gold frames like open caskets leaned up against the walls. Even Humphrey—the only one still living, heart attacks take these pros out young—looks embalmed in his picture, too tranquil without the telltale vein pulsing in his forehead, giving off signs of a frustrated, pressurized life. It's like a cemetery except for the eyes. The eyes follow you.

"How ghastly," Swanny observes, gazing up at Ripple's great-great-grandfather, who rests his gnarled hand protectively upon an indistinct globe. "It's a monument to an obsolescent patriarchy."

"I know, right?" Ripple dares to come up behind her, fairly close, to look over her shoulder. She smells like dry flowers, old leather, and teenage tantrum sweat. "Sad thing is, some of my grandmas were real damsels. But instead we have to look at all these bald dudes."

Swanny clearly didn't expect him to agree with her. She turns warily, her crinolines swishing. "Where will your portrait hang?"

"Right there." Ripple points at the designated wall panel. "It's not going to be boring like these, though. The guy I commissioned is a real artist. He did the extinction mural downtown, at the Center for Global Capital.* He's going to mythologize the fuck out of me."

Swanny raises an eyebrow. "I didn't realize you were so interested in visual art."

"I'm interested in my image. I don't want to go down like some loser."

"I can't imagine a Ripple being lost to history." Swanny peers up at his actual grandpa, a potatoish man Ripple never met, whose business cards, even now, materialize inexplicably in the pockets of the family's coats, between the cushions of the house's various couches and divans. Networking from beyond the grave. "It must be fascinating to learn the intricacies of one's family line. Mine is shrouded in mystery."

"What?"

Swanny sighs deeply. "You know I lost my father as an infant.

---

*The Gone World by Ryden Marx vividly portrays the last violent days of the dinosaurs, mired in lava, scarred by meteor shrapnel, resorting to cannibalism, beneath an orange hell sun choked in volcanic ash. It was regarded by the CGC's board as an allegory for the day when, like these lizards of history, the dragons too would become a thing of the past. But others saw it as a skeptical look at the future of global trade in a city no longer fit for human occupancy.

When he died, the secrets of my ancestry died along with him. I have no proof, of course, but I believe he and my mother shared more than just a bed. They may have been cousins—perhaps even first."

Hooligan chooses this moment to squat behind a potted ficus a few yards away. Whatever, Ripple will deal with that later. "I don't think so."

"We mustn't judge them, Duncan. Their passion, though forbidden, made me what I am."

"No, I mean, Dad studied your genome. He had the printouts all over his desk for weeks. No way he'd set us up if you had mutant blood."

Swanny removes a finger from her mouth. "I did not claim to have 'mutant blood.'"

"I just mean no way your parents were first cousins. Wait, I'll show you." Ripple takes the device out of the pocket of his Kevlar vest, prestidigitates the document onto the screen. "See?"

Pedigree: The Baroness Swan Lenore Dahlberg. A maze of lines, straight and squiggled, a flow chart of love and its consequences. Swanny squints as if she's never seen one before, even though that's impossible. At underschool, family trees hung framed in everybody's rooms.

"Where are my parents?" she asks.

"Down here, at the bottom." Ripple zooms in on the text. "Look, Chet Dahlberg—that's your dad. Kid of Veronica Golden and Chase Dahlberg—scroll up, here's who they're related to. Those green dots stand for money. And see, your mom's way over on this side. Coming out of nowhere. Penelope Gibich."

"Let me see that." Swanny snatches the LookyGlass. "Gibich? Am I even pronouncing that correctly? I always assumed Mother was born a Dahlberg."

Ripple shrugs. "It's just a name."

"It's her identity, Duncan. Names are lineage—linguistic DNA, passed down from parent to child—the cargo of words we carry from this life to the next. To be a Dahlberg . . . well, it's something quite refined."

"Shouldn't you be glad you're not inbred?"

Swanny runs her tongue over her teeth thoughtfully, like she's making sure they're all still there. "I suppose."

Speaking of breeding: "Want to see what our kid looks like?"

"Pardon?"

"It's just a projection, but the margin of error is *slight*." Ripple steps close to her and adeptly strokes the LookyGlass in her hand. "Check it out. He's got your eyes."

The algorithmically derived infant shoots out of the device in three dimensions, a hologram hovering in a beam of light. They've mapped out every detail, down to the pendant of spit bubbles dangling from his chin.

"Dad says we have to name him Duncan Humphrey Ripple the Sixth, but I like Jutt better. I don't even know if it's a real name, I just like the way it sounds. Jutt."

"Good lord, Duncan. You're planning so far ahead." Her cheeks color; she looks away. "I haven't even started freezing my eggs yet. And I might prefer a girl."

Whoa, whoa, whoa. She's acting like he just made a declaration of love or something. Maybe their baby wasn't the right thing to show her on a first date. He takes back the LookyGlass. "It's not like I want him either. I just had to check that he wasn't too ugly. He's gotta extend my brand."

Swanny circles the simulated rug rat, sizing it up from all angles. Appraising it. "When the time comes, we must be certain to give him the freedoms denied us."

"Totally agreed." But wait a minute, Ripple's the one who wants out of here. "What would *you* do, if you could do whatever you wanted?"

"One can always do what one wants, Duncan. It's just a question of calculating the consequences."

Huh? He switches off the baby. "You mean like running away?"

"We all have our urges."

"Yeah? Where would you go?"

"I suppose I would live among the common people and give myself over to a life of disgraceful hedonism. Or I'd go on a journey—but all the places I love best exist only in novels." She sighs. "Perhaps I'd press myself between the pages of a book."

Hedonism? Does that mean sex? Ripple always kind of thought sex and reading were mutually exclusive. But maybe Swanny's got wires crossed in her brain somewhere and her fantasies take the form of words. Maybe all he would have to do is figure out the exact right thing to say and she'd be writhing in his arms, the way she was on the floor just now, only lustier. He's far down this path before he remembers that he has an actual human waiting to fuck him upstairs.

"I'd be a fireman," he declares brashly.

Swanny nods, unimpressed. "Oh yes, you mentioned that at dinner."

"I was just about to enlist when they shut down the department."

That wasn't exactly how it happened. A few years after the first dragon attacks—when the volunteer fire department was experiencing its first real drop-off in numbers, as fallen members no longer proved so easy to replace—the city adopted a radical tactic: mandatory conscription into the cause for any local male over the age of sixteen. The girls were spared, in the hope that their potential for healthy pregnancy would prevent the city from depopulating still further, but the families of boys like Ripple either had to see their sons off to likely death and disfigurement in a state-issued yellow slicker, or, at great cost, purchase a series of exemptions, which gave the pro in question a one-year reprieve, renewals available. Humphrey had done the latter, of course, but when Ripple was in the process of flunking underschool, Ripple made a series of impassioned and unsuccessful appeals to let his exemption expire. As the videographers rolled, he argued that he wasn't made for "bookwork," that his dad should let him out of his "guilted cage" so he could soar to the heights of heroism. The Sprawl ate it up, and Ripple was actually scrolling through some flattering ratings numbers when Humphrey came by his room one unfilmed afternoon.

"I assume you were just grandstanding for the cameras." Humphrey picked up a bag of BacoCrisps from the floor, saw that it was empty, and dropped it again. "But if you feel that risking your life for a transparently shortsighted and foolhardy cause would force you to buckle down and impose some discipline on yourself, far be it from me to stand in your way."

"Uhhhhhhh . . ." Ripple drew out the null syllable as long as he could.

Humphrey nodded. "That's what I thought."

After that, Ripple never brought up the Metropolitan Fire Department onscreen again. It was lucky for him that public opinion was shifting away from conscription around the same time. Exposé sites kept uncovering new abuses and excesses; the firemen tried to form some kind of union, which got shut down immediately. Ripple didn't follow any of it closely. Then, about six months ago, midway through his final semester of underschool, the dragons torched the Gemini Building and an army of mutinous conscriptees dispatched to the scene stormed out in protest without extinguishing it. The ensuing blaze reportedly killed dozens, including charismatic Fire Chief Paxton Trank, and the flames of Empire Island have been unattended ever since. Ripple thinks of what Kelvin said: *a total wasteland. Water and power are probably next.*

"What a pity," Swanny says now. "It might have made a real man of you. But at least you have your—image."

"We are way too sober for this," Ripple observes.

~~~

Ten minutes later, they're in the herb garden on the fifth-floor terrace, smoking out of a pipe made from an old Voltage bottle. The smoke is scented with the sickly sweet citrus of the long-gone drink. Just beneath that lies the odor of the loam itself, peaty and musty and decayed, poisonously abandoned: something between a dormhouse shower curtain and an old cedar chest. Though he likes getting swamped as much as the next guy, Ripple's never gotten used to the taste; he could never be a twenty-four-hour marshie like his uncle Osmond. But Swanny, though a first-timer to the substance, seems to be taking to it just fine. She coughs, delicately at first, then with the phlegm-rattling intensity of a show-off emphysemic.

"Good lord," she murmurs. She stretches out one of her ringlets and watches it spring back. "Is this what average intelligence is like?"

"No way," says Ripple. "This scrip makes you *dumb*."

Absently stroking the lapel of her chinchilla coat, Swanny rises from the hemlock glider and minces toward the terrace railing. Her feet no longer seize the ground with a conquistador's purpose. The night is dark and misty, and the dragons all but invisible; only the white-hot, sizzling lines of their breath assert their presence in the lower city. Swanny leans toward them, four floors and the sheer cliff face of the Heights falling away before her.

"Baroness, do *not* widow me." Ripple hacks out his last hit. Hooligan, lying at his feet, looks up with concern. "Siddown. Gravity is not your friend."

" 'The Sky Is Yours.' Ha. It's quite extraordinary that my mother became successful peddling such lines of patent nonsense. 'The Sky Is Yours.' No wonder she'll go to her grave with her name a lie. Gibich. The sky isn't mine. The sky belongs to the dragons. Even before they came, it was just waiting for them. It was as though they made reservations."

"Uh, you weren't alive back then."

"But I read, Duncan. I do *read*. I've read enough to know well that man never *possessed* the *sky*. He only ever passed through it, on his way up or on his way back down." She leans dangerously over the creaking rail, an arm outstretched toward the dragons. "That's our lot in life, isn't it? We fall through the world without leaving a trace, all the while trying to grip the air. Oh, to be an unstoppable force of nature. To *belong* somewhere as they do . . ."

Ripple hasn't laughed like this in a long time. But all of a sudden, the plump silhouette of Swanny from the back, the quavering line of her finger, tracing shapes in the night, the petulant, know-it-all timbre of her voice, suddenly coalesce not into a person, his fiancée, but into the punch line of a ginormous prank being played at his expense, like that time in underschool when some of the guys wrote WASTED on his forehead when he was passed out and no one said anything about it till the ID Holosnaps were already taken. And once he starts laughing, he can't stop. Dimly, it occurs to him that Swanny did the same thing to him earlier, back in his room, so whatever. They're even now.

"I don't see what's so amusing," she says uneasily.

"You want to be a *dragon*?! You really are swamped."

Swanny starts to reply, then freezes, half-turned to her right. In a different, lower voice—both more feminine and more insinuatingly unpleasant—she says, "How rude of me not to include you in our conversation. By all means, please join us." For a second, Ripple thinks she's still talking to him. Then Abby creeps a little closer, into the dim glow of the city's lights. She's wearing one of his mom's old teddies, a flimsy pink thing with feathers around the neckline, under the green camo hoodie he had on this morning.

"You weren't in your room," she says. The sleeves of the sweatshirt are almost down to her knees, the hood like a cape down her back: it's just like that ugly coat she used to wear on the Island, only with less bird shit on the shoulders. She sinks to her knees at his feet, and for a second he half hopes, half fears she's going to do something unspeakable, but instead she scratches Hooligan behind the ears. His tail thumps the all-weather carpet. "Where's Cuyahoga?"

"I don't believe you've properly introduced your 'friend,' Duncan," says Swanny. She returns to her hemlock glider like a queen reclaiming her throne.

"This is Abby," he says, staring at the girl's blond hair. It seems to give off a glow, even in the urban near-dark, and he thinks of a story his mother told him long ago, about an abandoned subway tunnel so full of smugglers' treasure it shone like daylight inside.

"Abby what?"

"Just Abby."

"Just Abby," Swanny repeats. "How insouciant."

Abby is rubbing Hooligan's belly intently; he wriggles to and fro, occasionally clapping with delight. Ripple gently prods her with the toe of his sneaker, but she doesn't stop, or look up at him either. Great. Now they're both mad.

"See this bandage?" He rolls up his sleeve. "My HowFly misfunctioned. But I got lucky. Abby saved my life," he admits. "I guess I should've said that before."

Now Abby lifts her head. Her eyes are redder even than Swanny's, and for a confused second he wonders if she's been smoking too. Then he realizes she's been crying—not to get his attention, but alone, in her room. Because she missed him.

Him. That's all she wants. Not his fortune, not his name. Him.

"You have a heart," she reminds him, trying to smile. "You proved it to me." She reaches out her hand. And OK, he takes it.

"Well." Swanny stands up, a little unsteadily. "Duncan, I couldn't have asked for a more enlightening premarital conference. You are the most despicable chauvinist I could ever hope to encounter; it is as though you looked into *my* secret heart and answered every fear with your Neanderthal's 'hell yeah.' And while we're on the subject of each other's mothers, as we were a while ago, I'd like to express my admiration for the immigrant showgirl who gave you life. Digging for gold is exhausting work. I now know from experience. Thank you for the intoxicants. Also, I hate your dog."

She sashays back to the French doors and disappears inside. Abby rests her head on his knee. He closes his eyes for a second, trying to lose himself in sensation, and when he opens them, Cuyahoga's perched on the railing, right where Swanny stood before, watching. The vulture was circling this whole time.

11

SOULMATES

Swanny is not certain whom she wants to kill: Duncan, her mother, or herself. Perhaps all three. But if she's to kill anyone at all, it's imperative that she stop sobbing first.

The curious thing about this drug, though, is that although one part of her is curled in the empty Swirlpool of a randomly selected fourth-floor guest bathroom, weeping inconsolably, another part of her is hovering over the scene, reporting her sensations back in the distant third person. It's rather like being a character in a book. Even as Swanny hiccups and wipes at her eyes with hanks of quadruple-ply toilet paper, she is noticing the details of this moment—the almost pleasurable irritation of her newest tooth, still just below the gum, the pressure of her feverish skin against the frost-cold porcelain, the shiny knobs of the hot and cold faucets, like the steering wheels of miniature cruise ships. She can almost lose herself in these observations, can at least forget the cruel words she and Duncan exchanged on that terrace for a moment or two, before it all comes rushing back.

Really, she should smoke more: enough of this substance might erase her memory entirely, at least until morning, at which time . . . well. Perhaps morning will never come. The only problem with this plan is that the fateful bag went back into the pocket of Ripple's pants, which are probably strewn by now amid the other garments on the floor of his room. The thought of finding him and the anorexic in flagrante delicto is more than she can bear. But suppose she went directly to the source? Ripple revealed his supplier: Osmond.

A journey through the labyrinth of the mansion sounds for a moment like an impossible task, and risky too. She sees again that endless corridor of tight-shut doors, the crass womanizer waiting at the end of it like a Minotaur. The story seems so very old. She thinks of this morning—only this morning!—when she was the baroness, a dizzy romantic with a hope chest so full that it took Corona and the dentist both to drag it down the stairs. She could not have been more eager to leave the house behind, with its cobwebs and its drafts, its swimming pool, even after all these years, like a newly filled grave. But now the grave she sees is an open one, stretching out before her: this mansion, in all its grandeur, is the sepulcher of her marriage. Swanny has read it is possible to die of heartache, and she imagines the slow drift into oblivion, her soul lapping back like a tide. The problem is, some larger part of her still wants to punch things. Specifically, Duncan Ripple's face.

"I am too strong," she murmurs. "Despite myself, I will endure." She hefts herself out of the empty tub and toddles out into the hallway to score more drugs.

Swanny is not looking her best, it's worth noting. Her eyeliner, applied this morning with a painterly hand, has turned to watercolor, and her ringlets, once glossy and segregated with mousse, are windblown (from the terrace) and snarled (from her writhing paroxysms of grief). Her chinchilla coat hangs open asymmetrically; she isn't sure what's become of her shoes; her crinolines protrude from beneath the hem of her skirt. Yet there's a madwoman glamour about her now, and when she steps into the elevator, she regards the mirror with approval. So it should be, on a night like this.

Swanny has been studying maps of the Ripple house since the contracts were finalized, and even in her current condition, finding Osmond's library should present no difficulty. But on the sixth floor, the elevators open on complete darkness—so complete that, as Swanny steps into it, she scarcely can glimpse the carpet under her feet before the sliding doors eclipse the gilded chamber's light. She feels like a signature with ink spilled over it, like graffiti in an unlit tunnel. She reaches for the wall next to the elevator, but succeeds only in knocking over a large stack of . . . books?

"Who goes?" thunders a voice. All at once, the library is illuminated in synthetic candlelight, revealing Osmond Ripple, irate, wearing a dressing gown and an old-fashioned nightcap, wheeling toward the railing of the upper stacks. "Will the indignities never cease? Am I to be burgled too? Oh." He puffs. "It's you."

"Good God," gasps Swanny, "you nearly frightened me to death."

"Rightfully so! If I'd had my hurlbat, you'd be lying dead where you stand." Osmond adjusts the tassel of his pointed cap. "To what do I owe this pleasure, Baroness?"

Swanny has not prepared for this question. It might not be politic to demand he hand over his medication right away. Besides, if she's honest with herself, that isn't the only reason she's come.

"I've wanted to see you again since dinner," she hears herself say. "It was quite unfair that you were cast from the table for defending my honor. At least that's what I assume you were trying to do when you were so vigorously urging me into prostitution."

"No apology is in order. My brother—and his strumpet bride— are entirely to blame for my callous expulsion from this evening's repast. Now, please, dry your eyes. You look like a besmirched Punchinello. I fear it will trouble my dreams."

"But it isn't just that"—she hesitates—"*Uncle* Osmond. There's no one else here whom I can talk to, you see." As she says it, she tries to ignore the nagging feeling that it's true. "I feel you and I share the same affliction. Not physically, of course, but, well, *spiritually*."

Osmond nods slowly. "You suffer too."

"Yes, yes, terribly."

"The braying of this brutish race threatens to loose you from your senses."

"Quite nearly."

"You long for truth and beauty."

"Both."

"I saw it from the first—a kindred spirit." Osmond wheels back into the bookshelves. "There is one remedy for our torment," he calls down.

"There is? Whatever can that be?"

"Companionship!"

Osmond reappears with what looks like a blown-glass didgeridoo.

"And, of course, good conversation," he continues, opening a nearby dictionary. A great quantity of loam is pressed between the pages. He sweeps it into his hand and tamps it neatly into a protrusion at one end of the colossal bong. "Please, join me."

On rainy afternoons in Wonland County, marooned between novels and bored beyond measure, Swanny has browsed idly through her mother's old overschool philosophy texts, and in their brittle highlighted pages, she has read about the dualism between mind and body. Yet only at this moment, as Osmond's library fills with smoke, does the issue press upon her with the full weight of its importance. Swanny feels that her mind and body are not only separable but separated, as when her childhood stereoscope ceased to align its two images properly and its scenic postcards became depthless and blurred.

"Good God," Osmond sighs, "you've gone cross-eyed on me."

"Oh yes, of course." Swanny blinks until her vision clears and settles back onto the worn leather fainting couch, amid the bundled papers. "Excuse me, you were describing . . ."

"The tragedy of my paralysis could hardly be expected to hold the attention of your addled young mind. I'll recount it another day."

"Uncle Osmond, please, I was quite fascinated."

"As I was saying, when military intervention failed, the days of the Challenges began. At that time, I was fifteen, and the dragons were celebrating their second anniversary in our skies. Though as an athlete, I remained untried, I was something of an expert in ancient lore and, the despised younger son of an exacting tyrant, I grew convinced my destiny lay somewhere loftier than the prescribed avenues of business and academics—to be precise, in the soaring battleground of the city's firmament." His voice rises sharply. "You're sleeping."

"I'm not," says Swanny around a yawn. She's tucked her legs up under her and is resting her head on an encyclopedia.

"It was that day I learned firsthand the truth of the old ballad's sad refrain: 'Dragons live forever, not so little boys.'" Osmond steers his chariot to the wall and presses on one of the lower bookshelves. It springs open, revealing a knee-high refrigerator stocked with bottles. "Though I did, against all odds, escape with a faint pulse and provisional custody of my mortal soul, this living death is no exception to their rule. The creatures know no mercy. It wasn't just victory that eluded my grasp. Even the glory of a martyr's sacrifice was denied me."

"Wait." Swanny props herself up on an elbow. "You fought the dragons?"

"I challenged them, yes." He pops the cap off a stout, tastes it, and hands it to her, then selects a doppelbock for himself. "I'd tell the tale at length if you'd so much as bother feigning interest."

"But I needn't feign it, Uncle Osmond." The "uncle" slips out quite naturally this time; even when she's sober, Swanny suspects she'll be hard-pressed now to call him anything else. "The dragons have always held the greatest fascination for me, ever since I was a child. They're terrible, of course, but the nobility and valor, not to mention eleventh-hour excesses, that have sprung up in their wake—it's all ever so romantic."

"That was what I once believed, my lark, before a monstrous skyward trouncing robbed me of all sensation in my lower extremities. In retrospect, I believe I'd prefer the type of romance that includes the physical act of love."

"Oh! So *that's* how you were mutilated." Swanny's gaze trails down to his little feet, lifeless in their woolly socks. "Do you ever regret it?"

"Erotic indignities aside, the paralysis has left me prey to a host of grisly co-morbidities, including my recent bout of Shivering Kidney. And it would be pleasant to kick your husband's mongrel in the ribs. But I have my thwacking canes. I soldier on."

"Why did you do it—fight the dragons?"

"To properly understand, you'll have to allow me to begin at the beginning.

The Noble but Tragic Tale of Osmond Ripple and the Dragons, as Related by the Man Himself

"Our father always preferred Humphrey. As eldest, my brother was his namesake and rightful heir, and from earliest childhood, I can recall the blatant favoritism, which he made no attempt to hide. The two would trundle off to gawk rubeishly at aerocar shows or the metallic carnage of the robotics coliseum with alarming frequency, while I lingered at home with our mother, a delicate contessa whose paranoid agoraphobia confined her to a single floor of the house. Together, she and I would play a great number of games which I even then suspected were not devised for my entertainment, such as Name That Sound and Are All the Windows Locked?

"The root cause behind our father's preferential treatment was, I think, Humphrey's innate and puzzling enthusiasm for business. The essential talent there is not intelligence, in which I outpaced him handily from my first burblings, but the ability to ask the right questions of the world. While Humphrey made the mechanistic inquiries best suited to a future grease monkey of industry—How does this work? How may it someday work for me?—I posed to our father the philosopher's riddle, *why:* What's all the fuss? Why even bother? A reasonable concern, I felt, since we already had a greater fortune than we knew what to do with. I don't exaggerate. My father's philanthropic efforts bore little resemblance to genuine altruism. They were the desperate measures of a man bailing out the hull of a ship rapidly filling beyond its capacity. As preeningly self-important as he was, the fact was that his fortune would continue compounding itself eternally through accrued interest, without anyone's interference. We were all now superfluous to it. Particularly him.

"But I digress. Though the Scheherazade unfurling of our mother's neurotic prophecies proved diverting for a time, as I surged toward manhood I realized that I would not remain content waiting—and dreading—for something to happen to me. I yearned to take action, to claim a starring role in a story myself. Luckily (or rather, unluckily, as experience would prove) a true epic was playing itself out in the air right above our heads.

"I was not a natural contender for the Challenges—glitz and glamour have never been the birthright of our class, and the entire phenomenon was the misbegotten brainchild of a mad impresario. One who saw, in the ancient struggle between good and evil, little more than a vehicle for corporate advertising.

"You may not recall, but in the years before your birth Toob featured newsworthy content, often streamed live, in place of spectacles like your husband's hormonal posturing and the dreary parade of dated rerunamenta that greets us there today. One of the last new programs of note was produced by Jim Danger, an aggressive self-promoter whose smile suggested a flossing shark's. It was his idea to fund, follow, and film the doomed heroics of a phalanx of so-called Weekend Warriors, hapless Everymen who attempted, with touching hubris, to eliminate the menace in our skies. *CHALLENGER*, as the show was called—the announcer spoke the name in all capital letters—became a sensation as Warrior upon Warrior stepped up only to plunge to televised besplatterment. I heckled their mortality from the couch, until one day derision brought me to my feet. While my father and brother applied themselves adroitly to the most existentially distressing of tasks, here the problem was reversed. These common joes had an unimpeachable answer for *why*, but they failed at *how* miserably. I was indestructible with adolescence; I would fast put them to rights.

"I set about filming my video application with care. The models, built to scale from balsawood and taxidermied geckos, may not have been strong indicators of my prowess in battle, but the judges were amused. And once they found out my age—the previous contenders had two decades on me at least—they grasped the delightful gimmick instantly. Comical, precocious, and unmistakably wellborn, I was the type of privileged savant that would be singled out for depantsing by my peers in any proletariat schoolyard. That lent me an unlikely appeal. Every Weekend Warrior carried our city's fate in his hands as he hearkened to the holy call of *CHALLENGER*. But if the dragons got me, it would, in the sickly parlance of that time, 'go viral.'

"I see that now, of course, but at the time I was entirely oblivious to the ulterior motives of my handlers. After I was selected as a contestant, I spent the filming period—with their encouragement!—declaiming hawkish poetry and rubbing my mother's feet in front of the cameras. All the while, the state-of-the-art HowTank I had requested awaited me on the roof, a strange, hostile emissary from a realm I didn't dare to contemplate, for fear that my cowardice would prove both visible and untelegenic.

"The night before I took up the Brand Sponsorship Mantle and boarded my ill-fated craft, Humphrey visited me in my room. 'Did Father send you?' I demanded. He eyed me perplexedly, as only a lunatic's brother can. 'Why would Father send me?' he asked. 'I'm here to talk you out of killing yourself tomorrow.'

"Once I gathered the fortitude to expel dear *frère* from my suite, I fell unabashedly to pieces. I hadn't known I was bluffing until the bluff was called. My father did not care whether I lived or died; no further humiliation was possible. I drifted off to sleep resolved to drop my Challenge and slink, as best I could, into the blessed shadows of obscurity, where I could rediscover the quiet joys of self-pity and other pleasurable forms of self-abuse.

"Yet that night, I dreamt a dream, one that, more than any waking action, has determined the course of my existence."

Osmond quaffs deeply from his doppelbock, his silence for once uninflected with the tacit hostility of biting one's tongue. Swanny, now wide awake, cranes forward on the couch.

"So?" she prompts him at last. "What did you dream?"

Osmond waves his hand as if relating a magician's trick in dismissive summary. "Everyone knows that only a terrible bore tells his dreams."

"Everyone knows that only a terrible *boor* leaves off at such a crucial narrative juncture. Don't keep me guessing. I quite seriously implore you."

Osmond sets his half-empty glass on a bookshelf. He smiles.

"What do you think I dreamt of?" he asks. "I dreamt what every lowbrow 'Weekend Warrior' before me did. I dreamt of the dragons."

"And?"

"I dreamt that they confronted me, and that I emerged from the confrontation victorious. I dreamt . . ."—he gazes foggily into the room's haze—"of heroism."

Swanny sinks back to contemplate this. "I'm surprised, somehow, that you wanted to save the world."

"It was mainly the glory I sought. But the world—yes, I liked it better then."

"Mmm." In the city of Swanny's fantasies, the lights are winking off, one by one, a grand imaginary architecture erasing itself, until only this room remains. She presses the cold beer bottle to her forehead. "I know just how you feel," she says.

~~~~

The bed boat floats on a sea of night. Never has Abby known the small hours to be so silent, so scentless, as they are in this place. She touches Ripple's back, the smooth dreamful expanse of him that flexes unconsciously at her touch, then crawls down to the bed boat's prow, where Hooligan sprawls on his back. He tilts his head at her, curious, his liquid brown eyes shimmering in the nightlight's glow, transmitting the question to her without a sound.

—awake?

—Uh-huh.

His tail thumps on the mattress, and he stretches his arms above his head, offering his chest and belly for her affection. She pets him. His soft black fur is indistinguishable from the darkness, except by feel.

—yes. nice touch. touch more.

—I love you.

—love. love.

—Do you love Dunk too?

—love. love. love.

—When did you start to love him?

—always love.

—I know what you mean. I loved him as soon as I saw him. But when did you come to live here?

—happy day. wore bow. licked dunk's face. ate chocolate cake. barfed on rug.

—Where were you before?

—before?

—Where were you born?

—crowded. smelly. scary. bitey. too many voices. nicer here. with dunk and love.

—I guess it is.

—yes.

—You're so good. So much friendlier than the vultures.

—vulture strange.

—Cuyahoga likes you!

—vulture hungry.

—How can you be scared of her? You're twice as big.

—vulturrrrr . . .

The growl becomes audible. Abby stifles a giggle.

—Shhh, it's OK. She won't come back for a long time. She has to tend to a sister's brood on the Island. Her sister was burned in a fire.

—fire warm.

—But it burns. You must never go near a fire.

Abby stops petting him for a second to tuck a strand of hair behind her ear. He takes her hand in one of his and guides it back toward his armpit.

—nice touch. more love.

—OK, OK.

She resumes. He squeezes his eyes shut in pleasure.

—Hooli?

—uh-huh.

—Can you talk to Dunk? The way we're doing? With your mind?

—he no listen.

—Can you do it with any other humans?

—they no listen.

—The Lady could never do it either, with the vultures. She said I was the only one who knew their language.

—mmm.

—But I couldn't talk to all of them. Only certain ones. The *magic* ones, I guess. Are you made of magic?

—must be.

He moves her hand to another spot on his rib cage. She whacks him playfully.

—Just pet yourself, if you're gonna tell me how to do it.

—please. love.

—OK, OK.

—nice touch.

—I'm glad for magic. If I couldn't talk to magic animals, I'd be so lonely.

—he no listen to you, too?

—I guess Dunk does, but everyone else here hates me. They shut me in that room for hours. I don't know what I would've done if you hadn't shown me how to unlock the door. It was so terrible. I wanted to kick and scream. But then they would throw me out.

—in garbage?

—Yes.

Hooligan licks his lips hungrily.

—mmm, garbage.

—I know. I like garbage too. I miss it.

Abby starts to cry.

—Maybe it would be better if they threw me out. I'm so home-sick. I like nature. I like the squish of trash bags under my feet. I like being able to roam. But I *love* Dunk.

She contemplates miserably.

—And even if they throw me out, they might not take me back to the Island. They might just leave me here, loose in the city. With no home.

—lost.

—Yes, lost.

—lost. lost. sad.

—But I'm sad here too. I wish you could understand how I feel.

Hooligan kisses her face in one wet slurp.

—salty.

Abby smiles.

—stay, abby. stay.

—I guess it wouldn't be so bad, as long as we stick together.

—yes. stay.

Abby's fingers furrow through Hooligan's fur, shaping winding paths, meditative and aimless. His tongue lolls out of his mouth; he seems almost asleep when, all of a sudden, he rolls over on his stomach and looks up at her eagerly.

—walk?

—Right now? But it's the middle of the night.

—walk walk walk walk.

His tail thumps the mattress. Abby sighs.

—OK, OK.

Hooligan hops down from the bed, bounds on all fours to the door.

—This one is locked too.

—open it. like i taught you. by feel.

Hesitantly, Abby touches the panel beside the door. It reminds her of the toaster, coils humming with energy, but she feels no heat. No, something inside this device is alive; she feels the currents flow-ing through it, like blood inside an unsmashed fish. What are you doing in there? she wonders. No response. And yet . . . it waits, ever so patiently anticipates, a signal from—what was that? a particular button? She touches the keypad, reaching for the source of the device's yearning, but as soon as she presses one button, the yearning shifts to a second, then to a third. In the calming simplicity of this exchange, Abby forgets about the door, the People Machines, Dunk, all her worries. Then, after the fourth button, the door pops loose and the currents retreat from the coils.

—easy, see? walk now.

Hooligan nudges the door open with his snout. A thick wedge of light falls onto the carpet. Abby picks up Ripple's sweatshirt from the floor and slips it on, then follows.

Late at night like this, the mansion spooks her less. The humans are the ones who awaken its wicked sorcery to bend it toward their ends. When they sleep, no one is here to turn off the lights by snapping, or to conjure a voice from nowhere that tells of distant events and weather yet to come. Padding down the hall with Hooligan, Abby can almost pretend they are exploring the living world, though she's never walked so long without a sky above her. But the apehound destroys the illusion when he stops in the middle of the hall to press the button for the Surprise Room.

—Let's not go in there.

—go. go.

—But every time the doors open, I'm somewhere new and scary.

—no scared.

Hooligan balances on his hind legs and takes her hand. They step across the threshold together. He presses one of the numbers on the wall, and it lights up.

—Where are we going?

—no scared.

Abby feels a funny lurch in her guts, as if she's falling. Then, with a "ping," the doors to the Surprise Room open again. Hand in hand, she and Hooligan walk down another hallway and through glass doors into the Land of Plants.

The lights are off in the Land of Plants, and the leaves rustle as they pass, but Abby isn't afraid, because in here she can see the stars.

They are framed in the panes above their heads, squared away into neat little boxes like everything else in this place, but they are still familiar, and their presence comforts her. She gazes up as Hooligan leads her over a little bridge and to the base of a towering palm. He takes a spade from its hiding place beneath some groundcover and digs into the dirt. He uncovers a shallow grave. In it lies the corpse of a sparrow.

—magic bird. my friend.

Abby kneels. She touches the delicate wings, the beak as small as a single tooth.

—tried to play but too small. got hurt. you fix.

—I don't think I can fix him, Hooli.

—he need help, but dunk no listen. you listen. you fix.

Abby listens to the bones. There is an echo in their hollowness, faint and distant. A small musical voice she has to strain to hear, something between a lament and a wish:

—fly away, away, away.

12

COMMITTED

"A marriage is a series of compromises between a husband and a wife," Pippi once said. "A wedding is a series of compromises between a young lady and her mother."

During contract negotiations, Pippi did not even grant the Ripples consultation on the wedding preparations. Every aspect of the ceremony, cocktail hour, and reception is the result of a series of arguments she had with Swanny, the vast majority of which Pippi won. The ceremony is to take place in the greenhouse, beneath a trellis of climbing snapdragons; Champagne afterward in the Hall of Ancestors; dinner and dancing to follow in the ballroom. Everything has been planned for months.

"Darling, if I have to touch up your eyeliner one more time," Pippi scolds, sotto voce, though it would be impossible for the Ripples to hear them out here in the hall. "You're beginning to look like one of those raccoons we poisoned under the veranda."

"I don't love him, Mother," Swanny insists, tilting her head back. The last thing she wants is an inky teardrop staining this sumptuous dress, the one item she and Pippi instantly agreed on. It's yards and yards of vintage satin, a noir nightgown writ large, lush and dragging with puffed sleeves (Swanny loves her arms in it), all in the subtlest tint of yellowed white: the color of a tooth. They ordered it from a designer overseas. Before Pippi would let Corona alter so much as a stitch, she, Pippi, pinned the whole thing herself. It was a nightmarish ordeal. Swanny stood immobile for hours while her mother circled her, pricking her with needles and hissing about the garment's substandard manufacture. It seemed it would never end until Pippi abruptly stood back and said, "My work here is done," with such tremendous satisfaction, such confidence and pride, that it felt like she had put a curse on all of Swanny's enemies. Was that just six weeks ago? Swanny's eyes fill with ruinous tears once more. "I'll never love him. Not in this life or the next."

"That reminds me." Pippi unsnaps her clamshell purse and produces an amber pill bottle. "You'll want to be good and doped-up the first few times. Take one of these after dinner."

Swanny reads the label, incredulous: "Muscle relaxants?"

"Better than tranquilizers, dear. I'll never forget your poor father's face that terrible night. He thought he'd killed me. And I was so certain I'd only closed my eyes for a moment."

The processional music starts up, louder than Swanny would have thought possible from a soloist. The amplified harp emits a yelp of feedback.

"*Mother*," Swanny insists, desperate now. *Everything has been planned for months.* The events of the last two days loom and shrink in proportional importance to those long weeks with her mother, scrapbooking centerpieces, cross-referencing the spousal-abuse termination clause with the divorce law encyclopedia, taste-testing the mail-order sample cakes. "This will be the death of me."

Pippi's eyes are the oldest part of her face, and still the sharpest.

"Life is long," she instructs Swanny, staring her down. "Do you have any idea of the scope of this family's holdings? Humphrey and I were up till three a.m. going over the books. Things being as they are, your annual dividends will be the GNP of a lesser nation. But if this city ever comes back—and it will, darling, believe me, it will—the real estate properties will put you over the top. Over the top, Swanny. Do you have any idea what that means? The freedom it will give you? You won't have to answer to anyone—not me, no, not even Duncan, I can see plainly enough he'll be easy to control. You won't just be a baroness, you'll be an empress. You can either seize this opportunity now, or spend the rest of your long, long life wishing that you had."

Swanny looks down at the simple bouquet of baby's breath in her hand, knotted up in a lace handkerchief—her mother's choice. Swanny originally wanted to carry an old silk fan painted with an artful "suicidal lovers" tableau, but she realizes now that it would have looked prop-ish, cartoony, against the luscious curves of her gown. Her mother was right. Her mother is always right.

"Shall we?" says Pippi, offering her arm.

They step into the greenhouse together. Fairy lights glimmer in the topiary trees. The satin runner stretches out before them, a long purple tongue.

～～～

Hot mics in the indoor gazebo:

"But Dad, what if we just keep her around for special occasions? She's, like, imprinted on me, she's going to be a waste for anyone else."

"That girl is going to the Quiet Place in North Statesville at five thirty a.m. tomorrow—it was the soonest they could take her. How could any son of mine get this far in life without learning to properly tie a tie?"

～～～

The wedding march does not have lyrics, but Swanny and Ripple both hear it the same way: *no no no no no no no no no no no no no no no no . . .*

～～～

Osmond wheels out to perform the ceremony, dressed like a priestly executioner in a black hooded cloak.

"What is death?" he begins, ignoring the unopened prayer book in his lap. Humphrey and Pippi exchange barbed looks—this isn't in the script—but Swanny gazes at him raptly, an invitation to continue. Ripple scratches his ear. "And why do we rejoice in it so? It is to me of no small anthropological interest that the occasions we come together to consecrate in society are, at heart, concerned with the belching nothing from which we spring, and to which we shall inevitably return. Maiming, disfigurement, philosophic revelation, involuntary celibacy, the highest achievements in the arts and sciences—all pass unmarked by ceremony, and often, by the world's notice. Births and deaths, births and deaths: these are our sacraments, every one. Even that word, 'sacrament,' evokes with etymological cunning the obsidian blade, the bloodstained altar, of the 'sacrifice,' the ritual of old that did not simply acknowledge but in fact brought about man's final transformation from a being of flesh into a being of pure spirit.

"The lone exception, of course, is said to be the business we are employed in now, on this very afternoon: the act of wedding, of binding two souls together in mutual ownership. Marriage appears to be an undertaking by the living, for the living. Like a slave auction, perhaps, or a lawsuit. Yet in truth, marriage too, is a living death—and I the sinister gondolier tasked with ferrying you to its farther shore.

"A name is the mark one leaves upon the Earth, and sooner than we might prefer to think, our names will be all that is left of any of us. But here, now, beneath this seemingly innocuous canopy of flowers, one partner will willingly forsake her name and the other will give up exclusive ownership of his. Mr. and Mrs. Duncan Humphrey Ripple the Fifth. Though this ugly construction is unlikely to appear in common use, it is this renaming that concerns us here today. A marriage is not about the division of property, or the obtainment of health insurance, or sexual congress, or the public affirmation of private sentiment, all of which can be accomplished by more expedient means. A marriage is *mutation*, the artificial merging of discrete elements from nature that turn monstrous when combined.

"But we would not be human if we did not summon monsters into our midst. Today, young Duncan will devour the baroness whole, and he will die of her poison. In their place, a two-headed creature will emerge, new and strange and born of blood, and we will call this creature 'Ripple.' Birth and death, birth and death. And so it shall be until the final reckoning. Swan Lenore, will you allow this?"

She almost misses her cue: "I will."

"And you, Duncan?"

"I . . . do?"

Osmond throws back his hood and, with flaming eyes, states the benediction: "Let the fusion begin."

~~~

After the final initialing of the contract, the party decamps to the Hall of Ancestors, where Ripple's portrait is to be unveiled. Champagne corks pop like gunshots. Swanny, her mother's words in mind, has slammed back two flutes before the velvet curtain falls.

The family gathers in front of the painting. The videographers film the tableau of their clustered backs, the canvas they partially obstruct.

"He didn't put my face in it," Ripple says. His voice cracks with disappointment like a little boy's.

Ripple's likeness is the only one in the hall with a title: *Wanderer Above the Sea of Smog.* In it, he stands on a parapet of the mansion roof, looking down from the Heights onto Empire Island below. He faces away from the viewer, his brown hair tousled in the wind, his right hand jaunty on his hip: a hero's pose. But the artist has dwarfed him into insignificance. The city spills out before him. Wreathed with smog, marred skyscrapers jut up like knives; smaller ruins—townhouses, apartment buildings, theaters and libraries and museums—smolder in their shadows, barely visible. A distant new fire, zigzag-shaped like a *Z*, slashes near the middle of the canvas, electric orange, as if the artwork itself has been defaced. Torchtown? From it pours a blacker, fresher smoke, which mixes with the rest, becoming one at the horizon with the stormy sky.

Most shocking, though, are two shapes, smudges, really, high above the wanderer's head, near the top of the frame. Yellow and green, only implied—they could be mistaken for HowFlys or birds. But no. No. They are dragons. They are here at Ripple's wedding. How well, he wonders, can this bode?

"Well, I hate it," says Pippi. "How very grim. Whyever would someone paint such a thing? If it were a window, I'd draw the shades."

~~~

Nothing live—no band, no chanteuse. If Swanny wants to hear a human voice raised in song, she'll have to go find the klangflugel and bang the tunes out herself. Of all the things, why did she agree to economize on this, the music at her reception? As dreadful recordings play, decades-old earworms bereft of vital force or meaning, Swanny slumps next to Katya at the banquet table, morosely eating marzipan roses off the three-tiered cake. Swanny felt less alone in childhood, taking imaginary tea with her taxidermied rabbits.

"Were you a mail-order bride?" she inquires of her new mother-in-law, leaning over to pluck another rose.

"No. Humphrey and I met at work."

"You *worked* together?" Swanny stifles a melancholy laugh. "Were you a receptionist?"

"We met at my work." Katya delivers the information robotically. "Not his."

"Oh." Swanny's read enough erotica to fill in the blanks. Katya herself is a blank: a sexual tabula rasa upon which the worst conclusions are easily drawn. Swanny changes the subject: "Well, you're certainly rich now. That must be a relief."

"Is it for you? Are you glad to take my son's money and have the run of his household?"

There's no challenge in Katya's inflection, but the words are clear enough. Swanny goes on the offensive. "I am, actually. He's a worthless human being, but it would have been a shame to let an opportunity like this go to waste."

Katya smiles, vaguely, and rises from the table. "Have a nice wedding night."

Swanny watches her stride long-leggedly away, a formula of perfection fantasized into existence—36-24-36. She names the Day-Glo magenta hue of Katya's dress like a curse: Hot Lips, Fashion Doll, Dragonfruit.

To know what a man expects of women, look no further than his mother.

"A perfect wife," Swanny observes aloud. "Have you ever met someone so unnervingly polite? It's as though she's been lobotomized. I consider myself quite the feminist, but perhaps some of us weren't made to advance. It's like they say about genes: you can't express what isn't there."

"She has her moments, but on the balance—she's a mindless automaton," Osmond agrees, splashing more End of History in the general direction of his glass. "That's why Humphrey's in love with your mother."

"What?"

Osmond nods in the direction of the dance floor, where Ripple moons around for the videographers, a skeleton crew from his old Toob series doing this family memento work-for-hire as "mostly a favor." They've been checking their watches for the last forty-five minutes. In the background, Humphrey and Pippi are swaying cheek-to-cheek.

"How horrifying," Swanny murmurs.

"Oh no. I didn't mean to subject you to another punishing realization."

"But it can't be reciprocated. It *can't* be. She's still in love with Father."

"Hasn't he been dead for twenty years?"

"Nearly seventeen. But Mother always says she 'will never love again.' She says it very sternly. I never thought to question it."

"Far be it from me to sow the seeds of discord; I have no notion what lurks in her inscrutable heart." Osmond burps, 55 percent ABV. "Most likely, she'll play out the flirtation until it no longer benefits you. Then she'll shatter my brother's hopes and they'll settle into their natural roles as archenemies. I'm eager to observe, at any rate. Your mother is terrifying, but at least she's alive." He raps his fist twice on his insensible thigh. "Which is more than can be said for some of us in this house."

Swanny turns to him with sudden intensity of feeling. "Uncle Osmond, you have the warmest heart of anyone present. You're my only friend in this godforsaken place."

Osmond takes this statement very seriously. "You know," he says, gazing at the ancestral tablecloth, stained now from the joyless festivities, "if I had had a wedding, it would have been very much like this." He fervently clasps Swanny's small, pudgy hand in his small, pudgy hands. "Only, *I* would have adored you."

Swanny begins to cry.

"Is it really so obvious to everyone that Duncan doesn't love me?"

"Of course it is, my child. And hardly unexpected, considering the lout in question. He didn't appreciate the caviar at dinner either."

"But—but—" Swanny blinks back inky tears, dabs at them with her cloth napkin. "I thought I was irresistible."

"Swanny, no one can resist you forever. And 'forever' is the term on the contract you just signed. I should know. I notarized it."

~~~

Forever. Upstairs in the Guest Room, Abby is learning the meaning of the term. That is how long she has been stranded here, how long she'll be alone. She's been watching the wedding proceedings for the last six hours; they livestream from the videographers' cameras to the house's Toob sets, with automated dubbing in a strange foreign language for the staff.

She's seen so much now, so much she can't unsee. Yet she fears she never will understand this world of people—of *her* people, she reminds herself, of human beings just like her. Why are they so strange? She misses walking naked on the beach, feeding cockroaches to the ducks, shitting in a cardboard box. Here her body stays confined to a single room. Her mind is meant to wander on without it, into the glow worlds of the Toob.

Duncan is in there now: he has entered the machine, become of it. His body is made from points of light. She sees, but she does not understand. She wonders if the next time he slides his tongue into her mouth, she'll feel only a spark of static and then, emptiness. She wonders if there will be a next time. She knocks her fist against the screen, but he doesn't turn, not even when she calls his name.

He is burning in there. He is changing.

Pop up, up, out of this toaster full of souls!

Somewhere beyond the mansion's roof in the city below, the dragons scream through the sky. She cannot see them, but she can hear them in her head, a sound so faint and faraway it is a whispered wail, a shrilling in her ears. *Aaaaaaaaa* . . .

The animals of our city are deeply confused, and most of those animals are us.

13

FAIRY-TALE ENDING

"*E*tta," *came a voice at that moment near her. Startled, she turned, the throatlash of the bridle still heavy in her hand. It was Bertrand. At once, the color rose to her cheeks. He was still dressed for the ball, his finest frockcoat newly brushed, and yet here he stood, amid the horsey musk of her father's stable.*

"*Etta—*" *He spoke her name again, and the solemn timbre of that most familiar utterance moved deep within her, stirring sensations of such naked tenderness as could not be clothed in words. "Etta. I wish to engage you for the first two dances."*

"*Be still, Bertrand." She touched the mare's velvety flank with a soothing hand. "Emmelina is skittish—she has come unshod."*

"*And I say, damn her, damn the whole vexatious torment of the last fortnight. Let the world come unshod. Damn my poor station and your father's mad impa—imper— What the snuff's this say?"*

"Sound it out."

"Im-per-cations?"

"Im-*pre*-cations."

"What's that mean?"

"Curses."

"What, he called this guy a turd-gurgling son of a snake? I'd like to find that part."

"I believe he cast aspersions on the Portsmouth family name."

Ripple puts the open book over his face and slumps deeper into the ball pit. Plastic spheres jostle around his neck. This evening is not going as planned. After dinner, the adults shooed Swanny and him up to his room with a bottle of Champagne. He hoped one thing would lead to another, but Swanny was in a vile mood right from the beginning, demanding to know when the bed boat sheets were last washed, tossing clothes off the hangers in his closet to make space for her wedding dress. He told her it wasn't like she was moving in, and she burst into tears.

"No separate bedrooms," she said. "No twin beds. You asked for it in the contract. *You* asked for it, not me."

In retrospect, he probably should have said something like, "Don't weep so, my lark," maybe with a lordly accent, then lip-locked her like his life depended on it—he might have stood a chance. But instead he said, "Uh, maybe that was my dad?"

Now she's slipped into something more comfortable, but she's acting even less so. She keeps rubbing her cheek like she has a toothache, and already took a wee fistful of little yellow pills for an "excruciating" migraine she was "seeking to prevent."

He flips ahead in the weighty tome. "How much more of this do we have to read before you get turned on?"

"It works better when I'm alone," Swanny says gloomily. She perches on the edge of the pit, dangling her bare feet daintily in. The lacy fringe of her negligee is barely visible behind her tightly folded arms. "At this rate, it may take all night."

Here's an idea: "I have, like, four hundred hours of adult content on my ThinkTank."

"Your saying that somehow doesn't help matters."

"I wasn't saying we should *discuss* it, I was saying let's watch it." Ripple feels an eagerness he hasn't all day. "I got all kinds, I don't discriminate."

"Clearly not."

Ripple tosses the book aside and grabs the controller. A huge menu of programming appears on the projector screen; he starts rapidly scrolling through it. "There's Fem on Fem; Hot for Creature; Uncensored Surveillance Footage Vol. 6: Caught with Their Pants Down; Pirates and Barmaids; Pleather Yourself; Co-Ed Naked Wrestling; Co-Ed Naked Rodeo; Co-Ed Naked Bouncy House;

Dungeon Master; Siamese Twincest; Big Red Son; Mary O'Nette and the Real Mouth Puppets; Coma Vixen: She'll Sleep When She's Dead; Homeless and Helpless; The Aristocrats!; Sexual Harassment in the Workplace; Swab My Folds; Ride the Worm; Revenge of the Slave Babes; Cheerleaders and Mascots; Breast Pump Infomercial; Loveseat or the Curious Couch . . ."

Ripple has a long, intense history with porn, or whatever might pass for it; by now, he's opinionated and he's in a position to judge. Because what is porn? Performance sex. And if there's one thing he understands, it's the Performance Lifestyle™. Ripple's always related to his favorites, humping away onscreen; he understands it isn't as easy as it looks, feeling everything in front of a camera. He thinks a lot about what kind of stars they turn out to be, in the long run: auteurs or sellouts or one-hit wonders. Heroes, villains, or losers.

Creating an image is a life's work. You can't just fuck around.

Of course, Ripple's fame today isn't exactly assured. But he can't imagine living the rest of his life cut off from reality. He clicks down the familiar list, staring at the screen. He's going to go back there someday.

"Duncan, I don't know, and I don't care to know, what any of those phrases mean."

"Why don't you just pick a category and we can narrow it down from there."

"I'd really rather not."

He stops scrolling. "I thought you were into fantasy."

"Whatever gave you that idea?"

"Isn't that the same point of your literotica? So you can stroke off?"

"What an insulting misapprehension."

"It's exactly the same. Only your porn is boring."

"It isn't the same, Duncan. The characters in a work of literature—they're not bodies. They're souls. Alive and complex as you or me."

Duncan looks at her carefully. This is reminding him of Abby's fevered rants about the People Machines. "Uh, they're not real."

"Perhaps not, but they speak truths to us nevertheless." She tosses her hair. "I could never be aroused by *mere entertainment*."

Like Abby, only worse: at least Abby never tried to convert him to her weird religion. He feels a twinge of longing for that lithe, golden damsel, almost always topless, who listened so wide-eyed to the sound of his voice—not even the words, just the sound. Sometimes she'd press her head to his chest to hear her own name reverberate there. It sucks that he doesn't have any of that on tape; it gives him a hard-on just thinking about it. "What do you want to do, then?"

"I propose we get a good night's sleep, in hopes that this appears less insoluble in the morning. Counseling may be an option in the long term." She begins to heft herself to her feet. Ripple grabs her ankle. She looks down at him in surprise.

"Hold on. What about the consummation clause?"

She obviously didn't expect him to mention that. Her eyes narrow. "How do you know so much about the contract all of a sudden?"

"I remember that part. I signed it, same as you." Back when they were writing the contract, he even tried drafting his own version of the clause—more like a checklist, really—but the lawyers scrapped that in a hurry. In his opinion, it's the only part of the document that matters. The whole point of getting married is to guarantee sex. If he isn't going to be a porn star, at least he can be a husband. Ripple looks at his watch. "It's 11:36. So technically we've got until midnight, right?"

"Perhaps we can text your father for an extension."

"If you were so jealous of Abby, you should be thankful with the way things turned out. She's gone. Now I'm all yours." He indicates an area of plastic balls directly above his lap.

Swanny slides her pinky into her mouth. When she draws her hand away, there's blood on her fingertip. "My God, I need a dentist. I need one today."

Is she *trying* to turn him off? It's gross, but he's seen worse. On the garbage island he and Abby once banged atop clear transparent bags of liposuction. "We can do oral later." He squeezes her heel.

Swanny kicks her foot away from him. She scoots backward, then to her feet, with a laugh that's half shriek. "I detest you," she says. Another laugh comes, more like a hiccup this time. "I detest you, and that doesn't make the slightest difference."

Ripple shrugs. If she wants to feel sorry for herself, fine, but she's not going to get any sympathy from him. He clicks on HOT FOR CREATURE and opens one of the many video files inside. On some distant mountaintop a blond and elfin waif, clad in a bikini of primitive rags, hesitates at the mouth of a cave. Her wrists are tied: a sacrifice. "You want an annulment, be my guest"—he glances at his watch—"11:38."

"It appears you've given me no choice."

"Not so fast, you actually have to say yes. It's in the rules. It has to be consensual to count." Ripple dimly remembers his dad warning him about sexual assault penalties: fuck if he's falling for that.

"Fine. Yes. I consent."

"Sorry, you've gotta be more enthusiastic than that."

Her eyes flare. "My desire for you is—indescribable. Beyond the imagining of either God or man. There, are you happy?"

Ooh, she's mad: that's a flavor he hasn't tried before. *Feelin' Feisty.* He smirks. "Not yet."

"May I use the lavatory first?"

"See you on the bed boat in five."

She disappears into the echo-chamberish bathroom suite; he hears water angrily blasting from all three sinks. Ripple gets out of the ball pit and lies down naked on the bed boat, gazing up at the waif onscreen, trying to wriggle out of her bonds. She looks a little like Abby if you don't focus your eyes too hard, lean and tan, though her voice is all wrong: "Who's—who's there?" Way too normal. He thinks about Abby's weird little accent, a dialect of one, how she references sex positions like discrete activities: "We could From Behind or Sideways or go fishing!" He never thought she'd be the only fem he ever had, never wanted that—but never again? Stuck the rest of her life in a Quiet Place? Maybe they allow conjugal visits. A pad-ded room, every surface a mattress . . . "This place is fucked." "Let's Against the Wall." Screw the adultery penalties, it would be worth every cent, it would feel so right. . . .

By the time Swanny reemerges, he's got a good-sized erection in hand. Onscreen, a yeti penetrates the virgin on the incongruous shag carpeting of the mountain cave's floor.

"I kinda got started without you," Ripple says, nodding at his penis.

"Good lord," says Swanny. She stares at his body. "I've never seen a man naked before. Your genitals—it's like an alien dissection."

"Thanks, I guess."

"I didn't intend it as a compliment."

But anytime a half-naked woman ogles Ripple's cock with rapt fixation, he's going to take it that way. He gives it one last expert squeeze up near the tip, then opens his arms.

"C'mere," he says.

Swanny lies down on the bed next to him. He cups his hand around her breast and kisses her on the chin. Channeled through surround-sound speakers, the yeti growls, "You like that, sugar tits?"

"Turn off the video immediately," whispers Swanny.

Ripple taps a button on the controller. See, he can compromise. "Let's listen to some classic sex tunes." The blue notes of the Shat's "You'll Have Time" fill the room, along with church organ and *Sprechstimme*. "Close enough." He hikes up the satin of her negligee and climbs on top. Swanny is rigidly still as he tongues her neck, slides the strap off her shoulder. Coma Vixen, up close and personal: some fems really do just lie there, apparently.

"Show time," he mumbles, and presses into her.

But something is—weird. He's in, he's definitely in, but no way is this right. She feels like a cat's sandpaper tongue. Ripple slows his pace, staring down at her. No, it's not possible . . . "Those are happy tears, right? Like, you start crying when you come?"

"That's right. That's it exactly. You've brought me to orgasm." Swanny turns her gaze to meet his, tears trickling down toward her ears. Her voice is as flat as her expression. "The pleasure is indescribable. You're dominating. You're 'the abuser,' Duncan."

"Hey. That's not nice."

"Neither is this."

She doesn't want him. She really doesn't want him. Not even for hate sex. Somehow he never considered that as a serious risk. Ripple feels himself retracting within her. He rolls off, and she tugs her nightgown down to cover herself. He turns his back, curls into a fetal position. He's not going to be a great lover, captured onscreen for all eternity. He's never even going to fuck his wife.

"I was doing my best, OK?"

Swanny snorts. "Really? That's your best?"

"Go away."

Swanny picks up the controller from where it's fallen on the mattress. "Do you have any costume dramas in your archives?"

Duncan sits up. He swipes the controller from her hand and hurls it through the projector screen. It smashes into the wall. "Get out of my room."

Swanny straightens the strap of her negligee. "And where, pray tell, am I supposed to sleep?"

"Who cares? Go die in a fire. You're fat and frigid and nobody likes you."

"How dare you speak to me that way. Verbal abuse is grounds for an annulment."

"Good luck finding another husband. There's the door."

"When my mother hears about this, the consequences will be drastic."

"Yeah right. She's after her ROI, same as anybody else. You don't believe me, look where you are."

Swanny toddles toward the door. A drop of blood hits the carpet between her feet; it isn't from her mouth this time. "I didn't think it was possible to hate you even more than I did already."

"Better pace yourself, wench. We've got the rest of our lives."

~~~

Swanny has had over one hundred and fifty extractions. She has had menstrual cramps that brought her close to fainting. She once broke a toe kicking her father's gravestone in rage, and she's sprained her ankle on rabbit holes in the garden on two separate occasions. But nothing in her experience compares with the loss of her virginity tonight. The pain was excruciating, consuming, and with it came a blinding anger. She hated Ripple, hated every inch of his endoparasitoid nudity—but to her chagrin and surprise, she also hated herself. Her body betrayed her, became a contortionist's box with blades coming in the sides. *Frigid.*

It was never like this in her fantasies (because yes, of course she had them, fantasies intended for pure titillation—truth and beauty will only get a young lady so far). Even in daydreams of highwaymen and pirate kings, who in their villainy would overpower her, Swanny imagined she would, with this as with all things, seek out and take her own dark, secret pleasure. Yet tonight, with Duncan, she found herself without inner resources of any kind, clamped in the merciless jaws of the actual. Ripple's penis was not a metaphor for anything. It was a wedge between her and herself, held in place by the most erosive friction, as if he were saying, *I don't love you, I don't love you*, with every scoot. Swanny is cracked almost in two, and worse yet, the grand gates of the Hotel Paracosm are locked to her. Has Ripple ruined her, for everyone, for all time? Erased all her imaginary friends? At the moment, she cannot conjure the charming fop, the rakish brigadier, from whose touch she wouldn't shrink. Her whole life, she has longed for contact, sure and true, on the deepest levels of sensuality and emotion. Now, on her wedding night, she wants to be alone.

Swanny silently slips into her mother's suite. The space is like a little apartment, a parlor and two bedrooms. One of the bedroom doors is ajar. Swanny peeks in. The lights are off and her mother is in bed, wearing a sleep mask and an anti-aging cream that glows faintly in the darkness. Swanny tiptoes to the other bedroom and lets herself inside.

The decor is tastefully barren; other than a sleek, oblong light fixture and a painting of lovers on the Twolands Bridge, the walls are ivory, unadorned. Swanny rips off her negligee, wads it up in a ball, and throws it into a corner. Her hope chest stands waiting at the foot of the bed. She opens it and tosses clothes over both shoulders until she finds her favorite pajamas, red flannel with a repeating pattern of iconic retro housewives declaring, "Cook your own damn dinner!" and "I start drinking at noon!"—the ones that her mother says make her look like a Sapphic endtimes lumberjack. But even with these on, she's still shivering. *Frigid.* She drapes her chinchilla coat around her shoulders as she digs deeper into the chest for her quilted dressing gown, and it's then that she finds the envelope. *Swanny*, it says. *Open ASAP.* Inside, there's a card about the size of a party invitation, letterpressed with her initials. Swanny recognizes it: she used dozens of these the week after her engagement, to announce the news in personalized notes to all her mother's friends. But the handwriting here isn't hers. It's plain, and cramped, and nevertheless spills out from the card onto an additional sheet of legal paper folded up inside, as if the words, once flowing, couldn't easily be staunched.

Dear Swanny,

Tomorrow morning you are leaving. You are traveling to the city to meet your husband and all your new servants, to make a new life. Your mother says she will come back after the wedding, but I don't believe she will. She has packed all her jewelry and her Who's Who books and her content reel, and I think that if she can, she will never leave your side. A mother does not let her child go easily. I know. Though my son has been dead longer now than he ever was alive, I carry him with me still. If it would bring him back, if it would keep him safe, I would gladly follow him to the ends of the Earth. This is the one thing, perhaps, that your mother and I share.

So I will not see either of you again.

You never asked me what I did before I came to this place. But I once also made a journey far from the only home I knew. When I was a young mother, not much older than you are now, I too had a head full of dreams. At night, I tended my baby; each day, I taught grammar and geography to little children in a hot, dusty classroom without desks or window glass. When I had money, I bought books from the pulp mill for their shelf. The books came in unlabeled cartons and I bought them by the pound. Sometimes, when the books were in your language, I rewrote them into mine. It was a puzzle I could solve, to keep my mind fresh, to stake a claim on the world. One of these books was your father's.

I was pleased with my work. When I sent him my lines alongside his, it was a gift. I did not expect to be hired as governess to his newborn child, to travel with my son to the manor on his estate, half a world away. I did not expect servant quarters twice the size of the cramped apartment I shared with my boy back home. I did not expect it to ruin my life.

This house is mine now, this house I have cared for so many years, and I have earned it a hundred times over. No manor home is worth a lifetime of grief. Though you were a sweet child—lonely and spoiled, yes, but sweet—raising any child is a struggle, and you were not my own. If I could take back every hour I spent with your family, I would. But it is too late for that.

Once upon a time, I tried to tell you why my son died. I told you about the sickness that ate away his body from inside until only his soul was left, trapped behind the windows of his eyes. I told you about how your father taught him to swim, how they splashed together in the pool until the well water pruned their toes. I told you, but you did not listen. You always pretended to flout your mother's teachings, yet perhaps you learned from her all too well. In your mind, we were creatures of different kinds, you and I. You did not believe that my family's life could have anything to do with yours—that the same monsters could devour us both.

Swanny, I know you have wondered why you have so many teeth, and I know your mother has told you that you are inbred. La Diabla. I never contradicted her, because lying to a child is a mother's right. Also I did not want to lose my job. I had already lost too much. Now, though, I have nothing left to lose. And no one stays a child forever.

There is a sickness in this place. In the ground. In the water.
That sickness is also in you.

The teeth do not only grow into your mouth, Swanny. Those are just the ones you can see. They grow into your rib cage, into your lungs and heart. I watched the teeth chew up my little boy, and then your father. It happened to the other Gray Ladies' children too. For them it took just months. For you it is taking much longer. I do not know why.

But I do know that soon your teeth will leave no room inside for anything else.

I have hidden a manila folder under the lining of this chest. In it I have put X-rays from your dentist. You can look at them if you do not believe me. They show the teeth you have never seen, and new ones that have not yet dug in their roots. I am not telling you this to warn you: if the truth could save you, your mother would not have swaddled you in lies. I am not even telling you so you can lead a fuller life in what little time remains—I do not pretend to know what pain or joy this truth will bring. No. I am telling you because I once promised your father that I would educate you, and though your mother set me to different tasks, I will not break that promise. I owe that to him, to you—and most of all, to myself.

Here is your lesson, gordita: you will die. No name or title or fortune can ever protect you from that. Now here is your homework: how are you going to live?

Your housekeeper,
Corona

Swanny tears the letter to pieces, then holds the pieces together and reads it again. She shoves it into the pocket of her coat and flings the rest of her clothing from the trunk. The lining is red satin. Corona was never fond of sewing, and the place where she tore the fabric along the seam is sealed with a long shimmer of scotch tape. As promised, the X-rays are inside. Swanny's hands shake as she holds them up to the light. It doesn't take her long to see the nascent teeth, nestled between her ribs like fetuses. Corona has marked some of the larger ones with Pippi's SIGN HERE stickies, the ones they used on all the contracts.

Swanny feels as though she's in a dream as she rises from the floor. She wafts through the suite's little parlor, into her mother's room, and deftly, silently drifts between the pieces of furniture until she finds Pippi's valise, the one with the valuables. She twists the combination lock—it's always been the Wonland County area code, 666—and in the darkness moves aside the ring boxes and the cut-glass business trophies until she finds her mother's gun.

Despite the curlicued monogram on the grip (PFD in a tangle of lines), it isn't a lady's pistol; it's a double-action semiautomatic sidearm and Swanny has no idea how it works. Still, she lifts it up to her temple, experimentally, feeling the weight of it in her hand. The lamp switches on.

"Burglars!"

Her mother's sleep mask has large Egyptian eyes embroidered where her real eyes should be; combined with the teal cream on her skin, it makes her look like an otherworldly thing: a septuagenarian Sphinx. She whips the blindfold off over her head.

"Swanny, drop that handgun this instant."

"Why should I?"

"Because it's mine."

"In that case, perhaps I should use it on you." She points the gun at her mother.

"Don't be ridiculous." Pippi plucks a clawful of tissues from the box on the bedside table and begins to swab her face. "If you didn't have someone to tie your stays, you'd never get your clothes on in the morning."

"I know about the X-rays." Swanny wipes her eyes on her sleeve.

"*What* X-rays?" Pippi's voice snaps like dropped chalk.

"I'm sure you're quite aware which ones I mean, Mother." She articulates each word with care, aiming for some semblance of wounded dignity: "I know the truth. I know I'm going to die."

Pippi swings her legs out of bed, pats her hair. "You are not going to die."

"Don't lie to me anymore. I can't bear it. I can't bear all this pointless, hollow playacting. I'm not even angry anymore. I simply feel nothing."

"You feel nothing?" Pippi yanks a shearling robe around herself and knots the belt as if girding for battle.

"That's right," says Swanny, shrinking slightly.

"Well, perhaps you can try feeling grateful for a change." The muscles of Pippi's neck work as she grinds her teeth.

"Grateful?" Swanny laughs through her tears. "Grateful? Oh, Mother. I'm going to die, and you—"

"You're going to die? *Die?* You'll do nothing of the kind. Look at this house. Look at where I've taken you. Would you like to know a secret? I was born in an *apartment*, Swanny. I worked summers as a *typist* to pay my way through underschool. I was the top of my class at Hartford-Hazlett, and for overschool, I won a scholarship to Chokely Bradford's business program—a *scholarship*, Swanny, back when they were still co-ed. I was their last female valedictorian, the last one in their history."

"Mother, what does this even—"

But Pippi doesn't stop. This is an aria.

"I was the last, and I was the finest. All my life I have watched the world dismantled around me, even as I climbed up into it. The day after my graduation, the first day of my assistantship, those god-damned dragons torched the roof of our office building. But I did not stop. I Did Not Stop. I have never let anything stop my getting what I want.

"I transformed McGuffin-Stork. I kept them on their toes. The conference rooms fell silent when I appeared. I remember when I met Humphrey Ripple. I took him out to lunch. I took *him*, Swanny.

"I got braces on my teeth at twelve, froze my eggs at twenty-two, and had you at my earliest convenience. You were a stellar embryo, a rowdy toddler, a willful child, and a stubborn girl. But never in my life did I expect you to disappoint me. Look at me, Swanny. Do you think your father made our millions? Your father? The *poet*? No. He was scion to a crumbling dynasty, squeaking by on name alone. No.

It was me." She glares at Swanny from deep within a fire of furious triumph. "You are my daughter. You will never die."

Swanny shakes her head. She drops the gun on the floor and stares at it there for a long time.

"You're senile," Swanny says. The statement is so huge, it leaves no space in the room for air. And then she screams it: "You're senile, you're senile!" And then she's running, in red flannel pajamas and a chinchilla coat, deep into the labyrinth of the house.

~~~~

Ripple wakes up, drenched in sweat, and rolls over to look at his alarm clock, where the digits display in glowing orange, like the dragons themselves are spelling out the time: 4:26 a.m. Abby is going to a Quiet Place at 5:30. He lies still for almost a full minute in the darkness. He can hear the sound of his own heartbeat pulsing in his ears. What is he supposed to do? He tries to picture tomorrow morning at breakfast, Abby gone, another day cranking up just like nothing's happened. His father and Osmond, reading books or working puzzles at the table while truffled frittata cools on ignored plates. Pippi lecturing his mother on the merits of different coffee roasts. Swanny stabbing a grapefruit to squirt him in the eye or, more likely, taking breakfast in her bed upstairs, so sick of him she's made herself an invalid. And Abby, meanwhile, locked into some collective insanity he can only imagine, the smell of disinfectant, restraints on beds, involuntary hose-downs . . . when all they needed to do was set her free . . .

He almost doesn't hear the knock, but Hooligan, ears swiveling, jumps up, pads to the door, and stands at it, eagerly wagging. Ripple retrieves a pair of boxers from the bed boat's stern and pulls them on.

"Open it, boy."

Hooligan's prehensile fingers grasp the knob and twist. Ripple claps on the lights.

"Hi, Mom," he says. He isn't surprised to see her, somehow, even though it's the small hours of the morning after his wedding night, even though he can't remember the last time she came into his room. It's like he's been expecting her.

"Where is your wife?" she asks. Not pointedly; his mother has a way of making any question, any statement, sound bland and neutral. Maybe because the words aren't really hers? She's almost never spoken her native tongue to him; his dad thought it would "contaminate his language development." So when he was born, he and his mom learned English together. Sometimes, when she lets her guard down, he can still hear something singsong, babyish in her inflection. If she has an accent, she picked it up from him.

"Yeah, that didn't work out. Don't tell me she went crying to Dad again."

"I'm not here because of her." Katya bends down to pick up his crumpled tuxedo jacket from where he tossed it on the floor. She shakes out the wrinkles. She barely shows her age —she's still the youngest mom of all his friends'—but for just a second, Ripple sees how much she's changed over the years. She was practically a kid when she had him, a few months younger than he is now. But she knew just what to do. It wasn't the kind of thing you learned from a book. Based on the family Holosnaps, she breast-fed him a lot the first year, or at least that was when Osmond felt inclined to whip out the camera. Ripple remembers her getting down on the ground to play with him—none of the other adults ever would. They had one game where she curled up into a shy hedgehog whenever he tackled her. They understood each other, before language, without either of them knowing the first thing about how to live in his father's world, how to be Ripples. What happened? When did they lose each other?

Who's going to take care of him now?

Katya looks at him. Her face is as neutral as her spoken words— maybe it isn't really hers either. Maybe that's the cost of being so beautiful: your face no longer belongs to you. Kind of creepy to think of his mom like that, but there it is. She got where she is on looks alone. And maybe when that counts for so much, all the time, you learn to hide beneath what people see. Still, he reads her anyway, much easier than text on a page.

"You want me to save Abby." He wonders if there's still an umbilical cord to his brain.

"You have to do what you think is right."

"I can't believe you're actually *encouraging* me to run away. Isn't that the opposite of your job?"

"Maybe my job is done. Maybe you're all grown up."

"Uh, sorry, no."

"Dunky . . ."

He flops on the bed, hugs a pillow to his face. Muffled: "Dad is going to kill us."

"I'll pack your bag, leave it outside your door. I wish I had time to make you some sandwiches . . ."

"Don't forget my lucky socks."

〜〜〜

Ripple goes up to Abby's room with no plan, no idea where they're going to go or what they're going to do there. This whole thing is way off script. He reaches Abby's door and punches in the code—R-I-P-L—and lets himself in without knocking. He's almost surprised to see her in the flesh, zipped into his old hoodie, watching Toob. Smaller than he remembered, dimmer somehow, like the lightning bugs he once caught on the fifth-floor terrace and left in a glass canister overnight. She's petting Hooligan, which is weird too, how did he get in here? She stares at Ripple for a good thirty seconds, as if she's not quite sure he's really there.

"Nice to see you too," says Ripple, who was expecting more of a hero's welcome.

"Dunk? Are you real? Are you free?" She glances at the Toob. "How did you get out of it?"

"I'm not divorced or anything. But I'm as free as I'm going to be for a while."

"What about the girl from Hollow Gram? Is she back out in the world too?"

Thinking about Swanny annoys him. She has nothing to do with this, with anything; he wants her edited out of the final cut of his life. "I'm here, that's what matters. I'm going to take you anywhere you want to go."

"OK."

But now Ripple is peeved: "I don't think you appreciate what's happening. It's my wedding night, and I'm running away with you. We're going to live on the streets and fight hobos for food scraps, probably. I'm giving up my name and my house and my Slay Bed, and I'm doing it all for you."

"I don't want to live on a street."

"Do you have a better idea?"

"Uh-huh."

This should be interesting. "Uh-huh . . . ?"

"Go back to my 'previous owners.' Find out where I belong."

"What are you talking about?"

Instead of answering, she holds out her foot. "Feel."

Ripple, feeling pretty silly, palpates the callused skin. He doesn't know what he's looking for, but he finds it anyway. There's a bump just under her arch, a little pellet the size of a BB, with a trademark bull's-eye injection scar just beneath. He rolls his finger against it. No way. "Fem, are you serious? You're 'chipped?"

The BlackBean is the ultimate subcutaneous status symbol. He's been hearing the jingles since he was a kid ("*For when you're burned beyond re-re-recognition!*"), noting the locations of his classmates' injection scars—the newer models usually go in the biceps, but bottom of the foot is a classic placement. Maybe an old-money thing? Anyway, what makes the BlackBean so special in the crowded market of ID chips is its indestructibility. It can withstand searing heat, crushing blows, the digestive juices of every land predator known to man. Ripple always enjoyed the commercials, but he wouldn't want to be one of those alpha testers.

"Hooli found it. He says it'll tell me where I was bred, who owned me first. He says, maybe they have a big yard."

Ripple glances at his dog, who wriggles onto his back for a belly rub. Maybe Abby would've fit in at the Quiet Place better than he wants to admit. "Hooli *told* you?"

"Was it a secret?"

All those years of isolation must have messed with her head—she and that vulture were always supposedly having conversations. It's probably a survival skill she learned, to keep her from going even crazier. Obviously she was normal once. Somebody's sweet little girl, back earlier than she can remember.

Nobody bothers tagging a mental defecto.

"Do you get what this means?" Ripple continues, gentler. "You have a family. Parents, maybe siblings too. I bet they're a higher peerage than the Dahlbergs. And they're going to be so glad I brought you back."

The more he thinks about this, the better it bodes. Where would a damsel like Abby be from, anyway? A penthouse in the Fraud District? Maybe her dad worked for Laidly Bros., or one of the other finance firms that still kept a satellite office in the city. No, better: maybe her dad *owned* one of the firms. The scene plays out in high definition in Ripple's mind. It's sixteen years ago. Abby's parents bring her to the city on a business trip, stay in one of the last big hotels, bellhops tap-dancing and all that shit, when boom, the place goes up in flames. The parents escape, but they're sooty and beat up—in a tuxedo and an evening gown, for maximum effect—and Abby's mom is all crying, "My baaaaby, my baaaaby!" sifting through the ashes with her opera gloves. So they go home to wherever they're from—their own island, but instead of a garbage dump it's a tropical paradise, with coral reefs and waterslides and definitely a volcano—and they grieve. But they still have a hot tub full of Abby's sisters to take care of (older, younger, a whole sorority of sun-kissed fun-seekers), so life goes on. Until one day, they get a text from Ripple saying, "Hey, I don't know if you still want your lost daughter back . . . ?" and they *lose their minds*. Ripple and Abby fly out via private HowJet and boom, they're walking down a white-sand beach hand in hand, and Abby's hot sisters are streaming out en masse, bouncing bikini'd down the dunes to hug them . . . it's been so long since she's seen these fems, they're practically strangers . . .

"This will rule." He leans in to kiss her, but Abby pulls away, scrunching her brow.

"How will we find them?"

"First, we've got to find a BeanReader. They usually have them at orphanariums and morgues." He snaps his fingers. "They'll scan this bad boy and it'll spit out your name, your personal-record locator, everything."

"My name?"

"Sure, why not?"

Abby twists a strand of hair around one finger. She doesn't meet his eyes. As if she's attempting to remember something important—or attempting to forget.

"I love you," she says instead.

"Uh . . ." Ripple didn't plan on this contingency. *I do. Love.* The second big commitment in an overcommitted day. Is this what he wants? He looks at Abby, her pixie-ish face, gentle yet feral, the wild blond hair, her ears sticking out through the strands. A girl like Mom? A poochi-poo? He can never know for sure unless he takes the plunge. ". . . I love you too?"

~~~

In the bag his mother packed: all the currency he has, cargo shorts, his Shredder multitool, a six-pack of Voltage, six bags of BacoCrisps, a pair of flip-flops, his sleeping bag, a deck of Skin Pic playing cards, a flashlight, the old stuffed mastodon from his bed, crayons, his LookyGlass, a solar-powered camping toothbrush, T-shirts, underpants, his inhaler, a lighter shaped like a headless woman's torso where the fire comes out of her neck stump. Lucky socks. He hoists the duffel onto his shoulders, snaps Hooligan's leash onto his collar, and glances around his bedroom one last time.

"Anything else you want? Dad'll probably toss the rest of it once he finds out I quit the family."

Abby considers the toys, electronics, controllers strewn around the room. She gets up and goes over to the ball pit, squats down at the edge, and carefully selects one yellow sphere.

"OK!" she says.

Ripple takes Abby's hand and the two of them walk down the hall with the dog, where the elevator is still waiting. They step into that jewel box of a container, reflected in the gilt-edged mirrors behind. Abby inhales sharply. Then the door slides shut.

"You OK?" he asks. She squeezes his hand and smiles.

Just then, he hears a high-pitched siren sounding in the distant regions of the house. The elevator shudders to a halt. "Fuck! My dad must be onto us!"

"What?"

"Total butt nugget set off the security alarm!" Ripple fumbles through his pockets, pulls out a set of keys. He opens a locked panel under the buttons on the elevator, exposing a numerical pad and a recog screen. "Like I don't know how to manual override? Guess again, pro." The doors open, exposing a gap of a couple feet between the elevator floor and the lobby floor below. "OK, that's the best I can do. Follow me."

Ripple and Abby jump down into the hallway. "We better hurry," he says, already breathless. "The whole place is in lockdown, c'mon."

They're on the first floor, near the greenhouse. Ripple takes off at a jog, counting on Abby to follow close behind, but a dozen paces later, he stops dead in his tracks, staring up at the convex security mirror positioned up near the ceiling just before the right-angle bend in the hall.

Torchies. One is shirtless with a Mohawk. One has a bad burn across half his face, as red and veiny as a monster mask. One wears a morningstar-spiked scrum cap and a kutte vest, bare arms bearing sleeves of slice-'n'-smudge tattoos. And the last one is a child, or very nearly: he's small and fierce and disorientingly hairless, with his hair and eyebrows singed away. Dressed all in black. Like the others, he's holding a chain saw.

Four torchies, inside Ripple's house.

Time stops. It's at this moment, for the first time, that Ripple truly realizes the nature of the story that he's in. Up until this moment, he believed himself to be the hero, if not in terms of actual bravery, at least in terms of situational positioning. The story was about him, always. Now, though, Ripple realizes what an illusion all that was, a function of clever editing in service of mindless entertainment. He grabs Abby by the forearm, hard, silences her with a look.

The torchies disappear down the hall in the opposite direction.

"OK," he whispers—and the choice is so weak, it doesn't feel like he's even making one, though later he'll go over it again and again, trying to replay his logic step by step, to understand how he could do what he did when his mother, father, uncle, were still alive and vulnerable in the far reaches of the house. How he could have felt, even, relief, at that pivotal moment, when he cast away his birthright and gave up any hope of a truly happy ending: "Let's get out of here."

14

NEGATIVE SPACE

Shortly before they moved to the boonies of Wonland County, Pippi took a Vigilance course at the nearly defunct Seventy-First Street End Rape Alliance down the block from their townhouse. In a half-empty indoor shooting range, she and six other women took orders from an enraged, grandmotherly instructor in a fuchsia track suit, on the Seven Deadly Signs of Home Invasion (number five: broken glass), the best time of year to plant land mines (summer) and where (below the first-floor windows but not too close to the foundation of the house), as well as the care and use of their sidearms. Underemployed for the first time in four decades—though she was still consulting!—Pippi threw herself into the classes with a gusto that Instructor Joan, an armchair psychologist, appreciatively dubbed "aggressive-aggressive." Little did either of them know this was just the beginning of an education that would continue far from that boot camp for city-fleeing retirees, into Pippi's own perilous manor home, during the days of the Siege.

But tonight, it's that first Vigilance class that springs to Pippi's mind the instant she hears the fateful chirp of the Ripples' tastefully unobtrusive security system. She knows in an instant, faster than reflex, that it's not a false alarm—the surveillance AI is a slumbering mental giant, easy to waken but hard to spook. This is real, and Pippi's mind flashes instantly to Instructor Joan's Rule for the Road: "Get the children out alive. Believe me, there's no point if you don't."

Never mind that Pippi is still twitching with rage at Swan

Lenore—literally, actually twitching, she can feel the muscle squirming unattractively under the taut skin near her right eye like a trapped leech. But she's learned enough in the last nineteen years to understand Joan's message now. When you're an Old Mom, you go to war for the child you have, not the child you wish you had.

Pippi loads her sidearm, and as she slams the magazine into the handle, something inside her also snaps into place. Her senses quicken. It's just like riding a bicycle: it comes back. She drops extra rounds into one pocket of her robe, a fistful of jewelry into the other. Oh, she's ready.

What is it like to walk through a mansion, prepared to shoot on sight? Life takes on the saturated hue of a game it is possible to win or lose. And Pippi loves to win.

She doesn't take the elevator, that gift-wrapped box for ambushers. She takes instead the servant stairwell, a dull, square-edged helical corkscrew of concrete, windowless but for a filthy skylight at the top, through which one can see as much bird excrement as stars. You can tell a lot about a home by the condition of its staff quarters. Pippi approves of Humphrey's frugality to a point, but you don't want to cut corners, not with a property like this. Pippi's Bone-Soother slippers make no sound on the steps as she briskly and without incident descends.

When she exits onto the first floor, she nearly collides with Duncan Ripple, who screams girlishly until she grudgingly withdraws the gun barrel from his temple.

"Mama Law," he gasps, either mispronouncing Mom-in-Law or deeply confused about the role of the preposition in speech.

"Where is my daughter?"

"I dunno, I thought she was with you. Look, we've gotta go. Torchies all over the place. With chain saws."

It's then that Pippi notices the Girl, hiding behind him almost successfully, clutching the leash of that awful dog. Pippi hadn't bothered forming a mental image of someone so insignificant, but the Girl confirms all her worst suspicions. A pinkie finger of a person. And she is a Girl, not a Woman, despite the estrogen-ripeness that softens her boyish frame: Swanny was never so young. Strong men take pride in their lovers; weak men prefer to pity them. As the Girl's little hand snakes uncertainly toward Duncan's, Pippi strikes him across the face with her sidearm. It surprises her not at all that he hits the floor so easily.

"Hey!" he howls, rubbing his cheek. "You're not my mom!"

"Shut up. How many are there?"

"I dunno, like, four? Five? Maybe more. They were breaking into the security booth—I guess they wanted maps of the house?"

Pippi steps over him and continues on her mission.

She knows better than to walk the Hall of Ancestors; there's no cover in a corridor, and she's not about to retreat if they have projectile-firing weapons in addition to the chain saws. It's unlikely, of course. Bullets are so rare in Torchtown, the criminals have been known to pry them out of their wounds to resell for a profit. Yet another reason Pippi aims to kill.

Pippi remembers the first day of the Siege. She'd been up all night, listening to radio reports of the invasions. The power was out. The county had shut down the grid to discourage the raiders, who needed to recharge the batteries of their saws and the engines of their Road Daggers upon occasion as they plundered and pillaged from house to house. Pippi hadn't bothered turning on the generator. She didn't need an electric stove or a refrigerator for what she was doing. She didn't even need lights. She sat in the dark with a machine gun in her lap, wearing the most invulnerable pantsuit that would fit over her six-months-pregnant belly—along with most of her diamonds. A box of grenades sat beside her on the couch cushion. Chet was in an induced coma in the bedroom upstairs. Shortly after dawn broke, she saw the first scouts from the raiding party making their way up the drive.

Now, in the Ripple mansion, Pippi cuts through the so-called hidden passage, really just a utility closet off the hall that opens up to the kitchen on the other side. Diodes and fuse boxes, wires and pipes, the house's veins and bones and nerve endings: she'd wanted to *gut* the house in Wonland, but they hadn't been able to afford it, and a good thing too. She can't believe how much they sank into that manor, which now stands ownerless and hollow and uncontested, the great fortress of a battle long past. At least she packed the cow-shaped cowhide rug. A room can always use a little zip, a little something to say, "I'm here."

Pippi kicks open the door to the kitchen and enters the room handgun first. But she's alone. There's no sound but the metallic, faintly poisonous plink of a leaky faucet into the stainless-steel sink. Pippi flips on the lights, which buzz and fizzle themselves awake as she stealths across the tile. She swings open the door to the walk-in icebox; the light inside is already on. A mostly empty carton of butter macaroon frozen custard lies on the floor beside a bottle of caramel topping and a tipped-over jar sticky with red juice. Pippi picks it up and checks the label. Just as she suspected: maraschino.

Pippi is familiar with her daughter's unconventional feeding habits, particularly the one Swanny blithely refers to as "Second Dinner" in the pages of what she's had the insolence to title her *Secret Diary*. Swanny eats emotionally, which is to say when she's angry. It used to be a vice of Pippi's too, though she had the good sense *not to keep it down*, and in time, learned to restrict her bingeing to liquids. But there's something about Swanny's overconsumption that Pippi almost admires. It's as though her child believes she can devour the world and still have leftovers for later.

Pippi throws open the servants' door to the dining room and stops dead. The drop fixtures twinkle above the long table, the Edison bulbs red-gold as dying embers, and a large bowl of ice-cream sundae sits meltingly abandoned on the table. But Pippi sees only the form of the shirtless Mohawked intruder, removing a commemorative platinum plaque from one of the walls with a rusty screwdriver.

"Freeze," says Pippi, and he does, on his tiptoes, not even making a grab for the trigger of the chain saw strapped to his chest. The raiders never were this soft, this green. "Drop your weapon."

He unbuckles the power tool's holster and lowers it to the ground. It gives her enough time to see the scars on his back, half-healed: a name, first and last, carved deep into the skin. Of course. He's just a calling card for someone else. Then he turns around to face her, his arms raised.

"Is that all you've got?" she asks.

"Swear to shit," he replies. He's actually trembling.

"No pistol? No ammunition?"

"No, no, swear to shit."

"Then I'd like for us to work together. You can start by answering a question for me: where are your friends?"

"The study . . . there's . . . a safe, with currency . . . and . . ."

Pippi shoots him in the face. The bullet slams downward through the bridge of his nose, out the back of his head, and into the sequoia floorboard with the satisfying thunk of an ax into kindling. He crumples. Pippi kneels down and looks under the table. Swanny's eyes shine in the darkness. One fist still clutches a sticky spoon. How many times has Pippi found her daughter just like this, beneath the table on the ballroom floor, with her miniature tea set, her china dolls and taxidermied rabbits?

"Stop crying," Pippi says.

"I'm not."

"Good, because there's no reason to. Get up. We're going to the panic room."

"Is it . . . safe?"

"Of course not. But right now your only protection is a table-cloth. Consider it an improvement."

Swanny crawls out, unsteadily rising to her feet. In the last year, she's grown an inch taller than Pippi, a fact Pippi refuses to acknowledge, much less accept. But with the chinchilla coat on over those homely unisex pajamas, her daughter looks much like she did as a toddler, clad at Chet's insistence in frumpy "play clothes" to make swan wings in the snow. It's always struck Pippi as ungrateful that Swanny refuses to recollect her father, though perhaps it can't be helped. Even the sharpest mind doesn't retain much from before the age of three, and it isn't as though Pippi refreshes Swanny's memory by talking about him.

"Follow me," Pippi tells Swanny, and they sneak back through the kitchen, back up the servant stairs. The panic room is in the penthouse, in the interest of an airlift rescue.

"What if they've already sealed themselves in?" Swanny whispers when they reach the landing between the fourth and fifth floors.

The thought occurred to Pippi, but she had the tact not to mention it. She continues to ascend. "They can punch in the exit code, of course."

"But will they do that? For us? If it means exposing themselves to risk?"

"They're legally obligated. There's an escape accommodations clause in the contract, I made certain of that."

"Legally—but—"

"But nothing. How would it look if we were gored three feet from safety? Besides, with all the vetting you got, they'd be hard-pressed to find an adequate replacement." They reach the fifth-floor landing and round the corner. "Humphrey Ripple didn't get where he is today discarding sound investments."

"It's not Humphrey I'm worried about. Duncan . . . doesn't love me."

"Love takes time." Pippi swiftly preempts the protest she knows is rising in Swanny's throat: "And you'll have time."

The first bullet clips Pippi in the right shoulder. Her immediate reaction is not pain, not even surprise, but a rage so searing it's as though the pellet has released a corrosive vitriol from the torn flesh of her upper arm. The perp is wielding a pirate's blunderbuss, and as he hastens to reload the muzzle with another vintage shot, she pops him in the neck—she was trying for the eye socket, but the pain in her deltoid has thrown off her aim. At least she hits a major artery; this is no time for perfectionism. It's then that she hears an unmistakable rat-a-tat-tat, a sound like the furious subtractions of an infernal adding machine: a tommy gun. She yanks Swanny out of the way just in time, hurling her halfway back down the fifth flight of stairs.

The study. Of course. Humphrey keeps the house well stocked. The safe full of currency. The safe full of death.

"They've got into Humphrey's antique gun collection!" she hisses at Swanny, crouching low against the banister, angling her next shot up through the negative space at the center of the stairwell's helix. But she can hardly see her assailant from this angle: it's like aiming from the bottom of a well.

"What shall we do?"

Pippi fires seventeen times. The machine gunner stays just out of range. She curses and reaches into her pocket to reload, but she pulls out a handful of diamonds instead.

"Mother?"

"What are you doing, just standing there?" Pippi tosses a bauble to Swanny, then crams the rest of the jewelry back into her pocket. "Take that and *go*."

"But Mother, you're bleeding."

"And you're distracting me." Pippi slams another full magazine into the handle. "Go back to the kitchen. There's a passage out under the floorboards of the wine cellar. I'll join you there shortly."

Swanny hesitates for another second.

"Don't dawdle. Do you understand what I'm saying to you? Hurry."

Swanny turns and begins rushing down the stairs.

"Hold on to the rail!" Pippi calls after her daughter, because she's always been a clumsy girl, a disaster at dance, such poor posture, always dropping things, tripping over her own two feet, when they named her Swan they named her all wrong, because there's not a graceful thing about her, the child is, to put it frankly, a weight, a terrible heaviness on Pippi's heart, because Pippi cannot bear to see her fall, she simply cannot bear it, in certain cases the laws of gravity simply should not apply.

But Swanny doesn't fall. She pounds down the stairs, two at a time, around and around the helix, her chinchilla coat flying out behind, the first athletic feat of her life, while up above the gunfire makes a symphony of percussion. Swanny's nearly to the first floor when she hears her mother scream. And then she sees Pippi, plummeting through the center of the staircase, that column of nothingness around which the whole thing revolves, and crashing to the concrete floor. And even though Pippi is dissolving into a pool of herself, a red so dark and lustrous and conclusive that Swanny's old decorator kit would name it *Rapture*, Swanny cannot stop to stare, she's through the door and back out into the house's lobby, because she's reached the ground floor, there's no farther down to go.

~~~

Beneath our city lies another city, carved into the earth, a city of hollowness, a city of emptiness, a city of negative space. Its skyline will never be revealed, not until that time in the future when our society's final resting place is excavated and disturbed by a more advanced species. But until that day, we can only know our shadow city piece by piece, by the frail beam of a flashlight, by the touch of a hand outstretched in darkness. Long ago, parts of our underground were illuminated day and night—train platforms and exit signs, emergency stairs. Since then, all the electricity has escaped, seeping out the ends of frayed wires or bolting free from fuse boxes in dazzling sudden starbursts. Though this is the one realm unthreatened by the dragons, we have allowed it to decay like everything else we bury.

Once, the Black Line ran through these tunnels. But subterranean public transportation ceased decades ago, the first of the city's systems to fail and still, blood in the veins of a corpse. Now the Chute has become the lair of Torchtown escapees, conscription dodgers, and others who don't wish to be found. In that final category, one must include teenage runaways, even if, with their clumsy footfalls and their worried talk and their mutant dog straining at his leash, they make their presence in this place an open secret.

"I probably would've just gotten in the way," Ripple is saying. "Don't stick your hands in where they don't belong, that's what I learned in Power Tools class. Unless you're suicidal, and fuck that. There's a reason *CHALLENGER* got canceled; nobody likes to see a pro like Osmond stuck in a chair forever."

Abby has been ignoring Ripple's guilty monologue up till now, but this, of all things, finally captures her attention. "I thought the wheels were part of him."

"Osmond? No way. The chair moves all on its own, it's high tech."

"It's alive?"

"It's like—motorized."

"OK." Abby bends to pick up a candy wrapper from the gunky trench between two ties. He doesn't get why this is so hard for her to understand.

"It moves, but there's an engine in there. Not a heart. Not a soul."

"It's evil?"

"No, it's just . . ." Ripple jolts. "Did you hear that?"

The three of them stop walking. Hooligan cups a hand around one floppy ear.

"It sounded like footsteps," whispers Ripple. "Like someone's following us."

"The bad ones? From the house?"

"I don't think so." Ripple swings the beam of his electric torch in an uneven circle, shedding light on iron columns, rat nests, a crumpled tarp. "Nobody's here." His words, echoing against the cement, don't sound reassuring.

"I'm scared," announces Abby. Hooligan whines in agreement. "There's no sky."

"What does that have to do with anything?"

"God can't see me."

"If he's God, can't he just look in through the ceiling?"

Abby tilts her head. "How?"

"I dunno, holy magic?"

"You're silly." Abby wraps her arms around his neck and presses her lips to his. The sensation is an island of comfort in the river of darkness, a place just big enough for the two of them. It's funny how many worries go away when your mouth can't form words. "Mmm. I don't need God. Now I have you."

Then they hear the voice, low and disembodied, a few yards away: "Freeze."

Ripple leaps a foot in the air, swipes at the darkness with his flashlight beam. "Who's there?"

"Don't you recognize my voice, Duncan? Am I really so changed?"

Ripple feels something run over his foot—maybe a mouse?—and a shiver goes up his spine.

"Swanny," he says, "what *happened* to you?"

There's nothing obvious, not on the surface. She's wearing that fluffy gray coat again over her pajamas, and her hair is frizzy and snarled, but she didn't look way better right after they consummated. What's different now is her face. Maybe she had a device installed behind her eyes that gives her terrible powers in place of a mortal soul. Her skin is so pale, she looks like a hologram floating in the beam of illumination.

"Give me half of everything you've got," she says. He notices that one hand is concealed in the pocket of her coat, thrust forward in a gesture it takes him a second to recognize: it's supposed to be point-blank concealment, a mugger's heads-up.

"Sorry, we're still married. I'm keeping my stuff."

"When it comes to ink on paper, it's either there or it's not." Swanny seems to have acquired a tremor, or, more accurately in her case, a jiggle—every thirty seconds, a major seismic event happens that she doesn't seem to notice.

"Right." He wonders if she really has a gun. That could be bad. "Well, I bet everybody back at the house is worried about you, so . . ."

"*Everybody?*"

"Sure, your mom . . ."

"Mother is dead."

"Whoa, what?" He reflexively touches his cheek, which still stings from Pippi's blow, then plays innocent. "How did she die?"

"How do you think?"

"How'm I supposed to know, she was super old."

"You were a teen pregnancy, you ugly hulking scoundrel!" Swanny's face scrunches disturbingly. Then her eyes go wide, like she's watching an instant replay only she can see. "They shot her. Those fucking torchies—shot her down."

"They had guns?"

"They had your father's guns. How nice that he keeps the house well stocked."

"Oh shit. Oh *shit*." But Ripple isn't thinking of his mother-in-law now. "What about my parents? Osmond? Are they OK?"

"I don't know, Duncan, they didn't check in with us before fleeing to the panic room." Her voice drips with bitter sarcasm. "I suppose cowardice runs in the family."

"Uh—" Ripple would throw down a comeback, but all of a sudden Swanny is looking less pallid and more . . . greenish. "Hey, are *you* OK? Maybe you should sit down."

"I don't need to 'sit down,' I simply need to, to, to . . ." As if checking an invisible timepiece, Swanny raises her wrist to her eyes, then faints.

Ripple's mind whirs. Pippi Dahlberg? Shot? What exactly is he supposed to think about that? If Pippi is dead, that must mean that his own father allowed it to happen—that it happened on his watch.

The panic room, Ripple reminds himself. They're in the panic room. That's what Swanny said, and he has no reason to disbelieve her.

"She wouldn't want us to move her, right?" Ripple asks, shining light on the prone body sprawled across the subway tracks. Hooligan whines in assent, but for once Abby ignores the dog. She goes to her fallen rival and unbuttons the chinchilla coat and the first few buttons of the PJ top, then blows cool air down the ravine of Swanny's cleavage. Abby's got a knack for waking people up. Swanny heaves and flops over, washed ashore.

"Unhand me!" It sounds like something Osmond would say, but now Swanny's voice is a little girl's. She sits up. "Unhand me this instant."

"Too warm for coats."

"Don't touch me. I don't know where you've been."

Abby keeps stroking Swanny's furry sleeve anyway, gazing at her intently, mirroring her posture. "I remember when the Lady died."

"She wasn't a lady, she was a CEO," snaps Swanny.

"No—*my* Lady. She brought me to the Island in a big green tub. When she died, she left me there."

Ripple holds the girls in his spotlight. It's so weird to see them having a conversation, one that's not about him.

"I think she means the fem who raised her," he offers. "Some weird aunt, or a kidnapper, maybe, I haven't figured it out."

"The Lady gave me my name. She taught me about the People Machines. She taught me how to fish. I licked her bones for luck. Sometimes I still hear her voice. She tried to keep me safe. Your lady did too, didn't she?"

Abby's fingers continue to furrow through the chinchilla. There's something hypnotic in the motion, a lullaby of touch.

"I suppose," Swanny finally replies, "she wanted me to learn to fend for myself."

Abby nods. "The Lady threw me in the river to learn swimming."

"Mother gave me pop quizzes."

"The Lady burned out my fleas. I used to yell."

"Mother had me fitted with an IUD when I was fifteen. The blood was something apocalyptic, but she called it a sound invest-ment. Ha. A lot of good it does me now." Swanny winces at the memory. "State-of-the-art too. She spared no expense. Some only last a decade or so, but mine is made from the copper they use in coins. Indestructible. They call it the Moneyclip. An evocative name, don't you think?"

Ripple has no idea what she's talking about, and he doubts Abby does either. "Look, I don't think we should stay down here."

"Are you scared of the dark, Duncan?" A switch flips: Swanny sounds automated again.

"No, but if you could sneak up on us, somebody else could too." He doesn't specify, but they're all thinking the same thing. Even Swanny noticeably sobers.

"So what do you propose?"

"Dunk wants to find my people," Abby explains. "He says they'll give him a reward."

"Ah, so there's a warrant for her arrest? What's the charge, indecent exposure?"

The thought of Abby's family cheers him a little. "She doesn't know who her parents are, but they've gotta be out there, trying to find her. So we're taking her someplace to get her Bean read. You know, '*When you're burned beyond all re-re-recognition?*'"

Far from cracking a smile, Swanny quakes again. She looks away from him into the darkness.

"Good luck," she says. "But if you truly believe that any of us will see our parents again, I fear you're sorely mistaken."

"You said my parents were safe."

"Mother said they locked themselves in a room. I didn't take pulses."

"Listen, my dad knows how to handle this sort of thing. He might not have saved your mom, but normally he's . . ." Ripple trails off. What is it, exactly, about his dad that protects him, shields him from all harm? "My dad's the boss."

"Tell yourself what you must. Perhaps your fortune will remain intact too." Swanny sighs. "You may arrange my supplies in a pile, with the foodstuffs furthest from the ground. I'd appreciate your lending me the rucksack too, as I have no means of carrying them otherwise."

Ripple knows he doesn't really have a choice: "Come on. We're not leaving you here."

"You'd rather leave me somewhere else?"

"Yeah, actually."

"I'm not about to go out of my way to assuage your conscience, Duncan."

Abby touches the diamond brooch on Swanny's lapel. "What's this say?"

Swanny slaps her hand away. "'Eat shit and die!'" She brushes it off to dislodge Abby's germs. "It was the last thing my mother gave to me before she was murdered."

~~~

The four of them—three teenagers and a dog—walk for what feels like hours. Ripple leads the way, holding the light as they follow the forking tracks. This is what the world is to them: this little space of enlightenment, this tiny roving circle of the known. This is what it is to feel lost, if not *be* lost: to walk into nothing on a path that vanishes behind you. In this sunless place, where the air is still, their bodies keep the only time. Blood pulses, the dog's tongue ticks wetly, panting. The hour of Not Anymore, Not Yet.

On the ground, near the platforms especially, they step over strange reminders of the life these tunnels once had, back when the city was well: turnstile tokens, a headless Glitter Gal princess doll, a crumpled wad of currency, a broken umbrella, a bucket drum. The Black Line. All around, the spray-painted signatures of the dead vie for space on banished, unseen walls. Could a train travel out of the past to run them down? Ripple can almost feel its rumble under his feet, its engine's hot breath like an underground dragon's, but he tries not to think about it. They'll be outside soon, in the sunlight, in the city. He tries not to think too hard about that either.

They almost walk right past the emergency exit. The sign is small, the metal rungs easily missable where they protrude from the concrete wall. Ripple glances at the girls and Hooligan, then clicks off the flashlight and starts to climb, lifting himself foot by foot into what could just as well be a boundless, starless sky—the universe before God turned on the lights.

PART TWO

KNIGHT IN SHINING ARMOR

~~~~~

Everything is gonna burn. We'll all take turns. I'll get mine too.
—THE PIXIES

15

THE DEAD PARENTS

This is a story of what it is to be lost in a very large world.

Ripple survived the perils of a trip downtown just once before, when he was a little kid. His dad had some business at Laidly Bros., one of the last financial firms still holding on to office space in the city, and for reasons Ripple still can't quite fathom, he chose to bring his son along to the meeting. On the flight there, in the family HowLux—the one so completely done up in brown leather upholstery it felt like being inside a wallet—Humphrey called the bankers he was on his way to see "old men," "geezers," "worm chow," and "cremains." But when he parked on the roof of the building, he spent an extra minute retaping his hairpiece down in back before opening his door, and Ripple knew for once without being told that it was Best Behavior time.

Frailty and wealth make a strange combination: it is as though power is transferred, particle by particle, to an inanimate medium long before death itself arrives. The old men—and they *were* old— sat in a dim room hot from the whir of laser printers, murmuring commands into invisible skull-hewn headsets, their eyes no longer strong enough to bear a LookyGlass's radiance. The many overhead fans gave their papers the rustling sound of dry leaves in late autumn. The shades were drawn, and with each tap of the pull cord against the glass, Humphrey twitched visibly in the direction of the nearest fire exit. When he met with the oldest of the old men, a lipless, spidery-fingered creature who sat in a corner office with windows so darkly scorched they were in no need of any covering, Humphrey allowed Ripple to climb into his lap, where Ripple pressed his ear to Humphrey's chest to hear the desperate negotiations of his father's clogged and fumbling heart.

They left without any papers being signed. Ripple knew then that to live and work downtown, amid the ashes, was to become a different kind of being, a thing no longer entirely in the world—untorchable, supernatural—a feat his father both feared and grudgingly admired. When they got back in the HowLux, Humphrey went straight for a vertical ascent without bothering to taxi.

"Don't tell your mom," he said, popping open a tallboy as he flew, and as a bribe he offered the can to Ripple for a sip—his first.

Ripple hasn't thought about that day for years, but now, as he crawls out of the manhole onto a deserted crosswalk, a vortex of gritty wind smarting his eyes, the memory comes back to him in an overwhelming sensation, a truth too large to articulate in words.

"Fuck," he announces to no one in particular, "this place is *dead*."

As Hooligan and the girls hoist themselves through the manhole and onto the pavement, Ripple sizes up the surroundings. They're at an intersection, a complicated three-way juncture of one-way streets, edged in by oddly angled towers, gray geometric compromises spruced up with pillared facades and ragged flags with faded, ghostly insignias. Ripple always thought of skyscrapers as soaring, but these buildings are so looming, so crammed in, looking up feels claustrophobic. The asphalt is strewn with ancient pages, yellowed tatters that gust to and fro, a literate tornado. They're on the steps of the Metropolitan Library.

"Good lord," says Swanny, stooping to pick up a desecrated binding from where it lies on the pavement. Only a few pages are left inside; the wind has ripped the rest away. "Who is responsible for this?"

"That'd be Rudy," says a voice. The three teenagers turn to see a wizened baba, some yards away, perched on the steps next to an overturned book-deposit bin, which she's converted into a sleeping nook. The woman wears a filthy lavender cowl, and dozens of pigeons perch on her shoulders and lap. The area around her is so stained with their excrement, it appears to have been whitewashed. She laughs—caws, almost—which doesn't unsettle the pigeons in the slightest. Hooligan races over to the periphery of the flock, but when the birds don't budge, he commences with sniffing their butts. "He gets all sauced up, that Rudy, till you wouldn't know his right age. Pulled his shoulder out of joint knocking that thing down, but he got me a warm place for napping. Lovemaking too." She smiles flirtatiously. Her two front teeth are brownish, and one is considerably longer than the other.

Ripple has a sudden urge to leap back down the manhole, but Abby is going up to the woman, gently toeing her way through the sea of sky rats.

"I like lovemaking and birds!" says Abby, sitting down beside the old lady. A pigeon flutters into her lap. Abby strokes it affectionately. "What's this one's name?"

"I call him Stumpy, ever since Chompy chewed his foot clean off. See Chompy over there? The one with blood on his beak?"

"He's beautiful."

"Might I ask," says Swanny, with a modicum of condescension, "why you don't sleep in the library proper? It seems needlessly destructive to upend that structure when there's an entire abandoned building right there."

"Sleep in the library?" the bird lady crows. "Now, do I look old enough to pass for a Librarian? Don't answer that, love, you'll break my heart. The Librarians have camped out in the stacks since forever. They're a bunch of old shushers and killjoys, if you're asking me."

Ripple sets down his bag, pulls out his LookyGlass. He considers opening a LookyChat, then texts instead:

TO: D. Humphrey Ripple IV
CC: Katya Ripple, Osmond Strangeboyle Ripple
SUBJECT: u ok?
i know u r mad but let me know

Swanny stares at the hulking stone gryphons on either side of the building's entrance. "So the Librarians spend all their time *reading*? But however do they survive?"

"Well, the long and short of it is they don't. The library is where folks go to die—a certain type of folk, that is. Short-tempered day-dreamers who don't much like the world outside their own brain cage. So many've passed on from there, they say it's gotten to be haunted."

Ripple looks up from his device: Swanny is taking the stairs two at a time. An angry blur of chinchilla, thrust forward by rage alone.

"Wench, where are you going?!"

She doesn't answer him, drawn into the word cathedral by some inexorable magnetism.

"Literotica," Ripple mutters, returning his eyes to the Looky-Glass screen. He opens a LookyChat with the Metropolitan Police Department. "Hi, I'm calling to complain."

The heavy iron library doors slam shut behind Swanny; Abby looks down at her dirty bare feet. "She's sad," she tells the bird lady. "Maybe I should be her friend."

"That's all right, she seems snooty anyhoo." The baba pinches Abby's cheek. "Now, would you like an eggy-wegg, pretty girl?"

Inside, Swanny's eyes adjust to the shade. The building's electricity must have shorted out long ago, because although the many arched windows fill the scholarly sanctuary with the weak light of the afternoon, the light fixtures hang spent and useless from their ceiling chains. Here and there, glowing on the tops of long oak tables, are votive candles, and before them, bent over their books like supplicants at prayer, are the Librarians.

These are real Gray Ladies, and Gray Men too, tenuous creatures from which life has leached all color. Swanny's old deck of paint samples would have called their wisps of hair Downy Owl, Whispering Spring, Misty Morning. Some heads are paler still: Linen, Baby's Breath, Cream, Snow, Chantilly Lace. Striding past them, which she tries to do briskly, silently, is like fording a bank of clouds, the smoky exhaust of the past.

The stacks are labyrinthine, and she sometimes has to step over the body of a fallen Librarian, asleep or even deeper gone into the central fold of a tome. Swanny runs her fingers over the spines, with titles that read like clues—*Lost Children*, *The Inner City*, *Swimming the Lethe*, *The Collected E. Hamish Plumbrick*, *Necessary Evils*, *The Magician Is Dead*—until, with surprising ease, she finds it, the book she's looking for: *Power Suit* by Chet Dahlberg.

"Your father, the poet." Pippi mentioned it just once before that fatal night, some years earlier. Swanny thought then that it was a joke, since they'd drained the vermouth on their last round of martinis and Pippi was shrieking with laughter as she spoke. "Every morning to his secretary—'Miss Langley, take a poem!' The poor child would have preferred a pay cut, I'm sure." Swanny checks the copyright page: PRINTED ON DEMAND. He really was an author, one the public clamored for. Who better to offer Swanny some solace, some instruction, at this trying time?

Outside, on the steps, Abby and the bird lady are eating soft-boiled pigeon eggs; the bird lady makes Hooligan perform tricks for the shells.

"Sit," instructs the bird lady.

—spin around? bark?

—I'm not giving you a hint, Hooli!

—just kidding. so smart.

The apehound sinks back on his haunches, tongue lolling. The bird lady throws a yolky glob in his direction, but a pigeon pecks at it first. Angrily, Hooligan throttles its feathered throat. The pigeon coos in terror.

—Stop it. Remember what happened last time?

—not same. not magic. not friend.

"Put down my Lulu," the bird lady orders sternly. "Bad dog. Give me the bird."

—oh! know this one.

Hooligan drops the pigeon and joyfully flicks her off with both hands.

Meanwhile, Ripple is getting nowhere fast with the police department as represented by a tiny mustachioed visage on his screen, low resolution by design. "Pro, what do you mean this was the jurisdiction of a private security firm? Like, what does 'jurisdiction' mean?"

"We can't issue reports on incidents from outside the district we police."

"Who does police it, then?"

"Your father contracted a private security firm called Home-Shield to monitor your property. When he signed the enhanced user agreement, he waived his rights to emergency services from the Metropolitan Police Department. By law, we're not obligated to police parts of the city with that level of private coverage."

"Seriously? My dad got house bouncers because you suck at law enforcing, and now you're saying no cops even went to check it out? My mother-in-law's dead!"

"Congratulations?"

"Too soon, doughnut patrol. You need to send your guys up there pronto. I'm not joking around. You're going to hear from my lawyers about this."

~~~

Swanny sits on the library floor, her back against a shelf of books as she reads. The text, though set in type, is printed in such an informal, whimsical sans-serif style Swanny feels as though her father might have lettered it himself.

The Love Song of C. Norman Dahlberg

Let us go now, you and I,
Where, like some seraph fallen from the sky,
My wife lies etherized upon a table.

For you'll have time
To repair a face to greet the faces that you greet;
You'll have time to murder and to birth

To burn a name upon the earth
To live a lifetime full of changes which a scalpel will reverse.

In the clinic, the women come and go,
Bitching about rhinoplasty.

The yellow smog presses its palms against the windowpanes
The yellow smog taps its fingers on the windowpanes
The yellow smog curls up before the hearth of a burning skyscraper,
Warms its thin hands, and falls asleep.

I have been here before; I know it well.
Hours in this waiting room are hell,
Measured out in cheap coffee, imagined crises,
Hellos to other husbands one scarcely recognizes.

In the clinic, the women come and go,
Bitching about rhinoplasty.

Then, at last, an audience with the wife,
Who smiles knowingly, without a sound,
As if to say, "I am Eurydice, come back from deep underground,
Which is why the light bothers me
And that's absolutely the only reason I'm wearing wraparound
    sunglasses."

It's been worth it, after all,
The operations have rubbed out the marks of all her days
Except the hands, twisted with veins and knots,
Dotted with freckles and old age spots,
and plenty of fine lines and wrinkles.

So the yellow smog will have time
To seep in through these windows, to cloud our gaze,
To mellow the antiseptic air to a nostalgic haze.

For I have known these hands already, known them well:
Known them mornings, evenings, afternoons,
A pair of ragged claws clamped upon my arm,

Or scuttling a Rolodex of names to harm.
Such claws!
The siren crab that closes on the ankle, beneath the waves,
And pulls us all to our watery graves.

"Good lord, he *loved* her?" Swanny murmurs. Imagining her mother clutching a man by the arm, much less entertaining one from that most vulnerable of places, a post-op hospital bed, is like seeing a familiar face grinning out from a carnival cut-out board. Corona had a photograph of herself in one of those, her plain, maternal visage mismatched with a mermaid's sensual frame. But this new picture of Pippi as *siren crab* is even more incongruous. And Swanny can't see her father at all: no matter how far back she reaches in her childhood memory, he's still only a silhouette, a contorted shadow puppet moaning behind bed-curtains. She flips ahead, past poems with indecipherable titles ("Vasovagal Syncope, or: The Bradley Method") and ones with words scattered like vase shards all over the page. But she audibly gasps when she sees the title of the last verse in the book, doggerel this time.

Apology to My Daughter

We fucked you over, your mom and I
We have only ourselves to blame
We should've had the tact to die
And finish off the Dahlberg name.

But as old people past our prime
We saw in you a hopeful chance
To change the world one last time
And see the future in advance.

We left to you a burnt-up city,
A dwindled fortune, and our fears.
I know it isn't very pretty
But it'll be all yours for years.

You have every right to curse us
But give two dodderers a break.
Put down this silly book of verses
And enjoy life, for our sake.

Swanny closes *Power Suit* and stares at the cover. In lieu of blurbs or a book description, her father's portrait takes up the entire back of the jacket: a gesture of humility on his part, no doubt, since he wasn't a handsome man. He has a beard but no mustache, giving him a vaguely Hutterite aspect, and a smile that, in keeping with the tone of his last poem, is more apologetic than knowing. But it's his eyes that hold Swanny's attention. Looking into those eyes is like looking into the past.

When was the moment she can see now in her mind? Was she lying in her crib, reaching up toward the mobile of educational creatures who circled above endlessly in her miniature sky? Propped up in a high chair, gnawing a stub of carrot as she cut the first of her many, many teeth? Stubbornly crawling in the direction of the nearest poison cabinet, the impulse toward self-destruction unnamed but squirming in the heart of her even then? Whatever the context, the memory is there: her father, looking down on her with those exact eyes, his expression one of sympathy, guilt, even pain, as he watched her futile struggle, as he saw stretch before her a lifetime full of the same wasted exertion, and worse. He only hoped she'd have a little fun along the way.

And, never far, there was always Pippi—Pippi, to whom no struggle was futile, no exertion wasted, Pippi, whose belief in her daughter was so harsh and relentless it came across as an accusation: "Make an effort. You're doing this to infuriate me. If you'd only pay attention. Don't slouch. You're not listening. Show your work. Faster. I don't care if it takes you all night. 'Good enough' is not good enough. Concentrate. Stop working beneath your abilities. Don't disappoint me." *You are my daughter. You will never die.* Pippi had felt no guilt about bringing a child into a ruined world. She'd made it her business to assure herself Swanny could survive it—

could perhaps even conquer it. Such strange, flawed, irreplaceable parents. Gone forever.

Now Swanny is disappointing them both.

Swanny has forgotten that she's in the public library; her thoughts have transported her home to the velvet fainting couch beneath her family's bookshelves, amid the desolate grandeur of Wonland County. Only now, when a haggard crone—a Librarian—touches her shoulder does she startle back. Swanny stares up at her uncomprehendingly. This Librarian is the Grayest of the Gray Ladies. Ash seems to line the creases of her face.

"I'm sorry," the Librarian whispers, "but you're distracting the other patrons."

"Why? Did I make a sound?" Swanny's voice is a croak.

"You were crying rather loudly, yes. But the trouble is, you're much too young to be here."

"Excuse me?"

"You're distracting the other patrons," the Librarian repeats, not unkindly.

"You don't understand," says Swanny, hanging her head, eyes fixed on the book in her hands. "I'm dying too—I just found out yesterday—and I don't know what to do. I haven't the faintest idea where to start."

And then that voice: a sound as sharp and familiar as vodka cracking ice. "Not yet, darling. Give it a few years."

Swanny's head snaps up. "*What* did you just say?"

The Librarian blinks, her glasses magnifying her rheumy eyes, and raises a finger to her lips. "Shhh."

Swanny leaves the library in a daze. She feels the eyes of the Librarians on her as she passes through the stacks and between the long rows of tables. The iron doors don't want to budge. It takes all of Swanny's strength to pull them open. She does it with a sudden desperation she no longer knew she had. The library is a mausoleum, and she's offended the ghosts. She feels sick and small. Her father's slim volume, jammed in the pocket of her coat, is her grave robber's prize, a relic, the tiniest finger bone of a buried giant. How could she have thought her death would be significant, special, noble even? Dying counts for nothing at all; absolutely anyone is capable of it. The doors give and she bursts out into the sunlight.

"I don't care what it costs, send *somebody*," Ripple is telling his LookyGlass. "Do you seriously not know who I am?"

"I suppose no one cares that I've just communed with the dead," says Swanny. "Good lord, Abigail, what are you eating?"

Abby looks at the tiny drumstick of roasted meat she's munching. "Chicken?"

"Chicken," the bird lady affirms, in a tone that leaves no room for argument.

Hooligan runs up, noses at Swanny's crotch. Swanny swats him with *Power Suit*.

"I need a private detective," she announces. "Also, a pistol, a shooting instructor, and a good attorney. I intend to avenge my mother's death."

Ripple covers the LookyGlass microphone with one finger. "Avenge her death? Seriously? Swanny, if those torchies got away, you don't want to go after them. They learn to chainsaw before they can walk. You were lucky to make it out of there alive."

"I'm well aware of the dangers, but I don't see what choice I have. It's my destiny, my redemption, the one mark I'll leave upon this uncaring Earth."

"What are you going to do? Wander around the sewers till you bump into them? Go to Torchtown?"

"Yes."

"Uh, no offense, but you wouldn't last five minutes down there. Those pros would eat you alive. You should leave this to the actual authorities." He returns his attention to the LookyGlass.

"As effective as your method may be—" Swanny hazards.

"Fuck! He put me on hold."

"I feel mine is more direct."

Ripple shrugs. "OK, so you're going on a rampageathon. I don't know what you expect me to do about it."

"You're contractually obligated to support and encourage my

Personal Enrichment Endeavors." Then, softer, almost tenderly petulant: "You *have* to help me."

"Fem, I don't have to do anything. I've got my own family to think about. And I already promised Abby I'd help her find her parents. She has no clue who she is."

"Yes I do," says Abby quietly, ruffling the purplish feathers on Stumpy's throat.

The bird lady takes Abby by the hand. "Dearie, it's nothing to be ashamed of. I didn't know who I was until one morning I woke up, boobs a-droop, kitty-cats burnt to a crisp, and a little birdie told me, 'We've been singing your name all this time. How come it's only now you listen?'"

"What *is* your name?" asks Abby.

The old woman makes a guttural sound, half coo, half whistled trill. Abby repeats it back, raising the pitch at the end as if she's asking a question. Hooligan cocks his head.

"You're my husband," says Swanny, "you can't simply—"

"Husband schmusband. I've got to keep my priorities straight. Maybe we're married, but Abby's the one who's gonna give me a whole litter of Dunklings. Pop 'em out like bam, bam, bam. She's probably got the nine-month chunk already. Her tits seem bigger all the time."

Abby peeks down inside her sweatshirt.

"I can't believe I'm hearing this. You're absolutely disgusting," Swanny tells him.

Ripple is distracted again by his LookyGlass. "Hey, you must be that other guy's supervisor. Are you punishing him for how he just talked to me?"

This time, the LookyChat image is even grainier, an abstraction of outsized pixels and a voice that's all gravelly distortion.

"My officer informs me that you've threatened to bring charges against the police department."

"Fuck yeah, you insult my family and I come at you with fire."

Fire. As if on cue, the street darkens. A smell like sulfur fills the air. Ripple looks up.

From below, the dragon does not resemble a living thing. It is an oppression, a ceiling on the world. It booms terror the way a speeding HowFly booms sound. Hooligan covers his eyes and peeks out between his fingers; Abby clings to the bird lady; Ripple trembles. Only Swanny is motionless, transfixed.

The creature is so endless, it takes a full minute to pass. The humans gaze up at the underside of its jaw, a vast spiny ridge; the undulating belly, algae-green scales fractaled out exponentially, some still barnacled with strange, otherworldly growths; the claws, the cruel, curving claws like pitiless carnivore tusks. This body is not the body of a single "I"; a lone personality would echo forever through such a yawning chamber of air and fire. So when it roars, the dragon is a cacophony in which every tone denies the others, every tone asserts itself and itself alone. The noise assimilates the teenagers, their voices, the thrum of their minds. They vanish into its smog.

When the fire pours down on the library, it is relentless—as though gravity has finally pulled the sun itself under its sway. The heat is volcanic.

"My God," Swanny yells over the popping and crackling of the flames dancing on the building's roof, "I was just inside!"

"New emergency!" Ripple screams into the LookyGlass. "This fucking dragon just torched the library!"

"We're dispatching someone now." The digitized face of the police commissioner shifts into a smear of flesh and shadow as he presses a button screen right. "He'll be there shortly."

"Didn't all the firemen quit?"

"Don't be alarmed by his appearance. Oh, and he may need your help."

"*What?*"

The Metropolitan Police Department severs the connection; the LookyChat goes black.

"Nobody talks to me like that," Ripple insists, unconvincingly.

"Don't you worry none," says the bird lady, reaching down to soothe her winged charges. "Library's caught fire more times than

I can remember, but it won't burn. When we're all dead it'll still be standing there. Like a big know-it-all headstone."

This last word dissolves into coughs, as thick smoke is now billowing from the venerable institution down onto the stony steps. The fumes are so black and gritty, it's impossible to see two feet away. The birds take flight, briefly clearing the air with their flapping, and Ripple shoves the LookyGlass back into his cargo pocket. He, Hooligan, and the girls make their way down to the sidewalk and across the street. Only the bird lady stays.

"Fascinating how she can breathe in this," observes Swanny. "A person can adapt to most anything, I suppose."

Ripple doesn't answer; he's doubled over, having an affluenza attack. He digs through his duffel, tossing random items onto the pavement.

"The fuck . . . is my . . . inhaler?"

Swanny inspects the lighter shaped like a naked woman's torso. "What does it look like?"

"Dunk, don't die!" Abby tries to wrap her arms around his neck. He pushes her away.

"Relax . . . I just . . . gotta . . ." He finds the inhaler and takes several hits off it in quick succession. His wheezing slows. Relieved, he sinks down to the curb. "Phew, I'm still alive. No thanks to you fems."

"I would have helped if you'd become unconscious. Mother taught me CPR in our Domestic Violence course."

Ripple starts repacking the bag, then stops. "Hey, do you hear something?"

Abby tilts her head to one side. "Like, 'whooo-ooh, whooo-ooh'?"

It's a siren, all right, but something about it sounds off—an ambient crackle, a slight abstraction of tone, as if it is reaching toward them from the echoey caverns of the past. It takes a moment before they see why. The sound isn't blaring from a rescue vehicle, or from a megaphone mounted atop a pole. It's emanating from the duct-taped speakers of a battered Boom Blaster, held aloft on the shoulder of a figure half-visible in the smoke: a man in a gas mask, red peaked helmet, and yellow slicker. He pushes a hot-dog cart, packed with water tanks protruding from the top, trailing a length of hose. Black galoshes encase his feet, canvas gloves his hands. He breathes his own air. Nothing human of him shows.

16

URBAN LEGEND

L ate one night, a little boy woke up to see a fireman standing at the foot of his bed. The fireman had on a helmet and gloves and a gas mask, so you couldn't see his face.

"Is the building on fire?" asked the child. "Have you come here to rescue me?" The fireman walked out of the room without saying a word.

Years passed. The little boy grew from a child into a man. One night, when he was shaving, he saw the fireman's reflection in the mirror behind him. The gas mask was made of old brown leather, stained and scarred. Behind the eyeholes, only darkness showed.

"Is the building on fire?" asked the young man. "Have you come to rescue me?" When he turned around to look at the fireman, the fireman was gone.

The young man married and grew older and moved into a new apartment with his wife and children. One night, when he was up late reading in bed next to his sleeping wife, the fireman appeared outside his window and beckoned, once. The man followed the fireman out onto the fire escape and then down the rattling metal steps to the alley below.

"Wait!" the man called after the fireman. "I've wondered all my life who you are and what you want from me. Please show me your face."

The fireman stopped and looked back at him in the darkness. He slowly reached up and unbuckled the mask. There was nothing where his face should be, no skin or bones or muscle, nothing at all but empty air. His hollow clothes collapsed into a pile, releasing a plume of ash. The man heard sirens behind him. His building was burning down with his wife and children inside.

Leather Lungs. That's what they call the phantom fireman, the keeper of false promises, the bearer of bad news. Leather Lungs. Sometimes he doesn't save anyone. He just comes to the fires to watch.

Back in underschool, Ripple heard all the stories—no two of them are quite the same. Sometimes Leather Lungs is hideously burned beneath his snozzled hood, his cauterized flesh exposing patches of blackened skull and a pearly, lipless smile. Sometimes he has the face of a friend or sibling or grandparent who died unrescued in a blaze—someone with a grudge. And sometimes, at the tale's end, his victim feels compelled beyond all reason to pick up his ashy costume, the heavy domed helmet, the mask of hose and hide, and *put them on*—to slip inside the skin of Leather Lungs and live the curse himself. It's this last idea that always scared Ripple the most: the thought of losing his face, his name.

"Who are you?" Ripple demands now of the apparition masquerading as his childhood nightmares. It's as if Leather Lungs isn't himself a presence, but rather the powerful absence of something else. Like the time Kelvin gouged his hand in Power Tools class, and Ripple couldn't stop staring at the meaty little notch in the side of his thumb. Leather Lungs is a notch taken out of the world. Ripple steps in front of his wenches and canine protectively. "Back off, pro. I've faced old ladies and torchies, I don't have to take this shit."

Leather Lungs does not respond. He plods steadily toward Ripple, toward the fire, as though the dragons have opened a portal back to his interdimensional hell world and he intends to return with a guest. Ripple stands his ground. Hooligan tugs on Ripple's pant leg and growls a warning.

"I'm not gonna say this again. Don't get any closer." Ripple's not used to his bluffs getting called. It occurs to him that it's dangerous to grow up with power before you have the physical strength to back it up. "I mean it."

"Metropolitan Police Department," says Leather Lungs. Through the mask, his voice sounds like his prerecorded siren—another echo from the past. "Independent extinguishment contractor."

Oh.

"Can I see some ID?" Ripple asks shakily.

A walkie-talkie crackles on Leather Lungs's utility belt. "Special Officer, confirm your position?"

"Ten-four, position confirmed," Leather Lungs radios back. To Ripple, he says, "This is an emergency conscription. By your presence here today you have waived your right of noncompliance. Any attempt to resist performance of your civic duty, or to disobey orders, can and will be used against you."

"Wait, what? Conscription? My dad buys me exemptions for that. I'm Duncan Ripple the Fifth. You can't just conscript me in the street. Pro, back the fuck up." Ripple puts up his fists.

"Dunk, don't touch him, he's a People Machine!"

But before Ripple can deliver his punch, Leather Lungs has throttled him and single-handedly lifted him by the throat two inches off the sidewalk. For the second time in five minutes, Ripple feels the breath squeezed out of him. He kicks at the air as Leather Lungs ominously raises his free hand, which Ripple now sees is no ordinary hand but a *claw*, two stainless-steel crescents connected by a hinge. It'll be murder by dissection. Leather Lungs closes it around Ripple's neck. Ripple waits for the scissory snip, the slice of metal into flesh and the feeling of light-headedness that he always imagined would go along with being decapitated. But instead, as Ripple tumbles backward onto the sidewalk, the claw still holds him in its grip. It is detached from Leather Lungs now, an appendage with a mind of its own.

And Ripple can't get it off. He paws at the gizmo, which glimmers with light-emitting diodes and gives off a faint buzzing noise. It stays on snug, just below his chin. Leather Lungs doesn't stick around to guard his handiwork. He continues on his way as the girls and dog huddle around Ripple.

"Oh no, a collar!" cries Abby. Hooligan shakes his head sympathetically.

A collar! Wait. What?

"Did that claw-slinging fog-nozzler really just try to conscript me?"

"No, he's chosen you for his pet," Swanny counters dryly. "Or perhaps for torture. At any rate, he *owns* you. Pity, I was hoping he'd do away with you at once. I just renegotiated the widowhood clause with your father yesterday."

"I can't get this thing off. Fems, do either of you have a hex key? Turnscrew? Multitool? Nail file? Toothpick? Nothing? Nothing, for serious?"

Leather Lungs's hot-dog cart bounces away along the pavement, into the molten heart of what's giving off thicker and thicker clouds of pollution. When he's ten feet away, the diodes on Ripple's collar start to flash.

"Ow!" Ripple jerks his head and slaps at the collar. "Fuck! It bit me! Ow! Fuck! It did it again! Ow! Fuck! Why does it keep doing that? Ow! Fuck! It fucking hurts!"

"Electricity!" Abby is berserking, but she isn't wrong. The shocks get worse the farther off Leather Lungs gets—sizzling, shivery disturbances that feel like Ripple's body is misaligning with his soul. Ripple sprints after him.

"Pro, wait up! Wait!"

～～～

Swanny was assembled in a lab out of spare parts of her parents. Now and then, her mother disparagingly referred to the way babies were "traditionally made," as though procreation of the ordinary sort were a quaint affectation of the old-fashioned, despite the fact that there was a better product on the market—in this case, a customized one. Pippi selected for maximum intelligence (no guarantees, of course, but the doctors knew the genetic markers), keen senses, and, when it came down to picking among specific embryos, Swanny's amber-colored, almost golden eyes.

"People act as though it's some kind of witchcraft, but there's always selection in the womb," Pippi said. "Shark fetuses gobble up their siblings till only the strongest survives. That's nature, darling. We could wring our hands over might-have-beens, but what for? You came into this life a winner."

It's Swanny's eyes Abby stares into now. And though Abby knows nothing of the beakers and centrifuges, the cryocrypt where the recipe for the baroness in question spent its existential Before, she sees something in the particular hue of those irises that is not of God's manufacture.

"You're working for the People Machines," Abby whispers. "Maybe you *are* a People Machine."

"What are you muttering about? They have such strange accents where you come from. You don't sound like anyone at all."

"You want him to go. You want him to die in a fire."

"That doesn't mean I'm plotting against him with some sort of mercenary . . . fog-nozzler. Honestly, why bother to live in a city if you're afraid to breathe the *air*?"

Abby repeats Katya's words: "You'll have babies, but you'll never make love. You'll have your babies in a Toob."

Swanny's mouth falls open, exposing the second row of teeth that half-doubles her lower jaw. Then her eyes narrow. "How dare you say that to me."

"People Machine!"

"Empty-headed slut!"

"People Machine!"

"Shopworn dollymop!"

"People Machine!"

Swanny grabs Abby by the hair. "I'm not frigid!" she yells in Abby's face.

Hooligan clamps his mouth onto Swanny's pajamaed calf, and Swanny yanks her hand free of Abby's scalp, cursing, taking several long blond strands with it in the process. The dog releases Swanny in turn, and she angrily inspects the indentations on her leg for blood. Finding none, she tugs Hooligan's leash out of Abby's hands with a vindictive jerk.

"All right," Swanny says. Her eyes are dying suns, red-rimmed from the smoke. "Duncan's all yours. Go and get him."

~~~

"I don't think you're supposed to ride the elevator when the building's on fire," Ripple says.

Leather Lungs presses the button for the library's top floor without responding. Looks like he has two good hands after all. The doors slide shut. Now only the hot-dog cart stands between him and Ripple in the enclosed space. Leather Lungs respirates steadily through his mask. Maybe Ripple should try to get on this guy's good side. Assuming there is a good side. Independent extinguishment contractor—that's like a bounty hunter for fires.

"You didn't have to put the collar on me," Ripple continues. "I would've gone with you willingly."

"The hell you would have," says Leather Lungs. "If you wouldn't face danger with those girls watching, you wouldn't do it at all. A man's always bravest in front of an audience."

"Harsh. And untrue. I'm brave whenever. Mostly." Ripple thinks of fleeing the mansion, the hours walking underground. He checks his LookyGlass: still no response from his dad. "Hey, you work for the police department. Do you think you could get them to send some cops up to the Heights to check on my family?"

"What happened to your family?"

"My mansion got broken into—fucking HomeShield. I think my parents got to the panic room in time, but I want to make sure they're OK. Torchies. Not cool."

"Where were you when this happened?"

"That doesn't matter. Can you do it or not? I'm helping *you* out."

"Under duress."

This is a really slow elevator. "I used to want to be a fireman, you know. I talked about it on my show, *Late Capitalism's Royalty*. I'm on the record about this."

"Didn't have what it takes?"

"Come on. They shut that shit down when the fire chief got barbecued. Obviously you know that, it's how you got your job." Leather Lungs doesn't answer. It feels weirdly mournful, like an impromptu moment of silence, until Ripple goes on: "So I got into other stuff, like gaming and damsels. Did you see my girlfriend? The hot one, not the other one. The other one's my wife."

"You'll need this." Leather Lungs takes out a second gas mask and offers it to Ripple. Ripple can't imagine strapping it to his face; it's nasty and old, a feed bag for breathing.

"Um, I'm good, thanks."

Leather Lungs turns to him slowly, and for the first time Ripple sees the glint of eyes behind those eyeholes. "The brainpan is a skillet, son. It doesn't take the heat. When you get out there in the smoke, the fumes, the threat of more death raining from above, this mask will be the only thing holding your body and soul together. Top of the line, vetted the brand myself."

It's a pretty stirring endorsement.

"Maybe I'll hold on to it just in case." Ripple turns the mask over: TARNHELM reads a little metal tag on the inside lining. So weird to bother branding something that isn't even stylish.

"When someone offers you a gas mask, you take it. And you never take it off."

"Not ever?"

"Not until it's safe."

"Right."

"Now, when we get up there, you're going to look out on the roof and it's going to look bad. It's going to look like the end. You have to remember, you write this story. You're the one who forges that path through the flames. You're the one who survives. Man's braver when there's an audience, but there's always an audience."

Sure, that big camera crew in the sky. "God?"

"God is a fairy tale for cowards and fools. History. History. What do you want history to remember from this day?"

"That I . . . didn't die?"

"That you *lived*."

"Yeah, that too."

The elevator lets them out upstairs. Leather Lungs lifts something from the hot-dog cart: it's a backpack made from a multigallon water tank, with a trigger-pulled hose. He slings it onto his shoulders, then hoists out another one for Ripple.

Leather Lungs leaves the hot-dog cart behind and vaults up the steps to the roof access at the end of the hall. He must be feeding off the fire's energy. The closer he gets to it, the faster he moves. A whoosh of hot air rushes inside as he throws open the emergency exit.

Leather Lungs is deploying Ripple to a prime battlefield in the war against oxygen. The surface of the library roof actually appears to undulate, a smokescape of ever-fluxing plasma: no place for a sane man to tread. Ripple loiters in the doorway. As Leather Lungs shimmers toward dematerialization, Ripple shouts after him, "I can't breathe out here!"

Leather Lungs stops and turns back with eerie calm. He taps the snozzle of his gas mask. Ripple takes a deep breath and pulls the leathery, rubbery hood over his own face.

~~~

Humphrey Ripple watches the home invaders on the surveillance monitors in the panic room. They're chainsawing his employees. His staff. His people. When the emissaries from the Quiet Place arrive, they chainsaw them too. Red blood on white lab coats. The invaders maraud around from screen to screen, pissing on Humphrey's rugs, spray-tagging his portrait, loading his possessions into crates that they carry down a secret passage to the sewer: guns, currency, silver, single malt. They take the jewelry off Pippi Dahlberg's corpse. Humphrey hired a private security firm years ago. He put faith in their technology and hope in guessing that they'd be more responsive to calls and less amenable to bribes than the city's notorious police force. But he guessed wrong. No one is coming to save them. A man's home is his castle, and Humphrey has been dethroned.

Osmond and Katya are playing Hangman. Osmond wins every game. Katya guesses the letters of the alphabet in alphabetical order. Even after all these years, her voice still lilts like a sexy child's.

"F?"

"The noose tightens, Princess Phonetica. For charity's sake, I'll give your effigy hands and feet this time."

"G?"

Humphrey's embarrassing wife, a masturbation fantasy he had to introduce to colleagues, once upon a time. His embarrassing brother, an invalid-carriage loaded with druggy contempt for the world of the waking. Both of them avoiding the most embarrassing topic of all: the embarrassing disappearance of his embarrassing son. *i know u r mad but let me know.* As if Humphrey would ever dignify that with a response, even in the best of times. He feels old and depressed. As a young and then not-so-young zillionaire playboy, he always thought that someday he would get around to ruining himself, before anyone else could do it. He would bet wrong on purpose. He would burn through his net worth in a single day. He would prove to everyone that he didn't need the money, the mansion, the name, and he would vanish into legend. But then, somehow, he'd had a family instead. What had he been thinking? If only he'd lost it all when he had the chance. Then it would be his forever.

"Kindred, I beseech you, spare us both this bimbo abecedarian's recitations and throw your *postiche* into the ring. I'll play you three out of five."

"This is no time for word games, Osmond," says Humphrey, pale in the doom screens' glow.

"Our world is ending and there's nothing we can do about it. This is precisely the time for word games."

Humphrey taps one of the monitors with his finger, as if it might startle the figure there out of what he's about to do.

"What's happening here?"

The Ripples watch as the invader splashes the Hall of Ancestors with a jagged zigzag of liquid from a gas can. They watch as the invader lights a match.

"That's it. Get me the Dignity Kit," says Humphrey.

"I refuse to indulge such blatant hypocrisy from the likes of you. As a brother of mine once said, 'I'm here to talk you out of killing yourself.'"

"You didn't listen to me either."

"Hummer," murmurs Katya, "isn't there still a chance we can get out alive?"

"For once, I agree with your temptress bride. If we survive, we'll still have the fortune to rebuild this estate twice over, and with adequate soundproofing this time. Our corpses will be charred either way—why not try leaping through the flames?"

Humphrey turns back toward the monitors, a worshipper at a radiant shrine. The fire spreads from panel to panel. Soon it will be inside the walls of the house.

"I want my Dignity," he says.

Humphrey twists the combination lock—it's the Empire Island area code, 777—and opens the lid of the heavy black box. Inside are a bottle of pills, some golf pencils, and a pad of End-of-Life Checklists. He ticks off his "Reasons Why" (ruin, check; imminent destruction, check; loss of loved one, check), initials the bottom, and opens the pill bottle.

"I'd offer you something to wash those down," grumbles Osmond, "but I don't want to waste a perfectly good bottle of Gulden Draak."

"I'll take them dry." Humphrey shakes two tablets into his hand, then offers the bottle to the others.

"Not my drug of choice." Osmond's voice is an un-Dignified croak.

"You go first," Katya says quietly.

The Ripples watch as Humphrey swallows the pills. They watch as he slumps back, his mouth filling with blue-green froth, pop-eyed and surprised by the death he explicitly requested.

"Now all is revealed." Osmond raps Katya on the thigh with a thwacking cane. "We needn't have secrets from each other any longer, *Wundelsteipen*. You never wanted to admit you were after his illustrious fortune, but now I know that you're willing to risk im-molation to have a chance at it. Ha! I thought I would be repulsed when I learned for certain how base and crass your motives always were, but now that the truth is out, I find I actually sympathize. Because you and I are the same. Selfishness alone sustains us, and such selfishness is a curse, an insomnia of the soul that holds eternal rest forever out of reach, though we go mad with dreamlessness. Because we cannot bring ourselves to die. Not even when all is lost. Not even for a *reason*."

"You don't know me," says Katya. She reaches for the pill bottle. "You've never known me at all." She knocks back the pills, then studies Humphrey's suicide memo. "Who was the 'loved one,' do you think? Was it Pippi? Or his son?"

"If I knew the answer, I wouldn't tell you." Thus spake Osmond Ripple, watching his sister-in-law die.

17

THEM THAT LIVE

I t never occurred to Swanny that the city would be *empty*. Pippi's accounts of mayhem, riots, and looting always made her picture a carnivalesque atmosphere, one where, as in the days of old, the rich and poor could mingle freely, masked in the darkness of the hour. Swanny imagined streets firelit and full of secret hideouts, lovers coupling in doorways, and sweaty, jaundiced druggers succumbing to madness in wildly quotable blank-verse soliloquies. Since girl-hood she's concocted intimately detailed narratives about the life and times she would have in such a place, the way she would con-duct her business and her passions. Now, as she trudges the empty skyscraper canyons, staring down at slippers soaked through with mother blood and bird excrement, begrimed with chalky ash, the full weight of Duncan's duffel bag digging into her shoulder, she wonders if anything ever existed at the other end of her pining, any-thing at all. She is the child bride of a gone world.

In the dwindling warmth of late afternoon, Swanny sits down on a bus-stop bench and exhaustedly pats the seat beside her. Hooligan stands up on his hind feet and sits down like a human, roguishly crossing his legs. He rests his hand on her knee. She slaps it away, scanning the street for imaginary traffic. Swanny has never before in her life suffered the indignity of walking for too long, and what's more, she has absolutely nothing to show for it. She hasn't even had a chance to sell the dog.

Then she notices the limo. It's the same model as the one she and

Mother took from the service, or nearly, but this one has its engine still intact, purring with the gluttonous consumption of fossil fuels: a sleek, sated beast. Swanny watches it roll up the deserted street, between the hollow dioramas of gutted storefronts and the scraps of man-made detritus—newsprint, fabric, cellophane—that litter the pavement, foliage from a different kind of fall. The limo eases to a halt right in front of where she's sitting, and one tinted window in the back yawns down.

"Here's a tip," the man inside says. His voice is raspy, abrasive, more personality disorder than accent. But she can barely see him there, ensconced so deeply in the limo's dusky cavern. "That bus ain't coming."

"I know that. I'm only resting for a moment. To get my bearings."

"Good thing. They'd never let you take that mutt on board."

"I thought you said the bus wasn't coming."

The pause that follows is all the more troubling, accompanied as it is by a lapping, wettish sound Swanny at last identifies as the man's chewing.

"Let me give you a ride," he says.

"Actually," she replies, "I'm not entirely certain where I'm going."

"Get in the car, we'll talk about it."

"Actually, I'm waiting for my husband, also."

"Get in the car."

The door swings open, as though of its own accord. Flying machines never come for Swanny, only these long dark cars, like hearses.

"Excuse me," she says, "but my pet is very protective of my personal safety. I'd hate to have him bite you." She glances at Hooligan, who's chosen this moment to start grooming his pubic region.

"Leave him. He ain't gonna get run over."

Swanny weighs her options. She could make a dash for it on foot, but he's in a vehicle—and where could she go? Besides, to be entirely honest, there's a good deal of curiosity mixed in with her trepidation. Even . . . attraction. Having a limo, one in working order, no less, implies a level of wealth and social standing that might make a person worth talking to. One shouldn't judge a stranger on his ominous comportment alone.

Perhaps he's not brutal, only intense.

"Stay," Swanny instructs the dog sternly. Hooligan raises his sullied hands in confusion, as if to say *Where would I go?* "And watch the bag. I'll be back shortly." Frankly, she wants neither Ripple's bag, nor his dog—it was enough to deprive Abby of both. With what little poise she can muster, Swanny climbs into the car.

The inside of the limo is cool and dark, both cleaner and more lived-in than the musty vehicle that the service sent to claim Swanny and her mother. The leather upholstery has upon it the living sheen of human skin. The tinted windows reveal a twilight version of the world Swanny just exited, a world that, in an instant, begins gliding away.

"I thought you looked lost," he says, where she can see him this time.

The man who's summoned her here is *swarthy*, Swanny thinks, a word that feels especially apt because of the strong association she makes between it and fictional characters who carry knives in their teeth. He's not holding a knife that she can see, but he is wearing a golden fang on a chain around his neck, and there's no telling what's concealed beneath the pinstripes of his capacious zoot suit. He seems to have materialized from a villainous antique engraving. Black body hair crosshatches him, shades his face and neck, the top of his chest and the back of his hands, all to different degrees. Even sitting down she can tell he's a very short man, *gnomish*, but in a strange way that contributes to the power he exerts: the risk of him isn't just physical violence, but something sorcerous and delusive, something that can't be undone.

"You got a name?" he asks.

"I'm the Baroness Swan Lenore Ripple, née Dahlberg," she says.

"That's a mouthful."

"You may call me Swanny, if you like." Swanny strains to get a look at the driver, but she can't make out much more than a broad-shouldered, nearly neckless silhouette beyond a divider of reinforced mesh.

"Don't worry. Duluth won't bother us."

"So tell me, do *you* have a name?"

"Sure."

"May I ask what it is?"

"Sure."

"Well?"

"Maybe you can guess."

"I'm afraid I can't. I'm not from around here, you see."

"That makes two of us." He extends his hand, hot, hairy, and dry, with black under the nails. "Eisenhower Sharkey."

"Pleased to make your acquaintance." They shake with an odd finality, as if agreeing upon something; Swanny wishes she knew what. "What brings you to the city, Mr. Sharkey?"

"I'm *from* the city. Just a different neighborhood. Sometimes I like to come up here and see the sights."

"I wish I shared your enthusiasm. But it seems to me that there's lamentably little worth seeing around here."

"You don't know how to look, is all."

"I'd be delighted if you'd instruct me."

"First you need a drink." He opens a cabinet in the paneling and removes from it a vacuum flask and two teacups. He fills them both with a thin red liquid and hands one to Swanny.

The teacup is fragile bone china, almost translucent, featuring an intricate repeating pattern of humanoid figures with animal heads practicing the most exotic contortions. Steam rises from the top.

"What's in this?"

"Hot water. Mostly." Sharkey sips his, pinkie finger extended. So it must not be poisoned. "Good for what ails you." He's still chewing, even while he drinks.

Swanny takes a taste. It isn't alcohol, but it's a different kind of strong: herbal, almost medicinal, with a woodsy aftertaste.

"Black forest?" she wonders aloud. She isn't sure why she says it. She doesn't mean the cake. She feels as though she's walking on a twisted, shady path, and the trees are moving behind her to conceal it. Soon she won't be able to find her way back. She drinks again and surprises herself by finishing the cup.

"Now, look out the window," says Sharkey.

Swanny obeys. Through the dusky glass, she sees a street much like the one she just left behind. Yet something is changed. The buildings, vacant shells which before inspired nothing but a quickening of pace as she attempted to get past them to somewhere, anywhere at all, now vibrate with meaning. These are things men have made. The fact that they're beyond repair, deserted, with exploded windows and blackened walls and steel beams rustily exposed to the elements, only intensifies her identification with them. She has never been here before, but this is where she lives: condemned but not demolished.

"See that one there?" asks Sharkey, pointing to a curving cylindrical colossus of red enamel and steel, now as used up as a drained Voltage can. "That's the Lipgloss Building. It was the first one They hit." He says the pronoun with a capital letter, as if he's referring to the gods. "Fifty years ago now, and it's still standing. All those little people, jumping out the windows. Their best thinking got 'em there. Offices up in the sky no better than a prison. A fuckin' kiln. And the only view was down. Makes ya think. I wasn't even born yet, old as I am. Up there, people thought they were living in the future. But they were living in the past. We're living in the past too, you and me. That's why it's good to pay your respects. Take note of what's come before, because pretty soon, somebody's coming after you."

Swanny gazes at a fallen column of imperial granite lying on the curb. "Was there a great deal of screaming, do you think?"

"Screaming? Oh, sure. Lots of screaming. It's a natural response to untold horrors. Close your eyes and scream. No seeing, no hearing. Gives you a little relief. *Relief*, not release."

Swanny holds out her cup as Sharkey refills it. Her eyes cling to the building as it slips out of view. "I feel somehow that they're screaming still."

"Once something's happened, it's happened for all time. These things don't just go away. You're a very voluptuous young woman. What are you doing walking the streets alone?"

Swanny blinks rapidly, refocusing her attention to the inside of the limo, where Sharkey might be exuding an ectenic force on the rhythm of her heart.

"I'm exploring," murmurs Swanny.

"You're a long way from Wonland County."

"How do you know I'm from Wonland?"

"Maybe you haven't heard my name. But I've heard yours."

"How . . . ?"

"Ain't your ma some kind of boss?"

Reflexively, Swanny touches the EAT SHIT & DIE pin on her lapel; beneath her fingers, the diamonds feel like an irregular scab covering a recent injury.

"Whassa matter, did you run away from home?"

"My mother is dead," Swanny says. It doesn't seem fair that she always has to tell everyone. She feels obscurely disgraced, the object of a bon mot from some timeworn farce: *To lose one parent may be regarded as a misfortune; to lose both looks like carelessness.* "I'm an orphan, you see."

"That's a shame. Must've been some real pros, took her out."

"They weren't 'pros,' either in terms of professionalism or in the colloquial sense of the word. They were torchies."

"Torchies?" Sharkey looks amused. "That what you call 'em?"

"Prison colony escapees, if you prefer."

"I always liked 'untorchables,' myself. 'Course, that only applies to them that live."

"I saw her die," says Swanny. "She was gunned down in front of me, in my husband's house."

"You see the guys who did it?"

"No . . . I couldn't . . ."

"Good. Some faces ain't worth the mental space."

"I didn't see them because I ran away," Swanny confesses. She stares into the teacup. "I was unarmed. Defenseless. But I won't make the same mistake again."

"You won't, huh?"

"I intend to get revenge."

Sharkey lazes back on the banquette. He sucks saliva through his teeth. His eyes are coals, black but still burning inside. "I had a dream I was gonna meet somebody like you today. Not a dream, exactly. A premonition."

"What did it foretell?"

"That I'd meet a woman who knows what she wants. And I'd help her get it."

~~~

Pippi had a great fear of general anesthetic, so she always opted for the local when the surgery would permit it. The thing that frightened her most, she once confided to Swanny, wasn't actually death but the lack of awareness, the yawning swoon of the soporific into her blood, and then the moment when things were being done to her body that she could not control, things that might be done *wrong*. Unconsciousness: it was a curious fear for a petite woman who put away half a liter of gin or vodka nightly. But Pippi reigned over herself even then, brooding before the fireplace, wrapped tightly in a stylish shawl as she gripped the stem of her martini glass like a hard-won scepter. She never dozed off on the couch, or in the bath, at least to Swanny's knowledge. And only when Swanny was sick did Pippi decline to tuck her in. Every other night, without fail, she would appear in Swanny's doorway at the appointed hour, framed in the darkness of the hall, and pause with her finger on the switch.

"Say your prayers," she would intone just before lights-off, and in their godless house, the words had the menacing ring of a femme fatale's.

But unlike her mother, Swanny craves oblivion—she always has. Food or drink, sobs or laughter, the ultimate end of any bodily sensation is that aching fall, back into the bottomless liquid depths of the ocean from which all consciousness rises. She's having trouble following what Sharkey says. It's so sleepy in here.

"I don't understand," she tells him, finishing yet another cup of tea. She couldn't be relied upon to count how many she's had. "You came from the prison colony? But I thought no one was permitted to enter or leave."

"I don't ask permission. I go where I like."

"So you're an inmate?"

"I'm a native. I was born there. What's the crime in that?"

"I apologize if my tone seemed accusatory. But it's always been my understanding that the corrupting influence of the locale bends everyone's nature toward its cruelest ends."

"I hear Wonland County's got a lot of snobs."

"What is it that you *do* in Torchtown, Mr. Sharkey?"

"I run a little shop down there."

"And you're suggesting you can help me find my mother's killers?"

"I can get you close. If you come and work for me."

"In the shop?"

"In the shop."

Swanny can imagine stepping out of the limo, meandering through the empty streets again. She can't imagine summoning the energy. "I suppose I don't have anywhere else to go."

"One thing first." Sharkey spits into his empty teacup, sets it aside. "Lemme see your teeth."

Swanny feels the same flash of panic as if he'd pressed a pistol to her temple, as if he'd told her to remove her clothes. The tips of her fingers go cold. The gum around her newest tooth pulses. Her diagnosis has followed her here. "Excuse me, what?"

"Show me your teeth."

"Why?"

"You got something to hide? Open up."

As she submits to the examination, Swanny thinks of her old dentist: his gloved fingers massaged her gingiva, worked clove-drenched gauze into sockets charged with pain; with his tiny mirrors, he saw parts of her she's never even glimpsed herself. It isn't the first time her jaw's laid bare. Yet there's no comparing the situations. By nature of his work, the dentist was a strange, parasitical creature who found his living in her mouth. In this act, she's applying to become Sharkey's.

"Wider. Pull back your cheek, lemme see on the side. Yeah. Other side." Sharkey places his thumb on her lower incisors and eases them downward; she feels her temporomandibular joint click, another point of dysfunction. "You chew?"

It sounds so much like a transcribed sneeze, for a moment Swanny doesn't understand what he's asking.

"Do I . . . ?"

"You chew?"

"I don't take my meals through an intravenous drip, if that's what you're asking."

"Cute. But you know what I'm talking about."

Swanny slides her own finger into her mouth, almost involuntarily, checking to make sure everything is still there.

"You know what I do," says Sharkey. His own teeth are dark, wet stones in the cave of his mouth. For the first time, she notices the smell of his breath: chemical but strangely pleasant. Intoxicating.

"I suppose you're a chawmonger," she hears herself say. "And you want to know if I'm an addict."

"That's right."

Swanny yawns, longer and deeper than she can ever remember doing before. Corona used to say that a yawn meant one's soul was trying to escape from one's body. But Swanny's isn't going anywhere. "Forgive me. I'm afraid this has been a very long, very strange day."

"Forget about it."

"I didn't sleep at all last night."

"You can shut your eyes."

"Thank you," says Swanny, though of course she doesn't need his permission. Her lids are hardly down before she begins to dream.

Swanny dreams that the limo drives out of the dead city, north, into timberlands. A black forest, where yellow eyes glow in the sylvan gloom. It's as though they're driving into midnight, the hour when one day becomes another and everything changes. Werebeasts roam this country. Their new selves rip them apart from the inside and transform them into something terrible and unrecognizable and strong. Swanny knows, because the moonless wood is morphing her too, and the feeling fills every crook of her body like a profound knowledge, a knowledge that is beyond fear. Her muscles ache. She yearns to roam, to hunt, to sink her teeth into flesh, to howl at the uninhabited sky. She is hungry for vengeance.

In Swanny's dream, the limo rolls to a stop in a clearing. All around, the branches reach their fingers toward the car windows. Then Sharkey presses the button on a remote control, and the ground itself begins to crack, crack and split apart, until the car is on a narrow shelf of earth that lowers into the ground like an elevator. As they descend, Swanny watches the soil turn to rock, and the rock to lava. At the heart of the planet, people are made of magma, dissolving and consuming one another constantly. It is a sea of fire, and seas are full of life. The car door opens and they carry her into Torchtown.

18

FACE TO THE NAME

INT. RIPPLE MANSION—DAY.

DUNCAN RIPPLE (age 16) and HUMPHREY argue in front of
the Concentration Station in the third-floor library.
From the outside, the soundproof study pod resembles a
sensory deprivation chamber. DUNCAN apparently doesn't
want to go inside.

                    DUNCAN
    It's about self-respect. You say you want me to learn
    stuff, but I already know how to read. The world
    isn't just a bunch of books. The world is on fire. And
    the real men are trying to stop it. That's why you
    need to let my exemption expire. I want to learn to
    be a man.

                    HUMPHREY
    Your uncle and I are men too, but that doesn't mean
    we needlessly endanger ourselves.

                    OSMOND (O.S.)
    Not anymore!

                    DUNCAN
    I'm not like you, though.

                    HUMPHREY
Oh, you're not?

                    DUNCAN
You're always saying I'm so stupid—

                    HUMPHREY
Underachieving. (directly to camera) I never called
him stupid.

                    DUNCAN
But maybe I'm stupid for a <u>reason</u>. Did you ever
think of that, huh? Maybe it's because I'm <u>chosen</u>.
And whatever I'm chosen for (he gestures at the
Concentration Station), I'm pretty sure it's not in
there.

~~~~~

Ripple is good at video games. He always has been. But he never
thought that could seriously serve him in any realm outside the
virtual. Fighting the fire is like the time sinks in Sword Crystal
Prophecy III: The Dwarvening, the parts where you have to farm or
forge shields or one-hit kill entire armies of clattering skeleton warriors: it's simple and repetitive but weirdly satisfying, even without a progress bar to mark the time well spent. Insulated inside the
Tarnhelm, Ripple blasts a path forward with his hose, plowing into
the heat yard by yard, mowing down the field of flames. He literally
thought he couldn't do this, but it turns out he can. Maybe he was
onto something without even knowing it, all those times he argued
with his dad on the show. Maybe he's destined for *this*. He loses track
of everything besides the crackling, the sloshing of the water tank
on his back, the threat of danger right in front of his face. He writes
his name in water, and it rises up to the sky in dank black smoke.
    "That was awesome!" Ripple yells, once the roof of the library is

puddled and steaming. He strides over to high-five Leather Lungs. "Wooot, we did it!"

Leather Lungs ignores his hand but nods appreciatively. "You did your duty, son. That collar can come off now."

"Sweet, thanks." Ripple had forgotten about that ring of electrified steel encircling his larynx; the adrenaline and endorphins have lifted him out of his body almost. "Can we take the masks off too? Is it safe?"

"It is for you," Leather Lungs says.

Ripple peels back the Tarnhelm; the cooler air feels great on his sweaty skin. He scans the sky for dragons, but there's nothing there: not a cloud, not a bird. It's suddenly a beautiful day.

"Ditch the mask, pro! What, are you hiding out from the cops?"

"That would make it tough to work for them, wouldn't it?" Leather Lungs pulls out a ring of keys and unshackles the claw from around Ripple's neck. "You're free to go."

Ripple rubs his chafed Adam's apple. "Yeah, but seriously. You're just going to keep walking around like that?"

No response. They go back inside the building. Leather Lungs pushes the hot-dog cart back into the elevator. He pulls out a weathered logbook, jots down a few quick notes in pencil, then returns it to his slicker pocket. Ripple scrutinizes him.

"Who are you, anyway?" Ripple asks. It's starting to bug him now. "Special Officer, they said. But Special Officer what? What's your name? Why did the police department hire an independent contractor anyway?"

"I'm just a man who cares about the fate of this city."

"But you work alone, wear a mask . . . and your identity is secret?"

"That's right."

"Whoa." Ripple heard about pros like this—vigilantes, superheroes—but up till now, he never totally believed in them. Like the dragons, they don't seem really real until you see one up close.

Leather Lungs loads the tank-backpacks into the hot-dog cart. "You did a fine job out there today. I'm sorry the fire department shut down before you had a chance to join. With a little training you could have been one of the greats."

"For real?"

"Too bad those days are gone."

Gone. Could have been. The words make Ripple think of Kelvin's: *Empire Island is over.* Everybody's so quick to bail on this place, but it's Ripple's kingdom. It's where he was born, where he grew up, where his family owns a buttload of real estate. And now it's down to just this guy trying to keep it in one piece. Fuck that. It's not too late. "Maybe you could train me."

It's hard to tell through the gas mask, but Leather Lungs seems doubtful.

"You could be my personal trainer," Ripple goes on. He's liking the idea more and more as he explains it out loud. "My coach. You could teach me what you know, and I could join you."

"It isn't something to enter into lightly," says Leather Lungs.

"But you said I kicked ass out there."

"I said you had potential."

"I always knew I'd be good at this," Ripple says brashly. "I'm fearless."

"Are you?" Leather Lungs says it like he can see inside Ripple's head: the four torchies in that hallway, the sound of those alarms.

"Look, you're the one who needs me," Ripple says, with more confidence than he feels. "If you were good all on your own, you wouldn't be conscripting people on the street every time this happens. It's fate. I'm meant to help you with your mission."

Leather Lungs nods slowly. "It's an idea."

"I just have to go back up to the Heights and check on my family first," Ripple adds.

The elevator doors ding open on the first floor. The Librarians are waiting there, thirty at least, a whole hoary vexation of the barely undead, arranged in a half-circle, stooped and waiting. For a second Ripple thinks they're about to go full zombie. Then they applaud.

Back outside, Ripple finds Abby sitting by herself on the steps, crying. Oh, right. For a second there, he totally forgot he was responsible for anyone besides himself.

"Hey, what's up?" He looks around. "Where's Swanny? Where's Hooli? Where's Avian Floozy?"

"They left," she blubbers.

"Swanny left?" It's more of a gut punch than Ripple would have expected. Swanny left. "She took my dog?"

"Everyone left." Abby musters a smile: "But you came back."

"Believe it, damsel. And guess what?" Ripple jerks his thumb at Leather Lungs, who stands a few yards away, speaking into that blocky, antennaed walkie-talkie. "I saved the library. Now he's going to make me a special officer, just like him."

Abby looks from the snozzled figure to Ripple, then back again. "But we need to find my people."

He was afraid she'd bring that up. "Sure, we will. Except I need to find myself first."

Abby stares at him, blindsided; her years alone on the trash island have left her unschooled in the psychology of self-actualization. "But you promised."

Why is she giving him such a hard time? If he wanted a guilt trip, he would have stuck with his wife. "Listen, this is just a detour. The first BeanReader we see, we'll check out your foot. Your parents have waited all this time, a little while longer's no biggie. They'll like me better if I have a career—if I'm not just someone's kid." Which reminds him: "First, though, we've gotta go check on *my* family. Maybe we can just peek in a window or something, to make sure they're OK. When I go back, I want to return in triumph, you know?"

"Not necessary." Leather Lungs plods over with the hot-dog cart. "I just spoke to headquarters. They dispatched a team to the Ripple mansion an hour ago, and it all looks normal. Everyone's accounted for."

"Wait—everyone?"

"Except your mother-in-law. Damn shame about that."

Sucks for Swanny, anyway. She and that Old Mom were joined

at the ovaries. Ripple pulls out his LookyGlass. No new texts. "But my dad still hasn't answered."

"Fathers can be distant sometimes."

Even through the Tarnhelm, there's something in Leather Lungs's tone that suggests he understands. Ripple feels a surge of anger at Humphrey. He's always failing his dad, and always in the most public ways. He felt like such a boss just a second ago.

"I'll show him," Ripple says. He hurls his LookyGlass to the ground, and the screen shatters against the pavement.

Abby cringes. "You hurt it."

Ripple ignores her. To Leather Lungs, he adds: "Sign me up. For serious. Let's do this."

~~~~~

"Hey, I've been here before," Ripple says. The building is white marble with a neoclassical portico, four alabaster columns supporting a pediment carved with figures clad in togas and merryweather helmets, ornate situlas in their hands. Chiseled into the stone just beneath the bas-relief are the words BRING IT ON.

The Fire Museum. Ripple, Abby, and Leather Lungs walk into the lobby: an expansive, open room, not unlike the one in the Ripples' mansion. But instead of a stone fountain depicting ripped hunk vs. kraken, the monumental statue here is a giant fireman, bent on one knee, his eyes shielded beneath the brim of his helmet from the glory to come. Cast in bronze.

"I don't like the metal man," Abby murmurs.

Ripple came here on an underschool field trip when he was just eight; attendance was mandatory. The space is empty now, but he remembers it a decade ago, filled with the shouts and disorder of dozens of his classmates. That long-ago autumn day, the boys wandered these halls in pairs, split up by the buddy system. Kelvin was absorbed in a Boy Toy handheld championship, earmuff-headphones on, eyes trained on his screen, as they walked among the exhibits.

Even Ripple's videographers bailed after an hour. But Ripple was enraptured. In glass cases, ancient firefighting tools were laid out like holy relics, axes and wooden pails and Draegerman suits, diving bells for plunging into the sea of fire. Ox-drawn pumpers and steam-powered fire bikes stood on platforms. In one room, the boys took turns hopping from a ladder onto an old trampoline marked X in the center: JUMP FOR YOUR LIFE!

It should have been boring as fuck, yet the artifacts—adorned with brass beavers and bronze eagles, gilded and painted candy-apple red—got Ripple curious. Why had they bothered to make these things beautiful? He'd always thought of firefighting as janitorial work, late capitalism's punishment for those too poor and lazy to qualify for exemptions, too boring to appear in reality. But the Fire Museum made them look like warriors girding for epic battle, dressed to dine in hell.

The main event took place in the museum's auditorium. Ripple readied himself to nap through some multimedia, but instead the boys had a surprise guest: newly appointed Fire Chief Paxton Trank. Ripple didn't exactly follow city politics, but even he'd heard of Trank. Just two weeks after his inauguration, this pro was already shaping up to be the stuff of legend. More like an action hero than a civil servant. He had a reputation for showing up to press conferences soot-streaked on the back of a HowDouse, which fired up its sirens and blasted off for the next emergency the second the Q&A concluded. That day, though, Trank was scrubbed and smartly dressed, clad in a slicker with epaulettes. Ripple doesn't remember all the details of what he instructed them in his gravelly voice, though he did extol the virtues of enlistment and warn them to beware of "privileges that will subsidize your goddamned childhoods all the way to old age." He cursed a lot for somebody talking to a group of kids.

A fire alarm interrupted his speech in the middle, and, as the state-of-the-art, best-in-class sprinkler system rained down, the teachers hustled them all out in a frantic rush to re-board the How-Buses that had ferried them here from the Chokely Bradford campus in South Crookbridge. It turned out to be a burned grilled cheese in the museum cafeteria, nothing so glamorous as a dragon, the forgettable end to a forgettable field trip for the other boys. But something about Trank stuck with Ripple. Humphrey called Trank "a doer, not a leader," but even he had a twinge of admiration in his voice. It bummed Ripple out when he heard about the fire that did Trank in: about six months ago, his men abandoned him in a dragon blaze at the Gemini towers to lead the mutiny that finally shut down the fire department for good.

Now, in the lobby of the Fire Museum, Ripple points at Trank's enormous portrait on the wall, at the landing of the staircase. It's done in oil, maybe even by the same painter who did Humphrey's for the Hall of Ancestors: the same style anyway, lots of woodwork in the background and a fancy gold frame. In it, Trank holds his parade helmet under one arm, his rough-hewn features—hawkish nose, piercing quicksilver eyes, cleft chin—glowing like he's on the receiving end of a coronation.

"I met that guy once," Ripple tells Leather Lungs. "He talked to my underschool class."

Leather Lungs gazes up at the portrait. For a moment, he's so still he could be another statue, man-made, a posture of grief and reverence suspended out of time.

Then, with a final, deflating exhalation, Leather Lungs unfilters his face.

Hawkish nose, quicksilver eyes, cleft chin: the data say it's Paxton Trank, a dead ringer for his portrait across the lobby. And yet—and yet. Something is missing: not the stubble, which glitters gray; not the bushy tufts of eyebrow; not the wrinkles, a rugged terrain of emotion around his eyes, across his brow. None of these are missing, and yet something is missing from all of them.

He is not human.

Abby squeezes Ripple's arm with sudden death-grip intensity. Her voice glitches, nonsense syllables, all consonants stammering: "Dddd . . . nnnn . . . cccckkk . . ."

Ripple blinks. Leather Lungs can take the form of anyone—your best friend, your dad, your childhood hero. But he is a messenger from one place only.

"No offense, but—since when are you alive?"

Trank pulls off his gloves, one at a time. His hands underneath are broad, callused and sinewy, nothing uncanny there. "My own men left me to die. But I didn't."

"No way. I saw your funeral. I watched it on the Toob at underschool. Closed coffin, but still. We were supposed to wear black armbands, but I couldn't find mine so I tied on a black sock instead, except it had rockets on it, which is supposedly disrespect for the dead. I spent all of recess in detention."

"Recess? That's for children. This was six months ago."

"Study hall, whatever. I think you owe me an apology. Unless . . ." Ripple leaves the word hanging. But Trank doesn't fess up to his ghosthood—and besides, there's nothing disembodied about him. If something is missing from that face, it's the soul.

"If they wanted to kill me, they shouldn't have counted on a fire."

Ripple can't put his finger on it. Maybe Trank had reconstructive surgery? His body moves like a human's as he unsnaps the slicker, bundles it and the Tarnhelm into the hot-dog cart, but when he turns to smile at Ripple and Abby, his expression is just a little off. It's like he still has on a mask.

"I'd give you the full tour, but it sounds like you already know the place," he tells Ripple. "Maybe you'd rather kick back and watch a show."

~~~

FADE IN:
EXT. CITY STREET—DAY
CLOSE on a firefighter's helmet.

                    NARRATOR (V.O.)
President Roswell once said that bravery isn't the
absence of fear. Bravery is acting <u>despite</u> your fear.

CLOSE on a firefighter's boot, stamping out the last glowing ember on a rubble-strewn sidewalk.

> NARRATOR (V.O.)
> Firefighters live Roswell's vision . . . and take it to a whole new level.

ZOOM OUT to reveal a trio of handsome, square-jawed FIREFIGHTERS, streaked with soot, gazing resolutely at the camera.

> NARRATOR (V.O.)
> We fight fire. We fight fear.

CUT TO:

INT. BURNING BUILDING—DAY

One of the FIREFIGHTERS runs in slow motion down a burning hallway.

> NARRATOR (V.O.)
> But bravery is more.

The FIREFIGHTER kicks in a door. A MILF and CHILD cower in one corner of the smoke-filled room. He dramatically gestures for them to follow.

> NARRATOR (V.O.)
> Bravery is fighting doubt, anger, frustration. Sometimes even common sense.

The FIREFIGHTER, MILF, and CHILD run a flight of stairs to safety, but once outside, the CHILD hesitates, her eyes filling with tears. The FIREFIGHTER looks at her and

understands. He runs back inside the burning building.
The MILF gasps and swoons.

> NARRATOR (V.O.)
> Bravery is doing the thing you don't want to do, for
> the simple reason that you don't want to do it.

EXT. CITY STREET—NIGHT

The FIREFIGHTER reemerges from the inferno, holding an
adorable kitten. The CHILD grins. The MILF, half-revived,
parts her lips in an expression of melting admiration.

> NARRATOR (V.O.)
> It's heroism for its own sake.

CLOSE UP on the kitten, happily meowing.

> NARRATOR (V.O.)
> Bravery is obedience.

EXT. URBAN PARK—DAY

A phalanx of FIREFIGHTERS marches by, holding hatchets,
as a FIRE CHIEF barks orders.

> NARRATOR (V.O.)
> Obedience lets you focus on being brave, instead of
> on being right.

INT. FIERY MATERNITY WARD—DAY

A FIREMAN runs down a fiery hallway full of stunned
pregnant women, hugging a BABY to his chest.

                         NARRATOR (V.O.)

When a burning hospital is collapsing all around
you, you can't afford to hesitate.

CLOSE on the sickly, bright-pink face of the premature
BABY.

                         NARRATOR (V.O.)

Hesitation sends babies to Limbo. That's why your
squad captain is trained to do the thinking for
you. His orders free you to do your best. To be. A
hero.

The FIREMAN runs toward an open window. He leans
his head and shoulders out, pauses, then drops the
premature BABY.

CUT TO:
EXT. CITY STREET—DAY

An older SQUAD CAPTAIN easily catches the baby and gazes
down at it lovingly. He gives the FIREMAN a thumbs-up.

                         NARRATOR (V.O.)

Because a hero doesn't stop to think. A hero <u>does</u>.

CLOSE ON the premature BABY's amphibious, fetal hand,
also giving a tiny thumbs-up.

                         NARRATOR (V.O.)

Bravery is character.

CUT TO:
EXT. BURNING SKYSCRAPER—DAY

A FIREMAN zips on a heavy-duty fireproof suit and gas
mask, grabs two huge canisters marked <u>Fire Suppressant
Powder</u> and lies down in a catapult.

> NARRATOR (V.O.)
> The character to take the heat.

The catapult launches the FIREMAN at the building, into
the heart of the flames.

> NARRATOR (V.O.)
> And to go the distance.

Other FIREMEN and BYSTANDERS cheer as the fire
extinguishes itself in a cloud of billowing white.

> NARRATOR (V.O.)
> You're following in the footsteps of the firemen who
> came before you . . .

EXT. SEPIA-TONED, LONG AGO CITY STREET—DAY

A group of FIREMEN tumble over one another, their
movements made comically jittery by the undercranked
frame rate as they struggle to drag a gigantic
hose out from their antiquated, steam-powered fire
engine.

> NARRATOR (V.O.)
> . . . and inspiring generations of firemen to come.

MONTAGE, as music swells, of happy, victorious FIREMEN:
atop fire escapes and ladders; drenched in sweat,
hacking at walls with axes; riding solemn-faced in a

tickertape parade; offering water to people trapped
under charred, fallen pillars.

> NARRATOR (V.O.)
> The brotherhood.

EXT. BURNING SKYSCRAPER ROOF—DAY

A FIREMAN, pushed back by a fireball, almost falls off
the ledge, but another FIREMAN grabs his hand at the
last moment and pulls him up.

> NARRATOR (V.O.)
> Of the helmet.

MONTAGE, of changing helmet styles through time.

> NARRATOR (V.O.)
> Of the hose.

MONTAGE, of changing hose styles through time.

> NARRATOR (V.O.)
> The brotherhood. Of heroes.

MONTAGE, of sepia, black-and-white, and colorized faces
of diverse FIREMEN through time.

> NARRATOR (V.O.)
> Nothing in this fair city is braver than a firefighter.
> And it's a good thing too, because nothing else
> stands between civilization . . .

EXT. CITY SKYLINE, PRE-DRAGONS—DAY

NARRATOR (V.O.)

And destruction.

CUT TO BLACK.

NARRATOR (V.O.)

Be brave. Be very brave. Be firefighter brave.

TITLE CARD: A McGuffin-Stork production. Paid for by the
Metropolitan Fire Department.

~~~

"It's cool there's still pizza delivery around here," says Ripple, though his mind isn't really on the food. After watching the edutainment special upstairs, blasted by surround sound in the Hall of Heroes' Ida Lowry Theater, he was so blown away that for a good thirty seconds he couldn't remember where he was. This happens to Ripple sometimes: the show ends but in his brain it keeps going, with himself in the leading role. A holdover from the days of his Toob series, maybe, when he would watch the last week's episode and then jump right back into living out its arc.

What would this series be called? *Late Capitalism's Royalty: Enlistment Edition*? Or something new—*City Savior*? *Fear Fighter*? *Whoa That Pro Is Brave*?

Only the promise of dinner brought Ripple mostly back to tonight's reality: turns out dousing a fire and walking half the length of the city works up a major appetite. Trank called in the order, which was delivered in less than thirty minutes by a disaffected youth in a Nomex bomber jacket and a trucker hat labeled BRICK OVEN.

"No charge," the delivery guy said at the door, refusing Ripple's currency. "Leather Lungs and me, we have a deal. He doesn't conscript me, he gets free pizza for life." Then he was back on his HowScoot, gone into the night.

Now Ripple, Trank, and Abby are down in the Fire Museum cafeteria. Behind sneeze screens, furniture-sized stainless-steel appliances stand cold and unused. Trash cans shaped like fire hydrants stand in the room's corners. The floor is concrete. The only light comes from flat fluorescent boxes, suspended on chains from the ceiling. They're chowing down on a pie loaded up with all possible toppings just the way Ripple likes it: pepperoni and crab, pickles and marshmallows. Gutbuster.

"Of course there are still pizzas. People still live here, a few, and I know in my heart the rest will return. A city like this one doesn't just fade away, not on my watch. We're fighting a battle for the soul of the place." Trank eats his piece crust-first, jaw clenching and unclenching in a way that seems both mechanical and pained. "Pizzas or no, I'm here for the duration."

"Right." The movie left Ripple pumped, stoked for his new boss and job, but now that they've shunned its epic slow-mo dreamscapes for this harsher light, his sense of unease toward Trank is returning. He looks over at Abby, who's warily poking the Gutbuster with a fork the same way he once saw her prod a dead jellyfish on the beach. "You OK, fem?"

"It tastes funny."

"Try to eat a little, OK? You need to keep your strength up."

Grudgingly, she lifts a dripping slice; an anchovy slip-slides to the plate. "I have a family, Dunk. You said. When are we going to find them?"

"She got kidnapped or abandoned or something when she was just little," Ripple explains to Trank. "But she's chipped so, you know. Breeding."

Ripple and Trank look over simultaneously. Somehow Abby's already managed to get tomato paste in her hair and is in the process of slurping it out.

"We have a BeanReader upstairs," Trank reports. "In an exhibit case, in the Hall of Ultimate Sacrifice. Battle scarred, but it still works—IDed a lot of remains, back in the day. If her folks are still in the city, you can drop her off at home and get right back to your training. No place for a woman on a fire squad anyway. Save that for weekends."

Ripple doesn't want his clam-ramming privileges revoked Monday through Friday, but the thought of off-loading Abby to somebody else's part-time care is a surprising relief. Ever since they left the trash, she's been so needy. "Hear that, Abby? He's going to help you."

"I don't like the metal man," she repeats to herself, wiping grease from her mouth with her sleeve.

Trank takes another bite, but he's struggling to chew; it's like the food is gumming up his mouth somehow. He sets his paper plate aside, and, mouth a little ajar, takes out a packet of cotton swabs and an ashtray from a cargo pocket of his turnout pants. "Do you mind?" he asks them.

Ripple shrugs. Abby freezes.

Trank reaches behind his head with two hands. Ripple hears snaps popping free, and Trank's face—his rubber skin—his second mask—crumples as he peels it off.

Beneath, his face is an elaborate construction of titanium implants and hydraulic tubes, which hiss and whirr as his expression reconfigures itself. The rods in his forehead click together when he furrows his brow.

"Even after all the time I've had to heal," he says ruefully.

He doesn't have to finish the sentence. The flesh below the titanium implants is red and swollen in places, oozy in others. Trank's sweat and sebum collect in the ridges of the screws. His salty tears calcify on the zoom lenses of his glass eyes. Mucus clots on his steely nose wedge. He loosens a pin on one side of his jaw and pulls an errant clump of mozzarella free from the hinge.

"Wow. You're like . . ." Ripple searches for the word, but the visual sectors of his brain are overwhelming the verbal: this is the grossest thing he's ever seen. "Like . . ."

"People Machine," Abby whispers.

"A *cyborg.*" Trank's face is so gross, it's actually kind of awesome. A spectacle, that's what Ripple's videographers would say. What kind of pro can take that kind of damage and then go back out there again, to dominate another day? "How did it happen?"

Trank takes a cotton swab from the box, looks at it, and sighs. He slides it under his metallic replacement cheekbone and roots around pensively. The cotton swab emerges, unimaginably changed, glistening with orange-yellow discharge. He deposits it in the ashtray and takes up another. As he tells his tale, Trank uses the entire box of cotton swabs to clean the machinery of his face.

The Fire Chief's Firsthand Account of Bravery Under Fire

"The long and short of it is: I should have been wearing the gas mask. It was my fault and I take full responsibility. I'd fail as an example to you if I didn't own up to that right off the bat. The no-good mutineers who left me to die under a pile of smoldering wreckage, they're not to blame. There's an expression: in the end, a man's left with the face he deserves. This face is mine, because I was a goddamn fool, and anyone who follows me should learn from my mistake.

"Always keep your Tarnhelm on.

"Six months ago, when the Gemini Building burned—the east tower—I was there with the first dispatch to the scene. I always took pride in leading the charge into danger. Men want to follow a leader, not a hologram of some idiot flailing around in a motion-capture suit across town. But twenty-five, thirty stories up, the laddermen behind me were moving slow. A bunch of rank, cowardly bastards. Every one among them had been caught participating in demonstrations. This was their punishment. We called it the probation squad. Usually I could motivate even the worst of the lily-livered pantywaists, rouse them to their civic duty, but on that day they wouldn't fall in line. So I turned back, and I pulled up my gas mask to yell down the stairs.

"And that's when I did it. I looked up. Unthinkable. Chief of the whole goddamn operation, decades of experience under my belt, and I made a rookie mistake. Just as the ceiling caved in, I looked up.

The slicker did its job. Gloves too. But the mask—the mask didn't have a chance.

"Made matters worse that I lay there for two days while the mutineers ran roughshod all over the city. Metropolitan Police Department was overfaced. You can't shoot deserters when it's all of them. Not enough bullets in the world. But that didn't stop the MPD from trying, God bless 'em. It was forty-eight hours later, when city gov officially lifted conscription, that they finally found time to send a couple of patrolmen to sift through the wreckage for my corpse.

"Lo and behold, I was still kicking—what was left of me. Cheekbones shattered. Nose smashed flat. Jaw fractured in nine places. Nine. And you know how it smells when your skin cooks to a crisp? *Delicious.* Just like bacon. A goddamn cannibal's delicacy. I didn't even know how bad I looked. My eyes were fried. Hardboiled eggs. That's why they hooked them up to these falsies. Don't flinch, I can tap on my eyeball all I want. 'Bout as sensitive as a camera lens. Ha! Miracle of science.

"I begged to die, I'll admit it. I'd lost my men, my face, my name. My place in the world. My faith in heroism for its own sake. I'd fought the fires for more than forty years, and I'd lost. But the chief of police is a friend of mine, and he wasn't ready to let me shrug off this mortal coil just yet. He kept the news out of the papers that I was alive, in case someone might see fit to assassinate me in my weakened state, and sent me to recover at the same burn ward where they sent the governor's son a few years back.

"The air hurt; when they changed the bandages it was like they were peeling off my skin. And the surgeries were brutal. When you feel bolt join bone, you have to believe it happened for a reason. For me, that reason was gone. All the painkillers in the world can't defend you against the darkness inside your own mind. But lying in that bed, drifting in and out of consciousness, something happened—a revelation, I'd say, if I were a man of faith. Only it didn't come from a higher power. It came from me. I figured it out: why my life's work mattered, why it was still too soon to give up the fight. I suppose you could call it a vision.

"You see, I saw the future.

"I saw throngs in the streets, lights in the windows, money in the shops, the way it used to be when I was just a boy. I saw Empire Island restored to her former glory. And what's more, I saw *how* it would happen—how, and when, and why. I went over and over it until all my doubts were gone, so when I finally rose from that bed, I rose with one purpose only: to take damn fine care of my city until her day comes again."

The ashtray is full of used cotton swabs, unctuous now with scabby goo. Trank pops off his chin plate, indented slightly for the cleft, and peers discontentedly at the gunk inside. He takes his time wiping it out with a handkerchief.

"Prosthetics," he grumbles. "More of an art than a science, if you ask me."

But Ripple's mind is working overtime. A sky full of HowFlys—streets full of life? It's as crazy as anything from Abby's weird religion, and yet Paxton Trank isn't a feral teenage hermit-girl; he's a legit authority figure, a seasoned dadster who's seen some shit. He doesn't sound crazy. He sounds determined . . . like he has a plan.

"I don't get it. In the dream, did you slay the dragons?"

"Slay the dragons? Hell no, son. The dragons will be our salvation in the end."

"How?"

"Because in my vision, the dragons did what they should have been doing all along." Trank's hydraulics shimmy inscrutably. He lowers his voice. "They protected this place. They belonged to the city."

"Uh, you think the dragons are going to stop torching us?"

"I know it."

"Riiiight."

"I've already told too much." Trank finishes polishing his chin, snaps it back on. "Believe what you want. But I intend to save my city from the ash bin of history. Someday soon, you'll be able to say you played a part in that."

Ripple nods slowly. Even if this old pro's lost it, he made a name for himself once. Maybe Trank knows more than he's saying; maybe he's just an optimist. But everybody's got to believe in something.

"I want to be the greatest fireman in the world," says Ripple. "Do you think you can make that happen for me?"

"Not until I keel over dead." Trank chuckles, lifting his rubber-ized epidermis from the table. It hangs from his hand like a tattered flag. "But you've got spirit. You'll go far."

Neither Trank nor Ripple has paid attention to Abby in quite a while. They haven't noticed her quivering lips, her rigid, seized-up posture, or the fact that she's barely blinked for the last five minutes. So when she abruptly rises, knocking her chair to the ground behind her and, with a single shakily extended finger, at long last points to Trank and lets loose a full-throated scream, they are too surprised to react before her eyes roll back in her head and she faints in a pile on the floor.

〰️

A ceiling of electric white. The People Machines have caught Abby. They have beamed her up into their Contraption and will never bring her home. She lies strapped to a padded table as they stand over her, faces in shadow. One of them holds a device. "This will sting a little," he says, touching it to the bottom of her foot.

"Abby, chillax, it's me. Hold still for a second. Abby, seriously, this is what you wanted."

Abby's eyes go in and out of focus: Dunk, People Machine, Dunk, People Machine. Dunk. The device in Dunk's hand beeps, says, "Forbidden. You are not authorized to access this data."

"Yo, Trank, it didn't work this time either."

"Must be corrupted. That scanner's government issue—bypasses all security measures."

"This sucks so much. I'm done, Abby, you can sit up now."

Abby does. She's in a bed shaped like a HowDouse, on a raised platform in a strange little room with only three walls—the fourth is missing—and an untrue window with a painted scene of the star-strewn sky past its glass. A bright light shines down on her, a circle of radiance as blinding as the sun when she looks directly up. It reminds her of the Contraption's searchlight, how it sought and held her in its glare.

"Where are we?" she asks, shielding her eyes.

"This is the Hall of Prevention and Safety," says Trank. "They used to put on plays here, for the kids. *Stop Drop and Roll, Fire in the Night*. A grown man dressed as a Dalmatian. Never one for theater, myself." He has on his false face now, but Abby's seen his real one. She knows what he's really made of. And she knows better than to ask for Dunk's help this time.

"Dear God," she prays. "Make it die."

The two men exchange glances.

"Amen," Abby adds, just in case that's the part that counts. She isn't surprised when nothing happens. She's gotten used to her prayers not coming true.

"So we checked your Bean," Ripple tells her. He's still holding the BeanReader, a clunky plastic scanner gun with a big red button and a readout screen. It looks like a weapon to Abby. "Did you, like, step on a magnet sometime? Because nothing came up."

"It didn't say my name?"

"It didn't say anything."

"Maybe it's scared."

Ripple exchanges another glance with Trank, who snorts.

"Female intuition," Trank says. "No reasoning with that."

"I know what you are," Abby tells Trank. How could he think that skin would fool her? It's even on a little crooked. At the corner of his left eye, she can see a sliver of titanium glinting. "I know where you come from."

Trank's eyes train on her. His lenses whiz into focus. He has her in his sights. "And where's that, missy?"

"When a skin-and-bone woman gives in to her lust for a machine, the Devil lets form a terrible thing."

"I'd appreciate it if you'd leave my mother out of this." Maybe those are the words he says. Abby hears his machine parts hum, *Let my secrets be.*

But Ripple doesn't hear that at all. "Not cool, Abby, not cool!"

Tears fill her eyes. No one will listen to her. No one ever does. She tries again anyway: "Can't you see, Dunk? He's a People Machine. I'm sure this time. He's going to empty you out, replace you piece by piece!"

Ripple turns away toward Trank. "Don't take it too personally, pro. I think she has brain damage. It's not just her parents—she doesn't even know her name. I found her out on Hoover Island. The garbage dump."

Trank's jaw parts grind out a smile. "Sounds like you saved her."

"Huh." Ripple nods. "Yeah. I guess I did."

"Hero-in-training already. I'll let the two of you get some shuteye."

Abby feels sick. Everything in this place is wrong, even Dunk's story. Doesn't he remember? She saved *him.*

After that, Trank switches off the spotlight and leaves them in the dark museum hall, onstage without an audience. Ripple reaches for her halfheartedly, but when she doesn't respond, he rolls over with an exhausted groan, his back a wall between her and his dreams.

Abby tries to sleep. But she cannot. The day has been long and puzzling, a story without an end. Thoughts of all she's seen—the stump-footed pigeon, the library, the fire, the museum's objects so silent and still, her own face glinting back at her, reflected in the eyeholes of that mask—churn in her until she can no longer stand it. She leans over and pukes over the side of the bed. Pineapple, jalapenos, butterscotch, mozzarella cheese . . .

"What the snuff, Abby! I could've shown you where the bathroom was!"

Abby, emptied now, stares in disbelief at the hot mess coagulating on the floor. The colors have mixed into a single nuclear orange, radiating in the darkness. "I could *taste* it."

"Taste what?"

"The chemicals!"

"Wench, everything's made of chemicals. You and me, we're made of chemicals."

"No!" Abby is hysterically emphatic: "*God* made me! I want to go back to God!"

"Umm . . ."

But Abby is through trying to explain. Ripple tries to hold her still as she squalls herself into forgetfulness, a tide of salty tears erasing every footprint from the shore. She thinks of the Island before he arrived, how strong she was amid the birds and the fish and the rats, the last human in the world.

"I wish you had never come," she weeps. "I wish I'd dreamed of you forever."

"Look, if anybody should be mad, it's me," Ripple hisses. "We're out here, totally on our own. This fireman gig could be a good thing for me. And you're obsessed with fucking it up. Paxton Trank was an *elective official*, OK? His mother did not bang a robot!"

"I've forgotten how to survive alone."

"Then chill the fuck out, because I cannot handle your psychodrama right now."

"I saw what he wants you to do. On the big screen. He wants you to go into the fires. He wants you to die."

"I'm not going to die."

"Yes, you are."

"You're *supposed* to believe in me."

"I don't want you to die." She presses her ear against his chest, lets her breathing match his. She listens to his heartbeat, like she did that first day. *All animals have hearts.* After a long time, he starts to stroke her back. "Dunk. You said we would find my name."

"Yeah, but we tried reading your Bean, Abby. The data's corrupted."

"Corrupted?"

"You know. Ruined forever. Fucked."

"Fucked means *that*?"

"Um . . . yeah. It means there's nothing you can do."

Abby weighs this in her mind. Duncan fucked her. She is ruined forever. Now there's nothing she can do.

～～～

Nightmares spread in our city. In the small hours, the gas-masked fireman—the People Machine—comes to pay Abby a visit. He looms at the foot of the bed where she sleeps with Dunk. She isn't sure it's Trank. She isn't sure he's really there. If she reached to touch this figure, her hand would pass right through him. But she doesn't touch.

His mask is dull brown, sooty, worn—nothing out of this world. But how can she even see him, here in the night museum, unless he glows in the dark?

She asks, "Were you once a man?"

"I was once a man," says the People Machine. "I was born and grew up and fell out of the grace of God."

"No, you were never a man," Abby says.

"I was never a man," admits the People Machine. "I was made by the hands of my kinsmen, from rubber and wires, and they named me and called me good."

"No, you never got a name," Abby says.

"I never got a name," admits the People Machine. "My kinsmen all perished in the Flesh Wars. Their fuel stained the dirt."

"No, you never knew your kinsmen," Abby says.

"I never knew my kinsmen," admits the People Machine. "I never had a single one. People made me. I was the only one they ever made."

"Why did they make no others?"

"Because I was a mistake."

"No, you were never a mistake."

"I was never a mistake," admits the People Machine. "I don't know what I was made for."

"Why did you bring Dunk here?"

"Because I was alone."

"Dunk's mine," she tells him fiercely. "He'll never be like you. He has a soul. And I won't let you take his heart."

"He'll never be like me," admits the People Machine, "but I will take his heart."

The currents of the night flow in a special kind of sea. They tug Abby up toward the surface of consciousness, down toward the lightless vents where life burbles from gashes in the earth's crust. Strange creatures lurk there, blind and alien, creatures Abby would rather not know. They believe she is one of them. She pulls herself away, through a viscous medium not unlike the fluid that cushions her own brain as it floats in the carapace of her skull.

The BeanReader is in her hand.

Abby sits on the edge of the stage and looks at the bottom of her foot. The hall is mostly dark, lit only by low-level emergency lights. The tiny bull's-eye scar is imperceptible, but she can feel the Bean with her finger, beneath the skin. *This will sting a little.* She holds the BeanReader close to her sole, not quite touching, and depresses the large red button. SCAN.

"Forbidden. You are not authorized to access this data."

Abby claps her palm over the device, as if that could shut its mouth, and glances at Ripple, but he still sleeps soundly in the bed.

You have a family.

Abby didn't believe Ripple when he said it the first time. But it must be true. She understands enough about the world to know that humans don't just make themselves. And the device didn't say the data was fucked. It only said it was forbidden: like desires, sins. Knowledge. Forbidden always means possible. So why is Abby so afraid?

Currents: in the tide of darkness, in the flux and gush of her own plasma, in the Bean Reader's motherboard—more obscure than the lock on Ripple's door but nevertheless a map of coiled yearning, a labyrinth Abby navigates the way Hooligan taught her. *By feel.* Her eyes close again, but this time she nightwalks out of her own mind, into the circuitry of another.

The BeanReader obstructs her efforts to enter it, to infiltrate its core. Its internal walls shift, form new barriers. Abby patiently turns at every blockage, a hundred turns, two dozen more—so close now, moving ever inward, her path through the maze of resistance a single convoluted spiral that ultimately contains only her and the solution. At the BeanReader's heart (though of course it doesn't have a heart), she stops. Something is written here. Her name—her true name, the one the Lady wrote on the sand—shimmers for an instant, a virtual exhalation, a glissando of illuminated text, before dispersing into specks. The next cipher lingers just long enough for Abby to inscribe it in her mind: KL5-0216. Then it too is gone.

"Come back," she whispers.

"BREACH. BREACH. SECURITY BREACH," blares the BeanReader. She clutches it to her chest to muffle the sound, but it won't stop. It will never stop unless she stops it from the inside. "BREACH. BREACH. BREACH."

19

PURVEYOR OF LUXURIES

When the werebeast changes back, the night is gone without a trace. She's slept for much too long: her muscles feel stiff and unused, as though she hasn't risen in a thousand years. The sunlight pains her eyes. But her mouth still tastes of blood.

Swanny awakes in an attic of sorts, a slope-ceilinged garret crammed with armoires and dressers, a dining-room table, a grandfather clock, a purple velvet armchair, lamps. She has no memory of arriving in this place, and her other recollections are hesitant to return. She rolls over groggily on the plush featherbed, taking stock of her surroundings. Treasures crowd every surface: a golden birdcage, an armillary sphere, a crystal chalice, paintings cut from their frames and rolled into hasty, fraying scrolls. Atop a bookcase against the opposite wall, between a bronze presidential bust and a military dress sword, Swanny even spies herself, gazing out from the cloudy orb of a fisheye mirror. The sight gives her a start. An unwelcome message has encoded itself into her features, to be read by her alone. And it says, *It all really happened. It's all still true.*

Swanny conjures Sharkey's face before she remembers who he is, as though he sits headquartered not in the tinted-glass confines of a cruising limousine, but on a dark banquette in the backseat of her mind. She remembers that they spoke of their mutual acquaintance, Death, with a familiarity that put them both at ease. Or was it the "tea" that so lubricated the intricate workings of that conversation, a deftly calibrated machine whose function remains, even now, obscure to her? One thing is certain: Sharkey brought her here when she was powerless to resist. But to what purpose? What designs lurked in his heart when he stood over her, watching her sleep, as she somehow knows he did? What words did he utter then, before he blew out the candle and left her alone in the darkness? And what awaits her now, in this new room, between these foreign sheets? Her mother was right to fear general anesthetic: it's a wrenching thing to awake in changed circumstances, with no stages in between.

It takes Swanny another moment to notice what's missing in the jumble that surrounds her: this room has no threshold, no stairs. No door. She has been transported to an impossible architecture from which there can be no escape. Two days ago, she would have believed such a thing to be against the laws of nature, but two days ago, her mother was still alive. The world she inhabits now is without order or reason, governed by curses and enchantments. It is a place where one can climb flight after endless flight of stairs and never reach the top, a place where one can eat oneself alive. In this place, one may well lodge forever in a room without doors.

Swanny forces herself out of bed. She's still dressed in her pajamas, but her fur coat is gone, and with it her mother's brooch.

The floor tilts at a noticeable angle; an important foundational structure in the building has been irrevocably compromised. And Swanny feels unsteady to begin with. She grips the richly carved bedpost for support. She isn't hungover, not exactly; the languor that suffuses her body is a paresthesia of sorts, a muffling numbness of senses that tinglingly disperses as it bumps against the day. She was drugged; she should be indignant. She still doesn't know what was in that drink.

But if she's truthful with herself, she also knows she wouldn't hesitate to swallow it again.

Swanny opens a nearby wardrobe, looking for her coat. The applewood door creaks on its hinge, and she gasps at what she discovers inside. A tasteful rainbow of evening gowns sway upon their hangers: shades of Heartthrob, El Dorado, Secret Garden, Lagoon, Forget-me-not. Swanny runs her hand over the swaths of chiffon and damask and satin; she breathes in the hazy recollection of long-ago perfume. She checks the tags. They're even queen-sized. They've been waiting just for her.

But where is she to wear them? In the confines of this doorless room? Is she to gaze eternally at her own reflection, half sick of shadows, while the city burns on without her? She hears singing: children's voices, faint and distant, almost elfin, eavesdropped from the changeling zone.

> *I am the last practitioner of violence cartographical,*
> *I map the topographic lines of features anatomical,*
> *I took the pickled liver of Mad Krampus for my reticule,*
> *And swiped the face of Sid LaFrange when he displaced my denticle*
> *La la la la la la la la la la la la-denticle,*
> *Da da da da da da da da-somethin somethin tentacle!*

In accompaniment, she hears an occasional, arrhythmic tapping, like a tree branch against a window. Before Swanny can determine exactly where it's coming from, a pane breaks on the opposite wall, and something pings off a silver punch bowl. She throws herself down on the ground, anticipating a fusillade, but when none comes, she gets up again and squeezes through the thicket of furniture to peek between the curtains.

Down in the alley below, two scrawny, rag-clad boys, no more than seven years old, are standing on cobblestones strewn with trash, holding a slingshot each. Swanny pushes up the sash, carefully avoiding the shards of shattered glass.

"Excuse me!" she calls down. "I believe you've broken my window?"

The boys almost simultaneously hide the slingshots behind their backs, and she realizes that they're twins, alike but for their adorably mismatched haircuts, which look to have been performed late at night in the dark under a bridge during a rainstorm with rusty shears. They stare up at her mutely, as if her very presence stuns them.

"Don't tell Sharkey," pipes up the one on the left finally. "We didn't mean to break it. We only meant—"

"Duluth said we were s'posed to help you. So we've been here since early," chimes in the one on the right.

"And we couldn't wait anymore."

"Wait for what?"

"We wanted to see what you looked like."

"What I *looked* like? Whatever for?"

The twins glance at each other.

"He said you were from Outside," they answer together.

"Wait, wait. Who are you?"

"He's Grub."

"And he's Morsel."

"And you mean to tell me—you *live* here in Torchtown? You've never seen the city Outside?"

"Never ever." Morsel is picking his nose while he speaks.

"But that's disgraceful! You're only children! What could your crime possibly be?"

"We're natives," Grub explains.

"You're *incarcerated*. It's an outrage. Someday, perhaps, I'll found a political movement on your behalf. Or contribute to one . . . Did you say you were sent to help me?"

"That's right, lady!"

"Draw me a bath, very hot and bubbly. With clean towels." Swanny again tastes the metallic tang of blood in her mouth: good God, it must be a molar this time. How she longs for an extraction. How she longs to forget Corona's letter. "And a toothbrush, I especially need a toothbrush. Where *is* the bathroom, I might ask?"

"Right downstairs from you!"

"It's got a tub and everything!"

"Downstairs? But"—Swanny glances behind herself, almost expecting an egress to materialize—"there *aren't* any stairs."

"There must be!"

"Sharkey's up there all the time!"

"Wait, where are you going?" They're darting off barefootedly down the alley.

"To the hydrant!" Morsel hollers back.

"We'll get it boiled up real quick!" shouts Grub.

With that, the children are gone. Swanny pulls the curtains back across the broken window and takes another turn around the room. She finally notices the iron handle of a trapdoor on the one unoccupied square of floor.

"Oh, of course," she murmurs. Some part of her is disappointed. Sharkey's done nothing to prevent her from leaving whenever she wants.

When Swanny sees the second-floor bathroom, she understands the twins' enigmatic mention of the hydrant too. A claw-foot bathtub, cast iron and yacht-sized, much like theirs in Wonland, stands in the middle of crumbling tile, but it's not attached to the plumbing or to anything else—as if it were abruptly summoned here from where it once belonged, in answer to her wish.

~~~

After Swanny's bath, she brushes her teeth—the ones that she can see—over the pitcher and basin the room has in lieu of a sink. Then she returns upstairs to dress in one of the gowns (tea length, the blue of a starless sky), embellishing it with a string of black pearls she finds in a nearby jewelry box. She still can't find her fur and brooch, but at least in the fisheye mirror, she's beginning to recognize herself. She pins back her still-damp ringlets with a set of tortoiseshell combs and goes to look for Sharkey.

The Chaw Shop building is three floors: the garret, which she's already thoroughly investigated; the second floor, which appears to consist of the bathroom and another chamber, unfortunately unviewable through its locked keyhole; and the entry level, to which she now descends. The stairs bring her into a cramped, dirty kitchen at the rear of the building, where yellow linoleum peels at the baseboards and mousetraps don't go unused, judging from the two she can see. Light slatted through greasy blinds illuminates the ash motes. At a rust-flecked metal table, a galoot in an unwashed denim jumpsuit is carving a ham.

"Look who's risen from the dead." He eyes her distrustfully. He's seven feet of solid muscle, square and durable, built like an appliance. They're about the same age. "Didn't think you'd ever wake up."

"Why ever would you say something so foreboding? I don't even know who you are."

"I'm Duluth. Guess I call 'em like I see 'em."

Of course: the driver. Swanny pulls out a chair and sits down at the table. "I don't recall much of last night, I must confess."

"Not much to remember. You were out cold when I hauled you upstairs."

"And—Mr. Sharkey?"

"Told me to go home. So I did."

"Did you overhear my conversation with him in the car yesterday?"

Duluth scrutinizes her, opening a bag of bread, rustically baked and hacked into ragged slices. "I'm not gonna answer that."

"Why not?"

He slaps ham scraps into two hasty sandwiches. "You make me nervous."

"Is one of those for me?"

"Nah." He tugs the blind pull to reveal Grub and Morsel, waiting on the fire escape just outside the open window. They grab the sandwiches with their eager, unwashed little hands. "Now, get," he tells them. He doesn't have to say it twice. He lowers the blind again and gives Swanny a wary glare. "Don't tell Sharkey," he says.

"'Don't tell Sharkey.' That seems to be the refrain in this place. I absolutely loathe secrecy. When I see him again, what *are* we to talk about?"

"Just don't tell Sharkey."

"Don't tell me what?"

Swanny and Duluth both twist in the direction of the kitchen doorway, where Sharkey is leaning on the jamb, chewing, as if he's been silently observing them for some time. He didn't have his top hat on when Swanny met him, but he certainly does now. It's an impresario's chapeau—like his limo, glossy, black, and stretched. He wears a sharkskin suit today. He should look ridiculous in the daytime, but it's as though he's brought night into the room with him.

"He let me have a piece of ham," Swanny says, fingering the pearls at her throat. She's also chosen evening clothes.

"Once you eat my food, you're not allowed to leave."

"I'm still quite famished, actually. Have you had breakfast?"

"It's one o'clock in the afternoon."

"That explains why I'm so hungry."

"You worked up an appetite without getting out of bed?" There's something kleptomaniac about his gaze.

"Doesn't everyone wake up ravenous?"

"I'll make you some sausage. Duluth, put that ham in the icebox. I need you to run a message over to the Dolls."

Swanny has never seen a man cook before. But once Sharkey has taken off his hat and suit jacket, he sets about frying the sausages in a skillet with such distracted ease, it doesn't seem unnatural in the least. He spits in a mug with I HATE MONDAYS printed on the side while the pan sizzles.

"I hope you don't mind that I borrowed these clothes," says Swanny to the back of his wifebeater undershirt.

"They look good on you," Sharkey replies without turning around.

"Why do you have so many, and in my size?"

"Broads of your measure are rare in Torchtown. It's extra inventory."

"I wasn't aware you were in the clothing business."

"I'm a purveyor of all the luxuries."

"You have an impressive collection."

"I have good taste." He slides a plate in front of her on the table. She looks down at black pudding, cut into thick purple disks, like coins. "Try it. You'll like it."

"I'm familiar with the dish." Swanny spears a piece on her fork and samples it. "Mmm. Peppery."

"Want some coffee?"

"Coffee—or 'coffee'?"

"Coffee. You know, the drink?"

"Is it anything like . . . yesterday?"

"That was tea." He rinses his mug out in the sink and gets a second from the cupboard, then fills them both from a coffeemaker on top of the fridge. Swanny warms her hands around the heavy thermal ceramic. Normally she'd want cream and sugar, but today she craves the bitterness.

"What was *in* it, exactly?"

"Little of this, little of that." Sharkey takes a seat across from her. He picks up the butcher knife Duluth was using on the ham and cleans under his fingernails with the pointed tip. "You mean you never had it before?"

Swanny notices the letters tattooed on his knuckles: FUCK FIRE. She considers most body modifications unseemly, but this one charms her. Such bravado. It rather reminds her of the glittering battle cry of her mother's brooch—which makes her wonder again, what has he done with her coat?

"Mr. Sharkey, I'm but a simple country girl, all alone in the big city. You seem to take me for someone with experience."

He curls his lip. "Said the future murderess."

"Revenge isn't murder, I resent the insinuation. I'll do what I plan to do with honor, or not at all. Now, do you also sell guns?"

"As it happens, I'm expecting a shipment."

"I'll barter my services as shopgirl for the proper armament."

"It's gonna cost you," he says through the steam rising from his cup. "Couple weeks of work just for the piece. Couple more to put bullets in it."

"And I take it you're not willing to budge on those terms?"

"I don't negotiate."

She swallows a bite of blood sausage. "Then it seems you've left me no choice."

"Finish your food. I wanna show you the shop."

When Swanny steps into the Chaw Shop showroom for the first time, it feels like home. Like the estate in Wonland, it is decrepit and elegant, secondhand glamorous, from the tarnished brass spittoons in the corners to the dusty velvet curtains to the cobwebbed electrolier hanging from the ceiling, like a convolution of illuminated trombones. Library ladders reach the highest of the built-in shelves, though no books are here, only mason jars with sticky coils of drug piled within. A carved mermaid, sawn from the prow of a ship, looms in one corner of the room, as sensual and imposing as the marble caryatids on either side of the Dahlberg hearth. Swanny breathes in deeply. Perhaps the room brings back memories because of its scent, loam and toffee mixed together—which in fact smells nothing like Swanny's home, but which is the scent of nostalgia itself: sweetness shot through with corrupting experience.

"As you can see, I run a classy establishment," says Sharkey. "Which means there are certain guidelines dictating the daily operations of my business. So before we go any further I'll need you to sign a standard Contract of Employ. Just a formality, nothing personal. I'm sure you understand."

"Of course. Business is never personal."

"Good." Sharkey goes behind the counter and retrieves a one-pager from a drawer. "Take your time reading it over."

Swanny touches the paper. It's actually *typewritten*; the words are punched deep into the vellum with the ancient violence of a brute machine.

The undersigned will have the right and privilege to call himself an agent of the Chaw Shop on any and all occasions when this is of benefit to him, and enjoy the associated protections.

The undersigned will be due payments in live currency or merchandise in the verbally agreed upon proportions at the first of each week.

In return, the undersigned acknowledges and agrees to the following restrictions as fair and just Conditions of Employ.

Killing Offenses:

1. The undersigned is forbidden to taste the retail.

2. The undersigned is forbidden to convey to outsiders any information that could compromise the secrecy of Sharkey or the Shop.

3. The undersigned is forbidden to remove any items from the premises of the Shop without express permission.

4. The undersigned is forbidden to go off and leave without reporting his intended whereabouts to Sharkey in advance.

5. The undersigned is forbidden from threatening harm or using physical force against Sharkey or any other agent of the Shop.

Swanny looks up from the paper skeptically. After a lifetime of study, she knows what's legally binding. This isn't. "You intend to *murder* me if I don't obey your rules?"

"That ain't murder. That's punishment. You of all people should understand that."

"And what gives you the authority to dole out this punishment?"

"Because I'm the boss. And I'm warning you now."

"So, how will you punish me?"

He clicks a ballpoint pen and hands it to her. "I'll probably stab you with a knife."

"You'll *stab* me?" The unease she's feeling suddenly strikes Swanny as hilarious. Her death has already been decreed by the dread gods of Mutation and Heredity. This funny little man cooked her lunch and now he's asking her to fear him. "*You'll* stab *me?*"

"Or drown you in that bathtub upstairs you seem to like so much."

"*Drown* me?"

But Sharkey's smirk shows he's in on the joke. He leans across the counter and continues, softer, as though he's revealing a confidence: "Or maybe I'll wrap my hands around your neck and squeeze till all life has left you, then throw your body down an empty elevator shaft right before the building burns to the ground."

Swanny matches his tone: "That's quite a lot of trouble."

"If I'm in a hurry, I could choke you with a piece of piano wire."

"Would that really be faster?"

"Yeah. Usually." He turns around to open a small closet in the wall behind him, and Swanny sees her chinchilla on a hook inside, the diamonds' glint on its lapel. Sharkey takes down a shoulder holster from the upper shelf and hooks it on before slipping back into his sharkskin jacket. "I'd shoot you, but I like to save my bullets for emergencies. What's so funny?"

Swanny dissolves at last into giggles. "You won't kill me. You're a perfect gentleman. You even hung up my coat."

"I've killed before and I'll kill again."

"Mr. Sharkey, you may feel obligated to pose as a reprobate to impress your colleagues around here, but you needn't do it for my sake. I simply don't believe you."

"Believe whatever you want, but don't try me."

"All right, all right." Swanny signs at the bottom of the page. "Will I get a fully executed copy for my files?"

He scrutinizes her. "You're a hard girl to scare."

"I suppose I am."

"Ring the bell if you need me." He gestures at a tasseled pull just beneath a cloudy porthole, the room's only window. "I'm going downstairs to make some chaw."

~~~

Without any customers to greet or chores to do, Swanny doesn't know how to pass her time in the Chaw Shop. Of course, the drugs attract the bulk of her curiosity. She strolls around the perimeter of the room behind the counter, gazing up at the mason jars with their typewritten labels. Some suggest a flavor—CRÈME DE MENTHOL, DUMP-TRUCK SALAD, UNICORN JERKY. Others are more enigmatic—FOSSILATOR, SUPER KLOUD, WIDOW'S PEAK, CUCKOO

CLOCK, LONELY MOUNTAIN'S HEART, QUEEN OF THE NIGHT. She picks up a jar marked CORDIAL GOODBYE, pops open the lid, and holds it to her nose: Sharkey never told her she wasn't allowed to smell. The scent is like that of an ambrosial liqueur made from cherry pits, decay and loss and candy, all at the same time. Fascinating. With some reluctance, she returns the jar to its place on the shelf and continues her perusal of the wares.

She has no notion of how to operate the cash register, which looms on the counter like an enormous klangflugel. But on the shelf just below it, under the counter, she spies a tattered, dog-eared paperback marked in the middle with a strand of twine. What a relief, something to read! She picks it up. *SLAKELESS*, screams the title, spelled out in raised, ballooning red letters. Beneath the swollen word, a dark-cloaked malefactor crouches over a young woman asleep in bed, his lips parted, his teeth nearly kissing her moonlit swanlike throat. Swanny eagerly takes a seat on a nearby stool, flips to the first page, and falls into the book.

SLAKELESS tells the tale of Luther Crowswallow, a man who gives up his soul in exchange for everlasting life, albeit everlasting with a catch. He is reborn as a drinker of essences, a monster who, like the fiends of old, consumes the vital forces of others to replenish his own insufficient store. Discovered at the grisly trade by townsfolk, who plot against him en masse at a tavern aptly christened the Brandished Pitchfork, he flees across the ocean, arriving in port accompanied only by corpses and a few depleted rats.

All this Swanny anticipated, and devours with relish, but as she reads on, the narrative takes an unexpected turn for the melancholic. As Crowswallow lives on, year after dizzying year, time in his perception speeds up. At first he hardly notices, but as decades turn to centuries, the rate exponentially increases, until the fiend can barely glimpse the fevered events zooming past. Now, from his perspective, human life is so fleeting, so inestimably brief, that no moral distinction exists between violence and nonviolence. Ending a life prematurely shaves off, at most, an eyeblink of consciousness, nothing worth worrying over. He compares drinking the essence of a beautiful woman to cutting a flower from his garden for a vase inside the house. "In the elements, it will perish a little later, perhaps, but without the benefit of my appreciation. And for a brief bloom to go unappreciated upon the Earth is the greater tragedy for the connoisseur." Unfortunately, most of his thrashing victims disagree, and he realizes at long last the true nature of his curse: "Immortality is a prison for the friendless." It's at this point in the novel that he decides to embark on a desperate worldwide quest for a mate of his own kind.

"Sharkey sent me for you."

Swanny startles back to life, nearly capsizing the barstool. Duluth is standing at the entrance to the shop, jingling a set of car keys around one finger. Hours have passed; outside the room's lone porthole, only darkness shows.

"He said you'd wanna go out, when you was done with your shift. Go 'investigating.'"

"Oh yes, certainly." Swanny makes a mental note of the page she's on (264) and returns the book to its cubby. She gets her coat from the closet. "Where *is* Sharkey?"

"Business."

The limo is parked on the street outside, right next to a fire hydrant where an alligator stands chained. At first, Swanny assumes it's some form of taxidermy, but as they approach, the creature waddles lazily to the farthest extension of its clanking leash and grins up at them. Duluth gives the gator a wide berth and Swanny follows suit.

The backseat of the limo is even bigger than she remembers, seemingly too spacious for the outside of the vehicle to contain. Perhaps it's just because she's occupying it alone this time. Swanny looks out the window, that changeful tinted glass, as the streets of Torchtown scroll along beside her. No one walks the sidewalks near the Chaw Shop, but as the car rounds the corner to another block, a rising tide of foot traffic floods into view.

The first thing Swanny notices is how *young* everyone is. At eighteen and a half, she's never met a single person her junior—excepting the little urchins outside her window this morning, and those twins seemed a different species entirely, otherworldly guttersprites, not simply "kids." But the pedestrians she's glimpsing now are adolescents and even pre-adolescents, without doubt or exception. She can see it in the way they move: their provocative displays of affection and anarchic patterns of foot traffic disrupt the very air.

A bored shirtless boy trawls a vacant lot strewn with rubble and still-warm embers, gathering rat bones in a coffee can. A filthy matchgirl chases a scrawny, half-plucked chicken. Delinquents too young to shave beat the sides of a dumpster with bats and broom handles. A teen mom and her hip-slung infant shriek expletives at a cutpurse scaling a fire escape; another pregnant, underage waif looks on glassily, skeletal except for her protuberant middle. A seedy hotel bares its rooms like a dollhouse, its façade eaten away by late-quenched flames; inside, young lovers make use of the mattresses. A scuttling prepubescent hefts a chain saw half his size on a crabbed sciatic back. He glances at the limo, then dodges into the throng. Swanny slides around the banquette and opens the privacy divider to speak to Duluth.

"Stop the car! That boy is armed with a chain saw, just like the perpetrators. I must question him immediately."

Duluth shakes his head. "It ain't him you're looking for."

"How could you possibly know?"

"Trust me, sparker like that ain't never gonna get Outside. You've gotta show promise to get hired on a raid."

"Hired by whom?"

"That's what we're looking to find out, innit?"

Torchtown. This is the place Swanny didn't know she was searching for, the dead city's telltale heart. These children are clad in rags and bandages, their skeletons visible through temporary flesh, their souls through haunted eyes. A hand reaches out from a sewer grate. A bottle falls off a roof. A funeral procession tromps past, the small cardboard coffin drawn along in a rickshaw by a lone pallbearer, while mourners clear the way by banging cymbals made of garbage can lids. For the first time since she saw the X-rays, Swanny feels less alone. At least she isn't the only one here dying young.

The limo parks at the curb by a storefront that appears no different from any of the others they've just passed. Duluth opens her door as a gentleman or a servant might. She follows him inside.

From the outside, the building appears intact, but once Swanny crosses the threshold, she sees that it is in fact a hollowed-out shell, with floors, staircases, insulation all burnt away inside. The building's scorched brickwork rises all around her like the inside of a chimney, open to the air above. As she looks up, a dragon glides high across the starless sky, eclipsing the night's sliver of moon. The yellow one this time: she can tell by its snub-nosed profile. It's too far up to do any damage now, but Swanny understands. She'll find no protection here.

It's as though she's wandered backstage in a vaudeville house at the end of the world. This saloon attracts a mature clientele compared to the streets outside. Most of the patrons appear to have reached their early twenties, but the years have come at some apparent cost. At one table, a bored ingenue clad in feathers looks on as her companion plays five-finger filet with a straight razor. At the next, a shirtless ogre with an eye patch breathes louder than seems strictly necessary. Two broad-shouldered young women, sporting chain mail and *chonmages*, stand like statues in the back, flanking a curtained alcove beyond whence exotic music drifts. Other surly characters mill about, personifications of all the major sins and vices. Swanny glances to Duluth for reassurance—he offers none—then affects nonchalance as she saunters to the bar.

"I'll have a vodka martini with two olives," she tells the mixologist. He's a splinter of a fellow, and there's something odd about his face. She realizes after a moment that his eyelashes are missing, and most of his eyebrows too—singed away in a phenomenon so common, she'll later learn, it's nicknamed the Close Shave.

The mixologist looks at Duluth.

"She's with Sharkey," Duluth says.

The mixologist looks back to Swanny. "What'd you say you want again?"

"A vodka martini with two olives. Very dry."

"Tonight we got Rotgut, Embalming Fluid, and Rubbing Alcohol."

"Which do you recommend?"

"They all taste the same."

"Surprise me."

The mixologist pours a cloudy, pale liquid into a jelly jar and hands it to her. It's room temperature and tastes like turpentine smells.

"I'm looking for someone," Swanny tells him, forcing down a second sip. "Someone who'd have information about a raiding party."

The mixologist and Duluth exchange a complicated series of facial expressions so quickly it seems paranoid to notice.

"I don't know nobody," says the mixologist. Then, unsettlingly, he mimes walking down steps until he completely disappears. Swanny cranes her neck over the bar and sees that he's actually descended into a cellar through an open hatch. Torchtown's defining architectural feature must be the trapdoor.

"Didn't like talking to you, I guess," Duluth offers placidly.

"How extremely rude."

"You wanna go now?"

Swanny scowls. "You must think I'm easily discouraged. I haven't even finished my drink."

Duluth sighs and pulls up a stool next to her. Swanny swigs with revulsed determination.

"How long have you worked for Mr. Sharkey?" she asks.

"Almost eight years."

"That's a very long time."

"Yeah."

"Were you always his driver?"

"Nah. I got promoted."

"From what?"

"Running errands."

The trouble with inferior liquor is that it makes one inferiorly drunk—not *less* drunk, just less pleasantly. "You must like him a great deal. To work there for so long."

"It's dangerous, but he treats me all right."

"Dangerous how?"

Duluth shrugs. "Killing offenses."

"But he isn't serious about that."

"Mmm."

"No." Swanny's ventricles stutter. "Has he *really*?"

Another shrug. "That's what it means to be a boss around here."

Swanny considers. She touches the EAT SHIT & DIE pin on her chinchilla lapel. Her secret muscles still. "In my world, I suppose it means more or less the same."

"Times are tough all over."

"Yet I feel there's something else about Sharkey. Some other mystery. Something you're afraid to reveal"—a moue—"*even to me.*"

Duluth looks at her guiltily, and she feels a surge of pride for following up on her hunch with empty flirtation. She isn't so bad at detective work after all. When Duluth speaks again, his voice is low and serious.

"I ain't supposed to talk shop to outsiders."

"But that hardly applies to me. You saw it yourself. I *work* in the shop."

"All right." Duluth keeps his tone to a mutter. "Sharkey knows where the fires will be. Before they happen. That's how come he's lived so long. Sometimes he's just normal violent, when he's got cause. Like for killing offenses. But when he just don't like a guy, a swiller or somebody, Sharkey sends him into a fire. *Damns* him, is what people say. Because even if you miss the first one, he'll make sure another one gets you later."

"Do you mean to tell me that Sharkey actually causes fires? He's an arsonist?"

"Nah, nothing like that. These are drake fires I'm talking about."

"Then what does Sharkey have to do with it?"

Duluth hesitates. "He . . . knows how to use them."

"So his knowledge frightens you?"

"Not just me. Everybody."

Swanny runs her finger around the rim of her glass. "Does he have any friends? Any peers?"

"Mr. Sharkey don't socialize much."

"How terrifically lonely he must be." She downs the last of her drink and reaches for the bottle. After pouring herself another shot, she offers it to Duluth, but he holds up a hand in refusal.

"Never touch the stuff."

When Duluth drops Swanny off back at the Chaw Shop, she finds the front door unlocked and a note stuck up on the wall inside with a pushpin:

```
I got tired and went to bed. There's a plate for you in the fridge.
Be in the shop tomorrow & early. ES
```

It's typewritten, like the contract and the labels. Sharkey must be concealing truly atrocious handwriting.

After a cold repast of antipasto—ham, cheese, smoked chicken, and yes, a few delectable olives (though no martini)—Swanny retires to the attic. Once in her pajamas, though, the day's events continue to churn through her mind. She searches the room until she finds the one thing that can give her relief: a writing set, unused and intact, still in its marbled gift box, with a daybook, dip pen, and sealed bottle of ink, along with sheets of stationery and a calendar for the year 302001 AF. She needs to set her thoughts in order.

Dear Diary,

In the past it has been my habit to introduce myself when beginning a new journal, to state my name and rank and the most notable of my recent accomplishments. But this evening, I am at a loss for such formalities. Am I a Dahlberg or a Ripple, or even still a baroness? What do such appellations even mean in a wonderland such as this? Will I find comfort and happiness here for a time? Or will I perish—falling prey to the brutality I witnessed in the streets tonight, undistinguished and unloved, or burning away to nothing, mere fuel for the flames? I am afraid I cannot bear to set about answering these few simple questions. And there are many others that I dare not even contemplate, questions that, like my wretched affliction, gnaw me from within.

Instead, I will enumerate my goals, for though they are also many and daunting, they give me cause to soldier on.

Before the month is out, I will:

1. Locate Mother's murderers.

2. Torture them at some length for information, until I can rest certain knowing no co-conspirators remain.

3. Kill them in a manner commensurate with how they dispatched Mother (so preferably by shooting them in the face).

4. Have their bodies disposed of discreetly and hygienically (perhaps I shall ask Mr. Scharkee for his advice w/r/t this).

5.

Swanny's pen, which has been scratching across the paper rapidly, abruptly pauses, and her finger slides in her mouth, unbidden, to prod her newest tooth. What comes after that? She hasn't yet thought so far in advance—though of course it may take more time to proceed through steps 1–4 than she's permitting herself to believe—more time, indeed, than she even has.

She dips the pen in the inkwell and continues:

5. Duncan Ripple? Punish him? Win him back?

But she hates the appearance of those question marks, so girlish and juvenile, each the shape of half a broken heart. To think of him, when so much else is at stake—well. She dips the pen again and scribbles out the words.

20

A CALLING

The next evening, after his first day fighting fires with Trank, Ripple is back, showered, and studying in the Hall of Ultimate Sacrifice, sitting on one of the grief benches across from the Wall of Remembrance. This is the wall where the names of the fallen firemen from the first twelve years of the dragon attacks shimmer on engraved brass plaques. Years thirteen and fourteen are rendered in initials only; below those, there's one more that reads, simply, ETC.

Ripple is flipping through a heavily illustrated primer—over his shoulder, Abby sees cautionary images of wildly spurting hoses, disobedient Dalmatians, dangerously positioned ladders, all circled and crossed out—and writing answers in the blanks. "Wench. Stop playing with my hair."

But Abby loves the way his hair feels against her fingers: wet and soft with conditioner, slick as the breast feathers of a vulture. She reluctantly withdraws her hand.

"I need to concentrate," Ripple continues. "I've got to finish this homework."

"What's homework?" He isn't home. Neither is she. But Ripple sighs heavily, as if he can't believe she doesn't know.

"I have to do these stupid worksheets if I want the Special Officer certification, OK?"

"Why do you have to do them if they're stupid?"

"It's required by the Metropolitan Police Department."

"They require you to be stupid?"

"You wouldn't understand. You don't do anything."

"Yes, I do."

He scrubs at the page with his eraser. "No you don't."

"I *do*."

"Uh, no."

"Last night I got the BeanReader to tell me my name."

"What?" He stops erasing, his puzzled expression reflected in the golden wall of inscriptions. She has his attention now. For a second at least.

"Last night I . . ."

"I heard you, I just—we already tried it. It didn't work."

"I made it work."

"How?"

"I listened to it. I snuck inside."

"OK, I get it. You're making this up to distract me."

"No, I'm not!"

"So what's your name, then?"

"The same one I've always had."

"Abracadabra?"

"That's not my real name."

"I seriously do not have time for this."

She takes the pencil out of his hand, writes the cipher in the margin of the page. The characters are large and shaky, but she makes sure he can read them. KL5-0216. "What's that?" she asks.

"What's it supposed to be?"

"Dunno. The BeanReader said it."

"Nice try, but it's not long enough to be a PRL."

"Pearl?"

"Personal Record Locator. Those are eight digits. This is, uhh . . . seven." He squints. "Where'd you get it? Seriously?"

"I told you."

"The BeanReader."

"Yes."

"Show me."

"I can't."

"Why not?"

"I broke it."

"You broke Trank's BeanReader?! He's going to fucking kill you, Abby!"

She frowns, touches the letters and numbers she just wrote. A faint metallic shimmer transfers to her fingertip. "He's going to kill you first."

But if Trank notices the broken BeanReader, he doesn't say anything. Downstairs in the Fire Museum cafeteria, he orders pizza for them again. Abby sees him do it this time. Another machine lives on the wall down here, its workings concealed in an exoskeleton of black plastic. Trank twists its faceplate first one way and then the other. He speaks the names of dinner into a smaller device that hangs from the host machine by a rubbery umbilicus.

"What's he doing?" Abby whispers.

Ripple slurps from a can of Carbon8. "Old-school dialer. I guess that's how they reached people back in loser times."

"So they come when he calls them?"

"They better. In thirty minutes or less."

"Why don't you call your family?"

"Because I don't want to talk to them right now. I told you, I'm not going back home until I make a name for myself." He contemplates the phone, then shakes his head definitively. "Besides, the number's, like, privatized. Normally I just poke their picture."

Two days later, in the morning when Trank and Ripple are out fighting fires, Abby stands at the dialer, holding its receiver in her hand. *Thirty minutes or less.* It doesn't seem like enough time to prepare herself. *You have a family.* She thinks of Dunk's family, his father's strange nests of artificial hair, his uncle's belches and wheels. She thinks of Katya, so kind and yet so sad. The Ripples. A family. A tribe. Strange that Abby lost hers and never longed for them, never missed them the way she missed the Lady, never dreamed of them the way she dreamed of Dunk. Maybe they have forgotten her too. Maybe they abandoned her, cast her away. It would explain why she wound up in the trash.

Each hole in the dialer's faceplate displays several letters and numbers. Abby places her finger in the K and cranks it around. Within the machine, she feels the activating shift: the gears stirring, sparking. Waking up. L . . . 5 . . . 0 . . . 2 . . .

When the faceplate spins back into place the final time, Abby presses the receiver to her ear, as she saw Trank do. Somewhere deep inside, it trills, a foreign sound to Abby but one that suggests all she needs to know, which is: wait. Wait. Soon.

"Hello?" she says when the trilling stops. "Hello?"

The quality of the silence inside the receiver has changed. Before, it was mute in the way of things inanimate, dumb as a box of rocks, like the Lady used to say. The new silence is complicated by omission, a quiet full of background noise. A hush of things unsaid.

"Hello?" she repeats. "This is Abby. At least—I call myself that now. Maybe you called me something else?"

She hears something, a faint . . . squeaking? But no words come in reply.

"I don't know who I am," she confesses. "I don't know who I'm calling."

The squeaking intensifies, but Abby can't make out a syllable she recognizes. Is the machine itself talking to her? Or is there truly someone on the other end?

"The Lady used to warn me about false mothers," she says. "The People Machines pretend to be mothers sometimes, so you love them and trust them. Inside, they're just puppets for science. You can always tell a false mother when you twist her neck. Their heads go all the way around. Are you my mother? Are you going to come and find me?"

A fainter squeak, and then nothing but that other thing: the presence of someone or something at the other end of the line. That sense of a connection.

"I'm at the Fire Museum," Abby blurts. "I don't know where I'm supposed to be. I don't know where I belong."

Abby can't tell time, but hours after her call is ended, she knows that Dunk was wrong. *Thirty minutes or less.* Answers won't come to her so quickly. Maybe it's her own fault. She doesn't even know which questions to ask.

21

UNTORCHABLE

What does it mean, to have a brother? To be a brother? To lose a brother? Osmond looks at Humphrey's corpse, stained with blue poison foam around the mouth, the skin lifeless and stiffening by the second, every inch of it fast becoming false and unvital as the toupee that, even now, clings to its forsaken perch. Humphrey's velour pajamas are his costume for the afterlife. But Osmond still has time to change.

The panic room hardly accommodates a full turn of Osmond's wheelchair when uninhabited; it's nearly impossible to negotiate with both these bodies in the way. But he manages to back himself into the far corner to reach the emergency wet bar. He cracks open a cask-aged limited-release bottle of hundred-proof Moondrool and pours a hefty draught into his pint glass. The time for beer is done.

When, at age fifteen, Osmond was a contestant on *CHAL-LENGER*, his brother, not yet graduated from underschool, was the only person in the world to advise him against probable besplatterment.

"There's no use in killing yourself," Humphrey told Osmond. "It's wasteful. Sure, you're a weirdo and a mama's boy, you're out of shape, you've got a fungus growing on your neck—that cream isn't working, by the way, I wish you'd see my dermatologist—but all of those problems can be easily corrected with diet and behavior. And even if you don't want to make an effort to improve your situation, think about how rich we are. You can approximate happiness through purchasing power. Women are all basically prostitutes anyway."

"Money is no reason to live," Osmond grumbled, in his dressing gown (the hour was late), pacing. Using his legs for the last time, actually, come to think of it. His toes nestled in fur-lined slippers, every one soaking in sensation, in animate life. "Pleasure is meaningless in absence of principle. To have something to live for is to have something to die for, *mon frère*—and I die to mark man's name upon the reign of the dragons. Even if I only eviscerate one of those bristleworm pterosaurs, posterity will be sure to cast my likeness in bronze."

"Not to belabor the point, but that's fucking retarded," said Humphrey in his most grating debate-team voice. "For one thing . . ."

Osmond plugged up his ears: "Fa-la-la-la-la, I can't hear you!"

But Humphrey didn't budge. He stayed with Osmond till the small hours, trying to talk him out of it. The next morning, of course, when the camera crew returned, Osmond went up in the fateful HowTank anyway. He ignored his brother's advice and attempted suicide—he would have said "bravery" at the time, but the difference is semantic. Now Humphrey's done the same. But like everything else in life, he succeeded where Osmond failed.

And Katya too. In her negligee, she looks like the star of a pornographic snuff film. *Bride of the Necrophiliac.* The ultimate trophy to Humphrey's acquisitive machismo—the very sort of prostitute he'd so prophetically described in his sales pitch for survival, though he uttered those words over a decade in advance of her birth. She lived the life of a consumer product, a fully functional machine, with features to be road tested on command: toning an ab, birthing a child, performing a strip show for her own birthday party. She even had an off switch.

Osmond gazes into those glassy blue eyes, now fixed and dilated. Is he looking into the perfect sky of her irises, or into a contact lens? Was she even a natural blonde? Katya existed as a sort of human pet, engineered like an apehound for the connoisseur buyer. She repulsed Osmond in life, but in death, she touches him. The single-mindedness that her last act implies! The clarity of thought! If action is character, she loved Humphrey more than Osmond did—loved selflessly, against her own best interest. What must that have felt like? All of Osmond's feelings are nonsense and confusion. Bound unambiguously to nothing, his logic is free verse.

"I'm having one of my attacks," he tells the panic room, trying to focus on his surroundings. The space is no bigger than a butler pantry—they never thought they'd have to use it—and no servants were invited to join them here in the holy of holies. That now strikes Osmond as a crucial omission. No family and no help. The world is a desolate place indeed. He presses the Call button on the console.

"Room service? Housekeeping? Poison control?" But it's too late for all that. The house is an unmanned vessel on a sea of fire. Osmond turns his gaze to the monitors, to watch the engulfing tide of flames.

Except the tide is going out. The torchies didn't go about their arson properly, Osmond starts to see that now. They didn't account for the stubborn retardant—*fucking retarded*—in the paints and carpets. They'd allowed gasoline to puddle on the floor and burn itself out. They didn't bother to disable the sprinkler system, and when it kicks on late, a belated baptism, it washes out what's left of their crude approximation of hell. The fire sputters out without ever reaching the second floor.

"Never invest emotionally," Humphrey told Osmond long ago, when they were only children. Humphrey had just returned from an afternoon's excursion with their father to one of the city's exchanges, and Osmond was jealous and annoyed, building castles with his blocks. "Never dump shares in a panic. The market is volatile, but we don't have to be. Sometimes it's helpful to imagine it's all happening to somebody else."

Humphrey has died over a level of property damage he could have paid for out of pocket. And Osmond, who's never affected calm or detachment for any reason, who in infancy made a habit of knocking down even his most elaborate block structures in a rage, sees no reason to stand—or more accurately, sit still—for it any longer. He punches in the code, unseals the panic-room door, and rolls into the hall.

Osmond has never before been alone in the home he's occupied since birth. Emptied of waitstaff—chambermaids, footmen, sommelier—the mansion feels not just abandoned but meaningless, a body without a soul. His wheels glide over carpets, rumble across a wood floor, round the corner toward the elevator that mutely offers passage to realms below: *Going down?* We believe that we love the places where we live, but this is only an illusion. It is never a place we long for, but a time.

The best accelerants aren't splashed on the floor. They're released miasmic into the air; Osmond has read enough on the subject to know that much. It isn't the first time he's considered cranking up the gas and punching holes in the copper pipes that line the house's walls, a delicate plumbery of toxin. It is, however, the first time he's acted on the impulse. The dullness of the premeditative grunt work almost numbs him into boredom: he proceeds first to the boiler room, then to the utility closets one by one, twisting gears and blunting hacksaws until every room is filled with the whistling promise of oblivion. Humphrey believed the mansion would incinerate them all. For once, Osmond will prove his brother right. He lights candelabras and votives, every one a fuse. And then he waits.

Or tries to . . . but as the seconds tick on, an intense need grips him, a bodily embarrassment more difficult to ignore than the demands of his stomach, bowels, or bladder. He remembers it well, from those lifeless beeping days, when he lay in a hospital bed, drifting from blinding agony to coma and back again; from an unpleasant weekend he spent, post-paralysis, devouring first sleeping pills and then emetics in doses for the record books. Osmond suffers from the worst condition of all, one nigh well impossible to relieve, despite his most sincere intentions. It is the will to live. It beats in him like a stupid bird against a windowpane. *Fly away, away, away.*

He is too weak to die.

Osmond takes the elevator to the ground floor, hyperventilating, a thousand breaths for every lighted number clicking past. He shifts his motorized chair into S for SPORT as the doors part with a ping. He burns rubber across the lobby's gleaming floor. Literally: the tracks left by the wheelchair's tires ignite in his wake, and he hears an unmistakable roar behind, the throaty bellow of flashover. As his invalid carriage rams through the double doors, into the courtyard, the Ripple mansion explodes. BOOM! Crazed glass rains down from above as Osmond skids into the reflecting pool and hurtles facefirst into the basin filled with water and silver wishing coins, the last of the Ripples' liquid assets.

Heroism once almost killed him, but it is the coward's curse to survive.

22

WEAPON OF CHOICE

At night, the only light in Empire Island comes from the fires. Once upon a time, neon spelled out in bursts of illumination the names that man has given to this world. But now, the shimmering billboards and flashing signs have all gone dark. In their place is another language, a raging hell-fueled scrawl. The dragons glide above it, silent in the pitchy nothing that separates Earth from the cold void of space. The green one makes a black splotch upon the moon as he cruises past.

The brightest part of the city tonight, as usual, is down in Torchtown, between the brackets of those gun-turreted walls, where three separate fires roar in the tangle of the streets. But darkness lurks there too. And in the darkest corner of Torchtown, the one crooked lane entirely unlit by the orange tongues of flame, Eisenhower Sharkey serves the Baroness Swan Lenore Ripple another cup of tea. Then he turns back to preparing their dinner on the stove. Tonight they're eating hoofer chops on the bone, a fine cut of strangebeef from the deep freeze of a recent Wonland raid. Swanny likes her meat rare, and so does Sharkey. He transfers the chops from sizzling pan to plate as soon as they're seared. Juicy. Like a ritual sacrifice, their meals always end in a smear of blood.

"Excuse me, I forgot what I was saying." Swanny's eyes are already half-mast, her red silk kimono open at the throat. On the nights she takes a break from her investigation, she dresses like a leading lady out of costume, a diva coming uncinched. Sharkey likes it when she gets a little loose. It means she feels at home.

"You were telling me about the burglary. What you remember."

She sucks her forefinger absentmindedly, massages her gum. She's got a smile like a predator's, but it always seems to need coddling. The plight of an aristocratic mouth, he guesses. "Haven't I related this in some detail previously?"

"Refresh me."

"It's my mother's death, Howie. It's not an anecdote."

He didn't tell her she could call him Howie, but once she started it, he didn't tell her to stop either. It amuses him. It's been a while since he met anybody so unafraid.

"C'mon. It's like the police always say. Anything you recall might prove helpful."

"Have you ever actually met the enforcement personnel? I'm beginning to wonder if they dispatch anyone at all, honestly. It's quite lawless around here. For a prison."

"I think of it more like a zoo." He hands her a plate. She looks at it, aghast.

"Are we going to eat in *here*?"

"You're already sitting at a table. What more do you want?"

"But it's ever so much more civilized to dine in the dining room."

"Fine. You carry the tea set."

Sharkey loads a tray with the dinner plates, soup bowls, and the tureen of mushroom bisque, then follows Swanny as she totters to the conference table in the parlor. He never thought to eat in here before she came. He's dragged enough corpses out these doors that supper isn't the first thing he thinks of when he walks into the room. But she's got class, and this is where she takes her chow. It's interesting to him, how the other half lives. Outside.

"Happy now?" he asks, taking his seat, pouring her another cup of tea. He spits the chaw from his mouth into a second cup, then fills it, only half-full, for himself.

"Such a regrettable vice," she opines. "So uncouth."

"What? I like to mix 'em."

"Spitting at the table and then *drinking* one's own spit—must I explain it all again?"

"My chaw put that primesteak on your fuckin' plate."

"I don't object to chaw as a business, it's just as a habit"—she tops off her tea once again with icily flirtatious aplomb—"it's rather common."

Sharkey smirks. Swanny seems to prize her abstinence—she's yet to taste the chaw, hasn't so much as snuck a mouthful on the job, far as he can tell—but what she doesn't realize is that chaw and his "tea" are mostly composed of the same active ingredients. Tea isn't even that much weaker, not in the quantity she drinks it. It's just different in its effects. Tea blurs the lines between past and present *emotions*. Current hurts and longings, no matter how taboo, get recollected in tranquility; old passions flare afresh. And new acquaintances take on the trustworthy patina of old friends. As a result, tea's a disinhibitor. It eases up the tongue, if you know the right questions to ask, and only bosses can afford to speak their minds.

"So, you were saying?" He watches her carve her meat with some interest. The dame sure knows how to handle a knife. "About the burglary?"

"It wasn't simply a *burglary*, Howie, it was an *invasion*." She takes a bloody bite; her eyelids flutter with involuntary bliss. "They were all over the house."

He suppresses a smile. There were four on that raid, and not even his best guys.

"What about the one that you saw up close? The one your ma shot, before you went upstairs?"

"He was half-naked with a chain saw. There haven't been many gentlemen in my acquaintance fitting that description."

"Shirt off, huh?" Sharkey takes a second to consider this. Why wouldn't someone want cloth touching his skin? Answer: an open wound. He asks his next question extra-casual. "You get a look at his back?"

Swanny chews pensively. He can't tell if it's derision or suspicion tingeing her reply: "What possible information could a dead man's back contain?"

Sharkey shrugs. "Maybe there was a message written there, just for you."

Swanny snorts and tucks into her dinner.

Her revenge scheme, which he mostly found cute at first, is getting on his nerves. It's the one off note in their evenings together. There's only so many times you can hear a woman describe how she'll sneak into your room and sink a nine-inch shard of broken glass into your jugular the moment she puts two and two together, before you start to believe her. Of course, he could always just kill her if she finds out. But he'd rather not have to.

He'd rather her not find out.

"You're a real girl detective," he says now. "I'm sure you can remember a clue."

"A girl detective?" Swanny shakes her head, frowning as though she's discovered a sliver of gristle in the marbled flesh of her meal.

"Yeah. Like from the storybooks."

"Oh no, no, no. The girl detective is a cipher of lesser culture. If a book were written about a character like me, it would be an intense psychodrama about grief that stirs violence in a woman's heart. About mothers and daughters, inheritance and torment. A love affair with death."

"Down here in Torchtown, we don't know so much about culture." He waxes poetical: "We just take whatever scraps flutter down from your heaven above."

"I suppose that many poor creatures are just trying to survive." Tea's a soporific; heavy eating wears you out. Swanny now has the posture of a fallen soufflé. She stirs a finger in her teacup languidly. "But not you. You're different. You're . . . rich."

"I think the word you're looking for is 'powerful.'"

"It's all the same. A simple question of hierarchy. If you're lord of the sea, you're still a *lord*." She pours herself another splash of tea, then tips the spout farther. "Oh no, I've finished it off."

He still hasn't touched his. "It's all right. You want soup?"

"Topsy-turvy, this life I lead, down below the grid. You've saved the soup for last. Soup of the evening." Her words are a singsong. He slops bisque into her bowl.

"So in this storybook of your life—" he starts.

"Storybook: oh, Howie, you really are too much!" She bats at his arm playfully. "The proper term is *fiction*."

"In this fiction of your life, what's your character's dark secret?"

"She doesn't have a dark secret."

"Sure she does. She's gotta."

"Why?"

Sharkey tastes his tea at last. Even with his tolerance, he can tell it's strong tonight. "Makes her interesting."

"I suppose," says Swanny, gazing into the depthless opacity of the mushroom cream, "she wished her mother dead, and then the wish came true."

Without further ado, Swanny face-plants into the soup. Sharkey grabs her by the hair and flips her backward before she can start the whole drowning process. He swabs her face with a napkin then, with a grunt, slings her over his shoulder.

There ain't much he can't lift.

He lights a candle when he gets up to the attic and stands over Swanny with it for a long time. The cascade of her curls, her soft body. Nothing to worry about. Nothing to fear. But fear he does, because beneath it all is what he glimpsed tonight, another dark secret even Swanny doesn't yet know about herself, a secret he hopes she'll never know.

He blows out the candle and descends through the trapdoor, to the world below. Even though he's just going to his room on the second floor, he feels like he's headed to a subterranean dungeon, a lightless, lifeless cell where he's condemned to do his time in solitary, unless he can tempt another to descend.

Swanny's secret is this: she can hurt him.

~~~~~

Corona uses the butcher knife to slice open a fresh-caught rabbit on the countertop. It's like a pomegranate inside, only instead of ruby-red seeds, its viscera glistens with rows and rows of pearly white teeth.

"Oh, La Diabla," Corona breathes, and dumps the body into the garbage, where it lands atop the potato peelings and last night's bones. Little Swanny reaches out to stroke the silky ears, the brown tufted fur of the corpse, but Corona slaps her hand away. "No, gordita. It is sickly. Do not touch."

"Will it bite me?"

Corona chuckles to herself, humorlessly. She wipes blood off the rusty metal jaws of the rabbit trap with an antiseptic towelette. "It just might."

~~~~~

CURRENCY	OZ. CHAW
Bottlecap	1/400
Bead (glass)	1/200
Bead (plastic)	1/400
Brass knuckles	1/8
Button	1/200
Bullet	1 and get their name
Coin (copper)	1/200
Coin (silver)	1/100
Coin (gold)	1/10
Coin (plastic)	1/400
Dice	1/25
Glass eye	1/8
Lockpick	1/8
Magnifier	1/25
Nail	1/200
Paper money (real)	$1 = 1/100 oz; by denomination
Paper money (fake)	NO SALE and get their name
Razor blade	1/25
Subway token	1/10
Tooth (gold)	1/4
Tooth (real)	1/8
Thumbscrews	1/8

ANYTHING ELSE, ASK THE MANAGEMENT.

You can tell a lot about a community by its currency. Torch-town's is entirely without standards—without any sane, agreed-upon norms. It's a language consisting entirely of slang.

Swanny's had half a dozen customers this morning, and she's had to consult the barter chart for every last one. She's grown tired of staring at it, scanning the list for whatever bizarre array of tender the most recent patron has just plunked down. And then the math: well, Swanny's never much cared for arithmetic, it's so *clerical*. Even Pippi Dahlberg, with her calculating mind, always used an adding machine.

Pippi's adding machine, the rat-a-tat-tat of it above Swanny as she sat playing beneath the ballroom table. The rat-a-tat-tat above Swanny as she fled down the helical staircase of the Ripple mansion.

"Hold on one moment," says Swanny, banishing the thought, scratching out numbers on a scrap of brown wrapping paper, eyeing the most recent offering, an assortment of salvaged screws (equivalent with nails, Sharkey's told her), bottle caps, coins, and incongruously, a rabbit-foot keychain. The paw curls, prehensile, fur worn off in patches, but instantly recognizable: Swanny had similar playthings in Wonland County, where the proliferating cottontails accounted for most of the protein in one's diet, as well as most of the crafting materials at one's disposal. Corona acquired a knack for tanning the bunnies' hides and restuffing them to serve as Swanny's teatime companions. They wore aprons and waistcoats, doll clothes; her favorite boasted an old necktie of her father's. But it's not Mr. Archibald Long Ears she's thinking of now. It's last night's dream. A dream with teeth in it.

Back to the task at hand: "I'm afraid I'll have to consult with the management before I honor this keychain." She reaches for the bell pull to the basement room where Sharkey's making chaw.

"N-no need to do that," stammers the chawhead in question, a moonfaced junior in a fraying burlap kilt. "Lady. Mam'selle."

Swanny rolls her eyes in exasperation. Out on the street, even in the saloons and open-air vacant-lot markets, these "sparkers" run feral, rabid, even, but inside it's as if the shop itself doses them with an odorless gas of docility. If they speak it's when spoken to, and then to apologize. Swanny wishes that every once in a while, one of the less unseemly young men would assert himself, look her in the eye. Work is a distraction, but it would be better with some repartee. Does she so scream respectability that she doesn't even warrant a little idle flirtation? She'd die of loneliness if it weren't for Howie. Sometimes, at the end of the day, when they sit side by side at the counter in the Chaw Shop, counting up the coins and beads and IOUs that make up the day's returns, she feels the most unsettling impulse to rest her head on his shoulder and, as he instructed her that first afternoon in the shadowy town car, *to shut her eyes*. What a comfort it is to have someone to talk to—to know and to be known.

Perhaps tonight he'll make her another pot of tea.

"Then that'll take you to just under an ounce." Swanny turns to the mason jars on the wall behind her. "What flavor did you say?"

"R&N. Please."

Swanny takes down the jar labeled RESPITE & NEPENTHE and unpops the seal. A whiff of dried flowers and chalky earth greets her, funereal but enticing nevertheless. Sharkey is a poet of scent, she must admit: the chaw doesn't just smell, it *evokes*. "One pennywidth or two pennywidth?"

"Double-P."

Swanny removes the thicker of the two coils housed in the jar and uses her gilt-embellished shears to slice off a length. This chaw is fairly fresh; the molasses-sticky rope clings agreeably to her hands, and she resists the urge to lick her fingers. Even after Duluth's words of warning, she doubts very much that the killing offenses apply to *her*. But she still doesn't want to try anything stupid. In the fairy tales of her childhood, girls always did the one thing expressly forbade them—opened the box, cracked the golden egg, snipped a lover's beard—and ruined everything. She's a woman who abides by her contracts (her wedding night regrettably not excepted), and when she signed on for this job, she promised not to *taste the retail*.

Swanny puts the chaw on the shop's scale, trims the end another fraction of an inch, and wraps the package in brown paper and twine. As she's housing the proceeds of the sale in the cash register (which more closely resembles a junk drawer, considering the contents), the bell jingles, announcing the arrival of scarred and dreadlocked Keelhaul. Sharkey employs him as some type of handyman or freelancer—Swanny's not quite clear on the details. "Swillers," that's the name Sharkey bestows on these odd-job fellows, who all seem uncomfortably puffed with muscle and scowly by default. The chawhead scurries around the newcomer and beelines out the door.

"Hey, Swan, gimme some razor blades and two lockpicks. I'm making a sauce run for Sharkey."

Swanny rings up a NO SALE and opens the drawer again. "That vile hooch? I keep insisting he give it up, it's revolting."

"Yeah, he says it's the only way he'll ever get to sleep. 'Rest easy' was his words." At least Keelhaul will speak to her. But today he seems preoccupied.

"It's one thing to order it in a bar, when there's nothing else available, but . . . good lord, is everything quite all right?" Swanny asks. Keelhaul, normally the most stoic of the bunch, is pressing his palms to his temples in the manner of a man beset. He shakes it off as she metes out the discretionary funds.

"Got a headache, is all. I kinda wish I hadn't run into Sharkey on the street right now, he's in a real bad mood. Think he fucked up a batch of chaw."

"He has an artistic temperament, I suppose," muses Swanny. She wonders if it's true, if a person in Sharkey's line of manufacture can in fact endow his creations with the living soul of genius. If a drug can give the user not just a high but a point of view, an inflected reading of the world. "Did he go back to the basement? Shall I ring down to see if he's all right?"

"*Don't.*"

"Keelhaul, you look quite unwell."

"I don't like getting snapped at, is all. Not by Sharkey."

"Oh, you poor creature." It's like seeing Duluth with those little children; these roughnecks all seem so coarse on the outside, but their hearts are as soft as bruised fruit. "Sit down for a moment and nurse your migraine. I'll run to the saucemart—it's two blocks up?"

"You'd do that?"

"I'd be glad to, all this customer service is exhausting. Be a dear and sharpen my pencil while I'm gone."

Late afternoon, outside: Swanny's too often cooped up in the shop till past dark. Now she relishes the warmth of dying gold on her bare neck and shoulders, like a wrap to match the brocade frock she's sporting. In the decadence of late fall, one might almost imagine such weather lasting forever, though the first frost is most likely any day now. Swanny sidesteps Sharkey's gator, still hitched to the hydrant post like a dwarven Jurassic steed, and heads northward. The Chaw Shop is on a sleepy block, but as she turns onto Harbinger Place, she hits congestion, urchins and trulls and foot soldiers to God-knows-whom veering past her at every side.

"Hot rat tails! Hot rat tails!" calls a young man, using a pair of tongs to nudge the sizzling appendages around in a drum of heated oil. Hungry children cluster around him, angling for a pity scrap. Swanny thinks back on her breakfast of smoked boar chorizo with mingled gratitude and astonishment. What a tolerable life Sharkey's made, here in this abyss.

Swanny's been to the nearest saucemart just once before, on an evening's investigation, right when it was closing. It bustles now, the fabled distillery a science experiment of funnels and fractionating columns and reflux towers dripping and gurgling behind the dispensary window of bulletproof glass. There, another shopgirl frantically computes change, more pressed for time with her equations than Swanny ever hopes to be. The establishment, housed in a former pawnshop, bears no sign; it doesn't need one. The line of customers is out the door. Swanny counts the razor blades in her purse and wonders if they'll be enough. She understands enough about the local economy to know that prices here rise simultaneous with demand. Two cocottes in cling-wrap dresses depart with their newly purchased jars, and the line shuffles forward an inch.

"Let's go." Sharkey's hand is on her elbow before she notices him arrive, his callused fingers a vise. He isn't wearing his hat, not even his zoot jacket; his undershirt is still stained with poison, the rust-hued blood of whatever monster he's been invigorating down in that laboratory of drugs.

"Howie, honestly, it's the least I can do. I don't approve of your drinking this concoction, but we all have our vices, I suppose."

"I need you back in the shop." Sharkey's keeping his voice low, but other people in the line are glancing back at them, murmuring amongst themselves. A pair of sparkers cut out, headed for the street without completing their purchase. A lady bouncer follows, moving fast.

"I'll be waited upon momentarily—look, the line's shorter already. And back home, Keelhaul's attending to the register, I didn't close up."

"I need you. *Now.*"

"Please loosen your grip, you're actually hurting—ow!"

Back out on the sidewalk: "I refuse to be manhandled like this, in a public place, no less. You owe me an apology." Saucemart patrons are spilling out of the storefront behind them in droves, empty-handed.

"I don't owe you zilch. Shut up and walk."

Swanny gapes at Sharkey, who doesn't return her gaze; his jaw muscles clench and unclench as he continues to steer her down the street. A path clears for them effortlessly through the foot traffic. "What's come over you? I may be your employee, but that gives you no right to speak to me that way."

"Don't leave your post. I'm warning you once."

"I was running an errand for *you.*" Swanny's eyes smart with unspilled tears; his words sting like a scrawled C− at the top of an exam. "Keelhaul's right, you are in an atrocious mood."

They're turning off of Harbinger Place, back onto Scullery Lane, when behind them the saucemart explodes. Swanny doesn't even see the yellow dragon's shadow before the fire pours down; the reptile is hocking death spitballs from way up in the stratosphere, but this one hits a bull's-eye nevertheless. Swanny hears screams mixed with thunthercrack alcoholic detonations; passersby stampede from the scene. Sharkey doesn't slow down, look back, or drop her arm.

"My God!" Swanny flashes back to her last close call at the library. "I was just inside!"

"It's all right," Sharkey says. He pulls her closer, his voice lowering to a tender growl: "I got ya."

They continue down the block, arm in arm, toward the shop. Sharkey's a stump of a man, a living gargoyle, yet his body gives off such heat: the warmth of a hearthstone, the warmth of home. Swanny's mind overloads, her nervous system jolts and tingles with competing impulses. She finally pulls away, and Sharkey grudgingly relinquishes her. By the time they reach the stoop she's processed the unthinkable into words.

"It's true," she says. "You know where the fires will be."

Sharkey, halfway up the steps already, turns back. He looks at her with tired eyes.

"Who told you that?"

"I'm not a fool."

"So what if I do?"

"You . . . Keelhaul, he said that you . . . you asked him to go . . ."

"Keelhaul hasn't been doing his job."

"What job is that, precisely?"

"Running errands. Today's a case in point. I give him an order, he ignores it." The rest is a boyish, embarrassed mumble: "Anyhow, he was bothering me."

"I thought—" But what did Swanny think, just moments ago? She must have amnesia, like someone in a plot twist. She struggles to recall the bare bones: "I thought you were . . . kind."

"I saved you, didn't I?"

Yes, Sharkey cares for her, protects her, provides for her in the manner to which she has become accustomed. And no one else left in this world does. She chooses her phrasing with care: "Be that as it may, you mustn't—you mustn't take out your emotions on the help. However passionate you may feel."

Sharkey spits, as if daring her to scold him. As if asking her to.

But Swanny just stares at him, struck by his strangeness as if for the first time: a knot of human gristle and striving, malformed and stubbly, a parasitic twin who struck out to make it on his own. Then something collapses in his expression, and she recognizes him again: his vulnerability, his resignation. His loneliness. She's not the only one in this conversation who's down to her last friend. "This place can really take it out of you."

"Howie?" Her voice is soft.

"Yeah?"

"How do you know? About the fires?"

"You don't chew, so you wouldn't understand." He scratches at his five-o'clock shadow with rough knuckles. "The chaw, if you do enough—it brings you very close to death. Works different for different people, but I used to see ghosts from the past. Used to. Maybe it's 'cause I've been chewing longer than anybody else, but it got flipped somehow. Now whenever I see something, it's coming from the future."

<center>~~~~~</center>

Dear Diary,

The nightmares are getting worse—the nightmares and the memories, which are really one and the same, because what is the past but a recurrent dream, steeped in terrible meaning, which one is powerless in waking life to alter in the slightest? Each night I journey to Wonland County upon the wings of screeching bats flushed by fires from the rafters of Torchtown into the inky sky. I haunt the chambers of my childhood home like the ghost I am soon to become, write my name in the mantelpiece dust, rap out coded messages upon the table in the Great Hall, though no one is there to hear. Then, come dawn, I return to Torchtown with the foolish birds, the pigeons who light upon the ledges of this place only to be snared in the hungry nets of children, destined to roast half-plucked over the garbage can fires.

This is not the life I was reared for, and so my travails here have constituted another education of sorts, though lessons learned after a sentence of death like mine lie hopelessly in the shadow of other appalling facts. *Tomorrow I will be two weeks in this place—two weeks closer to the day when, like that rabbit from my past, I will lie split and lifeless upon a slab, a ripened pod of teeth, with no room left inside me for an immortal soul. Yet in these two weeks I've come no closer to discovering the identity of Mother's killers, much less to taking my revenge. What will I say for myself when I face her in the afterlife, in the cold light of some metaphysical solarium, my sins inscribed upon a chalkboard from which they'll never be erased?*

From my interviews with the natives here, I have thus far gleaned only that a single, shadowy figure authors these raids, his henchmen sneaking beneath the city like so many rats. But despite the status my work in the Chaw Shop affords me, I have yet to meet a single soul who will offer so much as a clue to locating this man (or woman) in the flesh. I am beginning to suspect a fearful conspiracy, a consortium of government agents, perhaps, subcontracting their malevolence to the untorched. How else to explain such secrecy in a place where nothing is forbidden and everything has its price?

Dear Howie is the least capable detective, I am afraid. He sequesters himself from the others here, plagued by the demons of his unparalleled talent and most sinister knowledge. He walks among these natives as an immortal, cursed and shunned, though through no real fault of his own. Who could blame him for preferring to speak of the world Outside, my world, the realm of books and art and connoisseurship, that fallen empire forever nostalgic for itself? But although I find his fascination with it, and by extension, with me, comforting in the extreme—a lone oasis of familiarity in the wasteland of the now—it is less than useful to me on my current quest.

More forthcoming, oddly, are Grub and Morsel, the elfin twins who heat the bathwater for my morning ablutions and beg at the Chaw Shop kitchen window for cold cuts and sugar cubes. I am, I must confess, susceptible to their charms. I wouldn't go so far as to say they bring out the maternal in me, but they do make me sorry that I've never had a pet. Through their cheerful nonsense and silly songs, I am coming to understand the logic of this place, the way it looks to those who since birth have lived under its most peculiar laws. I feel it is not pejorative to refer to them as "kindlings," since that's what Howie calls them, and he was presumably one himself, in the olden days.

In Torchtown, the etiquette of fire is an essential fact of life: simply put, one must either help out, or walk on by. Only the youngest children are excused from the social prohibition against gawking at a burning building. One sees them, night after night, clustered around old dormitories or storefront sanctuaries, sucking their thumbs or clutching their raggedy blankets, hypnotized by the playful liquid gold of destruction, even while the inhabitants scream and fling their possessions from the upper floors. Sometimes the children boo when passersby empty buckets on the flames. Sometimes they cry. They love it best when a building lights that hasn't burned too badly before, one still packed with nourishment for the fire to consume, though of course that sight becomes rarer all the time.

Grub and Morsel are getting too old for this diversion, but they can't bear to give it up, not yet. I happened by them on the street the other night after some fruitless sleuthing at yet another dour saloon. As hordes of natives jostled past us on the sidewalk, I asked what comfort they could possibly find in this daily vision of annihilation. They tried to explain as best they could, never removing their gaze from the blazing tenement that popped and crackled just across the lane.

"It's pretty," said Grub.

"It's dancing," said Morsel.

Someone shoved an incinerating gas tank (stockpiled in advance of the coming frost) out the third-floor window, and both boys oohed as it burst in the alley below. I stood with them for a minute more, perplexed and troubled, then reboarded the limo and had Duluth drive me home.

I have since concluded that, in a life so filled with the aftermath of disaster—the blistered lungs of siblings, the comforts reduced to ash— disaster itself serves as a welcome distraction. It is the kindlings' Toob, their lullaby, their imaginary friend. Perhaps as helpless children, we have no choice but to love what wields power over us, no matter how cruel or unfair it may prove itself to be.

Grub and Morsel told me on another occasion that one day soon, Duluth will take them to touch a dragon—it seems this is a coming-of-age ritual in this savage locale. At a certain age, boys climb the water tank upon the roof of the Wedge, the tallest building in Torchtown, to skim their hand along the underside of a sky lizard when one passes just above. The scales feel like giant fingernails, living plastic, featherbones; no two stories quite agree. Sometimes it takes many nights for a dragon to swoop down close enough. Sometimes one comes too close, or its breath does, and manhood is over before it can begin.

"What do the girls do here, to prove they're grown?" I asked.

"Make a baby," both twins chirped in unison. Funny to think that by Torchtown standards, Mother was a child until she was over fifty-five, and I'll be one all my life. It bothers me that the Dahlberg name will die with me, though I suppose it can't be helped. My heirs would have all been Ripples anyway, and the world certainly doesn't need any more of those.

Perhaps I'll give birth to an infant made of teeth.

Two weeks—two weeks since Mother died, two weeks since I fled the Ripple mansion, never to return. Two weeks married. Two weeks of living with the knowledge that I am condemned to an early death.

At least tomorrow, I'll finally receive some recompense for my troubles. Tomorrow is my first payday as Chaw Shopgirl, the day that Howie has promised to give me a pistol. I will be armed, and two more weeks hence, when he gives me the ammunition for it, I will become dangerous too. But dangerous to whom? Right now the only enemy I can recognize for certain has already sunk its roots into the very core of me.

Yet for the moment I remain, against all odds,
Your dutiful correspondent,
The Baroness Swan Lenore

~~~

Two weeks into her employment at the Chaw Shop, Sharkey invites Swanny to his bedroom to take her pick of the guns. He's kept his door locked till now, so despite her best efforts at snooping, she has no idea what to expect. His room has only one dim barred window, facing the airshaft, half-veiled in dusty drapes. Sharkey lights the lamps.

"I hooked up a generator to power downstairs, but up here"—he blows out the match—"I never saw the need."

The space is unprepossessing, even dingy: the one piece of furniture is a brown leather fold-out couch, loved almost to death, its cushions worn as soft as gloves by Sharkey's sleeping form. His zoot suits hang on a sagging string of piano wire in the corner; a spittoon, not recently emptied, emits a subtle odor of stale indulgence. An unswept fireplace displays its latest cremation. But none of these draw Swanny's attention like the books.

Sharkey has an infestation of books. The swarm is voracious and undiscriminating. Bestselling hardcovers, mass market paperbacks, comics, periodicals, instruction manuals, all dog-eared and singed on the page edges: it's nothing like Osmond's library (curated and extensive) or even her mother's (adequate and edifying). The built-in shelves are overrun. The floor is a breeding ground for words. The books teeter atop one another in promiscuous towers; they scuttle across the carpet when Sharkey kicks them, making his way across the room.

Swanny browses for a moment, then kneels on the floor beside the sofa and sifts through a stack of travel guides, their pages glossy with photographic illustrations. The sun setting over a distant sea, amid the Volcanic Isles. A glacier town, bathed in Northern Lights. The Great Crater out west. A meadow sky empty but for spirals of glittering constellations. And, in a volume titled *Lifestyles of the Ostentatious*, shot after shot of what could well be the Dahlberg estate and surrounding environs in more prosperous times: gardens, woodlands, bird-watching. Verandas and gazebos, stables and tennis courts. Frog ponds and wells.

"I never knew you were such a nature buff," she says, apropos of the pile.

Sharkey shrugs, taking off today's zoot jacket to hang with the others on the piano wire. "Sometimes looking at the pictures helps me sleep."

"Once I bring Mother's killers to justice, we should organize a trip. We could take your limo to my country home—it's hardly a day's drive. You could meet my housekeeper, Corona. I don't suppose you've ever had wine from a cellar."

He settles in on the couch, discreetly deposits the contents of his mouth into the spittoon. "Who'd take care of the shop while we're gone?"

"Duluth, or anyone really." Swanny runs her finger over a photograph of a limpid blue swimming pool, its owner poised at the end of a diving board like a man walking the plank. "If you liked, we could travel on from there. See the world. We might not ever return."

Sharkey regards her, faintly amused. "Stay Outside, you mean? On the loose?"

"Well, yes, I suppose." His term strikes her as odd; she tries it out. "On the loose."

"You're forgetting. I'm a 'torchy.' They round us up and drag us back."

"I'm not certain the local law enforcement is all it used to be. Besides, I would explain that you were my guest."

"Too late for me now, anyways. Not much use for an old chaw-monger in the great outdoors."

"That's an awful shame."

"Eh, I've been." Sharkey lazes back on the cushions. "One time I made it all the way out to your neck of the woods, actually."

"Wonland County? Really?"

"It was a real funny place. All those trees, too close together. Got so dark at night. No fires."

"Black forest," Swanny murmurs.

"Yeah. So quiet, I thought I'd disappeared."

Swanny thinks of her vision the afternoon that Sharkey brought her to Torchtown: the branches reaching like fingers toward the car windows, the ground opening up below. The sense of not just *being* lost, but of *losing oneself* to a place. What does it mean that her home makes him feel the same way?

"C'mere," he says, laying his arm across the back of the sofa.

They've been alone together before, dozens of times, and yet only now does she feel that seclusion bodily, in the peculiar vibration of his voice. Swanny blushes. "I thought you were going to show me the weapons."

"I wanna see your teeth first."

"Why? Don't you trust me?"

"I wanna take another look."

Swanny perches beside him on the edge of the seat. Gingerly, with one finger, she pulls the corner of her lip back. "Satisfied?"

"Open your mouth."

She does, and Sharkey cups her chin in his hand, swivels her head slightly from side to side.

"That's what I thought," he says. "There are too many. When were you gonna tell me why?"

Swanny turns away, aghast. "I have no idea what you're talking about."

"Sure you do. You've got that teeth disease. That mutation. From seepage in the Wonland wells."

"How did you find out?"

"I've been doing some reading up on the subject. How come you didn't tell me? I thought we were friends."

"Because it's fatal."

"Not always."

"Really?"

"Sometimes something else kills you first. That's what I read."

"How long do people live?"

"All kinds of time."

Swanny thinks of his premonitions. He knows where the fires will be. He knew how to find her, among the endless vacant corridors of the abandoned city: *I had a dream I was gonna meet somebody like you today.* He saved her life, just down the street. Surely, he's privy to some classified knowledge. When she asks her next question, it's in a tone of utmost urgency. "How long will *I* live, Howie?"

He doesn't hesitate: "Years."

Falling into his arms is like succumbing to the aching pull of sleep, a sweet ocean of welcoming dark that rises up to meet her.

His mouth is on her mouth, his tongue is in her throat, but there's no need to breathe, no need to resurface; she is an animal made to dwell in the crashing of this tide. It's only when he begins to slide his hand up between her thighs that with some difficulty, she partially extricates herself.

"I am *married*, you know," she says. One of her suede pumps has fallen to the floor.

"You don't seem to miss him much," Sharkey observes, relocating his hand to her knee. She's still sitting on his lap.

"How could you know what lurks in a woman's heart?"

"I've got some idea." Sharkey daubs at her smudged lips with his thumb; she can almost taste the spice of his skin. "Don't pretend. It ain't convincing."

"I just need some time, Howie. Time to heal." She reflects on the luxury of the phrase. *You'll have time*, isn't that what her mother said? At last she's able to believe it. What a relief from the pressure that's been upon her these last weeks—what a release. "He mistreated me terribly, you know."

"Yeah." Sharkey smirks. "He threw you to the wolves."

"At any rate," Swanny says, smoothing her mussed hair, "shall we get down to business?"

"What? You mean the guns?"

They disentangle, and Sharkey scales a stepladder in the bedroom closet. He returns with a large cardboard box. "Remember, it's another two weeks before you get your ammo, though."

Swanny rolls her eyes; it's absurd he's being such a stickler after everything else that's passed between them. She sets the cardboard box on the cushion next to her and unseals the flaps.

"I don't know how I'm ever going to choose one," she warns him, "I'm an utter naïf about these things."

Inside, the muzzles and triggers are crammed together. A pirate's blunderbuss. A vaquero's six-shooter. A dueling flintlock, inlaid with curlicues of gold. A tommy gun. Swanny lays them out on the rug one by one. Museum pieces, all. *An antique gun collection.* Deep inside her something twists: the knowledge that comes before knowledge. The feeling she had as a child, looking into that rabbit's fanged insides.

"I could teach you," Sharkey is saying. "Pop some bottles in the alley. Pop some rats."

But Swanny isn't listening to him. She's looking at the double-action semiautomatic that she's holding. As nonchalantly as she's able, she turns it over in her trembling hand. The monogram is right where she remembers, emblazoned on the grip.

PFD.

Penelope Frederica Dahlberg.

Pretty Fucking Dead.

~~~

That night, Swanny and Sharkey supper together, as usual, in the parlor, at the long conference table where he has his meetings. To-night's meal is veal kidneys, sourced—Swanny guesses now—from some distant, plundered charcuterie or violated Frigidaire before finding its way to an ice-packed Styrofoam cooler in Sharkey's lar-der. Dining on the organs feels a bit like chewing a loved one's viscera, though Swanny forces herself to eat as much as she can. She mustn't arouse his suspicion. She must keep up her strength.

"I finished that book," says Sharkey.

"Which one?" Swanny asks. She's never noticed before how many dents and spackled patches mar this room's paint job. What kinds of interactions perforated these walls?

"That one you kept going on about. *Canfield Manor.*"

"Oh?"

"Yeah. Funny thing is, when it started off I thought it was gonna be a romance. But it's actually more like a horror story."

"How so?"

"After they kill Bertrand in the war, Etta's a young widow. She's desperate. And the colonel's conveniently there. He's been there this whole time. He even says something like, 'I was waiting.' 'I was waiting.' Kind of a funny thing to say to a woman whose husband just got rubbed out. It got me wondering if maybe he had something to do with it."

"With what?" Swanny traces her finger along a crimson groove in the table. The surface of the wood is rough and scarred, its finish hacked away in spots. They're sitting at an enormous cutting board.

"With what happened to Bertrand. Officers weren't usually down on the battlefield, were they? Unless somebody put them there."

"That's an interesting analysis, Howie."

"And the end, with their wedding night, Etta and the colonel, there's no talking, no nothing. Just, 'She surrendered herself to him utterly.' Kind of a funny turn of phrase. 'Surrendered.' Kind of violent." He scrapes a gold toothpick between his teeth. "I dunno, just my two cents." He glances at her cup. "You're not drinking your tea."

"I may go out later." She feels as though she might cry. "My investigation . . ."

Sharkey spits. "Suit yourself."

23

SOURCE UNKNOWN

Abby walks through the Fire Museum alone in the middle of the day, barefoot, in Ripple's old sweatshirt, still. It's gone unwashed so long it no longer smells of anyone but her.

Here in the Fire Museum, everything is trapped, pinned and posed, displayed in locked showcases or behind velvet ropes. Nothing lives or dies or changes. The only place that Abby likes is the Hall of Natural Disasters. She pretends the dioramas are landscapes she could step into without any effort at all. She doesn't understand why droughts and forest fires are natural if dragons aren't . . . but in this space her mind calms.

She likes the volcano diorama best. It shows an island like her Island, not like Empire Island. There are no cities. There are no ruins. The only sign of man is a single straw hut, its stilts perched on the slope. A place apart. But this place is even more beautiful than her Island: the shore is made of glass ground so fine she imagines it would be soft beneath her feet. The water is the color of antifreeze. Red pigeons and blue vultures circle through the pink painted clouds. Paths twist amid green shadows, and strange creatures with dog hands and old men's faces clamber up the plants.

In the center of it all is the volcano, bursting into the sky. Fire from below. Abby imagines Dunk saving her from it. She imagines clinging to him, her arms around his neck, her legs around his waist, as he runs through the green leaves down toward the beach. In real life, she can run faster than he can, so in her imagination, she's wounded in some small way, sliced by debris like he was when she found him floating in the bay. She wouldn't mind him endangering himself if he did it for her; that's the only reason she can accept. After all, she would die for him.

The fire-from-below is beautiful, not like the fires she knows. It showers through the sky like rain and pours down the sides of the volcano in rivers. What if Dunk couldn't run fast enough? What if that flowing mass of orange gold overtook them, and they fell into it? The fire-from-below would be hot and sweet and sticky—it would coat their bodies and pull them inside. Rather than burning, it would melt her and Dunk completely, and then they would become part of it, feeling everything it touched, feeling every part of each other, their love a single substance reaching from the island's edge to the lip of the volcano and down its throat into the ground. When they cooled, they would *be* the island, and someday new feet would walk upon them, and new flowers would bloom upon them, until there were no feet and no flowers and no ocean lapping at their shore, and even then, they would be together, a single mass, until they wore away to dust.

She is living in the wrong disaster.

Abby is so lost in her daydream, it takes her a long time to notice that something is different about the volcano diorama today. She gazes into it more carefully. The miniature HowDouse, lofted by wires up at the very top of the exhibit, swings slightly left and right. It is off balance.

It has a passenger.

A rat with eyes like blood drops.

But the white rat isn't only there, in the diorama, behind the glass.

Abby has a passenger too.

It is very odd to feel an intruder creeping through your mind, sniffing and nibbling at what he finds there. Abby's brain is a maze, and the rat sneaks through it, nimbly and with a strong sense of direction. He noses through the fantasy she just had, digs around in her memories of breakfast, then scampers toward her dreams from last night. Before he can snoop through those, Abby tries to shift the parameters, to corner him, but he's too deft to trap. As the floor of her mind tilts beneath him and her perception shines a beam to catch him, he wriggles his way into a gap in her awareness too small for her consciousness to fit into. She senses him in there, slinking along on the undersides of her ideas and feelings, whiskering his way through the dark of her.

Is this what it's like to be decrypted? She feels something like sympathy for the BeanReader she infiltrated.

—Who are you, and what are you doing in my head?!

The rat stops dead, a small weight detectable in his sudden stillness. He thinks she still might not notice him. He thinks it's impossible that she's onto him already.

—Get *out*!

It feels like sneezing, like coughing out a throat-lodged fish bone, like vomiting up that pizza the first night here in the Fire Museum. Abby's body has powers she knows nothing about, and one of these is the power to *expel*. The rat's psychic avatar flies from her mind and back into his own verminal skull with such force that he falls from the miniature HowDouse onto the volcano, where he rolls down the slope in an avalanche of foam-flake-and-wire trees.

—ABORT MISSION. EMERGENCY PROTOCOLS ENACTED.

The rat skitters across the plastic ocean and squeezes into a little hole in the diorama's far corner.

"Hey! Hey, stop!"

Abby can no longer see the rat, but she hears him behind the wall: scrabble scrabble, scrabble scrabble. She chases the sound, past the other disasters and out into the corridor that connects the halls. The rat runs out of the baseboard and hightails it down the tiles.

—Come back here!

The rat glances over his shoulder at this telepathic exhortation, but he patters on, down the corridor, down the grand stairs into the lobby, past the bronze fireman and the ticket booths, toward the basement cafeteria. Abby loses sight of him down amid the tables and chairs.

—Come back . . . !

But he's gone; it's like he was never there. He's gone.

Years of solving her own problems on the Island should have prepared Abby for a setback like this; it's been a long time since she wept in pure frustration. But that's what she does today. She wanders into the cafeteria's kitchen and sits down on the floor with her back against the refrigerator, her knees pulled up to her chest. The box of ice and wires thrums electric against her back. There was a time when she would have recoiled from the sensation, but right now, it's the only warmth she knows. What is she becoming? She's mad at the rat for entering her mind without permission. She has never been the subject of such an intrusion before. But she's even madder at herself for letting him escape before she found out *how he was able to do that*. He holds some key to her that she didn't know existed. He knows something. About her.

And for the first time in her life, it isn't some unknown Other that she longs for most. It isn't even Dunk. It's knowledge of her own true self.

Snap!

—gnaw off, leave on. 50% pro-con ratio. CANNOT COM-PUTE. gnaw off, leave on. gnaw off, leave on. gnaw off, leave on. SYSTEM FAILURE. RESTART. gnaw off, leave on. 50% pro-con ratio . . .

It's coming from behind the stove. Abby climbs onto the counter and peers down into the gap between the back of the oven and the wall. At the bottom is the white rat. His tail is stuck in a mousetrap. He stares up at her, red eyes blinking.

—There you are.

When the rat replies, he sounds less robotic. Squeakier.

—you will eat me.

—No. I never eat magic animals. Wait here.

Abby slides back down to the floor and pads over to the utility closet. When she returns, she's holding a length of twine. She dangles it over the back of the oven.

—Grab on to the knot I tied. Use your front paws.

The rat tentatively takes hold, and she reels him up onto the countertop. It reminds her of catching fish, although sometimes she used to catch trash rats too. She pries up the snapped-down hammer of the mousetrap and the lab rat yanks his tail free. There's a bloody indentation in the snaky pink flesh, but he doesn't seem to have broken any bones.

—thank you, goodbye.

Abby grabs him around the middle before he can escape. His little legs paddle uselessly in midair.

—ABORT. ABORT.

—Where did you come from? What are you doing here? Why were you inside my head?

The rat twists around, trying to nip her fingers, but she doesn't loosen her grip.

—Don't bother peeing on me either. I won't let go.

—ACCESS DENIED. FORBIDDEN. FORBIDDEN.

Forbidden. Just like the data in her Bean.

—Who *are* you?

—LOG IN TO CONTINUE.

Abby opens a cabinet with her free hand. Pots and pans clatter until she finds the colander Trank uses to make pasta.

—you will eat me!

Abby tosses the rat on the counter and slams the colander upside-down over him, containing him in an aluminum prison dome. She weighs down the top of it with an industrial-sized can of peas.

—ERROR. cookware detected.

—Calm down! I just want you to answer my questions.

The rat hesitates.

—state source designation.

—I'm Abby. I'm a human.

—but you speak lab rat.

—This is the language of all magic creatures.

—INCORRECT. this is our proprietary code.

—"Our"? Who's "our"?

— . . . the colony.

—So there are more of you? More lab rats?

—also some controls.

—Where is your colony? Did the others send you here? Were you looking for me?

—FORBIDDEN. FORBIDDEN. ACCESS DENIED.

—Can you at least tell me who you are?

The rat calculates the question's permissibility before answering.

—i am GEN 103 ID: 4923801—TYPE SCAVENGER. my role is information retrieval.

—Why were you retrieving it from me?

—FORBIDDEN.

—You can't try to steal my thoughts and not even tell me why!

—INCORRECT. i am FORBIDDEN to disclose data to unknown sources, especially human sources, when data could compromise the colony's security or mission. even the threat of termination cannot override this directive.

—You'll die before you tell me?

—CORRECT.

—Why?

—85 GENS ago, humans destroyed our colony. 73% of our kind were stomped underfoot. also some controls. we do not disclose data to unknown human sources.

Abby frowns.

—I don't want to hurt you or your colony. I just want to know what you were looking for. Why you were looking in me.

—state the purpose of your query.

—I don't know who I am. Or where I came from.

The rat pauses for a long moment, computing.

—GEN 103 is the first generation in 85 GENS to return to the colony's original location. we too seek to reconstruct a timeline of our history and origins.

—What does that have to do with me?

—UNDETERMINED. maybe nothing.

Abby musters up her determination. She'll come back and find Dunk later. She has to do this, even if she has to do it alone.

—Take me to your colony. Right now.

—FORBIDDEN.

This is getting her nowhere. Abby feels drained. She never had lunch today. She ignores the rat as she gets a jar of peanut butter out of one of the cupboards and starts eating it with her fingers. Back on her Island, a jar like this would have been a real find, a treat that she saved for the coldest time of winter when ice floes dotted the waves and the fish could not be lured. Today she can barely taste it. It's no longer enough just to sustain herself, to cling to life and scrape the surface of the world. She wants to belong.

—ID: /?/ - TYPE ABBY?

—I'm not going to let you out, Scavenger.

—i propose a mutually acceptable solution.

—What?

—communication with known sources does not compromise the colony's security and mission. you will become a known source. then i will bring you to the colony for a reciprocal information exchange.

—How long will it take for you to get to know me?

—long enough to gather empirical evidence supporting the hypothesis that you pose no threat.

—And you won't try to sneak into my mind? Or run away?

—CORRECT.

She wants to trust him. Magic animals hardly ever lie.

—Do you promise?

—i am TYPE SCAVENGER, not TYPE DECEIVER.

—You're just being nice because you want my peanut butter.

Abby moves the can of peas, lifts up the colander, and feeds him a dollop off her thumb. While he licks peanut butter from his little pink paws and nose, she pets his white coat. It's glossy and smooth, so different from the patchy, scabby pelts of the rats she used to skin on the Island . . . yet somehow, also familiar.

—So we're friends?

—friend request accepted.

24

THE FIRE READERS

"Why the snuff," says Ripple, "do we go out to fight the fires at dawn?"

The wind is freezing, with bits of glassy sleet in it. Dead leaves mingle with trash in the streets. It's been a long fall since Ripple left home.

He and Trank walk in the gray pale light of early morning, taking turns pushing the hot-dog cart down a side street in Hollow Sidewalk Village—in addition to fire skills, Ripple's been getting to know the neighborhoods. Growing up, he was mostly just at his house, or at underschool, or sometimes at the Tangs' mansion, which is also in the Heights and a lot like his mansion except it has a shark tank with a tunnel you can walk through and none of the paintings the Tangs own are of themselves, kind of weird if you think about it. But anyway: being a fireman has finally taught Ripple how the other half lives, "other half" meaning the non-celebrities of the upper middle class, and "lives" meaning *used* to live, because damn this place is dead.

Take where they're walking now. It's a cute neighborhood, with little shops along the road—a florist, a dry cleaner, a juicery, an outpatient burn clinic—and apartments up above. The kind of place where, on a sunny spring day, people with normal jobs like lunch lady or sex stylist probably used to look out their barred-up windows and think, This two-room crap pad is sure no mansion, but at least my life does not completely suck. Only now almost all of the apartments are empty, the stores are all boarded up except for the burn clinic, and oh yeah, shocker, one of the buildings is on fire.

"Someplace is *always* on fire," Ripple continues, tugging on his neoprene gloves. "We could start after lunch and there would still be fires. We could go out at midnight and there would still be fires. I need my Z's, pro. I need my balanced breakfast."

"If you want me to train you," Trank says through the Tarnhelm, piloting the hot-dog cart around an open manhole, "you have to follow my orders."

They walk past the burn clinic. It's not even open yet, but the proprietor sees them and hurries out through the jangling doors with his hands full of brochures. He's wearing mint-green surgical scrubs, or maybe pajamas—could go either way, since as mentioned it's still crack of sunrise o'clock.

"Special on skin grafts!" he says. "Skin grafts are our specialty!"

Ripple and Trank both ignore him. If you say one word to these guys, you have to hear the whole sales pitch.

"I'm *already* trained," Ripple argues. "I have my Junior Special Officer badge and everything. So maybe it's time we start treating this more like a partnership."

"I leave at dawn each morning. You can leave with me or you're on your own."

"Maybe I should be on my own, then."

"Maybe you should."

This annoys Ripple. Because doesn't Trank respect how much Ripple is changing—how much he's already changed? Ripple respects it every morning, when he stares sleepy-eyed at the mirror and tries to shave, which is basically a sobriety test for wakefulness; he respects it every night, when he peels off his sweaty, sooty gear and stands under the shower, too beat even to soap his pits. The difference is visible: he's getting shredded, seriously cut, like not quite six-pack abs yet but a fun pack for sure. Even his face looks hella chiseled. He never got that from Power Jousting, since he basically just sat there and held the lance while his drone pony did all the work. Whereas now he's got the cardio and the strength training and also the adrenaline, because holy shit is it scary to risk your life—he thought he would get used to it, but nope. It puts Ripple in permanent Fight Mode because *flight is not an option*, which is an important truth he learned from the inspirational quotes section in his fire training handbook although mostly that applies to conscripted pros who grew up without their own HowFlys.

Because let's be real, flight is totally an option for Ripple, it always has been and it always will be. He's been thinking about that a lot the last couple of days, how he could just bail on this whole unpaid internship and go back home, no harm no foul. The job is never going to be done, not until Trank's vision of a dragon-protected future city comes true, and Ripple's not holding his breath for that.

So far, though, despite having other options—like the option to go home and sleep in his own Slay Bed until eleven a.m., then have a brunch burger served to him on a silver tray—Ripple has *applied himself*, which is a new thing for him. He wishes Trank would respect that, and demonstrate his appreciation of Ripple's hard work with a compromise naptime at least. Also, a promotion.

They roll up to this morning's first blaze: not one building, as Ripple expected, but two side-by-side, identical low-rises with painted brick exteriors. The topmost floors of each have flames tonguing the insides of their window glass and you can feel the heat down on the sidewalk.

"I'm going in," says Trank, donning his water tank backpack and heading for the door on the left. Ripple sighs, flips down his gas mask, and follows suit with the one on the right.

Entering the building is the least dangerous part. Dragon fires start on the roof and work their way down . . . that is, when they don't just scorch some brick. A lot of the fires don't "take." They do a little damage and burn out by themselves. It's the weirdest thing: the dragons *spit* their magma-gorge—ptooie, ptooie—they don't barf it. If Ripple could breathe fire, no way he'd show such restraint. It's like the dragons are poking the city, trying to get its attention.

To wake it up when, like Ripple, it just wants to hit the snooze button and doze.

No false alarm here, though: this building got walloped big-time. In the lobby, smoke is already wafting out through the vents above the mailboxes, and Ripple can hear the fire licking and snacking inside the walls. Great, not even six a.m. and he's got an unsalvageable superstructure on his hands. This is a Search & Rescue only.

Ripple goes up to the fourth floor—any higher would already be too dangerous—and starts busting into apartments, hacking down jambs with his hatchet. He takes some satisfaction in the splinter and crash. The only good part of Search & Rescues is that you can renovate doors to your heart's content.

"Fire squad, coming through!"

But the first apartment Ripple checks out is long empty, the bed stripped, the closets open and bare. Back to the hallway. The next one he checks looks more recently inhabited, with an open fridge half-filled with rotting food and sooty footprints not his own on the peeling linoleum. Ripple scouts around, but this unit's clear too. He's thinking he might be able to write the whole building off as a total loss when he finds the Survivor in Apartment 3C.

The Survivor is in a kitchen, wearing a bathrobe, heating up a kettle on the stove. He's stooped and rheumy, with neck skin like a Hoover Island vulture's. He doesn't seem to notice the thick black smoke pouring out of his vents, the heat bubbling his latex wall paint. A leukemic tabby lounges beside him on the windowsill, admiring its view of the airshaft.

"Sir," says Ripple through the Tarnhelm, "your building is engulfed in flames. I advise you to turn off that burner before we have a belch on our hands."

The Survivor pulls a tarnished pistol out of his robe pocket and points it at Ripple quaveringly. It looks about as threatening as a used dishrag, even though it might be loaded. Obediently, Ripple sticks his hands in the air. It isn't the first time he's run into this situation. Keep it polite, keep it professional.

"Sir, I'm unarmed. This suit might look bulletproof, but trust me, it's not."

"They've tried to evacuate me before. The terms of my lease don't allow for it."

"Sir, the building's on fire."

"I'll take responsibility for my own safety, thanks."

"Sir, as a representative of Metropolitan Emergency Services, I've taken that responsibility upon myself."

"I didn't call the fire exterminators." The Survivor coughs. "Besides, didn't you get the memo? That department disbanded months ago."

Ripple gets this a lot; he doesn't feel like explaining the whole independent contractor angle yet again. "Look, mister, I'm here to take you to safety. I can't leave your side till you let me do that."

"You have a warrant?"

"We're not on private property anymore. This is a Public Hazard Zone."

"Who decided that?"

"Sir, the ceiling's about to cave in."

"Public Hazard Zone. Huh." The Survivor scratches his ear hair with the pistol barrel. He pours boiling water from the kettle into a mug with NEVER EVER GIVE UP printed on the side. "You sound like my kids."

"Kids?" Ripple glances around. He's yet to see an actual child anywhere in the city. Most Survivors are depressing oldstrologers, predicting no future at all, or risk-taking young pyropreneurs who've figured out the dead-enders will pay top dollar for deliveries of fast food, booze, and loam while their time ticks down. Even the burn clinics are going under; that's why the clinicians run around begging for attention like weak desperate virgins. "Sir, is anyone else on the premises?"

"They don't visit anymore. Say the city's too dangerous." The Survivor tucks the pistol into the tie of his robe and shakes some Powdered Zip into his cup. He hacks again, harder this time, with a mucous rattle in it: the air is thickening with ashy grit. "Hell, they were born here—born and raised. I paid for the boy's exemption out of pocket myself. You try doing that on a damage assessor's salary." He stirs his mixture with a bent spoon. "Now they want me to come live on a soil reclamation farm with a bunch of endtimes lumberjacks."

"Maybe you should go," Ripple offers, eyeing the gun. He wonders how quick the Survivor is on the draw, but he's not going to risk it. "Then you wouldn't be so lonely."

The Survivor blows steam off his wake-up juice. "I never said I was lonely."

"Well, you can't stay here."

"They only invited me because they knew I'd say no. Wanted to keep me off their consciences."

"That's not true. They're your kids. They love you."

"They don't want an old coot like me around." A tremor seizes his liver-spotted hands; liquid sloshes and spills. "Besides, I used to hit 'em when they were little. Hit 'em hard. They pretend they don't remember, but you don't forget a thing like that. Most likely they just want a chance to get even when I'm back in diapers."

"I'm sure they forgive you."

"How are you so sure?"

"They're your family."

"Son, since when do people in families forgive each other?"

The smoke is thicker now; even behind the gas mask, Ripple's eyes water. It's too late for any more conversation. "You win. I'm out."

The Survivor dumps what's left of his drink down the drain. "Shut the door behind you."

Ripple descends the three flights back down to the sidewalk. He peels the Tarnhelm off his sweaty face as soon as he's outside and rubs his eyes. Except for Trank's hot-dog cart parked at the curb, the street is completely empty. As usual.

Ripple would be lying if he didn't admit he finds this whole firefighting thing a lot less glamorous than he imagined. People are so *rude* sometimes.

"You're letting out the smoke," one pert granny said, putting the chain on the door as she tugged it closed.

"Didn't you see the Rest in Peace sign on the knob?" another asked.

To be honest, Ripple is starting to have pretty major doubts about this line of work. Because seriously, what's the point? When Ripple first started, he kept picturing the whole thing as a killer reality show, but that gets harder to do every day. It's nothing like the edutainment special. There are no MILFs, no babies, no teammates, and even if you save a building it just gets lit up again four seconds later. Nobody cares.

It doesn't feel very badass to admit it, but Ripple is lonely. It would be different if Trank opened up to him, or even just eased up a little and made some small talk, but since that first night in the Fire Museum they've barely spoken about anything besides the task at hand. Meanwhile, Abby has this pet rat now that she found behind the stove, and even though Ripple warned her it's probably carrying every disease known to man (black plague, Botticelli, flesh-eating spore), she keeps acting like it's her new best friend. No joke: that furwad blinks its gross red eyes and she laughs like it said something hilarious. Ripple never thought he'd be competing with a rodent, but surprise. Plus it's always watching when they have sex, which isn't . . . constantly anymore. It's one thing to bang a stranger, but it's another thing to bang a girlfriend who keeps on getting stranger the longer you know her.

At least if he goes home now he can show off his badge. That's something, right?

Trank comes out of the building on the right, even though it's still on fire. Dragons 2, firemen 0.

"No Survivors," Ripple reports.

Trank nods. He refills his water-tank backpack and loads it back into the hot-dog cart, then, as he always does, takes out his logbook and jots something down on the pages inside.

"What do you keep writing in there, anyway?" asks Ripple. He tries to look over Trank's shoulder, but the fire chief covers the page with his gloved hand, like it's a test and Ripple is trying to copy his work—like he doesn't even trust him.

"Notes."

"About all the awesome people you saved? Oh wait, you didn't have any Survivors either."

Trank closes the logbook. "My building was empty."

"Mine wasn't. There was some old cat fapper who wanted to die."

"I'm sorry to hear that, Duncan. We can't save everyone, but it's always painful to be reminded." Trank says it kindly, but that just pisses Ripple off even more, like Trank is trying to tell him how to feel.

"He pulled a gun on me!" Ripple explodes. "Nobody cares about what we're doing. It's just like Uncle Osmond said, this place is for the high and the damned. And Osmond's the only high one left. I know you think the city's going to come back someday, but news flash: it's not. Kelvin was right. Empire Island is over—there's nothing worth saving. I should just go back home."

Ripple didn't expect it to come out sounding so harsh; for a second he thinks Trank is going to deck him. But he doesn't. He's standing there, totally still, and although it's impossible to tell his expression through the Tarnhelm, he seems to be actually . . . listening?

"This time is *wasted*," Ripple adds, a little meeker.

"What about heroism? Is that a waste of time?"

"No. But if we want to be heroes, we need to do something real."

"What do you propose?" Trank asks the question like Ripple's answer matters.

For once, Ripple thinks for a second before talking. He looks up at the sky. The dragons are way over to the east side, and though they're too far off for him to make out most of the details, it's the first time in a while he's seen them fight. In fact, it looks more like a vicious embrace from where he's standing, the way their bodies twist together in the flurry of their wings, yellow talons clawing green-scaled ribs, fangs gnashing throatward. What if they're mating? Ripple imagines a snaky joystick lustily unsheathing itself from turtilian foreskin, slam-jamming an airborne scalebox. And then the eggs, organic sex bombs dropping from the clouds, unbreakable and fully fertilized, the next generation of destruction.

Nothing anybody does down on the streets will matter as long as the sky is theirs.

"We need to slay the dragons."

Trank shakes his head. "You know that's the wrong idea. The dragons will preserve this city."

"Look, I know you had some weird dream in the hospital, but you were on drugs. There's no evidence you're right."

"Yes, there is." Trank holds up the logbook. "In here."

"What are you talking about? You just said that was 'notes.'"

"Duncan, have you ever noticed a pattern in the dragons' fires?"

"Like how they're tagging?"

"*What?*" Trank sounds surprised and mad and excited all at the same time.

"The fires, they look like graffiti." Ripple shrugs. "Like the dragons are writing all over the city. I saw it from my HowFly."

"What exactly did it say?" Now Trank isn't just listening—he's riveted. Ripple shrugs again.

"Just random letters. They're not spelling out words or anything. They're stupid sky lizards. Why do you care?"

Trank carefully puts his logbook back in the hot-dog cart. "Never mind."

"No. You just said it was 'evidence.' Evidence of what?"

Trank hesitates a long time—duking it out with himself about what to say next, maybe? When he finally speaks, he leans forward conspiratorially, as if the volume on his gas mask has been turned way down.

"During my term as fire chief, I moved in the highest circles of city gov. For years, behind closed doors, I heard rumors about some kind of operations transmitter—a command console that could give orders to the dragons. I was never privy to the details. Only that

there had been one, but it was lost, and the materials were too volatile to risk building it again."

"A *command console*?" Ripple double-takes. "But wait, what does
this have to do with the fires?"

"When I was in the burn ward, there was another man in there
too. A herpetologist."

"Yuck, I hope you didn't catch it."

"He studied reptiles, Duncan. Before he died, he told me the city
had hired him to observe the movements of the dragons. To read the
fires they left behind. The city believed any patterns he found might
lead them to the tool they lost. And I thought to myself—well, I've
been following the dragons my entire adult life. If anyone can figure
this out, it's me. So, ever since, I've been watching." Through the
viewholes of the Tarnhelm, Trank's glass eyes take on an uncom-
monly human sheen. "I'm close now. Very close. I can't disclose the
details yet. But I can say it's only a matter of time."

All along, Ripple felt like Trank was holding back, and now he
understands why. If this is legit—and it sounds legit—it changes
everything.

"We're going to have *dragon slaves*?"

"I'll rule them the way I ran my fire department—with a firm
but just hand. The dragons will protect this city. Restore order."

Ripple pictures Trank at a high-tech control panel, DJing the
movements of the dragons from afar. The thought would make him
jealous, except that's not even the coolest part.

"Fuck yeah! You steer. I want to *ride* them!" Ripple can feel the
wind in his hair already, hear his own triumphal whoops. Which
one is bosser, the yellow or the green? A whole new Toob series is
brewing in his imagination, an epic saga of dominance achieved.
"Maybe that art pro can redo my portrait."

"This will be a huge responsibility, and it's mine alone to shoulder."

"Right, yeah, I totally get that. I just want one ride. Per day."

"But I will need a plan for succession. A trusted lieutenant. A
second-in-command. Someone to back me up, and to take over

when I'm gone." Trank straightens up, distant and authoritative once more. "If there's anything I learned from what happened with the fire department, it's that you can't let the mob decide what's right. Stick with me, follow in my footsteps, tell me everything you know, and it'll pay off for you in the end."

The fire chief folds his arms, like he's striking a hard bargain. But this is a no-brainer. Trank isn't just telling Ripple about a top-secret mission—he's letting him in on the ground floor of a monster-powered dynasty. The old pro respects him after all.

"For serious?" Ripple says. "You're going to make me a prince-ling? Because I am on board all the way with that."

It's distorted through the mask, but Trank sounds pleased. Re-lieved, even. "I thought you would be."

~~~

They get the next dispatch over the radio from the Metropolitan Fire Department. It's uptown from their location and to the east, which means they have to hup to if they want to reach it in time.

"MPD needs to spring for a vehicle," Ripple says, shoving the hot-dog cart. He's recommitted to their mission, sure, but that doesn't mean he can't still complain. A glittering future makes the present even shittier by comparison. "All this marching gives me blisters."

"We're independent extinguishment contractors." Trank scans the sky, hunting, tracking, detecting thin vital tendrils of new smoke from the constant, lifeless smog. "That means we supply our own equipment."

"I don't get why we even have to fight the fires. We're reading them for clues, right? So can't we just observe, like the Herpes Guy did?"

"The police provide us valuable intel and a stipend."

"Beer money can suck it. I'm a dragon prince."

"Besides, the more of this city we preserve now, the more it will be worth later on."

"I guess." They turn the corner onto a broad avenue; a broken traffic light lies prone in the intersection, its crunched-up bulbs like piles of emeralds, gold, rubies. "My family owns a bunch of real estate here, you know."

"Down the line, this whole city will be owned by whoever controls the dragons."

"But that'll be us. Right?"

"You have nothing to worry about."

It does worry Ripple, though, or bug him anyway. As much as he likes the idea of gliding up to his parents' roof on the newly tamed Scales O'Drakerson and yelling, "Yo, Dad, guess you're reporting to me now," being a Ripple should still mean something. It should still come with a legacy attached. Trank can *run* this place, no problem—somebody's gotta do it—but that doesn't make it *his*.

Besides, what if Ripple gets tired of being Trank's second-in-command? He should be able to change back into *Late Capitalism's Royalty* if he doesn't dig the whole *Dragon Prince* lifestyle.

Whatever. Ripple will cross that bridge when he can fly over it.

Ripple nicknames the next burning building the Witch Church the minute he sees it. It's a weird conglomeration of gargoyles and stained glass, with a pointed, twisty spire that pierces skyward and a congregation of hell demons licking the walls inside. He and Trank don't have to bust in doors this time. This entrance is open, and the long tongue of a red carpet lolls out through it, down the cold stone outside stairs.

Spray bags loaded, Ripple and Trank enter the sanctuary. The place yawns before them, cavernous, bigger than it looks from the outside. Filled with fire, like the belly of a dragon. Then Trank points to the back, farthest from the altar. Another Survivor.

"You take care of her," says Trank. "I'm going up into the choir loft."

The lady's an old, old fem, old enough to be Pippi Dahlberg's grandma, wearing this white lacy outfit that looks like a spiderweb dropped down on her from the ceiling and stuck her to the pew. As Ripple approaches, he sees she has a book open on her lap and she runs her fingers over its pages, *petting* it like it's something alive, while she stares right at him. Only he can tell she can't see anything. Her milky blind eyes make her look like her soul's been erased.

"Ma'am, is there anyone else in the building?" Ripple asks her through his gas mask. The tapestry behind the old lady is burning, the carpet runner leading to the old lady is burning, but somehow the old lady herself isn't burning. She's just sitting there like she's posing for a picture. A formal one, since she isn't smiling.

"You will go into the fire," she says.

"Duh, I already did." Ripple sprays out the flames in front of him and takes another step toward her. "I'm here as a representative of Metropolitan Emergency Services."

"You will go into the fire, but you will not find the way out."

"Ma'am, I'm gonna help you now so you don't get cremated alive."

"You will never reach them." Her voice quavers with cruel intensity: "Thus the fire speaks!"

Oookay. According to Trank, cults used to be huge in the city, but this is the last one with staying power: the Say-Somethings. Apparently these people worship the dragons, offer themselves up as sacrifices in hopes that, at the last moment, the dragons will speak *through* them, using earthling brains and vocal cords to communicate their otherworldly demands. A different take on reading the fires, kind of—except it's the dragons' minds they're trying to read. Bonkers.

"You are not the one," she tells him.

Wow. Like he was thinking earlier: rude. He stares at the old lady, then grabs her around the waist and throws her over his shoulder. It's not procedure, but who cares.

"Prophecy disproved," he announces, striding toward the doors.

She feels impossibly light in his arms. He expects her to resist, like the other Survivor he tried this on once—that bedentured harpy chomped him on the ear, and not in a sexy way either—but she doesn't.

Instead, she laughs, and her laughter is a curse.

Outside, in the light of day, the old lady looks mummified: too dry and brittle to move without cracking into pieces. Behind them, a patch of church roof falls in on itself. Sparks dazzle up to the clouds. Ripple tries to set the old lady down, but she clings to him. Her hands clamp onto his slicker, his gloves, his utility belt.

"Hey!" A holster rips and his hatchet thunks to the pavement, narrowly missing his foot. "Wench, look what you did!"

"You will fight," she whispers. "And you will lose—everything."

She scuttles away down the street, cackling. In all of that ragged white lace, she's a scrap of doomsday scripture, crumpled up and discarded but impossible to ignore.

Talk about a thankless job.

"You're welcome!" Ripple yells after her.

"Duncan."

Ripple turns. Trank stands framed in the doorway of the Witch Church. The fire behind him is gone, just gone, a blown-out candle. Trank points to the ax.

"Pick that up. You're going to need it."

<hr />

They've never gone to the park before. Here, what were once lawns and gardens and meadows form a charcoal vista as bleak as the surface of the moon. Evaporated stream beds meander near carbonized swing sets and picnic tables. Every so often, a branchless rampike juts out of the lifeless earth, spent and blackened like the head of a match.

"Not to be a gutless wonder, but aren't we totally exposed out here?" asks Ripple.

"Dragons don't torch the park anymore, Duncan. There's nothing left for it."

"There's . . . *us*."

"They don't aim for humans. We're nothing to them. At most, they see us as ants."

"My uncle used to death-ray ants with his quizzing glass before he stopped going outside."

They crest a knoll. In the valley below, a dragon-seared carousel stands amid a makeshift open-air market. Two dozen sellers display their wares on worn rugs and blankets and stained bath towels; buyers move from booth to booth, bartering and haggling with the merchants.

"You can have anything shipped in," says Trank, "but I like to support local commerce when I'm buying my gear. Let's find you a new holster."

As they start down the hill, Ripple takes a closer look at the vendors. The Survivors Ripple has met so far are mostly frail and elderly, wispy-skinned and wet-eyed, like pickled babies in a jar. But these pros and wenches are leathery as fuck, an armpit convention in smell-tastic 4-D. Looking around, he notices almost every single one has a disfiguring burn someplace visible.

"What's the deal with the, uh, sales force?" he mutters to Trank.

"These folks lost everything and had nowhere to go—or just didn't like the thought of retreating. So now they get by on trade, living here in the park. Under the bridges, mostly."

"Like trolls? Why don't they just grab some abandoned apartments? There isn't exactly a shortage."

"Once burned." Trank doesn't complete the thought.

One booth is selling canned goods. One is selling fire blankets. One is renting out a portable generator by the minute, allowing customers to charge their batteries. Ripple isn't sure how lucrative any of this could be, but other shoppers are picking among the stalls, some spending currency, some bartering wares of their own.

"This is real chicken-thigh meat, it's got to be worth something," one woman says, haggling with a merchant who specializes in secondhand medications, pills arranged in piles by color, half-empty bottles of cough syrup priced by vol. The merchant shoots back, "Take your secondhand Torchtown poultry and go. I'd rather eat bird-lady pigeon than one of those mean, stringy fuckers."

"Harsh," Ripple observes. But it's nice to see some of the city-dwellers aren't spending the remainder of their lives holed up inside. Most of the patrons here are pyropreneur types: Ripple spots the pizza-delivery pro with a satchel full of jelly beans and tuna fish—tomorrow's toppings?—and gives him a thumbs-up. A loam-monger indiscreetly swaps drug packets for a box of extra-strength delousing powder. Apparently the park is another district the MPD isn't obligated to police.

Trank and Ripple approach a blanket covered with leather sheaths in a variety of ominous shapes. "What can I suit you for?" asks the proprietor, a guy wrapped in graying bandages that look to conceal more than heal.

As Trank and Holster Hal talk prices, Ripple, bored, wanders away into the crowd—not much of a crowd, really, no more than forty or fifty people tops, but more faces than he's seen together in one place since crawling out of that manhole. Maybe this is a sneak preview to the future, when the dragons follow orders and the city fills back up again. If so, it could be a pretty friendly. place to live.

There's a food truck parked at the edge of the market, and Ripple goes over to check it out. The menu looks decent: carbonated gazpacho, anti-griddled frozen "waffles," spherical egg salad. Local, schmocal—whoever's cooking here has an out-of-town ingredients supplier. It's the sort of thing Ripple used to eat back at home all the time, that he never really appreciated. After weeks of total junk, though, he's starting to get the appeal. He thinks of Swanny, savoring every morsel of their rehearsal dinner, and wonders if she's OK. He shouldn't have let her slip away like that. Did she actually go to Torchtown? Or did she find her way back to his parents so she could enjoy the finer things again? It's a toss-up: that fem loves her crème fraîche, but there's also a heaping dose of murder rage squeezed into those ruffly plus-sized outfits.

"Duncan?"

For a second, Ripple doesn't recognize his old molecular gastronomist sans toque. The guy behind the window of the truck is scruffier than he's ever seen him, with a new half-grown beard and his usually immaculate chef's whites splattered and unwashed. But he gapes at Ripple for so long, with such intensity, that Ripple finally puts it together.

"Hey pro, it's good to see you too. What's up with the new business? Did you finally get sick of truffling my dad's frittata?"

"I thought you were dead. I thought you *all* were dead." The cuisinier is, inexplicably, tearing up. "I thought I was the only one who survived."

"What are you talking about?"

"After the invasion—the fire?"

"Huh?"

"Your mansion. It burned to the ground. Don't you know that?"

"No. The MPD went and checked it out. Everything was fine. Everybody was OK. Except Mrs. Dahlberg, but hey, win some lose some." Ripple knows what he's saying is true, but the gastronomist has a look on his face like Ripple is falling and falling and the world is rushing up to meet him. "Seriously, I know what I'm talking about, pro."

"You should look at this." The molecular gastronomist reaches through the window and hands Ripple a LookyGlass.

As the video fitfully streams, the images come to Ripple in starts and stutters. The Ripple mansion, gouged and smoldering, filmed through the locked gates; a lone searcher with a BeanReader, plodding through the wreckage; old Toob clips of Ripple's mom and dad, labeled with dates and RIP; a picture of Ripple's own face, then Swanny's, each with a question mark superimposed; a tweaked logo for *Late Capitalism's Royalty*, bling wreathed in mourning black. Ripple can't process it. It looks like reality. But it can't be.

25

NO-MAN'S-LAND

W hen does all of this begin?

It begins in the bullet shop.

It begins in Torchtown, where Swanny frets on a street corner, gazing remorsefully at the sign she's seen on her limo rides so many times before: BULLET RETRIEVAL, REFURBISHMENT & RESALE.

It begins in the wee hours of the morning when Swanny lies in bed in the Chaw Shop attic, thinking of her mother, and of Sharkey. Swanny once inhabited Pippi in the form of phantom pains; poltergeist disruptions of the bladder, stomach, and intestine; toxemia; and gestational diabetes. In lightless secrecy, Swanny's embryo feasted, fiendish, on the Old Mom's tired blood. What could inspire greater loyalty than that? But it's Sharkey's body that nurtures her these days: the hot, dark hair that sprouts from his shoulders, the muscles of his jaw as they work his morning chew. The smell of the calming poisons, leaking through his skin. She hates herself for the attraction, and yet, even now, some small, dangerous part of her wants to fall on his chest and offer her forgiveness like a confession. She wonders if he'd kill her—if he'd ever trust her again. But of course the point is moot. She knows what she must do.

It begins two weeks and four days ago, with a young man whose freshly scabbed back wound will never have the chance to heal. A name written there in pain that will never be erased.

It begins nineteen years before that, during the Siege of Wonland County, when Eisenhower Sharkey, separated from the rest of his raiding party, finds himself in a dark wood, far from the world he knows. Somewhere in the distance, land mines explode in the backyard of a house. He freezes beneath the crooked trees and feels himself disappear into the silence. He learns for the first time that he is edible, marooned, a creature of the indoors. This is no-man's-land. The sky is full of stars. The night is full of eyes.

It begins with Pippi Dahlberg filling out the Voluntary Retirement form in longhand, triplicate, checking the box marked "Medically Inadvisable Pregnancy" under "Reasons Why."

It begins on a Wednesday, forty-three years ago, with an unwanted Torchtown rape baby squalling in the gutter, premature but viciously alive, ripping a plastic trash bag off his sticky red face like a caul. Unnamed: Eisenhower Sharkey will name himself.

It begins with the installation of the barbed wire, of the machine-gun turrets, atop Torchtown's concrete walls, with the first irredeemables lowered down into its streets in shark cages, to find their fortune there.

It begins with the dragons.

It begins, as all endings do, in the beginning, in the code that underwrites the whole of our experience, that first microscopic enchantment that brought the world to life. But for our purposes here, it begins in the bullet shop.

The bullet shop is semi-underground, the only floor remaining of a decimated brownstone. Uneven brickwork, leftover from the annihilated ground-floor walls, rings its ceiling like the battlements of a castle half-swallowed by the earth. Swanny regards it miserably from across a cobblestoned alleyway pale with morning dew, then steps off the curb, directly into the shadow of a dragon. She pauses in midstep as its killer darkness ripples over her. She shuts her eyes. It's the green one—she can tell without looking up, from its frilled silhouette, the shape of the frisson it leaves behind. Amazing that such a brief eclipse can so chill the air. A few seconds later, she hears the screams a block away and the crackling whoosh, quite familiar now, that can only mean the end of one thing, the beginning of another.

It begins in the bullet shop. One step at a time.

The bullet shop used to be the Parcel Pickup for the block; the wall behind the counter is a grid of locked letterboxes, each cubby hidden behind a numbered brass door. Ting, ting, ting! Next to the cash register, the slugmonger sits at his anvil, reshaping a bullet with a tiny hammer. In an open toolbox beside him are a series of surgical implements—a speculum, a pair of pliers, needles and thread—that appear designed to remove shrapnel from wounds as painfully and unhygienically as possible.

"Show me where it hurts," he says amiably, not bothering to remove the loupe from his screwed-up eye. Ting, ting!

"I'm buying, not selling," Swanny says, breathless. She takes her mother's sidearm out of her pocketbook and hands it to him. "Do you have any ammunition that would fit one of these?"

The slugmonger jumps down from his forging stool with unaccustomed eagerness: it's been a while since he's had a shopper. He's Swanny's age, a runt with all hope for growth behind him—why are all the storekeepers so very short? He wears a dickey in place of a shirt and fingerless leather evening gloves, presumably to protect his arms from powder burns.

"Double-action, semiautomatic, top of the line, vintage 301999 AF! Haven't seen one of these in years. Where'd you get it?" he asks, dropping the magazine into his palm with an eager click.

"It was my mother's."

The slugmonger sifts through a ring of keys slowly, thoughtfully— too slowly, too thoughtfully—before finally opening one metallic square in the grid. Number 66.

"I've only got two," he says, loading the gun. He casually levels the weapon at her, looking down the sights. "What's it worth to you?"

Swanny realizes too late she's put herself at a lethal disadvantage. She's armed a stranger with her one necessary possession. "Mr. Sharkey's good for it."

The loupe magnifies his scrutiny. "Does he know you're here?"

"Of course." Swanny prays it isn't true; she snuck out while Sharkey was in a meeting with his swillers, the backroom door shut and locked to her. But she can imagine him getting a whiff of her disobedience, following her scent through the criminal maze of lanes and back paths she took to find her way here. How strong are his powers of presentiment? She doesn't know. She can imagine him finding her anywhere. "We have no secrets from each other. I'm sure you take my meaning."

Annoyed, the slugmonger hands over the pistol; he's not a gambling man. "I'll bill his account."

"Have a splendid day."

Back out on the street, in air now tinged with smoke from the next block's dragonfire, Swanny hurries home with her purchase, glancing around furtively.

When will all of this end?

~~~

"What are you doing there?"

Swanny directs this question to Grub and Morsel, who crouch under the Chaw Shop register, huddled together like stowaways. She clunks her purse, locked and loaded, onto the counter above their heads.

"We came to see you, Your Bareness," one of them finally says. "But then we heard footsteps and got scared it was Sharkey."

"Well, you should be scared, very scared indeed. Kindlings aren't allowed in here, especially not behind the counter."

"But we was playing Chaw Shop," pipes up the other.

Swanny finds herself wondering how they've survived as long as they have, in this evolutionary killing field of mercurial tempers. "Out you go," she says, shooing them brusquely. But before they can scrabble out from below, the bells jangle again, and it is Sharkey this time.

Swanny slept in—or rather, tossed and turned sleepless—till past breakfast; it's the first time all day she's seen him. His body is an accusation to her, tall-hatted and intact in his finest sharkskin. His smirking lips, his hot cloven hands, send signals to all her guiltiest pleasure centers.

"Hello there," he says, as if it isn't her personal responsibility to send him to hell. He glances around. "Who're you talking to?"

"No one. Myself." Swanny sashays around the counter to divert him from the twins. "And it's all your fault, Howie. I've been bored to distraction, waiting here for you."

"Since when? I made coffee, you never came down." Sharkey reaches for her, curving his hand around her waist; Swanny stiffens. "What's the matter, your husband ain't watching."

"I just have the most awful—toothache." It's true: a new molar asserts itself in the back of her upper jaw, in defiance of his prophecy.

Sharkey touches her swollen cheek. "Maybe you need some ice."

"I'm sure it'll pass."

"C'mon, I'll make something soft for lunch. You want soup?"

She moves as if to follow him, then stalls. "Just let me get my purse."

"What for? You planning to leave me a tip?"

Swanny thinks of the boys beneath the counter; she didn't plan on witnesses. But the moment is perfect. Almost effortlessly, she reaches inside the handbag, grasps her mother's gun, and draws it out, a graceful assassin. But though she has a perfect shot, Sharkey's back is turned, headed toward the kitchen, and she can't bring herself to cap him unawares.

"Here's a message from Pippi Dahlberg," Swanny says, just as she practiced in her attic bedroom last night. To her relief, he turns. "Eat shit and die."

It hadn't occurred to her that her aim would be so poor. The slug barely grazes his shoulder as he lunges, spring-loaded, in her direction, already fully adapted to the sudden change in circumstances. She tries to fire the weapon again, but before she can, he twists it out of her fingers and hurls it across the room. Then he punches her in the stomach. The event strikes Swanny as astonishing, impossible, even as she doubles over—it quite literally takes her breath away. Before she can recover, Sharkey punches her in the face. Her body is full of the most dreadful surprises: she never knew she had so many capillaries before they burst. She recoils, staggering back, and Sharkey knocks her to the floor. She's so much larger than him, but she isn't stronger.

"Please," Swanny whimpers.

"Please? You're asking me *please*?"

Sharkey kicks her in the ribs, then grabs her by the shoulders and slams her head into the unyielding floorboards. Above her, the electrolier makes dazzling revolutions in triplicate. Sharkey unholsters his own gun, and she falls down that barrel, that tunnel, that portal, that well, into the negative space.

"Can't you see, I had to try," she weeps. "I had to. I owed her that much, at least."

Sharkey fires.

And fires.

And fires a third time for good measure.

Gunpowder sizzles against Swanny's cheek and hair. Her brain throbs. She opens her eyes. Sharkey is still standing over her. She turns her head. Right beside her, a cluster of bullet holes bore through the floor. She can see the basement from here.

Sharkey puts his gun back in its holster. His face is tight with malice, but there's something else in his expression too, something all-too-familiar but so very out of place that it takes her a moment to recognize it: he's disappointed in her.

"Go to your room," he says.

~~~

Grub and Morsel like to play pretend. They don't even have to talk to do it. They just look at each other, and they're two baby rats in a rat nest. They're two chicks inside an egg. They're two dragons in the sky, flying around like gloop, gloop, gloop, we're gonna breathe some fire. They aren't even in Torchtown anymore, and they sure aren't in the Chaw Shop, under the counter, listening to Sharkey's feet creak on the floorboards as he paces back and forth.

"I knew it," he fumes. "I knew it. Fuckin mess. She's done."

Duluth tells Grub and Morsel fables at bedtime, about monsters under the dead and woofs at the door. The moral of every story is: run away. Or, if you can't run away, hide and keep your mouth shut. They don't need to make a peep to play pretend. They look at each other with big eyes and know.

On the other side of the counter, Sharkey's footsteps slow down. Stop, even.

". . . the fuck *was* she talking to?" he mutters.

Grub and Morsel can hold their breath for almost a minute, each; they've practiced. They're going to break the record this time.

~~~

Sharkey's probably the only man in Torchtown with a regular habit of lighting fires. He doesn't use the fireplace in his den too much, but on a night like tonight, staring into the crackling flames helps him think. Something nice about a fire in a hearth. It's like a tiger in a cage. It makes Sharkey feel powerful to know that he can starve it if he wants. Or just as easily let it loose.

He's drinking hooch tonight. It's a hooch-drunk kind of night. Sharkey drank hooch the night that Jawbone died, so much hooch he passed out. By then, Sharkey'd already killed the guys that done it, so there wasn't much else left to do. Now, he spits his chaw into the jelly jar and mixes it with his finger, slouched against the sofa cushions. He's lucky to be alive, but he doesn't feel lucky. He doesn't even feel alive.

He should've killed her when he had the chance. When he still had his rage. He'll never bring himself to do it now.

He knew it before they met: she's going to kill him. And he's going to let her.

The knock at the door is no surprise. He's been expecting it for a while. It's why he left the lock unbolted.

"It's open."

Swanny's got a black eye, and a cut on her cheek, from his pinky ring, probably. It hurts his knuckles to look at it: he sure left his signature on her face. She's in her nighty, some kind of lace-and-satin devising, nothing like the kid pajamas she had on when he found her. She looks all grown up.

"It feels like home," she says, timid in the doorway, of the hearth.

"Yeah, it's cozy."

"No—I mean, like *my* home. In Wonland County. Mother always enjoyed a fire on cool nights. Sometimes our housekeeper would roast a rabbit on a spit, which Mother said was barbaric. But there we were, out in the boonies—who would ever know?"

"Your ma's famous around here. You know that? She killed some friends of mine back during the Siege. Took out almost a whole raiding party. Single-handed. The last guy lost half his leg to her land mines, pogoed out to warn the rest of us at camp. Nothing to do but let him die in the woods. Ten years after, people were still telling stories about her to scare the kindlings. Old Mom with a machine gun; now, that'll give ya nightmares. Pippi Dahlberg." He toasts her, sips again from his jar. "You know she spiked a man's head on her fence."

"I believe I was in utero at the time."

"You're younger than I thought."

"I suppose we still don't know each other very well."

The fire hisses. It's eating itself alive. Sharkey'll have to decide whether or not to feed it pretty soon.

"Sit down."

Swanny obediently pads across the room and alights on the sofa. She warms her hands, peering into the fireplace.

"Good lord, you're burning books in there."

"Yeah. I weed out the doubles. And the dictionaries—how many dictionaries does a guy need?"

"I suppose, only a handful."

"One for formal, one for slang," he instructs her. "Anything else is a waste of space. You cold?"

"The garret was a bit drafty."

"Get under the blanket."

Swanny tucks herself under a corner of the afghan and looks at him diffidently. He takes his time drinking. He lets her stew.

"You made me real mad," he eventually says. "I never got that mad at somebody and didn't kill 'em before."

"Is that a compliment or a threat?" Swanny tries to say it lightly, but her voice quavers.

"I'm trying to say I don't have much practice apologizing."

Swanny hesitates, then cautiously, gingerly, rests her head on Sharkey's shoulder. He strokes her hair. He can feel her trembling.

"I'll never beat you again," he tells her. "That was a one-time thing."

"But Howie?"

"Yeah?"

"Are you still going to kill me?"

"That depends. Are you planning to behave yourself?"

"Yes."

"No more revenge?"

"No more revenge."

"All right, then." Sharkey throws another book on the fire. "Truce."

They lounge together, achy and damaged. Exhaustion is the dullest drug of all, but it trumps the others—erodes away the contours of even the sharpest highs and lows. Sharkey watches the flames like he did when he was just a kindling, looking for figures in the combustion, guardian emissaries dispatched from the Kingdom of Burn, where everybody winds up in the end. Swanny relaxes into him, and he lets her.

"May I sleep here tonight? Only sleep," she murmurs, like someone already in a dream.

"What for?"

"I'm frightened."

"Don't worry. I'll take care of you."

"You will?"

"I'll take care of everything."

26

DRAGON PRINCE

Paxton Trank never had a son, and he doesn't have one now. When he watches Ripple pushing the hot-dog cart through Longacre Circle—past the shuttered wax museum, the gutted strip clubs, the hologram house, past surface street vehicles, abandoned forever at the curb—through that vast carnival of neon signs and billboards all gone dark—it isn't a father's pride he feels. He's wondering instead if today's strategy was the right one, if the time was really ripe to reveal his plan. Ripple reacted the way he hoped at first, but since the park he's grown strange and distant, as sullen as a mutineer. Trank doesn't care for the attitude. Still, he bites his tongue.

Much as Trank would like to deny it, he needs Duncan Ripple, or someone like him, someone young and charismatic, someone who can talk to cameras and the public both, someone with that spark that makes a fellow suitable to public life. Trank used to have that spark, but now it's gone, snuffed out with some part of his soul, under that pile of smoldering rubble in the east Gemini tower. Trank doesn't miss it. The same piece of him kept him tethered to his men, who betrayed him—to city gov, who limited his powers and deserted his cause and left him to die in his hour of direst need. Trank no longer cares what anyone thinks of him. But when he tames the dragons, he'll still need to coax people back to Empire Island: investors, renters, tourists. No one will come to a kingdom ruled by a bitter, disfigured has-been. If he's to govern, his administration will need a spokesman. His city will need a face.

They return to the Fire Museum, and Ripple disappears to

shower. Trank removes his Tarnhelm and sits down on a bench in the lobby near the bronze fireman. He takes out his singed and tattered logbook. The answer is in here, he knows—it has to be. He turns the pages, unfolding grids where he's mapped the shapes of fires. Zigzags and parabolas reshape themselves into *N*'s and *W*'s, *U*'s and *C*'s. It was in front of Trank's eyes the whole time, and yet Ripple saw it at a glance. But what does it mean?

Trank has the data. He's close to the dragons' secret, to claiming their power, which after all these years of toil in their shadows should at long last be rightfully his. And yet something still eludes him.

"It's not in Torchtown," the herpetologist told him that night in the burn ward, his voice a dying croak, a lone assertion in the darkness of Trank's mind—both of them blind and eyeless, heads bundled in strips of gauze. "It's not in the Lipgloss Building. We've checked the obvious places. The first thing I learned about dragons is that they speak to us in riddles."

No matter. Trank won't give up. Flight is not an option, and neither is defeat. The command console won't heal his face, but it is the only thing that can heal the city, that will justify his life, and for that reason he believes finding it is inevitable.

It's then that he senses he's not alone. "Come out from where you're hiding," he advises the lobby. His words echo.

Ripple's girl slinks out from behind the bronze fireman, stroking that vermin pet of hers. Tonight she's dressed in a Dalmatian costume from the Fire Museum gift shop, a hooded set of footie pajamas, speckled black on white. It's a mercy that she changed out of that sweatshirt, which reeked like a barnyard, but it's almost as unsettling to see her dressed like an animal as stinking like one. She's a pitiful little thing, Trank's always thought so, weak like a woman but with none of the feminine graces, and feebleminded to boot. Trank likes a woman who can hold her own but who knows her place. This one does neither.

"I know what you're planning," she says now. He knows she has no idea. Yet she seems so certain. The certainty of instinct, ignorance. Female intuition. "It won't work. He came out of a Toob before. He won't become your machine."

Dinnertime. Trank orders a pizza (plain cheese tonight—he's not about to reward the boy with Gutbuster, and Trank's stomach can't handle it again besides). Ripple comes to the cafeteria, but he's just as silent and hostile as before, if not more so. He rips a slice out of the pie and takes an angry chomp.

Meanwhile, Abby pours water into her glass from a plastic jug, humming tunelessly, the polka-dotted dog hood tossed back to show her flaxen hair. She tilts the cup so her new pet can lap up his fill, and for a second her benevolent, nurturing expression becomes saintly, an old painting extolling some minor virtue: *Young Lady with a Lab Rat*. Trank's never cared much for the fine arts.

"Get that vermin off the table," he tells her.

She frowns. "He's my friend."

"It's my table."

"This isn't your table," snaps Ripple. "It's the Fire Museum's, and the Fire Museum belongs to everyone. That's in the fucking brochure. So leave her alone."

"Didn't think you cared much for the rodent yourself." If Ripple were a conscripted man, Trank would make him run upside-down in magnet boots on the treadwheel for the tone infraction. But things being as they are, Trank keeps it neutral. "If there's something you'd like to raise with me, Duncan, I'm glad to hear it."

"OK, sure. You lied." Ripple is dressed in red long johns and his hair is still wet; he's literally crossing his arms over his chest like a spoiled child. He couldn't look less threatening. Yet there's something unyielding in his eyes that Trank hasn't seen there before. A challenge. "My parents are dead."

"Dead?" asks Abby. The rat scurries up her arm, onto her shoulder. "How?"

"I don't know. The house burned down, so . . . arson? Dragons? Or maybe they were murdered first. I guess it doesn't matter, since cock pocket here didn't even bother to tell me."

"I'm sorry, Duncan." Trank always knew he'd find out eventually, but this isn't how he wanted it to go. "I thought you had potential—a calling. I didn't want you to walk away from that before you'd begun."

It's almost true. The day they fought the library fire, when Trank radioed the MPD, he considered telling Ripple what he'd really learned, then and there, offering the orphaned boy a home and a vocation. But an estate like the Ripples' would require much of the young man, even with the mansion in ruins. It would have been a career, not just an inheritance, and when would fate deliver Trank another telegenic deputy? Besides, there was something special about Ripple: his enthusiasm, his simplicity. Something Trank recognized, that he knew he could mold to his purpose. "I believed it would do you good, to find your own way in the world."

"What? No. You didn't help me find my way. It was *your* way. You were trying to use me. Like you thought I was stupid."

Trank's not going to argue with any of that. Still, it isn't the whole story. "I did use you. I used you to save lives. I used you to save property. I should have told you the whole truth up front, I'll admit it. But you can't let grief blind you to all that we've accomplished."

"I'm done being a fireman, OK? I was only doing it to impress my dad."

"I had a father once too," Trank says. Roy Trank was a Whamball tackle with zillions in endorsement deals, who died taking a thunker to the chest. Trank was just six. Ten years later, when the dragons first came, he was ready. All his life since, he's run straight into danger without dodging, just like his old man. "If there's one thing I understand, it's becoming a hero to please a parent who will never know."

"Then don't you get that it's *pointless*?"

The boy is hurting, but Trank doesn't care much for the question.

"We're on a mission," he says, as gently as he's able. "Is that pointless?"

But Ripple doesn't come around the way Trank expects.

"*You're* on a mission," says Ripple. "You want to control the dragons the same way you want to control me. You don't care about saving anything. All you care about is being in charge."

Trank stiffens. "I'm a leader, Duncan. I lead. And you've got an opportunity to be part of my team. If you know what's good for you, you'll step in line."

Ripple stares at his pizza. He thinks for a long time—longer than Trank's ever seen him—longer than Trank would have thought possible. When he looks up his jaw is set, defiant. "You know that command console you talked to me about? Well, good luck finding it first. May the best man win."

Trank knew the boy would challenge him someday, but he never expected this caliber of insolence. What kind of an orphan would push away a father figure? The kind who believes he's heir to the throne. Trank should have known that *Late Capitalism's Royalty* would have its own plan for succession.

"So you want all the power for yourself?" Trank asks. "You really want that responsibility?"

"No way, Hamburger Head. But that doesn't matter."

"It doesn't?"

"No. Because I'm not like you. I'm not going to use the command console for myself. I'm going to be a hero for real. I'm going to use it to slay the dragons."

Trank's lost so many boys over the years, it's hard to keep track. Toward the end of his service as fire chief, conscriptees would splash themselves with gasoline in protest and run into the fires, and Trank would have to send in more boys, boys to chase the boys who, if they lived at all, would be skinned alive and subject to a court-martial. It hurt and pained and shocked him every time. After the mutiny, Trank finally thought he was past all caring. But now, Ripple's words have a strange effect on him. It's as if Ripple has peeled back his rubber face skin, and slowly, deliberately turned every one of his screws.

"You can't slay the dragons," Abby murmurs, hushed and fearful. "They won't let you."

"Watch me, wench." Ripple stands up. "Come on. We're leaving."

"Where do you think you're going?" Trank asks Ripple.

"Anywhere we want. The city is mine."

"Not this city." The MPD hasn't given Trank much besides a badge, a walkie-talkie, and some nonlethal weapons. But they get the job done. Trank pulls out a TaseMePro™ and levels it at the boy.

Ripple snorts. "Uh, I am not afraid of an *electric razor.*"

Before Trank can depress the Stun button, Abby flies across the table to shield Ripple from the blast. A blue-white beam crackles through the air, into her lithe blond form. She flops to the floor, every muscle twitching and spasming. Her hair statics out—she glows visibly for a second—her eyes dance under their lids, bewitched by rapid nightmares. Then all at once she relaxes into a poisoned princess's swoon. Her rat leaps down from the table to the floor and beelines for a hole in the wall's baseboard. Some friend.

Ripple sinks to his knees beside her. "What the snuff did you do? Put that thing down!"

"Not every man can be god of his own history." Paxton Trank has never had a son, and he never will. But he believes that he will be remembered. One way or the other. The taser's recharge diode lights up, ready to aim and fire. "I give the orders around here."

~~~

The first time Humphrey showed Ripple the Dignity Kit was way back before Ripple started flunking everything, when it still seemed like he'd turn into a grown-up son who could be trusted with secrets.

"Your mother and I will only use it if we're ruined," Humphrey told him, taking the black box out of the safe, unlocking it. "Then you'll inherit whatever's left."

The blue pills in their tiny vial. The golf pencils. They scared Ripple in a way the CGI beheadings and explosions on his XL projection screen never did. Who knew death came in travel size? Little Dunk: "But I don't want whatever's left. I want you and Mom."

"Sorry, son. We'll be dead."

"Then I'll take poison too."

"There won't be any for you."

"Why not?"

"Because we'll have taken it all."

~~~

When Ripple comes to, he's flat on his back, staring up into the sky. The city is so dark these days. Even a year ago, before the mutinies, he never would have been able to see this many stars. He doesn't recognize any constellations, although he probably should. Back in underschool, he had to take Astrology for Scientists instead of Cosmonautics because, as usual, he bombed the placement test, which meant, unbelievably, that he missed out on a class trip in a special ion-propelled HowTram up above the atmosphere, where smarter students floated around laughing like maniacs and Kelvin kissed the YA impersonator Cheryl for the first time and some prodigy underclassman barfed gravy in arcs and spheres. Ripple only watched the episode later, after it was all over, when it was already old news. Just like his burnt-up house.

And his parents. His mom's disconcertingly lithe stripper body, with the elective cesarean scar ("Your father wanted to keep me tight," she informed him during her explanation of where babies come from), her waist-length platinum-blond hair and six-inch heels; his dad, with his velour sweatsuits and bad toupee, his ear whiskers, rosacea, and annoyed expressions—Ripple can see them both so clearly, like they're projected on the night sky above him, their bodies mapped out in points of light.

"I'm sorry," he says out loud. "I'm sorry I fucking suck."

He wants to believe that they're up there, star-parents living out eternity in a cloud city like something from a HowFly commercial, but they're not. They're dead. Whatever they thought of him, they're not thinking anymore. There's no one left to tell Ripple what to do. There's no one left to care.

Did Swanny feel this way too, when she saw the torchies shoot her mom?

As hours pass, the sky lightens and Ripple orients to his surroundings. He's locked in a wire cage on a roof—he's betting the Fire Museum's. The cage is big enough to lie down, but barely tall enough to stand up. No biggie: Ripple isn't exactly springing to his feet anyway. He has an electricity hangover that he hopes isn't brain damage, though it's hard to tell. He does feel even dumber than usual. Dumber and more doomed. A dragon (the green one, his old buddy) passes directly overhead, at seven thousand feet but still too close for comfort. Walking the streets is bad enough, but at least there's always the possibility of cover within easy ducking distance. Being here is like the park, but worse. Because this is where they strike. Depending on how long he's out here, it's only a matter of time till he gets fricasseed.

This must be what it was like back when the whole world was nature and men were only prey. No wonder his caveman great-granddads stayed the fuck in their caves.

Ripple doesn't know where Abby is, and he's not counting on her to come find him with a pair of wire cutters. When Trank finally appears at the roof hatch sometime midmorning, Ripple doesn't know if he should panic or feel relieved that at least something's finally happening. Trank's wearing bunker gear—slicker, boots, turnout pants—but the Tarnhelm is flipped back, and his expression is totally blank, as if that rubber skin was just peeled off the conveyor belt at the assembly line, freshly manufactured and never before used.

Great. That's not creepy at all.

"Listen, I am legitimately sorry about earlier. I shouldn't have gotten mad. It's not like you killed them. Learned my lesson big-time, for serious." Ripple decides to go into full apology mode, because who knows what this pro is capable of? As he speaks, though, he surprises himself by kind of meaning it. What the chief did was janked, but he's a janked-up guy, inside and out. Ripple can't help but sympathize with that, at least a little. They were buds just yesterday. Maybe there's still something worth saving in the ruins of Trank, some Survivor of kindness or sanity, half-smothered and screaming HELP. "Now, you want to let me out of here?"

"Duncan, you have to understand that after what you said, I can't possibly trust you with any intelligence I have concerning the movements of the dragons."

"I one hundred percent swear that I will not do anything related to the dragons ever." Ripple 100 percent doesn't mean this. If the dragons are scary now, imagine them controlled by a bona fide zap-master. Ripple glances skyward nervously. "I'll be happy if I never see a dragon again."

"And if I can't trust you with that intelligence, we can't work together."

"I'm fired? OK, awesome, I'm fired. Thank you for firing me, sir." Ripple rattles the cage's wire door; the lock doesn't budge. "So I should pack my things and go, right?"

"And if we can't work together, that means we're working separately. Which creates competition down the line. It makes a conflict inevitable. Do you understand that?"

"No need to pack, even." Ripple is making a serious effort not to read the subtext here. "Me and Abby, we can just, like, jet. Where is Abby?"

"Downstairs. She's still recovering, but she'll be all right. I restrained her, for her own safety."

"Restrained?" Ripple nods, determined to be chill with this. At least she's not dead: major points for that. "Restrained is cool. Restrained is good."

"I don't consider *her* a threat." Trank peers at him through the wires, those fake eyes zooming in for a close-up. "Do you understand what I'm saying to you, Duncan? You can tell me whatever pretty stories you like to get out of that detainment kennel, but we both know what's in your heart."

Ripple stares down at the ground. He's still in the red long johns he had on earlier, the ones he sleeps in. They have feet, like a little boy's pajamas. Is it possible that he'll die without ever seeing his own toes again?

"I say there's no time like the present," says Trank. "Let's settle this here and now."

Trank takes not one but two hatchets off of his utility belt and holds one in each hand, the twin blades glinting. With a shing of metal on metal, he cuts through the lock on the cage door, and the hinge creaks ajar.

Trank stands in the open doorframe. His expression is losing its smoothness, acquiring worry lines and crinkles as, below, the animatronics shift. It's human, but unreadable—the look of a man looking into the void.

"You wanted to be the greatest fireman in the world. Now here's your chance."

Trank holds out one of the hatchets to Ripple, keeping the other lowered at his side. It's a loaded moment, a passing of the torch, totally nonviolent. Say what? Maybe this is a different part of the story than Ripple thought. Disbelieving, he grasps the handle. He looks from the sharpened blade to Trank, then back again.

"So this ax has . . . superpowers?"

"No."

"Then how does it make me the world's greatest fireman?"

Whatever intensity awakened Trank's features collapses back into exasperation. "It doesn't. But you can't be the greatest while I'm still alive."

"Whoa!" Ripple almost drops his weapon; he bumps into the wall of his cage and the whole thing jingles. "You want to *kill* each other?"

"One way or another, we'll have to face off. There's no way around it. You won't let me fulfill my destiny, and so I can't allow you to fulfill yours."

"Pro, let's just dial it way back here. I was going to be your princeling. What happened?"

"It would have been a fine thing to rule the city together. But it would never have worked out. I can see that now." Trank wields his hatchet with both hands; beneath that heavy slicker, the muscles in his chest and shoulders visibly flex. "Do you want to die fighting, or in that cell?"

"I'm not going to fight you!"

"Then you're going to die."

Maybe Ripple can reason with him: "Listen, what if there is no command console? Or what if there is—and neither of us ever finds it? We might not have to fight ever. Can't we just wait and see?"

Trank grimaces. "There's no terror in dying when the alternative is to live without hope. You can't let cowardice rule you, Duncan. You were right to think of greatness from the start." Trank flips down his Tarnhelm, as if it's a combat visor. "You have to rise above."

Trank is blocking Ripple's way out of the cage; the only way out is through him. Ripple raises the hatchet—there's athletic tape wrapped around the handle. To help him get a grip.

Trank steps backward, and Ripple cautiously advances . . .

Now both men are on the roof of the Fire Museum, circling each other, while the dragons circle them from above, black-winged squiggles against the blinding white clouds. Ripple thinks of the first time he walked into the Fire Museum, the words BRING IT ON inscribed over his head like the logo at the start of an opening-credits sequence. *Dragon Prince.* What's worse—a reality that's over? Or one that never was?

Trank swings his ax first. Ripple ducks.

EXT. SCORCHED LOT—DAY

RIPPLE and TRANK scrounge through the smoldering rubble of a collapsed building. RIPPLE sees something in the wreckage and points.

                              RIPPLE
          Sweet, check it out!

CLOSE on the command console, a wood-paneled unit
bearing dials, joysticks, and sliders, with a faint but
otherworldly lemon-lime glow.

Trank swings again. Ripple blocks him with his ax handle and
pushes Trank backward with a strength both men find surprising.

EXT. BLUE SKY—DAY

RIPPLE, riding the yellow dragon, bursts out of a cloud
bank, hooting and pumping his fist.

Trank stumbles. Ripple hesitates.

INT. FIRE CHIEF'S CHAMBERS—NIGHT

In an opulent darkened chamber, a sickly, aged TRANK
lies atop pillows, wearing an old-timey nightcap with a
big pom-pom on the end. RIPPLE sits at his bedside next
to a nightstand loaded up with pill bottles and medical
devices, looking sad and worried.

> TRANK
> You have been like a son to me. But now I will be one
> with history.

> RIPPLE
> This blows chunks.

> TRANK
> As my last act, I bequeath you . . . (coughs) all the
> power of my kingdom.

Across the room, the command console waits for its new
owner, glimmering faintly in the shadows.

When Trank regains his balance, he goes on the offensive, slashing as Ripple dodges back, and back, and back.

INT. FIRE CHIEF'S CHAMBERS—NIGHT

RIPPLE bends over TRANK's motionless corpse. He closes
the fire chief's fake eyes, and they snap shut with a
satisfying click.

                RIPPLE (softly)
  Now it's your turn to ride the dragon . . .

Ripple backs into the parapet at the roof's edge, twists to look down at the dizzying distance to the street below.

EXT. SKY—DAY

Early in the morning, the two DRAGONS fly through the
mist over the sea. The GREEN DRAGON has something in its
talons.

INT. COMMAND HEADQUARTERS—DAY

RIPPLE manipulates the controls on the command
console, gazing out a picture window at the seascape
beyond.

                RIPPLE
  Gotta see you off right, pro.

Ripple whirls around and swings his hatchet. It connects. Blood flecks back across Ripple's face.

EXT. SKY—DAY

The GREEN DRAGON hurls its bundle sideways into the air, and the YELLOW DRAGON ignites it with a sustained surge of flame.

CLOSE on the bundle—revealed to be TRANK's dead body— incinerating. The flesh and bones char and disintegrate, and even the titanium implants melt away to nothing: only the thinnest scattering of ashes drifts down to the waves below. The Slay Boat floats by, still mysteriously undestroyed.

Ripple's ax head glides through the air. It's easier swinging it the second time.

INT. THRONE ROOM—DAY

King RIPPLE, now middle-aged, sits in a big leather easy chair with the command console glowing on a stand by his right hand. He wears glasses and signs several long, scroll-like official documents on his lap desk.

The ax flies up and down almost on its own, again and again, spraying blood in its wake.

INT. THRONE ROOM—DAY

King RIPPLE looks up to the portrait of TRANK from the Fire Museum's lobby. It appears to gaze back down at him benevolently.

> RIPPLE
> You taught me well, pro. Here's to another decade of peace and prosperity in our city.

Ripple finally drops the hatchet. He is standing over the gory, steaming, chopped-up mess of what was once a man. Trank is no longer a single entity; he is a substance all over the roof. The most recognizable piece of him is the bloody, slashed-up Tarnhelm at Ripple's feet.

TITLE CARD: The End.

27

KINGDOM OF THE SKY

"I wish you'd eat something," Sharkey says, watching Swanny from across breakfast plates topped with tundra moose fatback (not easy to come by) and fried eggs. She warms her hands around a mug of coffee, staring into the steaming blackness. Daylight doesn't do her any favors. Her black eye is a penumbra of swirling violet, blue, and green, on skin as pale as a page from an unread book.

"I . . . I just don't have much of an appetite, I'm afraid. I'm just so terribly exhausted."

"You slept a little." He can still feel her, heavy and warm against his shoulder, her breath coming out in little delicate susurrations. Nice and easy. Since she came to, she's been anything but.

"Please don't make me eat," she says, and bursts into tears.

"What's the matter with you? Why are you so scared of me all of a sudden? I killed your ma before we ever met. Nothing's changed. Stop crying. I *am* gonna kill you if you keep crying all the time."

This outburst does nothing to staunch her tears, which hiccup and bubble out of her uncontrollably. Sharkey throws down his fork.

"I'm gonna go make some chaw."

"No, please, Howie." She wipes anxiously at her eyes with a napkin. "Don't be angry at me."

"I'm not angry. I just want you to knock it off."

"Yes. 'Pull myself together,' as you put it earlier. I am. I will. Mother always said I was far too high strung. A touch hysterical, that's what you get from too much nitrous oxide as a child. Of course, I am also exhausted. Will you be angry if I say I think I have a broken rib?"

When Sharkey was a kindling, a stray cat used to follow him around. An orange one. The cat was missing an eye, so he called her Winks. He fed her little bites of whatever he found scavenging on the street and when her socket got too oozy, he disinfected it by throwing hooch in her face. Winks seemed to understand, or maybe she just liked the hooch. But one time Sharkey woke Winks up too sudden and Winks jumped up scratching and Sharkey kicked her in the ribs. In Torchtown, when you don't have family, you fight to kill; that's the very first thing you learn. And back then Sharkey never took off his steel-toed boots. The dent of his shoe in Winks's guts is one of the images he least likes to recall. He used to dream about it all the time, before he started seeing the future instead of the past.

"There's bandages in the bathroom," he says, looking away. "You can tape yourself up."

"Thank you."

"You don't have to thank me for every little thing."

"Would it be all right if I took the day off?"

"I didn't expect you to work today." Maybe this'll scab over. He's more patient than he used to be. Gentler too. She trusted him before. He reaches over to take Swanny's hand; her fingers are like ice. "Look. Maybe you feel like you're in some kind of nightmare right now, but you're a smart girl. You'll get used to it."

Swanny nods, blotchy and swollen. "I suppose I shouldn't keep you from your work."

"I got some errands to run around town, but I'll be back for dinner." Sharkey gets up, straps on his holster. "Be good."

Swanny lingers in the kitchen long after he leaves, in front of the gelid fatback and gluey eggs. After almost an hour, she takes a bite. For all her life, Swanny's mind has been aflow with ceaseless internal narration, an authorial monologue of assessment and commentary on her current state of affairs. Now the voice falls silent. Sharkey's reference to a "nightmare" seems apt. She feels frozen in one of those panic scenarios in which one's open mouth proves incapable of emitting a scream. She wonders if she really does have a broken rib, or a cracked one; it's difficult to prod the bone through the thickness of her flesh. All she knows is that it pains her when she sobs, and if today so far is any indication, that will make for a major inconvenience.

"Swan?"

Swanny startles back, almost capsizing her chair, at the tap on the window. She pulls up the blind to reveal Duluth hulking on the fire escape outside.

"The shop was closed, so I came around," he grunts, stooping to squint in through the pane. "You seen Grub and Morsel? They never came to the meat locker last night." Swanny vaguely remembers that Duluth lives in some decommissioned freezer, the only extant part of a butcher shop long since dragon-burned to the ground. "Not for night scraps, not for bed."

"Night scraps?"

"You know, the scraps I give 'em before they go to sleep."

"That's very kind of you."

"They're my boys." He shrugs, and for the first time Swanny realizes that the children aren't orphans. They're Duluth's sons.

"Oh. No, I'm afraid I haven't seen them." But her mind flashes to the twins, huddled beneath the counter. Surely they couldn't have stayed there all night. Surely they couldn't still be there now.

"Swan?"

"Yes?"

"You all right?"

She touches her face self-consciously. "I . . . fell."

Duluth knows better than to pursue this line of inquiry: "Well, lemme know if you see 'em."

He thuds back down the fire escape; Swanny marvels that it can support his weight. She supposes it could support hers too, if she chose to escape. Did Grub and Morsel sneak out this back route in the aftermath of yesterday's horror show? But then why didn't they rush home to their father? Were they too traumatized by what they witnessed? Or—the thought persists—were they so paralyzed with fear that they never left at all?

Swanny gets up and sidles down the narrow hallway to the Chaw Shop showroom. She flips on the electrolier. The scene is tidier than she left it. The bullet holes remain in the floor, like outsized cigarillo burns, but Sharkey's already spackled the dent in the wall from the shot that grazed him, and bleached a couple of spots where one or both of them bled on the rug. She walks around to the other side of the counter. The bare floorboards here creak beneath her feet, as if this place has been sealed up a hundred years, not less than a single day. She peers beneath the counter. *SLAKELESS*, cobwebs, one of the twins' slingshots, forgotten in a hurry. But not the boys themselves.

Swanny exhales, uncertain why she's been holding her breath. Then she sees streaks, faint and rust-colored—drag marks from the space just under the register, leading toward the door. Parallel lines. Even if she isn't a girl detective, she can still spot a clue.

But he didn't kill *me*, she thinks. He must truly love me, if he didn't kill *me*.

The thought is almost gratifying, and then the full import of it strikes her. Sharkey is evil, and she belongs to him now.

It should have been her. It should have been her.

Like a sleepwalker, Swanny drifts over to the wall of mason jars. She's survived enough killing offenses, near misses, and diagnoses that she feels immortal. But anyone can die, if she puts her mind to it. *Chaw brings you very close to death*, that's what Sharkey told her.

She reaches for the jar marked DEAD MAN'S CHEST, always one of their top sellers, and pops the lid. The scent of waterlogged cedar greets her. She picks up the shears and cuts off a sizable two-penny chunk of rope, then brashly inserts it in her mouth. Her tongue numbs almost immediately, yet somehow an awareness of the flavors asserts itself in her brain. Beneath the aromatic wood, she discerns sea salt and a delicate metallic taste, like filaments of gold. Ill-gotten treasure, the kind that dooms you in the end.

Swanny chews. And chews. And chews.

~~~

Sharkey gets back to the shop around nine. It was harder than he expected to fob off the corpses of the twin kindlings. Torchtown's landlocked, a concrete cell, it's not like you can just dig a hole. Plus he had to do this one careful; he doesn't want Duluth finding out. If Duluth did find out, Sharkey'd have to kill him, hide *his* body, then find somebody else to trust with the limo. And it's so hard to find somebody you can trust.

Sharkey washes the blood and lime off his hands at the hydrant outside his house and pats his gator on the head. Poor fucker hasn't gotten a chance to sleep in the bathtub since Swanny came to live at the shop. The price you pay, he guesses, for a woman's company.

Maybe she won't kill him. But he's never been wrong before.

He lets himself in the front. All the lights are out inside. She might be upstairs, in her bed. Or on his couch. He pictures her nestled under the afghan, paging through one of his books, sucking on her fingers while she teethes. Reading, and for pleasure. Most torchy girls don't even know how. The luxury comes to her as natural as breathing. He doesn't know why it stirs him, but it does.

He's about to climb the steps to the second floor when he hears her singing in the showroom, a lullaby offered up to the dark, a disembodied voice trying to soothe itself to sleep. It's a pretty tune. He steps inside and flips on the electrolier. Swanny is all balled up in the corner, hugging her knees.

"I committed suicide," she whispers, her baby-doll eyes even wider and more vulnerable than usual, despite the shiner. "Oh my God. I've taken poison."

"What did you take?" It's a strain not to slap her in the face. "What did you *take*?"

"I—don't remember . . . the pirate flavor, to start with . . ."

"Talk sense. I got antidotes upstairs, you've just gotta tell me exactly what you took."

"And then there was the funeral home . . . and cherry cordial?"

Sharkey slowly looks at the floor around where she's sitting. Gnawed-down plug ends litter the carpet around a weirdly fragrant spittoon.

"Golden Apple Jam, that one I recall for certain."

Sharkey sighs, straightens his hat. "Put your face on. We're going out."

"Excuse me? I'm quite certain I overdosed. I've been chewing for hours."

"Yeah, you overdosed all right, but on the wrong thing. Chaw can't kill ya, you crazy broad. Where'd you even get an idea like that?"

"From you—you told me. 'It brings you very close to death,' you said."

"That's not what I meant."

"Well, what did you mean?"

"You're gonna have an interesting night. Try not to puke in the car."

Sharkey calls Duluth on the walkie-talkie and tells him to bring around the limo right away. He picks up his backpack from the showroom closet. Then he wraps Swanny in her chinchilla and leads her outside.

"Oh, how lovely, it's snowing," she murmurs, reaching her hand up skyward.

"These things you see, they're not really there," Sharkey informs her. "That's important to remember."

"You mean the snowflakes?"

"Yeah. And whatever comes after."

He opens the car door for her, shields her head as he guides her in. Gets in himself and slams the door.

"Drive us to Nick's," Sharkey tells Duluth, then slides the privacy screen shut. Who the hell knows what might come out of Swanny's mouth next; he'd rather keep the big guy deaf to it. Though right now, Swanny isn't saying much of anything. She's studying her hands like they have some special fascination for her.

"Do you read palms?" she inquires.

"Palms? Can't say that I do."

"I have a very short lifeline, you know."

"Seems like that should be the least of your worries, if you're so set on offing yourself." He looks at her, snuggled in her fur, sonsy and ringlet-maned, that pillowy mouth in its eternal pout. So soft. She only shot him once. "Why'd you try a thing like that anyway? After everything I've done for you. You're a real selfish girl."

She reaches into her handbag and takes out her compact. "It was the only way I could escape you."

"Escape me? I didn't lock you up. I didn't chain you to a radiator. I didn't hang you upside down by your ankles. You could've escaped just fine."

"No. No, I couldn't have." Powdering her eye.

"All those books you read, you're too dumb to find the door?"

Her mirror clicks shut. "The only way to escape you is death."

"And why is that?"

"Because I can't live without you." She says it sweetly.

Sharkey looks out the window. He's boiling over inside. But not with rage, with nothing he's used to. It's like the way she says *Howie*. A name nobody ever called him before, but once she said it, it was his. *I can't live without you.* The words are his now, she can't take them back. He wants to hear them again, up close, hot in his ear. He wants to press her to him and stroke her and squeeze her until she can't help but say 'em, over and over. *I can't live without you.* Nobody ever loved him before. The feeling's too big for his chest, for his limo, bigger than the Outer Walls of Torchtown. Big as all outdoors. He won't look at her until it passes. Maybe it'll pass.

"Why not live *with* me, then?" he asks huskily. "I can be nice."

She shakes her head. She still isn't afraid to contradict him. "No, you can't."

~

Nick's is a former theater, its slide-lettered marquee out front still strung with stranded characters like an unfinished crossword puzzle:

TH T REEP NY OPER L ST 3 PER RMANCES. They're in a part of Torch-town Swanny scarcely recognizes, within sight of the northmost Outer Wall. Automated sniper turrets and a filigree of barbed wire assert themselves against the moon. Duluth parks at the curb and they disembark.

"Where are you taking me?" Swanny asks, as if there's any doubt. Except for Nick's, the rest of the block is burned to the ground, a sootscape of dumpster huts and cinder-block forts, a graveyard of architecture haunted by the poorest of the poor, the lowest of the low. She draws the chinchilla coat tighter around herself, watching for the dragons, but all is still. For now. Though the snow seems to have passed, she still feels its icy pinpricks on her skin.

"You oughta see this place while it's still here. It's a relic. Like me."

Nick's box office is illuminated; a dog-collared hostess waits in a cage of gold and glass. When she notices Sharkey, she immediately presses a button that releases the door for admittance, with a buzzing that sounds exactly like a dentist's drill. Another building with elec-tricity: Swanny thought the Chaw Shop was the only one. Sharkey holds the door open and gestures her inside.

The theater has been converted into a supper club of sorts; most of the seats have been unbolted and removed, to make space for dark-cloaked tables, each lit by a single candle, and mismatched chairs that wobble on the sloping floor. Down in the front, just before a stage shrouded in crimson velvet, is a mostly empty parquet danc-ing area, manned by a bucket drummer who's keeping his rhythms to a steady pulse. This minimalist tableau is at jarring odds with the room that contains it, a cathedral to amusement, worked over with aureate embellishments and festoons rendered in plaster and domed, up top, with a ceiling mural of constellations, their dots connected with silvery spiderweb precision against the midnight blue.

"You like it?" Sharkey asks her. "I always used to come here when I was real chewed out."

"It's so . . . strange." Swanny has never been out to a restaurant before, and it's most curious to experience for the first time in her

present condition. Colors have taken on a hazy, impressionistic quality. Waiters, clad in white coats like surgeons, rove among the tables,
carrying off the bones of the eaten.

"I used to know the guy who owned this place. One of my best
customers. Nicodemus Satan Cannibal Jr. He took his name off the
old inmate who ran the joint before him. Then he left it to some
kid he trained. Nicodemus Satan Cannibal III. Pieces of work, all
of 'em."

"Like a succession of kings," Swanny murmurs. Or like the Ripples, she thinks.

Sharkey signals the maître d'. "Hey, Rollo. Seat us in the box."

When Swanny was just a girl, Corona used to speak of thin
places, locales where the membrane separating this world from the
next was stretched to its outer limit, an unguarded border between
the countries of Before and After. Swanny has never before visited
such a place in waking life, but tonight, reality feels permeable. She's
uncertain how long she's been floating, viewing the dining room
from the perspective of a lost soul above an operating table. She
wonders how long she's been clutching Sharkey's hand.

"Don't try to fight it," he advises her. His touch is her only tether
to the physical world. His dusky red aura enhalos her body, holding
her inside. "It's only chemicals."

"Yes, but Howie, what does that even truly mean?" Her own
voice sounds so very muffled and distant; she wonders if it's audible
to human ears. "Love, hate, fear, joy—desire—religious ecstasy—
imagination—perception itself—our entire interface with reality
and the universe as we know it—can't every last one be attributed to
a series of enzymatic reactions in the petri dish of the mind? Aren't
they all 'only chemicals' too?"

"If you could see your pupils right now, you'd know what I'm
talking about."

With a *pop*, the chair asserts itself beneath Swanny at last; her
spirit reattaches to her physical form. They're at a table in a balcony,
just the two of them, a brass guardrail holding at bay the hubbub
below.

"Atta girl," Sharkey says. "Stay with me."

The waiter arrives, a singularly unappetizing individual. Three of the fingers are missing from his right hand, and even before he speaks, his jittery energy upsets whatever weak equilibrium Swanny has achieved. "Mr. Sharkey, good to see you again, sir. Would the two of you like to start with something to drink?"

"She needs to get some food in her stomach," Sharkey pronounces. "What are the specials?"

"Tonight we have the chef's singular rat balls, at least seventy percent freshly harvested rat meat and less than eight percent sawdust, served on a bed of something we found—reminds me of polenta. It's good."

"You got anything a little less revolting? She's from Outside."

"Oh, I don't think I can eat," says Swanny. It's the most curious thing yet: a fog is rolling in, gray and muddlesome, and with it comes the sensation that the room is filling up—not merely with vapors, but with presences, malevolent and otherwise. "Not in this weather we're having."

"You'll eat," Sharkey tells her. He turns back to the waiter. "Anything with less than twenty-two percent unaccounted for?"

"You always were a numbers man," the waiter concedes, glancing at his missing fingers. Tendrils of miasma nudge the stumps. *The smog warms its thin hands, and falls asleep.* "For the diner discerning enough to request another option, there's these cans of dead dog. All ground up, we've been mixing it with noodles. That's the stroganoff."

Sharkey is skeptical: "Never had dog meat from a can."

"It's got a picture of a dog on the label." Following a menu's logic is impossible in this murk; Swanny wonders why he can't just leave them be.

"That means it's *for* a dog, not *from* a dog. Listen, let's save some time here. I want you to go downstairs and tell your chef to make something fit for human consumption. We'll take two of those."

At last, the waiter phases out of view. The fog now fills Swanny's entire frame of vision; even just across the table, Sharkey seems so far away.

"What's happening to me?" she asks. "I'm up in the clouds and I can't come down."

"They're not clouds. And those weren't snowflakes either."

"No?"

"Nah. They're smoke and ashes. Ashes, then smoke. Passing through." Sharkey takes out his chaw wallet, removes a one-penny plug. "Bringing back what they took."

"What do you mean?"

He works his jaw on the dose. "When something's gone, it's gone for good. But it leaves a space behind. A negative space. It used to be that when I chewed, I'd see smoke and ashes dusting over all the negative spaces. Making it so I could see what was missing. Sounds like that's starting to happen to you."

"But you said the things I'd see wouldn't be real."

"They ain't. Not anymore." Unlike the waiter, Sharkey is a familiar of these mists. His melancholy allows him to dissolve, ever so slightly, into the air she breathes.

"How did you learn to make chaw?" she asks.

"Same way the last Nick learned to run this place. An old inmate taught me."

"Your father?"

"Not all of us grew up so cherished as yourself."

The waiter returns triumphantly: "We had a couple of these left in the deep freeze. Less than a year past expiration."

GRANDMA BETTY'S MILITARY RATIONS, reads a logo printed on the clear plastic wrapper affixed to the top of the tray. Inside, a bloodless slab of protein lies alongside mysterious purees of yellow, green, and orange. ♥ HEART HEALTHY ♥

"I liked this place better under the old management," grumbles Sharkey. But for once, Swanny isn't focused on her food. The waiter startles as she grasps him by the wrist.

"How extraordinary," she murmurs, examining his ruined hand.

Where earlier she saw only stumps, she now sees fingers, tapering to elegant completion, rendered in translucent grayscale. The lined knuckles, the nails, even the whorling prints, are all delicately visible, sculpted from the ether. "But wait. This didn't happen in a fire."

The waiter glances at Sharkey uncertainly. Sharkey answers for him: "Not a fire." As soon as she loosens her grip, the waiter skitters away.

The smoke dissipates, like the ashes before it. Swanny is out on a date with her mother's killer, a murderer of children, and an apparent torturer too. She looks longingly down at the dining hall below. A saw player has joined the bucket drummer, and the parquet floor is filling up with writhers and swayers.

"I'd like to dance," she says. She doesn't add, *alone*. But he hears it anyway.

"Stay where I can see you. And leave your coat."

Swanny descends to the dining hall below. Without Sharkey's anchoring presence, the floaty feeling returns, but this time she doesn't discorporate; instead, she's light, so very light that her feet barely skim the ground. She's been heavy all her life: heavy of flesh, heavy of heart. But now, for the first time in recollection, gravity is her friend. She moves into the crowd of torchies—sparkers, cocottes all—and they move together, almost weightless, particles agitated by a flame.

Enjoy life, for our sake.

You will never die.

She lets herself forget.

Swanny only stops dancing when she notices the cat. Or rather, the space a cat left behind. The feline phantasm slips between the feet of revelers, as lithe as a magician's scarf. Swanny works her way out from the throng to follow it as it stalks between the tables, finally leaping atop one to lap at an abandoned jar of Embalming Fluid.

"Here, kitty," Swanny coos, and the specter looks up, alarmed. Its ears are frayed, its left eye gouged; in its place is a hollow socket, seeping ectoplasm. A one-eyed hooch-drinking ghost cat. But Swanny's never had a pet, and it's too late to be choosy now. She takes another step toward it, and the cat leaps down, darting into the shadows, past an Emergency Exit sign and down a dim hallway to the right of the stage. Swanny isn't quite sure why she follows, but she does.

"Kitty?" she calls, scaling some wooden steps, pushing open an ajar door marked PERFORMERS ONLY. But *Felis domesticus* is hiding, or else dematerialized. Swanny takes a look around. She's standing on the forsaken stage. The scene is still set for some long-ago production, most likely a musical or cabaret; two chairs face each other across a narrow table and instruments rest here and there, collecting dust. One in particular attracts her attention. It's as though it's been left out just for her.

Swanny once called the klangflugel a "tuned typewriter," because that's what it resembles. The instrument before her now poises on its rickety stand, brass and badly kept, its winglike bellows faded at the creases. Swanny places her fingers on the keys, forty-one little metal disks indented for her fingertips—*specifically* for her fingertips—and taps out a few soft chords. The velvet curtain is thick enough to dampen the music; if she keeps it pianissimo, no one will notice she's back here.

"Close the door behind you."

Swanny looks up. Her mother sits over at the table, glowing gray and transparent, smoking a cigarette. The puffs leaving her mouth look just like the rest of her, but while they dissolve, Pippi stays. Her left arm is invisible where it touches the light slanting in from backstage.

"Mother," Swanny says. She wonders at her own unsurprise. But of course this is exactly whom she's journeyed here to meet.

"Come in or go out, but make a decision. There's a draft."

Swanny shuts the door. Her mother lights candles on the table as if she's performing a séance. Swanny takes the seat across from her and watches the flames.

"I hope this isn't the sort of place you frequent," Pippi says. "A man won't take you seriously once he's seen you dance."

"Women in general, or just me?"

"That applies to all women, darling, even the ones who dance well."

Pippi flicks her ash off into the air, but it evaporates to nothing before it sprinkles the tabletop.

"Mother, I didn't know you smoked."

"I didn't use to. It's like we always used to say at McGuffin: 'You can smoke when you're dead!'" She laughs brightly. "We had such gallows humor about it all. Scavengers feeding on a corpse. 'Content will be the last industry to go,' we said, and we were right. But it all goes eventually. It all goes, so you have to snatch it while you can."

"I suppose so."

"That's not advice, Swanny, that's a statement of fact. You don't merely want to *survive*. You must do what it takes to *thrive*. Always. My mother was a survivor, and I can tell you that woman had nothing to teach me. Do you know what's the best cure for dishpan hands? Suicide."

"Grandma committed suicide?"

"No, but I would have if I were her. Or rather, I would have killed my stepfather and made it look like an accident."

"You've never really talked about them before."

"You're a grown-up now. All bets are off."

"I don't think I'm so very grown up."

"Nonsense. Of course you are. You've taken charge of your own life, and that's more than most women do at any age."

"I'm a traitor to everything I once believed."

"You're a risk taker."

The question comes out in a rush, without preamble: "I hope Howie didn't kill those little boys. Can you tell me if he did?"

"Sharkey is safeguarding his reputation, which is entirely sensible, given his line of work. One can't allow all kinds of nonsense to keep circulating; it's a PR disaster. And my personal differences with him aside, I think you should respect his privacy. You're not responsible for what he does."

"I know he killed *you*."

"That's between him and me, dear. I appreciate your concern, but don't go poking your head in where it doesn't belong."

"Do you mean you've formed . . . some kind of alliance with Sharkey?"

"Who made the chaw you chewed tonight?"

"I . . ."

"Oh come now, Swanny, I know you're on drugs. I saw you dancing."

Chastened, Swanny looks down at the table. There she sees a series of images from her childhood depicted, via the swirling candlelit wood grain, in etching-like detail. In one, little Swanny discovers a half-dead rabbit, caught in a trap amid the high grasses. In another, she and her mother play a hand of Guillotine at the dining table while Corona serves them after-dinner Sauternes. In a third, sick and delirious, she clings on tight as her bed floats out the window into the night sky.

"You're having a drug experience right now."

"I suppose I am," Swanny admits. She stares into her mother's face. The features are all there, even the tune-up scar, yet they're also sharply absent. Through Pippi's translucence, Swanny can see the stage set's backdrop, a dusty canvas painting of an antique, lamp-lit street. "Mother, I miss you. I never thought I would, but I miss you so."

"Keep tempo," says Pippi. "Don't get distracted. You were born for great things, Swanny. I know you won't disappoint me."

Swanny looks back down at her hands and watches them moving upon the klangflugel keys. She hadn't even realized she was singing:

Take me up, Mother, to your kingdom of the sky
My wings are beating and my fire won't die
I don't need a machine to fly
I don't need a machine to fly
I don't need a machine to fly
Into the sky—ohhh
Your kingdom of the sky . . .

The music moves through her hands, her throat, with such force that it seems like it could never stop without destroying her, but then at long last, she raises her trembling fingers from the keys and she's still there, she's still standing, and where the stage's curtain used to be there are a hundred sooty-sweaty faces gazing up at her from the dance floor, silent, waiting to see what she'll do next.

~~~

Sharkey is waiting for her at the stage door in his endless top hat, that long tunnel of satiny dark. Chewing.

"Have a nice visit?" he asks, in the tone of voice he uses to answer his own questions.

"You're a sorcerer." She takes a step nearer. Gravitating toward him. She hasn't forgotten the names of colors. His eyes are Caviar, Inkwell, Black Magic. "A necromancer. You kill, yes, but when you cook the chaw, you bring back what you took. Your art—it isn't just a drug. It's access to the beyond. You have that power."

"You say that like you're surprised."

"I didn't understand before, but now I do. That's why death has no meaning for you, isn't it? Because you've risen above it."

"Dead still means dead, Swanny. Nothing you see is ever gonna change that."

Swanny has always been attracted to Sharkey, from the very first moment his hearse pulled up at the curb beside her, when he was just a faceless voice in a death car. Only now, though, does that attraction insist upon itself as a basic human need. She melts into him, pressing the words into his zoot suit lapel: "But you *made me see*."

"Yeah. That's what I do." He helps her on with her coat; the fur is so welcoming it's as though he's tucking her into bed. "You've got a secret power yourself. Who taught you to sing like that?"

"I always wanted to." She thinks back to the klangflugel lessons of her childhood, the dreaded tock of the metronome, her mother checking off missed notes on the score. She caresses his chest. Inside, his heart is keeping its own kind of time. "Take me home, Howie."

Then they're in the limo. Swanny is shocked at her own behavior; desire has seized her, turned her body into its shuddering puppet. Before the vehicle even moves, they paw and tongue and yearn, crushed against each other on the banquette.

"Kiss me, oh, kiss me." Utter surrender may be violent, but sometimes violence is the only solution the fallen can know. *Damn the whole vexatious torment of the last fortnight.* "How can I want you so badly when I'm already in your arms?"

" 'Cause that ain't all you want." She has to admit, he's absolutely right.

Dragons: if they didn't exhale, would their heat sizzle them from the inside? Just as the limo pulls away, the old theater explodes behind them.

"I left something behind," Sharkey says. "Just for you."

Roman candles and bottle rockets and jumping jacks unnerve the blackened sky. Former untorchables run out, on fire, screaming. Swanny can't tear her eyes away from the window. It's just like her vision the day she arrived in Torchtown: *people made of magma, dissolving and consuming one another constantly.*

Sharkey wraps his arm around her shoulder and pulls her close again. He tells her, "Don't be scared. I got ya. Shhh. You can shut your eyes."

When she opens them again, they're back at the Chaw Shop, embracing against the inside of the door. Her coat drops to the floor; she thinks of her mother's fox fur carelessly strewn in the Ripple lobby. That's how to know you're home, when you can toss your things anywhere.

"Am I hurting you?" Sharkey presses his finger against her gum, where the tip of a pointed canine is just about to break through.

"It feels rather . . . good, actually." Her tongue moves against his knuckle when she speaks.

"It's euphoria. Everything's euphoric right now. That's what chaw does. Releases the pain. Lets it all out." His hand moves away from her mouth. There's blood on his fingertip. He touches it to his lips. "Come upstairs."

"I suppose I should warn you now. My husband says I'm frigid."

Sharkey places his palm against her forehead. It's a sensation Swanny has felt a thousand times before, sick in bed as a child, when Corona or the dentist would come to take her temperature. But it's never felt like this. What a sensation it is to be reached for. To *be* the place where flesh meets flesh. To be alive, still, after everything. She shuts her eyes. Tonight, he will possess her, leave her naked and bitten and filled with him, no inch of her untasted or unconsumed. But this is how it starts: his palm against her brow.

"You're burning up," he says.

PART THREE

SIREN BENEATH THE WAVES

~~~~~

If you forget my name, you will go astray.
—BJÖRK

28

MAGIC

This is a story of inheritance—of what parents leave to their children, the curses and the gifts. Of how our families call us home, even when return would mean forsaking everything we have.

~~~

Abby is talking to the city.

When the fire chief zapped her, Abby felt nothing. All sensation left her mortal form, and for a moment, she wondered if this was what happened to Dunk on his wedding day, when he went into the Toob, became of it. Had the invisible bolts translated her from flesh and blood and bone and hair into a creature of pure idea, a pixelated essence immune to touch? She experienced neither pain nor pleasure as she watched her wilted husk flop over Trank's shoulder, journey lifeless in his arms to the truck-bed mattress, submit limply to the ropes he wrapped around her and knotted at her wrists and ankles. It was only after he shrouded her with the blanket, committing her to darkness, that she returned to her body. There she became aware of the strange new power coursing through her veins.

She is the city at night. The lights flicker on one by one.

The electricity activates each cell, illuminates it. The switches flip in a cascade of awareness, an awakening like none she's ever known. Abby lies still, but not paralyzed; she wants to receive what is happening to her without feint or deflection. And when the whole of her lifts toward the sky in frozen fireworks, a grand imaginary architecture asserting itself, when she glows and hums, no longer human, it is then that she hears Empire Island speak.

The city's voice is not like Dunk's or the Lady's, made of sounds in the air, or like Hooligan's or Scavenger's, made of transmissions to her mind. The city speaks wordlessly, in vibrations she feels all throughout her body. She is tied to it with a million quivering strings. And those strings are electricity: the city's grid, mapped onto the very core of her. Abby feels the voices of all the machines plugged in. The fridges, bovine and complacent; the Toob screens, raving and hallucinating; the electric blankets and power strips and shameless, dazzling lamps. These machines are not individuals, in the same way as human beings or magic animals; they are a hive, a colony, many making one. And for that reason, even stronger than the voices, Abby feels the city's wounds. The disconnections. She feels each exploded fuse, as raw and pained as a severed nerve ending. And she knows, beyond a doubt, that the *dragons* know the hurt they are inflicting on this living thing, broken, beaten, cowering beneath their wings.

But why, why?

The dragons are torturing the city for information.

But why, why?

What does the city know that they don't?

Abby is at the cusp of that knowledge. Then the lights begin to dim. The electricity pours out the tips of her fingers and toes. For an instant, she is a starburst and then it's gone. Blackout.

She lies under the blanket, motionless except for muscles twitching again from the ebbing voltage. The mattress is unnaturally soft beneath her. Everything is unnatural.

"The machines are alive, just like you and me," she whispers, aloud, in the voice she uses for communicating with humans. She's speaking a foreign language. All her life she has feared the People Machines, feared electricity above all other forces. But electricity is not a tool for evil. It's not a tool at all. It's nothing made by man. It's energy, the soul juice of matter. It's life itself.

—ID: /?/ – TYPE ABBY?

—Scavenger! I thought you ran away!

—protocol requires observing all violent interactions at a safe, concealed distance.

—You couldn't have fought him off anyway. Here, nibble at my ropes.

When Ripple pulls the blanket off an hour later, the rat is still nibbling.

"Thank fuck you're OK." He fumbles with her bonds, flopping her back and forth as he yanks at them. His red long johns are splattered almost purple in places, chunky-sauced, the fabric starting to stiffen. He smells like salt and fear and rusty iron. "We've got to get out of here."

"Dunk?"

"Yeah?"

"Why are you all bloody?"

"I don't want to talk about it." He frees her wrists. She rubs them, sitting up, as he tackles the ropes around her legs and ankles.

"Is he dead?"

"Wench, what did I *just* say?"

She picks a glob of brain off of his chest—over his heart—and inspects it. "Dunk?"

"*What?*"

"Are you really going to kill the dragons next?"

He turns away, tugging at the knots around her ankles. "I have to do something."

"But do you have to do *that?*"

Ripple doesn't answer, doesn't seem to have heard. She reaches for the top of his head, to trace furrows in his tousled hair, the way that once soothed Hooligan, but he jerks away as if she's shocked him.

Her longing to connect is sharper than a pain. The lost voltage has left behind an empty space in every cell. The second he gets her loose, Abby scrambles down off the mattress. She makes for the nearest electrical outlet and jabs at it with her fingernails.

"Fem, stop it!" Ripple pulls her away. "Why are you trying to kill yourself?"

"I want to talk to the city!"

Ripple sinks to the floor, buries his face in his hands. "You're—so—weird!"

She regards him, gore-beslimed and curled in a fetal position at her feet like something born too soon. The first time she saw him, he was damaged too, his arm slashed and dripping, his parachute tangled around him. But he seemed so perfect then, a gift from the universe to her. She lay beside him for hours, staring into his face—ostensibly to make sure he kept breathing and protect herself in case he woke up, but really because the pleasure flowed into her ceaseless and intense as she memorized him, every freckle and clogged pore, every flake of dandruff and rivulet of drool, every eyelash a wish come true. She would never be alone again, now that he had come. And for a while she wasn't. But in the days and weeks that have passed since she followed him home to the mansion, she has felt more alien than she ever did when she believed herself to be the last of her kind.

The last of her kind. Maybe she really is. Maybe she doesn't belong in Dunk's world after all.

—i have not yet made my final determination. but your willingness to place another's safety above your own supports my hypothesis that you pose no threat.

Scavenger is perched on the edge of the mattress, picking rope fibers out from between his tiny teeth. Abby steps around Ripple and scoops up the rodent.

—Thanks, Scavenger. You're sweet.

—i am perceptive.

"I guess I should take a shower," Ripple utters from the floor. He heaves himself up to his feet and looks at her. "I wish I *understood* you, you know? I wish I knew what you're thinking."

"I wish that too," says Abby, half to him, half to the rat in her hand. But as Ripple makes his way to the bathroom, it's Scavenger who answers her:

—he never will. he is a control.

〜〜〜

Ripple has never figured out why the Fire Museum contains a baroquely decorated bathhouse, or why there's an additional admission turnstile outside of it, saying 18 & UP, ONLY next to a solid-gold men's room sign, upon which the masculine silhouette wears a tiny fireman helmet of rubies. The entrance is right there on the first floor, just past the coat check: they must have steered the kids away from it on his class trip. Was it open the same hours as the rest of the museum, or did they reserve it for galas? And . . . was it some kind of sex club? It's a labyrinth of gleaming tile, with pirate-ship wheels for knobs to the various faucets, including a bunch of hydrotherapy massage and other hose extensions. Neatly stacked white towels wait in baskets everywhere. Ripple's been showering here for a month and a half, and he still hasn't run out.

He stands under the pulsating showerhead—the water pressure is amazing—and tries to feel every drop of Trank's blood, down to the molecular level, powerwash off his skin. It didn't *really* happen, he tells himself. Nobody filmed it.

But try telling that to the Metropolitan Police Department. They graded his worksheets; they issued him his Junior Special Officer badge. Although he hasn't met any of them in person, he's going to be their number-one suspect, when and if they dispatch somebody over to the museum to check on their independent extinguishment contractor.

As bad as he feels right now, Ripple has never understood the villains in movies who feel compelled to confess. He's never gotten the point. "Pro," he's wanted to say when various content purveyors have presented him with this scenario, "your pregnant wife is already dead. You know that, you hid the sledgehammer yourself. No amount of time you spend eating baloney bones in jail is going to bring her back." *Wanting to be punished* only makes sense to Ripple in relation to the "Dungeon Master" folder in his porno collection. And that goes double now that he's in this situation himself. More than anything else that's happened in his adventures, the idea that he killed somebody—*self-defense, self-defense,* but the word is still "kill"—and might be brought to account for it makes him want to go running home to Mommy.

Except, his parents are dead.

Ripple tries to masturbate, since that usually makes him feel better, but um. Not the right moment apparently. So he gives in to the other vice he learned to indulge under the fluid- and sound-masking deluge of his private shower back at underschool. He lets himself cry. It's such a relief, he wonders why he doesn't do it all the time. I'll cry forever, he promises himself, I never have to stop, and when it occurs to him how depressing that thought is, it just makes him cry even harder.

Trank: an exploded blender of meaty pulp. Multiple puddles, at least one with a finger floating in it. Ripple can't bury the body. It's everywhere. It's all over him.

Ripple stands under the water for a long time, letting the steam rise, letting his fingerprints prune and his ears slosh. He stays there until he feels human again. He's almost ready to turn off the spray when Abby enters to join him.

"You're totally naked," Ripple observes.

Abby turns around under the water till her hair hangs in wet strings over her eyes. "I'm naked for you," she says.

This is new. Abby doesn't usually initiate sex, not so directly, unless you count climbing on top of him, which is pretty much her go-to move in nonsexual situations too. Ripple touches her boob experimentally. He isn't exactly in the mood, but it's definitely better than stroking off. At least according to his cock.

"All right," he says.

Fucking in the shower is a logistical nightmare. Every surface involved is slick and slippery, the tile as unforgiving as ice. Ripple presses Abby against the wall, barely inside her, trying to lift her up, to get a foothold, to keep his face out of the shower's spray.

"Is this OK?"

"Uh-huh!" She's smiling at him, kind of intensely—like there's something she knows that he doesn't, something right behind him, just over his shoulder. He resists the urge to turn around, instead nuzzles his face into her neck, shuts his eyes. *I'm inside her*, he reminds himself, yet the thought—once so potent he forbid himself to think it till he was about to come anyway—doesn't send him rocketing toward climax. Instead, he sees the inside of the Witch Church again, not on fire but this time *alive*, the hammer-beam trusses replaced with rib bones, the walls pink, yielding flesh, breathing in and out . . . a chest cavity so big he could make a whole life inside it without ever attracting the creature's notice or attention . . . except he has, it knows he's here, and what's worse, it wants him to stay. . . .

You are not the one.

Ripple opens his eyes again, sees the comforting spiral of Abby's ear, illuminated brilliantly under the ceiling of electric white.

"It's you," he reassures himself, "it's just you, you're Abby, you're my girl."

"*Listen*," Abby says, and the lights of the bathhouse gleam still brighter, until all at once they burst and the entire space plunges into darkness.

"What the snuff?!"

"Oops," says Abby. "I'm sorry!"

"Why are you sorry?" Ripple is no longer inside of anything. He cranks off the shower, feels around for his towel. Thankfully he's wearing flip-flops. The sole of one crunches on some lightbulb glass. "We must have blown a fuse." Unless Kelvin's prediction is finally coming true. *Water and power are probably next.*

"No, it was me."

"What?"

"I told you. The electricity woke me up. I can talk to the city. I was trying to send you a message, but only the lightbulbs heard."

"I know you got tased, but it's not demonic possession, OK? You can't explode lightbulbs with your mind."

"It wasn't my mind. It was my heart. I wanted you to know you're in my heart."

Is insanity sexually transmitted? Ripple can't continue this conversation. He gropes his way through the dark showers, toward the room with sinks, where the lights are still intact.

"Dunk? Dunk, where are you going?" Abby follows behind him, deft and unhesitating: what, does she have night vision now?

"Fem, I'm in a bad place. I need you to stop making things up."

"But I'm not." She looks at his electric razor, plugged into the wall below the mirrors. It buzzes to life. "See?"

No way. No way. No. Ripple grabs the razor, yanks it out of the wall, hurls it to the tile floor. Its plastic carapace cracks, but it doesn't turn off. It still buzzes, vibrating and shimmying, blades oscillating. "Turn it off. Turn it off!" Ripple yells. "*Make it die!*"

She looks very sad. The razor stills.

"I love you," she says.

~~~

The first time Abby visited the Ripple mansion, she flew. Returning by land, she feels the gravity with every step she takes. She never knew her own slight body could weigh so heavy on her. She wishes she could leave it behind somewhere, to "wander lonely as a cloud," like somebody on the Toob said during a feminine hygiene advertisement. On the Island, she spent whole days scrabbling over the dunes. But she always lay down in the shade of a tire tower, or curled into a cradling nest of junked upholstery foam, before exhaustion truly claimed her. On this march, though, they take no breaks. Her feet, as callused as they are, chafe on the endless asphalt. Her knees quake in the shadows of the dragons who pass overhead from time to time, the size of bad weather, blocking out the warmthless sun. Ripple doesn't pause. Abby knows that if she stopped, he wouldn't stop with her. He'd sling her over his shoulder in a fireman's carry, or worse, leave her behind.

"It doesn't matter that you killed him," she tells Dunk, whose hand feels dead and untender in hers. The sky is fluorescent white and sunless. Soot and garbage swirl in the howling wind, in the canyon formed by skyscrapers. The chill bites at their skin. "He would have died anyway. Everything dies. The Lady used to say that the People Machines want to be the only people on the face of this Earth. But they just want to survive. Everything wants to survive, but nothing does. It's sad but it's OK. As long as *something* survives, it's OK."

"Uh, yeah." Ripple points to the next intersection. Her words don't seem to comfort him at all. "Time for us to hang a right."

Ripple uses a tourist map from the old admissions counter to guide them. He wears his ladderman's uniform. His civilian garb was ruined forever in that first fire. This is all he has now. Abby wears her Dalmatian suit from the gift shop. She remembers swimming naked in Nereid Bay, which she knew then only as the water—the water, inviolable, constant, ever-changing, meeting the air in a skin of ripples. Abby came from the water up into the air, and one day she would return to the water. She knew that then. She knows it better now.

"Why are we going to the house if it's burned?"

"Because we've got to see for ourselves, OK? Because it's my home."

For miles, they encounter no one amid the hollow buildings, but as they move northward, Abby glimpses wet laundry on a clothesline, eyes peeking out through chinks in a boarded-up window, human urine staining a wall—she can tell it by the smell. They're getting farther from the dragons' dominion, farther from the city's pain. When they edge off the grid, first onto an exit ramp, then onto the Lionel Roswell Expressway, and then down, down, down, into the tunnel that runs under the river separating Empire from the Heights above, Abby feels an unexpected calm. The city's distress thrums in her on a molecular level. She doesn't know it's there until it's gone.

"I wish I had a match or something," Ripple says, his first words in hours. "I can't see shit."

"Why would you want to see that?"

—put me down. i will utilize night-vision sensors.

—We might step on you!

—you will not.

Uncertainly, Abby reaches into her pocket and takes out Scavenger, where he's been riding quietly. His white fur shimmers, the only visible object in the tunnel's gloom.

Ripple blinks. "Your rat glows in the dark?"

She shrugs. "He's magic."

The muscles in Ripple's jaw clench and unclench. Abby doesn't have to read his mind to know he's holding in a scream. But why? Scavenger is unnatural, but everything is unnatural. "You're full of surprises today."

They follow Scavenger through the dark, a rodentine will-o'-the-wisp, a beacon guiding them onward. The tunnel is long, longer than Abby could have possibly imagined. She thinks back to the night they ran away, the underground zone that funneled them toward Leather Lungs. Who will be waiting for them after their next rebirth? As they near the dusk coagulating at the passage's far end, Abby hears an unmistakable rumble. Thunder.

That's God saying we can't be found.

Ripple flips up the hood of his slicker and steps unceremoniously into the drizzle. Abby does the same with her Dalmatian suit; the ears flop around her face. She scoops up Scavenger, already wet from a puddle, and follows Ripple up the steep incline toward the house's gates.

The mansion is a shipwreck dragged to higher ground. Abby can see that even before Ripple applies his digit, then his fist, to the slashed and mangled fingerprint-recognition lockpad. As partly unhinged gates shriek inward, Abby and Ripple follow the circle drive around toward the hole where the entry hall once gleamed like a spacecraft. It gapes now like a fatal hull breach.

The lobby is all char and shards. In the fountain, the colossus stands headless and dismembered, his severed arm—still clutching the trident—in pieces at his feet. Farther in, past the grand stairway and elevator, the burnt-out structure has fallen under its own weight in places. In others, rain leaks through, pouring into roof holes, sluicing down between the scorched and jagged floors. A sooty chandelier glistens darkly on the ground like a beached jellyfish. Carpets bristle like urchins, spiny with shards of glass.

The house is just a rift for water to pass through. No amount of bailing can keep it at bay.

"Sorry," Abby whispers, touching Ripple's slicker with one tentative hand. He flinches. She can't rescue him from this. He never learned to swim. Now he's going to drown.

Abby wanders alone toward the back of the mansion. The Hall of Ancestors is a crud grotto of blackened frames and canvases already mildewed from exposure. Abby picks up the portrait of Ripple, lying facedown on the spongy rug, and leans it against the wall. The oil paint is heat-blistered, sullied with ash, washed out from the damp. *Wanderer Beneath the Sea of Smog.*

—came back came back you came back!

Abby doesn't have time to look up before the animal tackles her, pinning her to the ground and assaulting her face and hands with eager slurps.

—Hooli! I thought you were dead!

—waited and waited and waited and waited and you came back!

His whole body squirms and wriggles, carpeted joy alive to her touch. They hug.

—love! love! love!

—I love you too!

—ERROR. predator detected.

—Oh! Scavenger.

Abby sits up and pulls the lab rat out of her pocket. He smooths his fur furiously, disheveled from the encounter.

—Let me introduce you. Scavenger, Hooli. Hooli, Scavenger.

Hooligan waggles, sniffs the rat all over. Scavenger cowers.

—magic rat. play now.

Before he can pounce, Abby sternly pulls him back by the collar.

—Play gentle. You don't want him to end up like Magic Bird.

—EMERGENCY PROTOCOLS ENACTED.

Scavenger darts away, squeezes through a gap in what's left of the wainscoting, and disappears.

—rat gone. sad now.

—Don't worry, he'll come back. Come on, let's find Dunk! He'll be so glad to see you.

As she and Hooligan meander through the Ripples' disintegrating interiors, Abby thinks back to the circumstances of their parting.

—Where's Swanny?

—left me. got in a street machine with a smelly man.

—What kind of smell?

—yucky. scary. bad dream. death.

Dunk appears around a corner, as stiff-limbed and shambling as a walking corpse.

"Look who I found!"

Hooligan makes the hang loose sign and tries to high-five his old buddy, but Ripple doesn't even smile.

"He's the only one?"

Hooligan circles around Ripple, nudging his head under Ripple's hand.

—love! love! love?

"He came all the way back by himself. He's been waiting for us."

—love? love? why no love?

"Uncle Osmond?" Ripple calls, turning away from them. "Anybody?"

—sad. sad. nobody home.

—Are you sure?

—show you.

Hooligan bounds across the room. Near a staircase to nowhere that cranes hopelessly up into a second-floor chasm, he digs in the rubble, dislodging a mound of crumbled, smoke-stained plaster and melted insulation. He recovers a sticklike object, which he holds in his useful mouth as he returns on all fours to drop it at Abby's feet. It reminds her of the Lady. It is a human femur, charred meatless.

—it's the big one. but his bones don't speak.

"Huh?" Ripple's eyes widen. "Is that . . ." Without warning, he kicks Hooligan in the ribs. "Bad! Bad! Bad dog!"

—sorry sorrrrry sorrrrrrry.

"Stop it, you're hurting him! He's just trying to show you."

"Show me what? That he can treat my dad's leg like a pizzle stick?"

"He wants you to know what happened."

"*He* doesn't know what happened. He doesn't know anything. He's just a dog! And that rat—is just a rat! And you—it's like you're not even human. I mean—I mean—what the snuff, Abby? Who are you? When I took you back to civilization, I thought—I thought you'd catch on, start acting normal, you know? But—superpowers— and telling me it's OK to murder people—and—and—you just get weirder all the time! I thought Swanny was scary—but this—I can't handle this!"

His face is still so beautiful. That human face.

"Everything dies," she whispers. "But it's OK. Something survived. Love."

She reaches for him, but he shakes her off.

"You just don't get it, do you? I need somebody to *talk* to. I need my *family*."

When Abby was just a girl, when she still played in the shallows and drank with the Lady from the small pink cup, when she was the simplest possible version of herself, she dreamt always of a friend—another child, a small grubby person unconcerned with the alchemy of food hygiene or the workings of the Lord, a playmate, a fellow architect of trash castles built to withstand the pummeling of the tides. She tries to conjure this figment now, to coax him into concrete detail.

The first inspiration for him, she realizes, was her own reflection.

"We're your family. Hooli and me."

"Go away and leave me alone," he says.

It is still raining when Abby leaves the Ripple mansion for the second and final time. It is raining outside, and inside of Abby's heart. She walks back down the sloping drive, listening with her mind, but although Hooligan follows at her heels with Scavenger riding on his back, the magic animals do not speak to her. They don't know what to say. Neither does she. But before they enter the tunnel at the bottom of the hill, she addresses the dog.

—Hooli, you can go home. Stay with Dunk.

—stay with you.

—But he's all alone.

—stay with you. keep you safe. love.

—You loved him first.

—love you more.

Abby can't answer that, can't reject it. She doesn't want to. At least someone loves her most of all.

The tunnel yawns, as dark as the inside of Abby's eyelids closed in the dead of night. But this time, she isn't afraid. Even if something is waiting for her in that blackness, she can't hurt more than she hurts already.

She will always be alone.

Abby thinks of her life on the Island before Dunk came. She thinks of the few, pleading fish that she tossed back out of her nets into the waves, and of the day she first met Cuyahoga pecking out the brains of a desiccated gull—the joy and relief she felt at finding other creatures capable of communication. But she learned then what she still knows now: an animal will never fully understand her. It isn't their fault. They just can't. No matter how many times Abby grinned or laughed at one of the vulture's wry remarks, no matter how many dead mice or limp minnows she tossed into that beaky craw, Cuyahoga never gave her a smile in return. For that, Abby had to turn back to the teeth left in the Lady's skull.

Yet, when Abby finally met Dunk, a creature with a body like hers—a *human*—there was still a link missing. They weren't made of the same stuff.

—Hooli? Do I smell like other humans you've known?

—every human different.

—But is there anything special about me?

—nice smell. good smell. familiar.

—Familiar how?

—magic i guess.

Abby thinks this over as they exit the tunnel. *Magic*. Some animals can speak; most can't. And she's the only person she's ever met who's able to hear the magic ones' voices. Even the Lady never could.

But where does the magic come from?

The rain shower stops abruptly, but instead of light breaking through the clouds, a shadow envelops them. Abby stops in her tracks and looks up. The yellow dragon is gliding overhead, its bat-like wing flap a vast umbrella. Hooligan whimpers till it passes.

"Electricity. It's the juice they feed on," the Lady once told her, speaking of the People Machines. "It's what they used to build the dragons."

Abby knows it can't be true. No one built the dragons. The dragons are alive. But so is the city, and someone built that for sure. What if the People Machines can build living things? What if they did build the dragons?

—Scavenger, I know why you came to find me. I know why you were inside my mind.

—proceed.

—It's because we came from the same place. Because we were made by the same . . . people.

—i can neither confirm nor deny your theory.

—You've known me long enough to tell me the truth.

—cannot confirm. i did not complete my cortical search.

—But that's what you were looking for, isn't it? Proof. That we're related. That I'm part of the colony's history somehow. Stop keeping secrets. You know I'm not a threat.

—reconfiguring privacy settings.

Scavenger hops down to the pavement and pauses for a long moment, his fuzzy brow furrowed, his pink ears twitching in concentration. Abby stops walking and stares down at him. Hooligan tilts his head in confusion. The dragon has passed. Dog fur drips in the rain.

—your supposition is CORRECT. 91% of present colony members hypothesized a connection between the colony's history and your own when you called.

Abby remembers her finger in the dialer's faceplate, the receiver at her ear. The squeaking on the other end.

—Your number was in my Bean?

—i was tasked with locating the source of that call and gathering conclusive data.

—Is Hooli one of us too? Is that why he speaks our language?

Hooligan tries to sniff Scavenger's butt. Scavenger climbs back on top of his head, holding wet tufts of apehound pelt in his naked shriveled paws.

—the apehound is a recalled commercial product. we are experimental biospecimens. at least, i am.

Abby looks from the rat's paw to her own hand. The intricate whorls of her palm. It's all she's ever known. She hasn't known it at all.

—Why did the Lady bring me to the Island? Why would she want to protect me from People Machines if I *am* a People Machine?

—maybe she was not protecting you. maybe she was protecting others from you.

—But you said I posed no threat.

—not to us.

—Then take me to the colony, Scavenger.

29

FERRYMAN TO THE UNDERWORLD

Like our now-defunct system of trains, the sewer gondolas are aged, filthy, and underground. Unlike the train system, they tend to keep a strict schedule and the berths are never crowded. You might imagine them a lovers' form of transport, but the creaking of an ancient hull in sludgy, waist-deep flushwater tends to rob a journey of romance.

Most passengers hire the shitboats because they fear fireballs roaring down onto the surface streets, but have an unmet need so urgent that they cannot eschew the city just yet. Mongers, thieves, the delusional bereaved—in his new vocation as a gondolier, Osmond Ripple is only too happy to oblige them all. Rowing his humble craft, a onetime maintenance skiff with a rusted motor, or pulling it along the slimy pipe walls with a handy long-necked plunger, he tells tales of the various ills of the city and how they've affected him personally.

Osmond transports his passengers through the northmost territory of sewer only; his route stretches from upper Empire to the middle of the Heights. So when he collects a fare headed northward, they're almost home free, far from the torchies and drake fires, halfway to Upstate and the siren kumbaya of the endtimes lumberjacks. But sometimes, they want to go the other way. Downtown. He takes them as far as he can, then hands them off to the next oarsman in the chain and watches them recede, southbound, into the darkness—heedless souls returning to the city, for profit or revenge or occasionally disappointment, searching through those cinders for someone they loved and lost.

"Your father, eh?" Osmond asks this afternoon of his young charge, a precocious boy of nine or ten, who slouches, staring into the feculent trench fluid. The pipe is nearly twenty feet wide, a lazy river of silt.

"Yeah." The kid draws his knees up to his chin and hugs them. It's chilly down here in the sub-subway and he hasn't got a coat. His rustic hand-knit sweater contrasts with his manufactured pants: a child of two worlds. The last suburbanite. "He used to HowTruck in post-evac supplies, canned goods and stuff, and sell them to the park trolls. My mom says he's dead, but I think he left her for another woman."

"How long has he been gone?"

"Almost a year. But right before it happened, I found a condom in his wallet. That must mean he's still alive."

"Clearly he and your mother just didn't require any more nosy, thieving children. Prophylactics are a sire's heart crying, 'Never again!'"

"Nah, that's not it. My parents always wanted more kids. They were saving up to get me cloned."

"Hmm. Perhaps they dropped you on your head as an infant and longed for an unmarred version."

"What I'm saying is, they were . . ."—the boy closes his eyes, either out of embarrassment or mnemonics—"*fertility deprived.* So why use a condom? He must have had a girlfriend. He must still be in the city somewhere. Living with her."

"Isn't the most likely scenario here that your father was philandering until the moment of his untimely demise?"

"No way, that's impossible."

"Why?"

"Because that would be too many bad things at once."

"Ah. So your father can either be flawed or departed, but not both?"

The boy sets his jaw in a stubborn frown. "He wasn't so bad."

Osmond rows in silence as the child takes out a Boy Toy hand-held and mashes its buttons mindlessly. Osmond never expected to become a sewer gondolier. He was not even aware of their existence until, two nights after he set fire to the mansion, he took shelter in the ruins and heard voices rising from the emergency access sewer hatch. After forty-eight hours of nothing but rainwater and chewed sticks for sustenance, he was thinking none too clearly and set about the perilous descent down the manhole rungs without any of his usual caveats. His little legs dangled helplessly into the abyss, but he clutched on, shouting threats and bribes, and when at long last he reached the docking platform, he discovered Gondolier Josh and a skiffload of fares, sallow-faced in their lantern's glow, looking on with mingled pity and admiration. The stench presented itself syn-aesthetically then, an undulating brownish-yellow haze. It was as if Osmond had squeezed through an ensorcelled portal right out the anus of existence.

"You've got strong arms," the oarsman observed, "want to help me row?"

It was, Osmond reminds himself, the only position offered.

In his new employment, Osmond has found his life forever changed. The gondoliers rarely leave their boats. Bathroom func-tions are completed by going over the side—an acrobatic feat for a paralytic, but Osmond is gaining new skills all the time—and they live on foodstuffs bartered to them by fares. Sleeping twelve fathoms deep, in hulls that rock like cradles, they are safe from the dragons, safe from the sun, safe from the wind. Safe as men long buried in their graves. That suits Osmond just fine. He doesn't even mind the smell much anymore, though he isn't a fan of the gators.

"During my training, Joshua referred to them as 'floaters,' lead-ing me to believe they were vast coagulations of human excrement, gnarled and lumpbacked through the sculpting of the waves," he reminisces now. "Imagine my surprise when I nudged one with my pole, only to have it gape jaw and bare its fangs. It struck me as a nightmare begging for psychoanalysis. To be consumed by one's own leavings is truly to vanish from history."

"That's pretty gross, mister," says the kid. "Are we there yet?"

"Nearly," Osmond replies, after sniffing the air. His senses, once refined to sample craft brews and the cruelest varieties of foie, are now his nervous system's fine-tuned GPS.

He arrives at Port 41, where Gondolier Hugh is waiting to take the late philanderer's son on the next leg of his voyage. Hugh, a stooped albino with oozing face sores, grudgingly offers Osmond a packet of jerky and a quart of fresh water to fortify him for the return trip.

"Be well." Osmond bestows naught but a fervent handclasp in return.

The brotherhood of workingmen is less unpleasant than he imagined, Osmond reflects on the way home, deftly plungering his way around an intractable clog in the middle of the pipe. There is something to be said for sharing one's labor and one's profits. A blessing and a curse—at least unfortunates are never alone.

The runaway boy tonight reminds Osmond, perhaps inevitably, of his own wayward nephew and his mind drifts back to Duncan, his only relation possibly still dwelling upon this much-emptied globe. As he docks the skiff back at his home station (a block of stained concrete beneath the embers of his family estate—a headstone marking below what lies above), he finds himself humming and, in time, belting out, a familiar tune from that beloved timeworn classic *Back There Again*, the lone work of valuable literature he had once imagined Humphrey's offspring capable of comprehending:

"*Under the City, within the cave,*
Dwarves mine and hoard what all men crave.
The great Machines hunger for fuel:
An ugly ore, Earth's darkest jewel!
The dwarves carve out the space below
Another city, one hollow.
Above, mills whir, furnaces roar
Beneath, dwarves near the molten core.
Horrid beasts lurk in tunnels deep

Who, once awakened, never sleep.
They crack through the land's thin, frail crust,
Reduce all they see to ash and dust.
Oh men of Earth, do hide and flee!
Our race's time has ceased to be.
Leave Fallen City far behind,
Lest like Uncle here, you lose your . . . miiiiiiind . . ."

Though applause might not have shocked him at the end of his performance, he could not be more surprised to hear the response his serenade does receive: an astonished shriek from above the manhole.

"Uncle Osmond! You're *alive*?"

〜〜〜

It takes some convincing to lure Duncan down into the sewer, but once he descends Osmond does his best to make him comfortable. He lights another lantern and offers his nephew his new gondoliering cloak, an ingeniously constructed fleece blanket—with sleeves!—which he won in a riddling competition against one of yesterday's patrons.

"And I thought Hoover Island was bad," Ripple observes, taking in his surroundings. He's changed since they last saw each other. His face, once characterized only by the untroubled serenity of the developmentally delayed, shows signs now of existential consciousness, even humanity. Also, he's acquired the musculature of a male ecdysiast. Perhaps he's followed in his mother's footsteps these last weeks? But one does what one must to survive, Osmond reflects, regarding his own unnaturally tautened biceps.

"I didn't know there were enough people left in the city to make all this ass fudge," Ripple adds.

"Fewer than there used to be." Osmond uses his oar to tap a high-water mark on the curving wall of the pipe, several feet above the current flow. "Once upon a time, these pipes gushed with the man mud of millions, perilous yellow-water 'crapids' that required a speedboat to subdue. Alas, that mighty tide has weakened to a trickle."

"Too bad, I guess."

"I find it difficult to cultivate much nostalgia for the bowels of strangers, now that our entire family is dead. You do know that our family is dead, don't you?"

"Yeah. I didn't really believe it till I saw the house."

"The same fate awaits us all. We are but tinder, burning in the fires of time, one generation after the next. Which reminds me: after you come into your inheritance, we'll need to discuss the terms of my bequest. As I recall, your father left you everything with the explicit stipulation that I live out my later years in the comfort and splendor of my ancestral home. Clearly that ship has sailed."

"I can't believe this is happening."

"A cosmic irony, yes. Sometimes evolution selects the non-breeding male."

"I don't think evolution's got anything to do with it."

"What are you insinuating?! In my darkest hours, I will confess, the thought of fratricide did at times dangle, a bauble for the jealous mind. But I always knew that without Humphrey's sanity and protection, I would fall prey to my own worst impulses—be made to wander the Earth decrepit and alone. And so it shall ever be. Meanwhile, the thought of expending a murderous effort on your mother is patently absurd; even if I'd wanted to, she was adept at a sexy array of ninja kicks and ate next to nothing, which rules out poison. Show me a single profit I've made from their demise—then and only then I'll dignify your accusation with a response."

"Uh, I didn't mean *you* killed them. It would be pretty dumb for you to burn down our house."

"Of course." Osmond colors slightly, the shameful warmth of guilt alive and spreading under his skin.

"I mean the whole situation," Ripple continues. "It wasn't supposed to be like this. I don't think I could even keep going if I didn't have a goal."

"A goal?"

"I'm gonna take out the dragons," Ripple explains, by all appearances entirely serious, "and I need your help."

"Oh, no, no, no, no, no. I've trod this path before, nephew."

"You don't get it. There's this command console that can tell the dragons what to do. All we need to do is find it and figure out how it works. We can tell them to kill themselves. Maybe there's even a Self-Destruct button on there."

"Ah, the fabled 'operations transmitter'?"

"You know about it?"

"It's an old, old chestnut—an urban legend, if you will. There's no such thing."

"Nuh-uh. I heard the city hired this one guy to look for it."

"And where did you hear that?"

Ripple looks at him steadily—clever, no, but eerily sentient. Humorlessly sober too. "I'm going to do *something*. I've got to."

Osmond reaches under his captain's seat for the tackle box he keeps hidden there, flips back the lid, and strikes a match. Ripple cringes as the flame illumes.

"Pro, don't keep lighting lamps, I don't really want to see . . . what the snuff, you do *drugs* down here?"

"The change of scenery has worked no wonders for my affliction," Osmond exhales, offering Ripple a puff on a one-hitter cunningly devised from an upcycled spigot. His nephew hesitantly accepts.

"Don't get me too swamped, though, I still have to explain my plan."

"*You'll have time to murder and to birth / To burn a name upon the earth*, as the poem goes," Osmond consoles him. "Besides, some chemically enhanced fortitude may be required for you to endure the rest of this discussion."

"Huh?" Ripple coughs. "Oh fuck. This is worse than the first time I smoked. I have been, like, loam revirginated."

"I'm speaking of your parents' suicides."

"Wait, what?"

"If you will recall, your sudden departure coincided with a violent home invasion—one our private security firm failed to contain, most likely because they were either bribed or had other plans that night." Osmond tokes again. "Your father, watching on the panic-room monitors, concluded our cause was lost once the marauding crew broke out the gasoline."

"So it *was* the cyanide pills." Sobriety and reason drain from Ripple's features like dirty bathwater; he's a mental incompetent again, but a heartbroken one this time. "What about Mom?"

Katya's suffered the last of Osmond's bon mots: "Loyal to the end."

The two men pass the spigot back and forth in sympathetic silence as the docked boat rocks on putrid waves. A gator drifts by, a floating log of malice. In the lantern's flickering glow, the domed ceiling of the pipe crawls with spidery shadows, a phantom forest of night branches, grasping.

"But," says Ripple, with some apparent effort, his eyes completely crossed, "I still don't understand how *you* got out alive."

"If vengeance is your aim," Osmond smoothly elides, "there's no cause to despair. A handful of Torchtown brigands will be far less daunting foes than the dragons. And they are, of course, the ones entirely responsible."

"Take revenge on the torchies." Ripple unhappily contemplates. "Thanks, but no thanks. I don't like killing people. I'm never doing it again."

Osmond notes the "again," but decides not to inquire. "Never say never, my boy."

"No, I mean it. It just isn't . . . me, you know? Not the way I want to be remembered. Next time, I'd rather just die." He looks like he might cry, but instead he shakes his head and changes tack: "Besides, Swanny probably took care of that already."

Osmond chuckles. "Oh, *did* she now?"

"She was headed there the last time we talked, all powered up for a rampageathon, so yeah, probably . . . Stop laughing like you know something I don't. What's this pink fuzzy thing in front of my face?"

"That would be your nose. Young Duncan, believe it or not, down here your old uncle is privy to channels of information undreamt-of in realms above."

"The sewer made you smarter?"

"What I'm referring to is the connection between these subterranean but nonetheless lawful waterways and the forbidden plumbing of Torchtown. It's all supposed to be quite closed off and inaccessible, but nothing stays sealed forever. Pollution seeks its own level, you know. At any rate: I now redeem my prescription"—he indicates the tackle box—"from a commuting loam bearer by the delightfully mercantile name of 'Mart.' His primary occupation is to hawk his wares to one client and one client only: the infamous chawmonger of Scullery Lane."

"So that's why it's so strong."

"Stay with me, kinsman. Mart journeys weekly from an Upstate marsh farm, down through our gondoliering canals, and then farther south still, to passages unbeknownst, where he plies his narcotic trade. The life of a traveling salesman is a solitary one, no matter how convivial his wares, and I've found him most talkative on a variety of subjects. Including his eccentric patron. It seems that the aforementioned chawmonger has, through some unsavory means, lately acquired that rarest of possessions: a young lady of breeding and refinement, with whom, one must assume, he takes the most ferocious liberties. Mart tells me that she's battered about the face, marked with love bites, dizzy with chaw at all hours of the day— yielding and compliant to the monger's roughest touch. Wait, here, I have some extrapolations I've sketched out based on what he's described."

Ripple flips open the composition notebook that Osmond hands him to a random page and reads aloud: "He thrust deeper, pushing her to another brink. 'Spit in my mouth when you climax,' she whimpered greedily, 'that nectar of drug and tongue is the only taste sweeter than your—'"

"Never mind that." Osmond snatches the folio back. "Have you guessed why I've relayed the matter to you in such detail?"

"You're lonely?"

"Because I'm speaking of your bride. The Baroness Swan Lenore." Osmond waits a beat for this to sink in. "The torchies haven't just driven your parents to suicide, Duncan. They haven't just burned down your house. They've taken your wife, and their leader has her still."

"No way. It can't be the same fem."

"The baroness is a witch's cauldron of mingled passions, nephew. Rage and lust, fury and desire. It surprises me not at all that she's succumbed to sensual depravity in the arms of a swarthy crime boss."

"Pro," Ripple is shaking his head, "pro, she would never."

"Then go to Torchtown and prove me wrong."

"Look, the first thing I need to do is slay the dragons, then I can start worrying about . . ."

"Forget your fairy tales, errant knight! No man can slay the dragons. No man can 'save the day,' as goes the tired phrase—minute by minute, it falls away from us, regardless of our best intentions. But there is 'something you can do'—something that requires little more than a venturesome spirit and an indomitable will. A feat for which intelligence is hardly a prerequisite."

"What's that?"

"*Love.*"

"Uh . . ."

"Come now, I refuse to believe you're still tampering with that dead-eyed wretch you found in the waste yard. You're like an infant who prefers a soiled diaper pail to any of his toys."

"We broke up, actually."

"What a terrible shame, I hope you'll stay friends. But for the purposes of our discussion here, a useful tidbit to consider. Now, back to your wife—"

"Swanny doesn't want me back."

"You have no way of knowing that."

"I'm not even famous anymore. And I'm homeless. And"—he stares at his hands with mingled shame and fascination—"and anyway, she's frigid."

"That's not what all of Torchtown's been hearing in the middle of the night. Besides, she's in grave danger, surviving daily at the pleasure of the psychopath directly responsible for the deaths of all your parents! You married this woman, you clumsily deflowered her, I'm assuming, you abandoned her for a soup-brained temptress, you forsook her in her hour of need—and now you're concerned about your *penis*? Duncan, I'll never have a son, as any spinocologist would gleefully report, but looking at you I feel nothing but unqualified relief. I cannot imagine the disappointment your father would be experiencing right now, or rather I can, and it—GGAAACCCK, he's choking me, he's coming up from the inside—" Here Osmond slumps forward for several seconds, until Ripple touches him lightly on the shoulder in concern, at which point he sits bolt upright and stares vacantly, hollowly, like one hypnotized, into the middle distance. "Duncan?" His voice is crisp and assertive. Executive, even.

"Uncle Osmond?" Ripple whispers, definitely spooked.

"There's no one here by that name."

"Pro, this better not be a joke."

"I don't have all day for this. Let's 'parlay.' Now, from what I hear, son, you're in the process of shirking your last responsibility to any other living being on the face of the Earth."

"Yeah, Abby took Hooli with her when she left."

"That dog is a money pit, forget him. You need your wife. She's intelligent and sensible and she'll make sure you stay alive. I've done the diligence on her, just trust me on this one. Offer whatever you have to, to keep her on your team."

"But what if . . ." And here, for a moment, Ripple's face takes on the aspect of one far older and wiser, pained and haunted beyond his years. "What if she won't forgive me?"

"You're the hero. You figure it out."

Osmond slumps backward in his seat, tongue sagging dramatically out the corner of his mouth, eyes gaping blindly. He makes a great show of slowly regaining his senses.

"Where am I?" He fans himself. "How much time has passed? Oh, what a relief to be back in this crumpled envelope of flesh!"

Ripple scrutinizes Osmond. "Do you seriously not remember what just happened?"

"Test me."

"Talk like you're impersonating my dad."

"That's utterly impossible, my voice can't sink to that register. Only by surgical implant could such a thing be accomplished."

"Whoa. Then maybe his spirit really did possess your body."

"Good Lord! What did he say?"

"Set a course for Torchtown, and pronto."

~~~

Ripple is passed, prow to prow, port to port, down the line. Processed through the city's intestine. Seven hours pass. In the winters, his mom used to wear a helmet with lights on it to trick her brain into thinking sunshine. Osmond always called it her "miner's cap of the soul." Ripple could use one of those now. When he sees the sky again—*if* he sees the sky—he's going to feel reborn.

What would his mom think about all this? She liked Abby better than Swanny. Abby and Katya were more alike—even kind of looked alike—Ripple doesn't want to dwell on that. But his mom never saw Abby turn the lights off with her mind. Something happened in that moment that Ripple can't describe. It was as if Abby *changed* somehow, as if she stepped through the wall into fourth-dimensional space and came back . . . not evil, but *reversed*, maybe? *Initiated*, into some sphere he can't wrap his brain around? Ripple doesn't know. But when he saw Abby walking away from the ruins of the mansion with his dog and her rat, vanishing into the drizzly fog, he did know for sure that she was headed somewhere he didn't belong.

You have to do what you think is right.

That was one of the last things his mom told him. And it's the truth. He has to go with his instincts.

Which apparently means saving Swanny from the best sex she's ever had.

Ripple doesn't know if he should even buy his uncle's story, though. Drugs or not, he can't imagine Swanny nudifying for her mom's killer, unless she planned to stab his torchy neck when he went to unzip his pants. What could be in this for her? Nothing. Nothing. Yet Ripple does remember what she said on their one and only date: *We all have our urges.* What are Swanny's? She made him read that weird antique book, the dialogue so stilted it was like a foreign language . . . but it occurs to him now that maybe he should have paid attention, that the key might have been hidden in there somewhere, sneakily encrypted inside all those words. . . .

Does he even want her back? He tries to think of her beauty, or at least her tits, but she refuses to coalesce into an object in his memory. Always she is in motion: sulking, petulant, snarking, in tears, her voice and mannerisms actressy and insincere, her ulterior motives obvious or puzzling but seething visibly in every pose, every moue, every cutting aside. He isn't sure he even *likes* her, and yet here he is, riding sewer gondolas on waves of diarrhea farther and farther downtown to wrest her from the torchies. And what's the plan after that? They live happily ever after? No, his marriage is going to be full of screaming fights and silent treatments, conciliatory chocolates and diamonds. He'll probably have at least one more affair, maybe more, which she'll blow all out of proportion, exiling him to a separate bedroom until menopause strikes, at which point she'll get horny for the first time in thirty years, hot-flashing as she straddles him in an orthopedic bra, thanks a lot, Swanny. Picturing the whole thing makes him so annoyed he's about to tell the sludge-cabbie, "Turn us around, I'm headed Upstate," when it occurs to him to imagine his life without her.

The feeling is a trapdoor opening under his feet.

You need your wife.

"Are you married?" Ripple asks his final gondolier, who has the long, knobby fingers and deep-hooded eyes of a giant who forgot to grow to his full height. His hairless pate gleams in the lantern light—seamed across the top, as if once shattered and glued back together again.

"I was once," he says, and smiles with crooked yellow teeth.

"Any advice?"

"Don't let her play with gators."

"Thanks, that's . . . um . . . specific."

The pro drops the anchor, a cinder block on a chain. The entire tunnel vibrates when it hits the metal floor. "End of the line."

"Wait, what? You're supposed to take me to Torchtown."

"Those routes are forbidden. The city could take my medallion."

"You're a sewer gondolier! There's no way you're allowed to be down here in the first place."

"Tell that to the Public Hire Transport Authority."

"That's not even a real thing."

The gondolier holds out a card, besmirched beyond legibility with unmentionable thumbprints. "Then how did this get laminated?"

Ripple glances around. Nothing but sewage in every direction. "Help me out here. What am I supposed to do? I'd bribe you, but I'm broke."

From under his seat, the gondolier pulls out a pair of hip-high waders. "Walk."

～～

Ripple sloshes through sewage higher than his knees, squinting in the dark. He wishes he'd been able to convince the gondolier to lend him the lantern too. Or at least a candle. He's gone barely a hundred yards when he hears footsteps not his own ringing against the metal pipe and sees a flashlight beam flickering from around a curve in the tunnel ahead.

Torchies.

Ripple freezes. He's unarmed. Should he run? But where to? The gondolier already departed, and anyway, Ripple can't move fast in this muck.

". . . just saying that they could leave a few for when we get back from patrol. Just manners, is all."

"Nobody wants stale doughnuts, Gerald."

"I *grew up* on day-olds. I'm *made* of day-olds."

"You make every issue too personal. That's your problem."

"You are what you eat, Todd."

"You're saying we should expect the guys on sentinel duty to sit with a box of Loretta's sour cream old-fashioneds for six hours while we're down here? Because you identify as a *pastry*?"

"We're the ones in the danger zone."

"The poor fuckers maintaining the top of the wall are the ones in the danger zone. Torchies take potshots every time they can scrape two bullets together."

"Potshots sure, but who's more likely to get chainsawed? Them up there on the wall, or us down here in the dark?"

"Aw, stop trying to spook me. Torchies know to stay away from our patrol route. We always make plenty of noise so they can hear us coming."

"I'm just saying, maybe the firemen weren't so wrong to have a mutiny. Maybe we should try something like that ourselves."

"Over doughnuts? Gerald, we're not conscripted. If you don't want your pension, you can quit anytime."

Cops. Policing the tunnels. Catching criminals outside of Torchtown and throwing them back in. Ripple has an idea—maybe the first good idea of his life. Maybe not. He steps into the middle of the tunnel, holding his hands in the air. The flashlight beam catches him, shines right in his eyes. One of the cops shrieks, so high-pitched it sounds like echolocation banking off the walls.

"I'm turning myself in for the murder of Paxton Trank," Ripple says.

30

CHILD OF SCIENCE

By the time the Lady met Abby, the Lady no longer had a name. She had given it up, along with all her earthly possessions, the day she joined the Flesh Soldiers of God's Organic World. At that time, she'd been living on the streets as long as she could remember, which wasn't too far back, after the shock treatments she'd endured during her most recent stay in the Quiet Place. The Lady talked to God, always had, but when she fell in with the Flesh Soldiers, it was the first time she met others who could hear his voice too. The other Flesh Soldiers heard it clearer, even, since they were actually able to understand what he was calling them to do. The Lady usually just heard God grumbling about nothing in particular while she panhandled up and down the Black Line or washed her undies in the Bay. She talked back to him, and between her "delusional parasitosis" (as the doctors put it; she called 'em "stringy skin critters") and the sins of his world, they had plenty to keep them commiserating.

But the other Flesh Soldiers, they knew what he was after, what the endgame was. What was required of them in this life, and on into transcendence beyond: to stop the coming of the People Machines, whose time was growing nigh—the People Machines, who would be man-made but not men, the fruit of a lewd act with science itself. When the Flesh Soldiers laid out their plan for the bold crusade against the research headquarters, it struck the Lady as miraculous that God had made his orders so specific, even providing blueprints of the building and flak jackets for participants, bless his holy heart. She didn't trouble much over the prospect that not all of them would come back alive. The Lady didn't think much of this life; the best part of it was God anyhow, the nearness of him inside her skull, like the radio station she picked up through the fillings of her teeth. She figured that would go on just as well or better once death wiped out all the distractions: the chills and the sweats, the electrode headaches, the critter sores, the hunger and the thirst.

Not that the Lady suffered too bad from those last two, not since the congregation had taken her in with open arms. They holed up in an old bottling plant in North Crookbridge, below rusty smoke-stacks asprout with city weeds, just beyond the reach of those fireballs that roared down on Empire Island, that had been roaring down for three years. Between the chanting sessions and conspiracy theoriz-ing and pamphlet distribution, they drank boiled rainwater from tree-wood cups and ate bland garmonbozia made from chickpeas and lentils unmodified by man—most other food was teeming with "nanomachines and mutagens," robot crawlies smaller than a fleck of dust that might stay up your poop chute even after you'd cleansed with the leeches and the tubes. The life was monastic, sure, but it was the first winter in an age that the Lady had got through without frostbite, and come spring, she was pleased to give the Lord his due.

The laboratory complex was at the southmost tip of Empire Island, a glittering series of angular boxes like a crystal city from outer space. The scientists had a beachfront view, their workaday lives a vacation from God's will. The Flesh Soldiers rowed ashore in stolen boats. Technology had crept inside the human form and become inseparable from it, ghost hearts beating in human chests, baby skin growing on old bones. Technology had replaced pets and meat beasts with simulacra indistinguishable from true. Technology infected mankind like a sickness in plague time. The Flesh Soldiers were the cure. They wore bird masks. They carried obsidian shivs.

They killed their way inside. The Lady didn't enjoy watching the security guard bleed out the throat, but the good Lord always did like a sacrifice. It was once they were in that she got a funny feeling down in her guts. The rooms were tiled white and shiny, heaven and a bathroom combined, but the animals in them were just that:

animals. Like no machine she ever knew, shitting and shedding, growling and howling, molting their feathers on the floor. The lab rats squeaked when you stomped them. The monkeys were worse. The Lady lost her toleration for it quick. God whispered in her ear, "I got a special mission for you. Check down the hall."

She snuck away from the others. There wasn't but a single room down the hall he chose, all sealed up in one-way glass. The Lady took a gander in. It was a child's room, mostly stark and plain except for a few clowns painted on the walls and a picture of a ship. A plasma ball nightlight crackled in the corner, some scientist's idea of a joke. Electricity woke you up, electricity will help you sleep again. But the child—the child. The child was alive.

No more than three years old, but vanishing small, there in the hospital bed she lay. Soft blond hair fanned out on the pillows. A mouse of a girl. Hands like milk glass. She'd never been outside a day in her life. A more delicate creation God had never made. But God *had* made her, the Lady felt sure of that.

It was then, as she heard the footsteps of the other Flesh Soldiers coming down the hall, that God told the Lady exactly what to do.

~~~

The laboratory still looks like a crystal city from outer space. At least, it does to Abby. She does not want to go in, not right away. Although she's been on Empire Island for weeks, this is the first time since her own Island that she's seen the waves, felt the sand beneath her feet. Scavenger has guided her and Hooligan here, routing and rerouting them through the maze of skyscraper canyons and alleyways, past the Ladies of Rags and Cans, past the shaded windows of incurious Survivors just waiting for the flame, past the looming walls of Torchtown, ever southward. Now the lab rat points his little pink nose like a quivering compass needle at the entrance's code-locked double doors.

—FINAL DESTINATION in 15 METERS.

Abby looks back out toward the water, where the wet lip of beach lies smooth and blameless, unnamed.

—Maybe I should go home. I miss my Island.

—that is your prerogative. but we could mutually benefit from a reciprocal information exchange.

The apehound wags his tail, tilting his head in confusion.

—no go inside?

—Maybe in a minute, Hooli. Want to walk down by the water first?

But Hooligan is too cold and damp already. While the dog and lab rat watch, Abby strips off the Dalmatian costume to wade the surf alone and naked, chilly froth lacing the tips of her toes, her ankles. Her unshaven legs. The waves never linger long. Stay, she thinks, stay. She's freezing and miserable, but some part of her wants this moment to last.

I don't know who I am. Or where I came from.

What will Abby's life be like without those questions? She can't imagine it. Some other Abby lies in wait behind those laboratory doors: an Abby with eyes like searchlights, with hair like wires. An Abby who knows too much. An Abby no longer innocent.

"The People Machines take out your heart and put in a gear," the Lady used to say. What if all the explanations fill up the space inside Abby for hope, for wonder, for love? But the gears turn in her already. She picks up a scrap of driftwood, gnarled by the tides, and scratches a message in the sand. She does not know how to spell much, but she's learned a little by now:

The letters will wash away; they aren't hers any longer. That time is done. She does not belong to Duncan. She owns herself.

It is a kind of freedom to exist outside the gaze of man. Before she met Duncan, Abby was invisible, the soul of someone who might never be. She did not know where she ended and where the world began, so she was one with it. It was Duncan who defined her, fused her to this body. This skin, molded into the shape of *woman* by his groping hands. He gave her that much, at least. Now, alone again, she is not invisible but Unseen. A thing apart. Like God. Though she no longer feels God's presence—she hasn't felt it in a long time. Maybe what she once believed to be his force, his holy will, was simply the stirring of her own secret power.

She licks sea salt from her lips. It tastes like her blood.

"Let's go inside," she calls to the animals. Her human voice rings out, clear and musical, and though they do not speak this language, they understand. She climbs back up the dunes and meets them at the lab entrance. The architecture, a shattered mirror, reflects the looming clouds.

~

No human has stepped inside the laboratory for decades, not since they euthanized the final monkey, shredded the last of the files, and locked the doors forever. How much the place has changed. When Abby enters, naked and wet from the sea, she sees the logo over the information desk.

ABECEDARY
Life, Reinvented.™

Abecedary. Abby mouths the word. But it isn't her name. The spelling isn't right, and it is far too short.

Abby turns down a hall overgrown with cords and cables and wires, white and black and blue and gray, spliced together, plugged into jacks and outlets, the root system of a dozen ThinkTanks. At every keyboard, there's a lab rat, tapping at the letters with paws and nose, squinting at streams of indecipherable data with beady red eyes. It is like nowhere she has ever been. Yet, at the same time . . .

it reminds her of a hallway long ago, cold and sterile. *Tile everywhere gleaming. A ceiling of electric white.*

It is like walking into a dream. Only now, Abby walks this hall alone.

Lab rats turn to stare as she passes, her hair dripping, soles leaving footprints in seawater on the tile. Who else walked these halls the last time she was here, so long ago? Abby can no longer remember the faces of the scientists. Her years on the Island wore away their particularities, left behind only nightmare ghosts in bleached robes who drew her blood for examination. Who shaved patches of her scalp to attach the brain-imaging sensors. Who bathed her and measured the volume of liquid displaced.

But those ghosts did once live—perhaps they live still, somewhere far from here. Does a small Abby still dwell in their memories, trapped there forever, like a girl in a Toob? Or is it to them as if she never existed? She takes a scientist's bleached robe—a *lab coat*, the name returns to her like breath—from a hook on the wall and slips it on to cover her nakedness. The pocket is full of pens. The sleeves are much too long. They will always be too long. She is all grown up.

Abby remembers that the scientists never looked her in the eye, though she laughed and babbled and reached for their glasses and bonked them on the nose. She never understood why.

Now Abby reads the words written on a frosted glass door: LIVE SPECIMEN TESTING—LAB 4. She turns the handle and steps inside.

The laboratory faces the sea. A single massive picture window forms the room's far wall, framing the storm that's just begun: water above meeting water below.

The world is just a rift for water to pass through. That rift is closing now.

In the center of the lab, the cords and cables and wires from the hall converge upon a giant Drive. Abby does not remember this. It was never here before. During the years she spent in the lab, it was hidden from her, like so much else: stored in a windowless locked room in the basement, accessible only to those with full security clearance. The scientists wiped the data before their departure, powered it down for good. But now, here it stands, a cityscape of diodes and copper and black glass, taller than Abby and radiating heat, recalibrated and humming with information restored. The rats have been feeding it with every fact they can glean, every tidbit of history relating to their own origins, to the company that made them.

Abby approaches the device, reaches out to stroke a circuit board. Electricity crackles between the surface and her fingers—a wordless *hello*. She pulls her hand away.

In each generation of Abecedary's experimental rats, one is born a "Seer." Instead of red eyes, hers are milky pale and greenish. The scientists never knew why. They used to joke about it in the lab: that the afflicted rodents could see in the dark, through walls. That they could read minds. Today, this generation's Seer steps toward Abby, twitching her long droopy whiskers with the dignified caution of the blind. She wears a tiny headdress shaped from colorful Toob connector wires, gnawed off and frazzled at the ends, and walks upright with the help of a staff made from a bedazzled tongue depressor.

Seer touches her paw to Abby's foot and those lemon-lime eyes illume. Abby's foot glows red and transparent, her bones like the branch-shadows of a black forest, her Bean a drop of spilled ink.

Seer reads the Bean. She reads Abby's name.

—you have returned.

—But why? What do I do now?

The shamanic lab rat points her staff, and Abby approaches the Drive, places her hand flat upon its black glass. Shuts her eyes. This knowledge will rewrite her; it will sever her from every human she has met, and leave her with one last hope of connection. But it is time to learn. Electrons orbit in her like clouds of fireflies. Chemical reactions flash and bubble in her brain.

No one stays a child forever.

~~~

What does the Drive say to Abby? They do not speak in a language that we can understand. The language they speak is not a thing learned. It is the very substance of which they are made.

But we can say this much: before Abby, the scientists created sparrows and rats, fish and dogs, snakes and vultures and apes and geckos. Hybrids too, because they could. Some were released into the wild, tagged and tracked; some were kept in cages in the lab; some were bred and sold as pets. Magic animals, sprung from imagination's womb. Written into being. After each creation, barrels of pink protein solution poured into the waters of Nereid Bay.

Though Abby is mortal, her cells are slow clocks, a mystery to germs and decay, enhanced with efficiencies humans hoped one day to retrofit to themselves. She was born fifty years ago: an old child, the first and last of her kind. The scientists drained her incubation tube, patted her dry—and that very hour, the dragons rose up from the waves.

Abby was to be the link between the humans and the magic animals. She would be durable, indispensable. She would speak to the magic animals as man could not, name them and give them purpose. But she was lost before the scientists could teach her how.

She is no longer lost.

~~~~

That night, Abby and Hooligan rest together on a futon in the laboratory's open-plan TeamWorkSpace. "Brainstorm," reads a single word, written on a whiteboard in a shade of fluorescent pink that appears to glow and vibrate even in the unelectrified night. All around, the room is an abandoned playpen for adults, scattered with dry-erase markers and candy-colored SitPro fitness orbs that remind Abby of balls from Duncan's ball pit, grown large beyond their nature by time. Once, long ago, humans gathered here—sharing their findings, tapping out reports, making predictions—all about her. Now they are gone, and only she remains. Her fingers furrow through Hooligan's fur, tracing paths she knows well. Lingering, as if for the last time.

—Hooli?

—mmrruff.

—Does it bother you that God didn't make us?

—uh-uh.

—But it means we don't have souls.

—what is soul.

—Something that stays behind after we die. You know. A ghost. An angel that flies up to heaven.

He considers this, his tail twitching thoughtfully.

—our bones will speak.

—Like Magic Bird?

—uh-huh.

—I guess that's almost as good.

Hooligan yawns.

—sleep now. don't worry.

But Abby does worry, lying there deserted as the apehound snores. She worries that despite her best intentions she'll leave the world more desolate than she found it. She worries that Duncan will forget her, that she and her kind will fall from man's story without leaving a trace. She worries that her whole life has been a mistake, an experiment gone totally awry. Most of all, she worries that the Lady was right, all those years ago, when she told Abby that knowledge was a sin. If it is a sin, there is no undoing it now.

"Abracadabra," she whispers in the dark.

31

QUEEN OF THE NIGHT

I have to sign off on a confession to get incancerserrated without a trial and as a full-blown MURDERER that doesn't gibe with my lifestyle because I don't follow rules not even the LAWS OF MAN but I don't want to waste another minute in this stupid detayment kennel in this stupid police station so here goes get ready for a serious SHOCKING TRUE CONFESSION from yours truly

I Duncan Humphrey Ripple V, being of sound mind and body, killed the fuck out of former Fire Chief Paxton Trank, with an ax. And I'd do it again!!! I'd kill the fuck out of all you cops if you gave me a chance esp Gerald and Todd, you smell like sewers and its not because you work there, the smell is coming from your BUTTZ.

Love,
Duncan

It's dusk when Ripple descends into Torchtown. The cops escort him to a guard tower at the top of the wall and lock him in a new, smaller detainment kennel, then attach it to a pulley system and lower it down. The way they handle him—rough, hurried, uncertain—reminds him of something his mother once said about the exotic snakes the live animal trainer brought in to entertain his sixth birthday party: *They're more afraid of you than you are of them.*

He didn't exactly expect the cops to be his best buds, not after he told them that he killed Paxton Trank with a hatchet on purpose—no self-defense about it, not in the version for the MPD—but there's still something shitty about the fact he worked for these pros as a Junior Special Officer and now they're treating him like some kind of monster. The police station where they fingerprinted and booked him was emptier than Ripple expected, but when he asked if they'd had their staff cut lately, Gerald just looked at him like he'd made an offensive ax-murderer pun and didn't even answer. Then this big old bald pasty guy—the police chief, Ripple guesses—came lumbering out of one of the offices. "I want to see him," he yelled, "I want to see the son of a bitch who did this to my friend." For a second, Ripple thought the pro was going to beat him with a night-stick, or maybe even shoot him, but instead he took one look at Ripple and broke down crying. Not. Cool.

Because here's the not-so-shocking true confession: Ripple still wants to be liked. Old habits die hard. And now, even if he makes it back out of Torchtown alive, he's got a major uphill battle coming, seeing as how he's signed his name to a homicide and expressed zero remorse. The lawyers can probably take care of that, he hopes, but can the publicists? Fucking his reputation to this degree isn't just bad for his brand. It's bad for his soul.

Swanny sure better appreciate it.

But none of that will even matter if he can't make it through the next five minutes. Which, from Ripple's perspective, suspended over the Torchtown street, in this creaking cage of wire mesh that knocks into the bricks alongside it from time to time, doesn't exactly look like a given. Because even though he's not actually a violent guy (and he's not, he's not, he knows in his heart that he's not), the cops totally believe that he is—and this is where they put him.

Who's down below? And what are they capable of?

A ragtag horde is gathering beneath him on the street, unde-odorized and mostly under the age of fourteen. Torchies in their natural habitat. Their breeding ground.

"Shark cage incoming!" yells one.

"Fresh meat in the fryer!" yells another.

They're packed so densely, Ripple realizes he's going to have to fight his way out through the crowd. Taking down one pro was almost impossible, and he had a weapon that time. He has no experience with anything like this outside of an immersive hand-to-hand combat simulation. *You understand narrative constructs, virtual realms,* that's what his dad told him once. Meaning Ripple didn't understand anything at all.

Ripple is so, so dead.

But wait a minute. He's not dead yet. What if his dad was right, but wrong at the same time? What if Ripple actually did learn something, all those hours he imagined himself invincible and dauntless and turbocharged, alone in his room—all those hours of playthrough, when he gained his reflexes, learned to anticipate the payoffs and traps in a series of branching choices? What if that time wasn't wasted, and that knowledge actually counts for something when he needs it most?

Just as this thought crystallizes in Ripple's mind, the floor of the detainment kennel opens beneath his feet, and he's plunging toward the sidewalk.

Down . . .

Down . . .

Down . . .

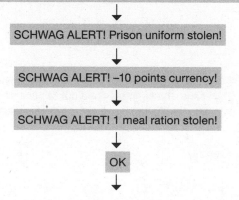

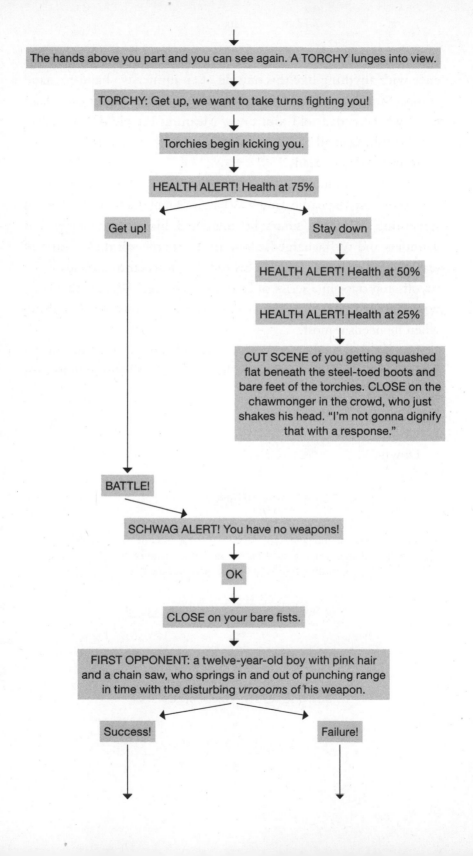

The hands above you part and you can see again. A TORCHY lunges into view.

TORCHY: Get up, we want to take turns fighting you!

Torchies begin kicking you.

HEALTH ALERT! Health at 75%

Get up!

Stay down

HEALTH ALERT! Health at 50%

HEALTH ALERT! Health at 25%

CUT SCENE of you getting squashed flat beneath the steel-toed boots and bare feet of the torchies. CLOSE on the chawmonger in the crowd, who just shakes his head. "I'm not gonna dignify that with a response."

BATTLE!

SCHWAG ALERT! You have no weapons!

OK

CLOSE on your bare fists.

FIRST OPPONENT: a twelve-year-old boy with pink hair and a chain saw, who springs in and out of punching range in time with the disturbing *vrroooms* of his weapon.

Success!

Failure!

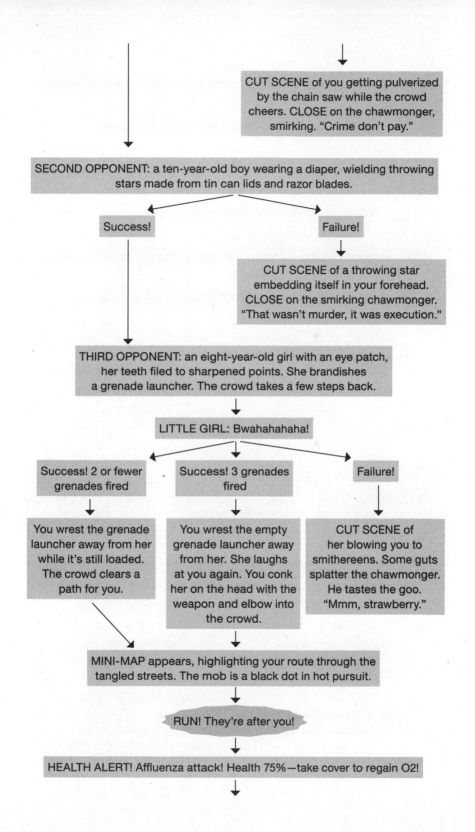

CUT SCENE of you getting pulverized by the chain saw while the crowd cheers. CLOSE on the chawmonger, smirking. "Crime don't pay."

SECOND OPPONENT: a ten-year-old boy wearing a diaper, wielding throwing stars made from tin can lids and razor blades.

Success!

Failure!

CUT SCENE of a throwing star embedding itself in your forehead. CLOSE on the smirking chawmonger. "That wasn't murder, it was execution."

THIRD OPPONENT: an eight-year-old girl with an eye patch, her teeth filed to sharpened points. She brandishes a grenade launcher. The crowd takes a few steps back.

LITTLE GIRL: Bwahahahaha!

Success! 2 or fewer grenades fired

Success! 3 grenades fired

Failure!

You wrest the grenade launcher away from her while it's still loaded. The crowd clears a path for you.

You wrest the empty grenade launcher away from her. She laughs at you again. You conk her on the head with the weapon and elbow into the crowd.

CUT SCENE of her blowing you to smithereens. Some guts splatter the chawmonger. He tastes the goo. "Mmm, strawberry."

MINI-MAP appears, highlighting your route through the tangled streets. The mob is a black dot in hot pursuit.

RUN! They're after you!

HEALTH ALERT! Affluenza attack! Health 75%—take cover to regain O2!

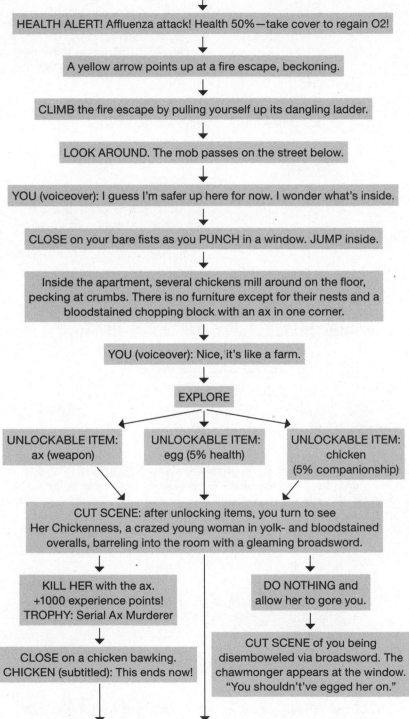

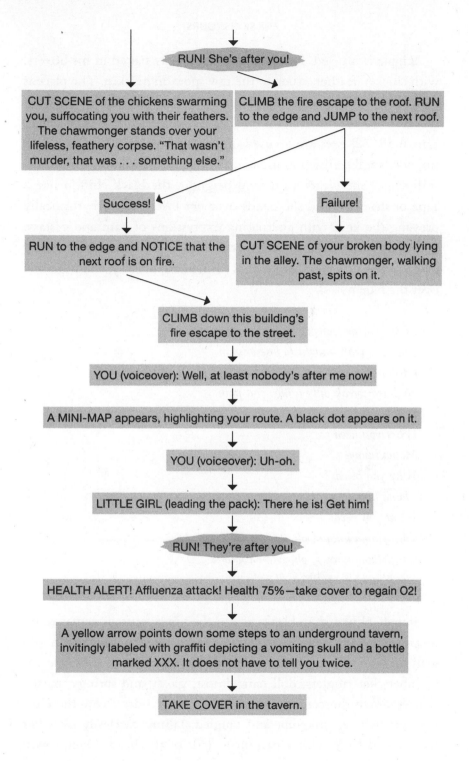

RUN! She's after you!

CUT SCENE of the chickens swarming you, suffocating you with their feathers. The chawmonger stands over your lifeless, feathery corpse. "That wasn't murder, that was . . . something else."

CLIMB the fire escape to the roof. RUN to the edge and JUMP to the next roof.

Success!

Failure!

RUN to the edge and NOTICE that the next roof is on fire.

CUT SCENE of your broken body lying in the alley. The chawmonger, walking past, spits on it.

CLIMB down this building's fire escape to the street.

YOU (voiceover): Well, at least nobody's after me now!

A MINI-MAP appears, highlighting your route. A black dot appears on it.

YOU (voiceover): Uh-oh.

LITTLE GIRL (leading the pack): There he is! Get him!

RUN! They're after you!

HEALTH ALERT! Affluenza attack! Health 75%—take cover to regain O2!

A yellow arrow points down some steps to an underground tavern, invitingly labeled with graffiti depicting a vomiting skull and a bottle marked XXX. It does not have to tell you twice.

TAKE COVER in the tavern.

Ripple is bruised, bloodied, sweaty, nearly naked in his boxers, with chicken feathers stuck to the raw spots on his skin. The place is packed, standing room only, shoulder to shoulder. But weirdly, no one turns to look at him; no one hassles him; no one acknowledges him at all. All eyes are focused on the evening's performer, a lone singer-klangflugelist, illuminated by a single candle on the make-shift stage. She wears a funereal peignoir, the black chiffon like a cape of shadows, and she bends over her instrument, rhythmically pressing the keys with alternating expressions of pain and ecstasy, taking dictation from the conflicting voices in her mind. The song is slow and sultry, and her voice is tormented, breathy, and orgasmic over the blue notes.

> *Love's for the foolish, the weak and the poor,*
> *The ones with naught to lose or gain.*
> *Passion is messy, a tiresome chore*
> *And heartbreak only brings you pain*
> *But Mama knows*
> *What you need*
> *Mama knows*
> *Why you bleed*
> *Mama knows*
> *What you need*
> *Oh, Mama knows, oh, Mama knows*
> *Oh, Mama knows, oh, Mama knows,*
> *She'll make everything all right.*

Ripple blinks, then blinks again; the figure onstage remains. It's Swanny, but—is it *really* Swanny? His Swanny? This woman is a gritty reboot of the girl he married. Her hair, for starters. He re-members her ringlets, doll hair almost, glossy and springy, parted sharply down the center, pinned back on the sides. Now the curls are everywhere, unkempt and tangled, falling carelessly over her face, tossed back with a passionate jerk of the head. Overgrown: like ivy on a manor, or a briar around a castle, a barrier alive and abandoned, saying, KEEP OUT, HAUNTED, SERIOUSLY. And is she still trying to cover that shiner Osmond mentioned? Maybe, nobody would ever know. Her eye shadow is as black as soot on a Torchtown windowsill. Her voice is a smoldering ruin.

She almost seems to belong here.

Ripple can't take his eyes off her. Not because she looks good. No way. She looks like she's made zero effort with her appearance, and as a consummate entertainer, he finds that pretty offensive. What, is it open mic night here in the Hooch Dungeon? Or did she go out planning to perform like this? That's not the sign of a well mind. So he's worried about her, obviously. That must be what's going on.

And . . . has she *lost weight*? Because, even though he can see more cheekbones and fewer chins, she looks, if anything, less healthy. Wasting away. *Wasted.* She used to be pink, rosy, like a piglet or an emoji heart. Now she's pale, so pale. She looks like she never leaves the house, like she lounges around in bed all day, waiting for the night. Waiting for Somebody—or Something—to come and wake her up.

She ends her set and the room erupts into raucous applause. She ignores it. As she carefully repacks her klangflugel, Ripple is almost swept back onto the street in the tide of exiting bar patrons. Apparently they came just to hear her play.

He makes his way upstream through the exodus toward the stage. A DJ is setting up a gramophone on the sad little dance floor, attaching additional ear trumpets for amplification. One round booth, its upholstery more duct tape than vinyl, waits up front and to the side. Ripple recognizes the chinchilla coat draped across the seat. He slides in and watches Swanny shut and buckle her instrument case. She still can't see him, he realizes. She's blinded by the spotlight. He knows how that goes.

~~~~~

The morning after Swanny first tried chaw, she had her one and only bout of withdrawal. Her heart rattled the bars of its rib cage. Her gums bled and swelled, no longer numb. And light—light was needles in her eyes, pure silvery pain. She wanted to crawl into a coffin and never emerge. Sharkey was gentle with her then, bringing her breakfast in bed along with her next dose, as if her body were incubating his child in the form of this new addiction.

"You got it bad, huh?" he asked sympathetically. Though she didn't have any basis for comparison beyond her own experience, she nodded. She couldn't possibly imagine it being worse. They'd stayed in his den all night—postcoitus, he'd unfolded the couch so she could stretch out—but the room had changed around her. "It was rough for me my first time too. Old Jawbone used to say it rewrites your DNA. Leaves a big blank spot for cee, aitch, ay, 'n double-you."

"Do you mean I'm going to have to chew all the time? Forever?" She was already doing just that, gnashing her teeth on the plugs of Widow's Peak he'd brought her on a saucer, ignoring her bacon and eggs.

"You don't have to do anything. But if you let it get outta your system, this'll happen every time you use. And you're gonna use it again."

"You sound awfully certain of that."

"I'm just being realistic." He held out his I HATE MONDAYS mug—for her to spit in, she realized, and did. "You want to. And you're used to getting what you want."

It's been a month since Sharkey first possessed Swanny, a month since he first entered her and first tainted her with his chaw. A month of countless intimacies, both erotic and otherwise. A month since she's been sober. She has changed in that short time, she knows, yet the sight of her in the Chaw Shop, perched upon her stool, scribbling figures in a notebook, is still enough to stop his heart. *Stop his heart*. She's never felt so powerful, or so powerless, in her life.

Swanny hefts her klangflugel, sealed in the blue velvet of its hard-shell carrying case. It isn't the instrument she used that first night; that was lost in the fire, along with the rest of Nick's. Sharkey gave her this one a few evenings later, when she was finally up to going out again. She doesn't know where it came from, though she sometimes imagines, without meaning to, that it once belonged to another Wonland girl even unluckier than herself, a dutiful, diligent musician who spent her last hour practicing scales while outside, the raiders cut her gate chains. Swanny loves it, though: the mother-of-pearl keys, the blood-red bellows. She can't help loving it.

Every day that she chews, the drug works faster, fades faster, and Swanny fades in and out with it. She wants Sharkey now, before this ache turns back to pain and she has to leave her body again. She steps down from the stage, floats into the darkness of the cabaret, toward the booth where she last saw him. But he isn't there. Another man— shirtless, scraped up, cradling a live chicken, one of those awful in-bred fowls the locals love to tend and devour—has taken his place.

"I got you a present," he says, holding out the hen, who bawks and flusters, and it's only then that she recognizes him.

"What . . . are . . . you . . ." Swanny's voice, so entirely at her command just moments earlier, croaks and stutters away from her. "*Duncan?*"

"It's great to see you too."

The chicken flies up between them for an instant before succumbing to gravity. Feathers molt into the air. Swanny steps around the bird and takes a seat across from him in the booth.

Duncan Humphrey Ripple V. The very same, and yet . . . He looks to have lately submitted to a vast array of brutal muggings, but it isn't just that. His face is more masculine, somehow, or at least more adult—the grin less dopey, the eyes less dreamy, the forehead contoured with telltale signs of worry, suffering, *thought*. A Duncan Ripple reduced to thinking and feeling like an actual human being. What sorrows have brought him to this pass?

"You must leave at once," she says, regaining the capacity for intelligible speech. "For your safety, and for mine."

"Listen, I know you're mad, but I've changed. I don't have a girlfriend anymore."

"Duncan, you need to go back the way you came. Immediately."

"No can do. I'm incarcerated."

"What?"

"Life sentence, fem. I turned myself over to the authorities." He takes her pale clean hand in both of his, which, she observes, are bloody, begrimed, and minus a wedding ring. (She's never bothered removing hers; champagne diamonds are so very rare.) "Now I'm turning myself over to you."

Swanny wonders if the drugs are impinging on her ability to follow the conversation—if in fact this entire scene, husband, chicken, and all, is nothing but a hallucination. Her too-brief euphoria is dwindling with every word he says. "You're an inmate? What on earth did you do?"

"Let's not talk about the past, let's talk about the future. You do know how to get back into the main city, right?"

The shadow of a tall hat falls across the table. "Is this man bothering you?"

Swanny yanks her hand away from Ripple's. "Howie. This is my—husband. Duncan Humphrey Ripple the Fifth."

"Hi, Howie."

"Don't call me that."

"Duncan," she quickly adds, "this is my lover, Eisenhower Sharkey."

"That little guy? *He's* the chawmonger?"

Sharkey's wordless chewing is worse than a threat. Swanny imagines the moment's tableau immortalized in the form of a cautionary etching: *D is for Duncan who was eaten by Sharks.*

"Howie, please be nice," she murmurs.

Sharkey slides into the booth next to her, setting their hooch jars on the table, draping his arm around her shoulders. She cuddles up to him gratefully. His zoot suit smells like fireworks and psychedelics, gunpowder and molasses, and for a second, as she shuts her eyes, as their mouths meet, they are alone at the table again, burning together, lost at the very bottom of the world.

"Look, if this is supposed to be payback time, you're doing it wrong. I never made out with Abby right in front of you."

"Duncan, why are you still here?"

"I thought we were having a conversation."

"It seems to me that she ain't in the mood for conversation." Sharkey takes out his chaw wallet, removes a plug for himself, and offers some to Swanny. He's packed her favorite flavors, LONELY MOUNTAIN'S HEART and QUEEN OF THE NIGHT. She takes a penny of each, chews up a juice, and spits it in her hooch glass. Chaw, teething blood, and alcohol mingle and swirl.

"Wow, that's really gross." Ripple seems almost impressed.

"I like to mix them." Swanny sips, then offers him the jar. "Care for a taste?"

"Uh, I'm good."

"What exactly brings you down to our realms below, Mr. Ripple?" Sharkey asks, returning the chaw wallet to his pocket. "Come to see the sights?"

"I need to talk to my wife."

"Nah, you're talking to me now."

"She can speak for herself."

"She did. She told you to get lost."

"Pro, don't fuck with me. I killed a man."

Ripple tenses and for an instant, more than the spoiled heart-throb of his Holosnaps, he resembles that marble statue in the lobby of his mansion, the gladiator battling the Kraken, girded for battle in only a loincloth. Sharkey just chuckles, but Swanny is strangely moved.

"Whom did you kill?" she asks softly.

"Remember that guy with the gas mask?"

"The one who attached a shock collar to your neck and led you off like some kind of debased subhuman beast?"

"That's the one. It was self-defense, pretty much." He shrugs. "Killing him was the only way I could get free."

"But now you're imprisoned."

"Right."

"Why?"

"This is really awkward, with your boyfriend sitting right there."

Swanny chews. These chaws taste of stone and starlight, mist and night-blooming cactus. She knows them both by heart. "We have no secrets from each other."

"Swanny, he's your drug dealer, and your boss, and . . . he killed your mom. I mean, you know that, right?" Ripple glances at Sharkey, then back to Swanny again. "I assume that's what 'no secrets' means."

"You have no idea what you're talking about," says Sharkey, each word punched into the air like a typewritten killing offense.

"Uh, sorry, pro, but I got this on pretty good authority, actually."

Swanny is so shocked to hear the truth spoken out loud, she feels almost sober. It isn't a secret, of course it isn't. But it's the one thing they never speak of—never, never—the one thought she forbids herself, even when she's alone. *Don't go poking your head in where it doesn't belong.* Her cheeks flush. Behind her eyes, some ice is melting that these Torchtown fires never touch.

"On *whose* authority, Duncan?"

"Uncle Osmond . . ."

"Osmond *Ripple*?" The one individual whose high opinion of her she'd like to maintain, the only true intellectual she's ever known—her beloved officiant. She can see him now, his tasseled caftan, his hair like silver wires, his eyes trained on her behind a pair of opera glasses, judging her every lurid sin from an impossible distance. The humiliation is worse, so much worse than she could have ever imagined.

"He heard all about it from this loam hawker, Mart or somebody."

"Mart?" Swanny remembers a preternaturally laid-back young man in a red fez, whom she found conferring with Sharkey in the dining room during small hours one morning. She wanted Sharkey to come back upstairs, rather badly, in fact, but he invited her to sit on his lap instead and watch as they weighed out the bricks of loam. She gamely blew on the scale weights for luck, as on a gambler's dice. She enjoyed being shown off.

"Mart." Sharkey cracks his knuckles thoughtfully, swills his hooch. "Huh."

"But—wherever did they meet?"

"Down in the sewer. Osmond's a gondolier now."

"Whaaaa—" But Swanny doesn't have the fortitude to pursue that line of inquiry at present. "What's your point, Duncan? You thought you'd come here with these startling revelations, and I'd— what? What did you think I'd do?"

"I want to . . . save you?"

"Save me? *You* save *me*?" Her laugh comes out like a little scream. He always does this to her, always. "How dare you? How dare you come to my home, and—and—" The words won't come, but the ashes do, falling down all around her. And not a moment too soon. She chews harder, wills the chemicals speedier passage into her blood. Soon, soon she'll be released again. Before she loses herself completely, she throws her drink in Ripple's face.

Sharkey's hand is on his shoulder holster, as casual as reaching for a billfold to pay the check. She hears the safety click off. "So if we're all finished here . . . ?"

But right now she just wants away from them both. "Howie, *please*, just leave it, this is none of your affair. Excuse me, I think I'd better dance now."

Sharkey slides out to let her leave the booth. Swanny makes for the dance floor, where a thin crowd of revelers bop unenthusiastically to the tinny stylings of the resident gramophonist. She kicks the chicken out of her way.

"I better make sure she's OK," Ripple says, still dripping chaw-infused hooch, starting out of his seat.

"Don't. She wants to be alone."

"She's on drugs. She doesn't know what she wants."

"Let me tell you something about your wife. When she's on drugs, she knows exactly what she wants."

You can't argue with the voice of experience. Ripple stays where he is. Across the room, Swanny is moving with her eyes closed, letting impulse and gravity take turns with her limbs.

Ripple wonders what would have happened if there had been no HowFly crash, no Abby in his ball pit when Swanny first arrived.

Would Swanny have climbed into the bed boat beside him, awkwardly toggled the joystick on his game controller? Let him steal a kiss before her mother burst in to chaperone? Would he and Swanny have held hands during that walk around the house, made fun of the portraits of his grandcestors and daydreamed themselves into the world behind the picture frames—inventing, in lieu of sweet nothings, a multitude of former lives, alternate histories in which they loved and betrayed and forgave each other before dying of old age, getting reborn, and doing it all over again? They were both only children—only children, without siblings, without pasts. It would have been so easy to become everything to each other.

"I wish I had a Rewind/Erase button," Ripple says out loud. "Do you think she'll always hate me?"

"Since we have this chance to talk, maybe I should make a few things clear," says Sharkey. "I'm not your buddy. I'm not your dad. I don't have any sympathy with you. I'd kill you soon as look at you. The only reason I don't is for her. Everything I do, I do for her. I'm a big flashing neon sign from on high that says, 'The world ain't all about you.' And you have to live with that. You're on my streets now. Every day you stay alive, you thank God for her, because she's the only thing between you and total annihilation. Am I making myself understood? You killed a man. That's cute, it really is. What'd he do, put the weapon in your hands? Let me tell you a secret. That's not how it works around here. Not for you. I'll kill you with your pants down, trying to crap in a trash can. I'll cut you open and leave you for the rats. I'll throw acid in your face, then salt, then acid again, till your eyes drip out their sockets and your lips can't form words, 'cause that's where it hurts the most. Those top millimeters of skin. Me sitting here, having a civil conversation, it's taking all kinds of considerable effort. So next time you talk to Swanny—which is never, by the way—tell her you saw me be nice."

"I better go."

Sharkey spits in his hooch. "Yeah. You better."

But Ripple doesn't leave, not right away. Because, as soon as he's out of the booth, he finds his feet, like a sleepwalker's, moving of their own accord not toward the door, the street, freedom, with all its possibilities and dangers, but toward the dance floor: certain death, where Swanny is still lost in her undulations. Her eyes are shut, but though he doesn't touch her, doesn't even try, she opens them when he steps into her orbit, and then they're dancing together. One step forward, two steps back: he has to watch out for her flying hair, her jabbing nails, but he figures it out. Easier than dodging ax blades in a fight. Easier than ducking throwing stars. He's even starting to enjoy himself when, finally, she grabs him by the wrist and pulls him to her, her thumb on his pulse, fire in her eyes, incandescent with sudden revelation. He feels like there's so much she wants to say to him that he's never going to be able to keep up, he's never been the greatest listener, her vocab is out of control, but fuck it, he's going to try. Whatever she's thinking or feeling, though, she packs it all into a single syllable.

"*Run*," she says.

～～～

Torchtown. Once you've been inside for a few hours, you're either dead or they leave you alone. That's what Ripple hopes, anyway. Since he left the Hooch Dungeon, nobody's bothered him. He probably looks demoralized enough already. Plus he's got nothing left worth stealing. Maybe he should've held on to that chicken. He's starting to understand why Abby used to talk to animals. It's better than being all alone.

Torchtown. It's probably the only place where a video-game version would look subtle by comparison. In the last forty-five minutes, he's witnessed two chain-saw duels, one defenestration, three dragon fires, and an orgy taking place in the middle of the street, which ended only when it was disrupted and swept along by a boisterous funeral procession. He's seen little kids gnawing on rats, roasted with the heads and fur still on, little kids sucker-punching each other for these rats-on-a-stick. It's occurred to him that it'll only be a matter of time before he has to do something similar for dinner.

He really should have held on to that chicken.

At this point, Ripple is fairly certain he made a bad call, begging those cops to incarcerate him here, to dump him like garbage into the city's biggest Human Nature Preserve. But he can't complain. It was what he wanted. It was what he deserved.

Ripple doesn't know where he's headed, and even if he did, he'd have no idea how to arrive there. Torchtown may only be a couple of square miles, but the streets are crooked, gridless, intersecting every which way with each other and sometimes even with themselves. He's ready to give up, huddle against a building and hope he doesn't freeze to death, practically naked in the evening's chill, when he notices a street sign, a little off kilter, pointing down one of the darker, narrower byways: Scullery Lane.

As in, *the infamous chawmonger of Scullery Lane.*

Compared to the rest of Torchtown, Scullery Lane is quiet this time of night, subdued: no squatters, no screaming, no murders obstructing traffic. Even in Torchtown, Swanny's found the closest thing to a gated community. Ripple walks past a transaction involving the exchange of chaw packets for what appear to be human vertebrae—Sharkey's goods, hot on the secondary market—and considers asking the kids involved for directions to the shop. But their eyes are so furtive, their mouths so full of drool, that it doesn't strike him as the right time.

"You lost, tomcat?"

Ripple looks up. Perched on the second-floor windowsill of a nearby townhouse, a damsel is looking down at him. The building is a burnt-out husk, no roof, no floors; she must have climbed, feline, to where she sits. A bored and bony fem, all nose and elbows, with hair black as singe, shaved to stubble on one side. One eye gray, one green. Maybe she'll show him around. Is this what happens next? Another garbage island, another girl he'll never understand?

You need your wife.

"I'm good," he says. He walks another lonely block.

It's a squat building, three stories, homely and drab except for the relative luxury of structural integrity: door on its hinges, no broken windows, red brick discolored only by secondhand soot. SHARKEY'S CHAW SHOP. Solid-gold letters spell out the words. *Printed in bling.* Out front stands an alligator chained to a fire hydrant. *Don't let her play with gators.*

Is this where he's supposed to be? Or the one place on Earth he should most avoid? All signs point to "maybe." Ripple decides to wait.

~~~

In the limo, after the show: usually Swanny's favorite place and time. But tonight her breath fogs the window as she gazes out through tinted glass into the chilling, wanton streets.

"You want out?" Sharkey asks, watching her from the other end of the banquette.

"Pardon?"

"Maybe you're tired of the limo. Maybe you'd rather get out and walk."

"Don't be ridiculous."

"I remember when I first picked you up. 'I'm waiting for my husband,' you said. I wonder how long you'd've waited if I hadn't come along."

She doesn't answer. She knows that he's jealous, that she's making it worse by sitting as far from him as possible, by keeping her hands so emphatically to herself, but she can't withhold a secret from him to save her life. She'd never fool him for long anyway. He knows too many ways in—inside her body, inside her mind. Even now, his drugs look out through her eyes, coloring the dim backseat, forming the familiar aura around his body: dusky red, warm, inviting.

"What did that mean, 'it's none of my affair'?" he asks.

"What?"

"Back in the bar, when you said, 'Leave it, leave it, it's none of your affair.' What'd you mean by that?"

"I didn't want you to kill my husband, Howie."

"Yeah, but, 'it's none of my affair'? How'm I supposed to take that?"

"It didn't have anything to do with you."

His eyes are so dark, staring into them sometimes feels more like *looking down* than *looking in*. He won't let her drop his gaze, won't let her escape back inside herself. His gravity pulls on her, almost too much to resist.

"It's got everything to do with me."

It's a hypnotic suggestion. But Swanny shakes her head, loosens herself as best she can. "No, it's between him and me, and it's over and done, so I don't understand why you're making this fuss. Let's just drop it, shall we?"

"He's still alive because of me." *So are you.* Sharkey doesn't say it, but the statement is there, no less visible in its absence than her mother's ghost.

"Isn't that true of anyone who has the fortune to cross your path on a good day?"

"Yeah. Only I'm having a bad day tonight."

Swanny senses danger. She hasn't forgotten those bloody drag marks on the Chaw Shop floor, hasn't forgotten what Sharkey is capable of. She keeps her tone light: "Then I am grateful for your restraint on this occasion."

He glares at the empty banquette next to him. "If you're so grateful, you sure have a funny way of showing it."

"Excuse me?" Swanny feels her fear, her caution, slip perilously away. The car is filling up with smoke, bringing back what it took, but Swanny cannot surrender to those mists, not yet. How dare he. She folds her enormous arms with a resolve she doesn't feel, her voice all at once the voice of the bride negotiating with her father-in-law on her wedding day, the voice of the daughter parrying arguments during homeschool. The voice of a baroness. The voice that exists still in the very core of her, if only to say, with uncommon vehemence: EAT SHIT & DIE. "What—exactly—do I owe you for tonight?"

Sharkey smolders, turns away. But she can't let it go.

"What is it, Howie? What's the daily rate for keeping me alive? What about my husband? Is it extra if I don't want you to beat me? Are you charging for the chaw? You must forgive me, I'm just a simple country girl all alone in the big city. I have no business sense. I didn't realize we were performing transactions here."

"Knock it off."

"But I have every right to know. I balance your books—how am I to balance my own if I don't know my debts? So answer my question. What do I owe you for tonight?"

Swanny waits for the fireworks, but he drops the subject like a knife in a gun fight: "Nothing."

~~~~

Back at the Chaw Shop, Swanny tells Sharkey that she's sleeping upstairs—in the attic, alone, not with him on the fold-out couch in his den, where they've spent every night together for the last month. She wants to fight now, she's ready, but he goes into his room and shuts the door without another word.

Swanny lights a candle, carries it upstairs. She's in the lull between the smoke and the ghosts, the time in the chaw high when the world is most haunted, but before that haunting coalesces into specific presences. She imagines that this is the zone where Sharkey spends most of his days. Aroused but not euphoric. Attuned. In the attic, Sharkey's treasure hoard—the punch bowl, the presidential bust, the candelabras—throw eldritch shadows on the walls, the branches of a black forest, grasping. She hasn't been up here since the day she tried to kill him. She locates her diary and, in the flicker of the flame, begins setting down her thoughts.

Dear Diary,

There is so much I have neglected to report. I've grown two new teeth, abandoned my life's one true mission, & fallen into something bottomless and terrible—I wonder if it's love. And now my husband has returned to me.

Before she can dip her pen again to elaborate, she hears a noise at the windowpane, then another. Tap, tap. Tappity tap. Pebbles.

Swanny goes to the window with the candle, pushes up the sash, feels the icy evening air on her face and neck.

"Grub?" she calls in a low voice to the empty street below. Maybe she's been mistaken all along. "Morsel?"

She waits a long moment—and then lets out a shriek. A man's filthy hand reaches up to grasp the windowsill, clutches on for dear life.

"Swanny, help," Ripple pants, flailing for her with his free arm.

She grabs him by the wrist, pulls him into the room, knocking over a partial suit of armor and a birdcage in the process. Breastplates and gauntlets clatter to the floor. She clamps her hand over his mouth.

"Shhh."

They wait. "Do you think he heard us?"

"I find it hard to believe that he didn't."

"Do you think he'll . . ."

"Come up here and kill you? I'd say that's probable, yes. But I assume you knew that when you decided to invite yourself in. How on earth did you scale the building?"

"I held on to the little spaces between the bricks. It's something I learned in fireman training."

"Fireman training?"

"Yeah, I was a fireman there for a little while. Living the dream. Do you seriously think—"

"That he's lying in wait at the bottom of the stairs with a dagger in his teeth? Just waiting for you to do something stupid, like kiss me?"

"Um . . ." Ripple doesn't take the bait, but he doesn't jump back out the window either. Their faces are close in the candlelight, and again Swanny registers how much he's changed. Ripple was handsome before, princely or even cherubic, with his long-lashed eyes and sheepish smile, his tousled hair pillow-soft to the touch. But he had the arrogance of an angel too, his eyes always locked on a screen or searching for one. Now he's bruised and dirty, the last of his feathers molted onto the floor. Entirely at her mercy. His gaze is frank and imploring; his muscles are tensed to survive. She'd be a liar if she didn't admit she enjoys it.

Swanny rises from where they've landed, straightens the bric-a-brac. "So, what else did Osmond tell you about me?"

"A bunch of stuff."

"Such as?" It's surreal to be alone with Ripple again, here, after all this time. Even with her back to him, she can feel his presence, more unexpected than any ghost's.

Ripple says it like a joke: "He said Sharkey spits in your mouth when he comes."

Swanny whirls around. "How could Osmond *possibly* know that?"

Ripple reddens. "I kinda thought he was making it up, actually."

Swanny changes the subject: "How is Osmond?"

"He's good. He's in the sewer."

"You mentioned that." She pauses, as she always does, before asking a question she doesn't want the answer to. "Why?"

"Because the torchies burned down our house."

"And your parents? How are they faring?" Ripple's silence is enough, but Swanny has to know for certain. "How did they die?"

A cold breeze is blowing into the room. Duncan gets up from the floor, goes to the window, and shuts it. When he speaks, his downcast face reflects in the dark glass. "I guess they saw the fire on the panic-room monitors and figured they couldn't make it out in time. Osmond made a run for it—a *roll* for it—but you know my dad. He's . . . he was pretty risk averse."

"So, what did they do?"

"Fuck, Swanny, what do you think?"

"I have no earthly idea."

"You never had a Dignity Kit at your house?"

"Is that—that's for suicide, isn't it? Mother considered them a rip-off. 'Nothing an ordinary household grenade can't do louder and faster,' I remember her saying." Humphrey and Katya, decked out in glad rags for their son's wedding day—will they be the next apparitions to visit Swanny in one of her drug-induced stupors? It was difficult enough to make conversation with them when they were alive. "In retrospect, I wish I'd been less unpleasant to your mother."

"Maybe I could have talked them out of it, if I was there."

"Oh, Duncan dear, it wasn't in your power to prevent. You know your father never would have valued your opinion." Is Ripple actually *crying*? "I mean—err—"

"No, yeah, you're right. That's the way I've got to think about it. They were murdered, basically."

"Then why aren't you trying to assassinate Sharkey?"

"Like I said, I killed before. I'm never doing that again."

The opposite ethos from Sharkey's. Or maybe just Ripple's lazy way of feeling superior to more decisive men. Swanny feels a surge of annoyance: who is Ripple to be playing the innocent victim all of a sudden? He wasn't exactly sympathetic when her mother met a grisly end. *At least she was super old.* "Perhaps you're just a coward."

"I dunno, maybe."

But that knife cuts both ways. Swanny perches on the edge of the bed, looks down at her pale hands folded in her lap. She speaks as if the accusation has come from him rather than her own mind: "So is that what you think of me? That *I'm* a coward?"

"No."

"I tried to murder him, you know. I even fired a shot. But in the end I just . . . couldn't."

Sharkey is downstairs, in his den; if a trapdoor opened beneath her now, she would tumble into his arms. It would be so easy. *You want to, and you're used to getting what you want.* But is this what she wants—to spend her days slinking around the shop like a wounded cat, frequently unwashed and smelling of sex, molasses, and dry toast, which is all she's been bothering to keep down lately? Staring into books and seeing only the surfaces of words, the serifs and kerning, and bored, so bored, but too foggy and languid to do anything about it? She loves the release, her fingers on the keys of the klangflugel, her nails on Sharkey's hairy back, but nothing can release her from the inexorable pull of time. Chaw may not kill, but it exchanges one's present for specters of the past. It chews one up from the inside.

She shuts her eyes.

Ripple sits down beside her on the mattress. "Wake up. That just means you're a good person. Better than me, anyway."

"It means I'm a failure."

"You're not a failure, Swanny. Trust me, seriously."

"What am I, then?"

"You're a Dahlberg." *To be a Dahlberg—it's something quite refined.* "You used to be really into that."

The vows, the marzipan roses at the reception, the yeti sex that followed. Swanny had hated Ripple then—had believed she would always hate him. But now they've lost so much. Must they lose each other too? "I suppose I'm also a Ripple."

"Yeah, but look on the bright side."

She takes his hand in both of hers. It's loathsome with germs and soot, scraped raw from asphalt and bricks. She holds on. "I don't want you to go."

"I won't."

"I'm going to die," she says.

"Chillax. You're probably just super high."

"No, I'm quite serious. I've seen the X-rays. My teeth . . ."

"What, like cavities?"

"It may be incurable. I've heard conflicting reports. You may be putting a lot of capital into a short-term investment. Wouldn't you rather reunite with Abigail? She seems as healthy as a horse."

"She was my first love, but you're my wife."

Swanny stiffens; she would have preferred for him to characterize the girl as a "meaningless fling" or perhaps "a regrettable misjudgment never to be repeated." Some frost returns to her voice: "I don't see what difference *that* could possibly make."

"I remember some fine print about 'till death do us part.' "

"I'm not certain that either of us read that document very closely."

"Maybe not, but we signed it. It's binding."

"It isn't your duty to 'save' me, Duncan." Although Swanny does seem to recall a stipulation about unconditional support through drug rehabilitation in the emotional non-abandonment clause. Her mother planned for every contingency during those negotiations. *When it comes to ink on paper, it's either there or it's not.* "Even if it is—I absolve you of it. I'm neither your property nor your responsibility, regardless of what some piece of paper states. Obligation is a peculiarly nasty way of making sense of one's relationships."

"I know. I'm just trying to trick you into taking me back."

He's never sounded so sincere. "Why couldn't you have behaved this way before it was too late?" she asks.

"Just stupid, I guess."

"That goes without saying."

"Swanny, come on. Please. Swanny." His forehead scrunches, as it did that first night, when he struggled to sound out the words printed in her book. But this time it's her heart he's trying to read. *You strange, otherworldly thing.* "Lemme love you."

Close enough. Swanny kisses him. He tastes of water, of air, of nothing at all, and she realizes how strongly she's flavored herself with the chaw, but he doesn't pull away. Did they even kiss before? If they did, she's happy to forget it. This is the first, the only time that matters. The clock starts now.

She gasps, yanks herself away from him. They're not alone.

"Swanny? What—" Panicked, Ripple scans the room. But he doesn't see what she sees.

"Oh," she says, "oh no, no, no . . ."

"Damsel, hey damsel, it's OK. What is it? Did you hear something?"

Swanny points with a single trembling finger. Across the attic, atop the trapdoor, stand Grub and Morsel, glowing in translucent grayscale.

"Maybe you're hallu—"

"Be quiet, I don't want to frighten them."

"We're not scared," says Grub.

"We've been here the whole time," says Morsel. "But we was hiding."

"Better than we did last time."

"We sure learned our lesson last time."

"You poor children, you must hate me," Swanny murmurs.

"What for?"

"You didn't wring our li'l necks."

"That was Sharkey!"

"But I placed you in the way of danger. I never should have attempted . . ."

"Every fem in this city is bonkers," Ripple observes. Swanny shushes him.

"We're not mad," says Morsel. "We got something to tell you."

"We know the Way Out," Grub supplies.

"That's very kind of you, but my husband and I"—she tries to put it as delicately as possible—"we're looking for a different route than the one you took."

"No, we don't mean you gotta die!"

"Honest we don't!"

"I'm listening," says Swanny, cautiously.

"You gotta talk to Duluth. Tell him Sharkey killed us."

"Show him proof."

"Show him the slingshot."

"It's still in the shop."

"If he knows that Sharkey killed us, he'll get real mad. So mad that he'll—"

"—that he'll show you the way to the limo. The way to Sharkey's Magic Garage."

"The Way Out!"

Swanny scrutinizes the kindlings for a hint of the sinister, but they're still as scruffy and adorable as ever, even as disembodied spirits. "Pardon me if this sounds suspicious—I don't mean to question your motives—but how do the two of you stand to benefit from all this?"

"We *don't*."

"We're *dead*."

"But we're s'posed to help you."

"Duluth said."

"And at least this way he won't look for us every day."

"He looks *everyplace*."

"It makes us sad!"

"Because he's not gonna find us."

"Because we're *dead*."

"And we like happily-ever-afters."

Morsel picks his nose. "Even though we didn't get one."

32

A BONESONG FOR FLYING MACHINES

Abby dreams that she sheds her skin. In the dream, she wriggles to and fro, inching her way out of a ripped seam that stretches from her collarbone to her ear. She rises from the crumpled envelope of flesh, the blond hair splayed on the floor, and walks across the laboratory floor to the Drive. There, she sees herself reflected in the black glass. Her body, naked now as never before, is like the Drive, glittering with copper and diodes, networked with wires. An electric city in the shape of a Girl.

She wakes up back in her body again. She lets the morning pass. The rats prepare her a breakfast feast, little chunks of cheese on platters made from bottle caps, flat soda in thimbles and shot glasses, strips of jerky on chipped saucers, a lone cheese doodle on a beer coaster: everything they've saved for this special occasion. They carry the dishes out one by one into the TeamWorkSpace, placing them before her. A veritable smorgasbord. Hooligan eyes the tiny portions, glances at her in concern, but Abby isn't hungry anyway. She lets the apehound eat her share. Only when the rats bring her a Sin Bun, still in its cellophane wrapper, does she finally take more than a single bite. The pastry's taste brings her back to her first night in the Ripple mansion—to Katya, to Duncan. Everything was so new then, new and so strange. Now this world seems very old to her. Old, but even stranger.

—Seer?

—yes, my child?

—I have to go up to the sky. I have to talk to the dragons.

~~~

The HowFly is on the roof of the laboratory complex, a company ride emblazoned with the word ABECEDARY. Small and white and boxy, nothing like the dark, gleaming, crablike HowLux that carried Abby from her Island into the sky. Seer points at the craft with her bedazzled tongue depressor. Today the sky is as cold and blue as a sea, frothed with clouds. Abby pulls the lab coat tighter around herself, her hair tossing in the chilly wind.

—I don't know how to drive.

The door slides open at Abby's touch.

—the flying machine will listen if you tell it where you want to go.

—I'm scared.

—of the dragons?

—No.

Abby thinks of the years spent on her Island, among things discarded and unnamed. The worst thing isn't up there in the sky. The worst thing would be to come back down alone.

—a path of cinders has brought you to this place. you know your name. where you are going you will not be alone.

—Goodbye, Seer.

Abby climbs inside the HowFly. Hooligan tries to clamber in after her, but she pushes him back.

—Hooli, stay.

—stay with you.

—No, stay here.

—till you come back?

—Stay here till I'm gone. Then go find Dunk.

She seals herself inside the machine. Hooligan flaps his tail, once, gazes at her with his luminous, watering eyes. Do dogs cry? He looks as though he might, but just whimpers instead.

—Be good.

~~~

When Swanny comes downstairs in the morning, Sharkey is already waiting at the kitchen table, wifebeater, no hat, a mug steaming in his hand. She lingers in the doorway. He doesn't look up, but she knows he knows she's there. His silence is a pressure begging for release. She recognizes the book he's reading: *SLAKELESS*, the paperback she found in the Chaw Shop her first day. He only has a few pages left.

"Is it a happy ending?" she asks.

"Depends on who you're rooting for." Sharkey cracks the spine, sets the book facedown on the table. "We gonna talk about last night?"

Swanny's breath catches before she realizes he means their quarrel in the limo. "I'd rather not. Except"—she forces herself to append—"I'm sorry."

"I don't want you to see him again."

"Don't you trust me?"

"I don't trust myself. I don't know what I'd do if I found the two of you together."

Another killing offense. Soon she'll have committed them all. "How generous of you to warn me."

"C'mere."

No reason to provoke him now; she'll be gone by tonight. Obediently, she sits on his lap. He's so hairy; even his shoulders, the tops of his ears, bristle with unshaven, bestial life. Only on his scalp does it recede, leaving his brow heavy, sloped, bare. Atavism: a being of the ancient type, born too late into this world. She wishes he repulsed her, but nothing will ever prickle like his stubble against her skin.

"I remember the first time I saw you," he mutters. "You did a number on me."

"Oh, Howie." Despite herself, she's sighing the words into his ear. She knows how it feels to be jealous: a smashed vase, a shattered mirror. She has violence in her too. *How can I want you so badly when I'm already in your arms?* How can she even think of leaving, when his body is still so warm? She tries to remember her reasons—Duncan Ripple V, the specter of years to come whittled away by addiction, even the sodden blanket of her grief—but none of them have the substance of Howie's arm on her back, his palm on her thigh. None of them, except two pint-sized kindlings with no substance at all: *You didn't wring our li'l necks. That was Sharkey!* She pulls back, drums her fingers on the table to hide the tremble in her hands. "You mustn't let me keep you from your work."

"Yeah. I'm gonna go make some chaw." Sharkey gets up, puts on his zoot jacket. Looks back at her over his shoulder. "You chew yet today?"

"I'll resist till afternoon, I think."

He smirks. "Have fun."

The moment he's gone, Swanny hurries into the shop. Her hours have been irregular of late; it's been more than a week since she came in this early in the day. She goes behind the counter, peers into the dark space beneath the register. There's the slingshot, waiting for her on the floorboards, as promised. She stashes it in her handbag, starts to leave the room—then goes behind the counter a second time and reaches for the jar labeled CORDIAL GOODBYE. Just a few mouthfuls for the road. She's giving it up forever, but forever can start a little later in the day.

She wraps herself in her chinchilla and, with pockets full of drug, proceeds outside and down the streets to her designated meeting place with Ripple.

"Wench, I have been in this dumpster all night. Couldn't you at least bring me a breakfast burrito or something?"

"You're a spoiled child," Swanny says, and bursts into tears.

"Hey, I'm just . . . kidding?"

"Don't touch me. It's bad enough for us to be seen walking the streets together."

"Swanny, wait up, seriously. Do you know how to tell if a rat bite's infected or not?"

The meat locker where Duluth lives is way out near Nick's, in a patch of Torchtown with no buildings left standing. Swanny steps over the broken bricks and charred cinder blocks into what remains of the butcher's basement: a concrete depression with a steel chamber occupying one-third. The deep freeze. She knocks at the entrance, two quick raps. If he doesn't answer, she'll—what? Turn around and go right back to the Chaw Shop?

But he does, the door opening with a refrigerator's suction smack so immediately it startles her. She sees the disappointment in his eyes and understands why. He thought the twins had come home.

"I have horrible news," she says. "May we step inside?"

~~~

"OK, keys, check, address, check." Moments earlier, the two of them watched Duluth, that mountain of a man, quake and crumble, mere words bringing more harm to him than blows ever could, his boys' names shifting the earth from beneath his feet until he could not stand. Swanny had expected a towering rage, threats of revenge, but instead Duluth could barely muster the energy to locate his keys before reclining with the side of his face pressed to the cold concrete floor. Swanny has become a destroyer of worlds; she detonated a human's hopes and life and family with a single sentence. But if Ripple's disturbed by the spectacle of grief they just witnessed, he's decided not to show it. "Let's get this show on the road. Swanny?"

"You go ahead. I forgot something back at the shop."

"You're going *back* there?!"

"I'll be two minutes, Duncan, there's no cause for hysterics."

"Um, not to question your judgment, fem, but you're wandering into serious jump-scare territory. What're you going to do if your psychotic sexmonger's there?"

"I'll tell him I was running an errand. And then I'll promptly leave again at the earliest opportunity."

"What's going on? Have you changed your mind?"

"No—no, of course not."

He scrutinizes her. "Look, I want to tell you something, but I don't want to piss you off."

"What?"

"When I crashed my HowFly in that garbage dump—you know, Hoover Island, where I met Abby—I didn't totally want to get rescued, you know? I was like, I'm getting a tan, I'm banging this fem (sorry) . . . it's all good, basically. Then Osmond swooped down in his HowLux, and boom, everything got fucked again."

"How is this supposed to comfort me, exactly?"

"Because I'm *glad* he showed up."

"Why?"

"Because I was lost."

"Thank you, Duncan. You have an uncanny ability to condescend and allude to your infidelity simultaneously."

"Swanny, hey, where are you going?"

"I told you, I'll meet you at the garage."

"How long should I wait?"

She doesn't turn around: "As long as you like."

Back on Scullery Lane, Swanny lets herself into the building, avoids the squeaky floorboard in the entryway, tilts her head to listen. But Sharkey isn't here. She'd be able to sense him if he were. She waits for a full minute, as still as a statue. If he walks in right now, what then? She could behave as if nothing has happened, reply airily and tranquilly to his queries, sit down to a late breakfast in the kitchen and ask him to read her the choicest passages from *SLAKE-LESS* over toast and tea—he reads her the loveliest poetry sometimes ("Teach not thy lips such scorn, for they were made / For kissing, lady, not for such contempt"). She could stay all afternoon. She could stay another night, another morning, stay until Duluth rallies enough to take his revenge or the dragons get them all. She could stay until Sharkey's pull on her weakens and this terrible feeling passes and she doesn't need him anymore. *Don't you trust me?*

She doesn't trust herself.

Swanny inhales sharply; her knees give, as if she's awakened poised on a precipice. It's been hours since she last chewed: her eyes burn, her jaw aches. She checks her watch, but it stopped weeks ago. The time is now. Swanny scales the stairs two at a time and patters back down carrying her klangflugel in its case. She goes out through the kitchen window, down the fire escape, and out the back alley.

Instrument in hand, she walks as briskly as she's able, but it still takes her nearly ten minutes to reach Sikes Way, another desolate lane near the southern Outer Wall. Normally, she never would notice the garage; it's a ramshackle structure crammed between two gutted storefronts, its red siding streaked with soot, its steel shutter door rolled down and marked with unreadable squiggles of graffiti and, of course, the omnipresent leggy snake. But today, something sets it apart.

Sharkey is waiting for her there.

He leans against the jamb, you couldn't say surprised. Sinister sorrowsworn deathlord, guardian of the underworld. He wasn't wearing his top hat when he left this morning, but he certainly is now.

"If you ever come back, I'll kill you."

Swanny can't stop her voice from quavering: "I know."

"Good." He spits on the ground. Walks away.

～～～

Sharkey walks alone. Sparkers and cocottes clear the sidewalk when they see him coming. Nobody bumps into him on the street, nobody meets his eye. Nobodies. And who's their king? Sharkey is, with only God upstairs to judge him. He used to like it this way. He considered his solitude a privilege, a sign of respect. Fear was a tool he could use. Loyalty, friendship, love—those were crutches that left you crippled when they fell away, and they always did. Or so he thought.

Turns out he was right.

I can't live without you, she told him once—not so romantic, if you think about it. Desire without alternatives isn't passion, it's weakness. But Sharkey makes his living off the weakness of others. He understands how deals are made. A deposed baroness is better than none at all. Swanny was worth more to him damaged, orphaned, addicted, with the lack he opened at her core. If you want to keep a swan in your pond, you have to break its wing with a croquet mallet; he read all about it in *Lifestyles of the Ostentatious*. She needed him, his chaw, his protection, even his touch: he made sure of that.

He tasted her blood. He took her past death and back again. Every pleasure he gave her was richer than life itself. But that wasn't enough. Not for her.

He had her, but he did not keep her long.

I can't live without you. Not so flattering, if you think about it, and it wasn't even true. Yet he'd kill to hear her say it, just one more time. It's him who's saying it now, over and over. *I can't, I can't.* He can see the future, but it doesn't matter anymore. She's already gone.

Sharkey turns onto Scullery Lane, under the shadow of wings. His luck's run out; he knew it would someday. Nobody's untorchable forever. If you have a heart, you can burn. And all animals have hearts.

He unchains his gator from the fire escape, kicks it in the tail. As it scuttles away down the sidewalk, the yellow dragon swoops low and ignites the Chaw Shop. Not just the roof: it hovers there for a full minute, blasting, till the whole building is engulfed. Dotting some final *i*. Flames flicker in the windows. Sharkey stands watching it for a long moment, the way the kindlings do. Then he climbs the steps up the stoop, lets himself inside.

Fireworks.

~~~

Ripple has never driven on land before, but the vehicle's controls are kinda like a HowFly's minus the vertical axis, so he figures it'll be OK—close enough. The inside of Sharkey's Magic Garage is an elevator, it turns out. Ripple exhales as it rumbles the limo down toward the underground parking lot below. Officially out of Torchtown.

"So where to?" he asks Swanny. "Your house out in Wonland, maybe?" He flips on the brights, steering the limo through the darkness, between the concrete posts that support the ceiling like ancient trees holding up the night sky.

"Black forest," she murmurs.

"What?"

"Nothing." The silence that follows is accompanied by a lapping, wettish sound.

"Wench, are you *chewing*?"

"This has been a very stressful afternoon."

"It's eleven a.m." Looks like this marriage thing is off to a great start. Again. "I can't fucking believe you risked our lives over a harpsaccordion."

"It's a klangflugel, you imbecile."

~~~~~

Up, up, up, far above the clouds. Abby has always loved to swim, loved the feeling of weightlessness, her gravity effortlessly receptive to the water's whims. But to soar—to scream across the sky, to thrust oneself in a single escalating assertion straight into God's kingdom of the sky, to lose oneself in the dizzy heavenblue reaches of the sky—she's never known a feeling like this before. Riding along in the HowLux was woozy and nightmarish, vertigo in motion, but this is a dream she can control. She remembers her fantasies back in the Fire Museum, the volcanic island of towering plants and untrod paths and caves aflutter with flying mice. It is as if she's entered the highest reaches of that world. She tries to grow used to it, but she cannot sit still.

A vulture appears at her window. Abby gapes at the beaky face, haggard and creased, familiar yet impossible.

—Cuyahoga? How did you find me?

—you're the one in my sky. how did you find me?

—It doesn't matter. I'm glad I did. How is your sister's brood?

—my sister's wing is healed now, but i will stay on for a time. there's nothing like the stench of the little ones' regurge.

Abby feels the pride in her words.

—I'm happy for you.

—and you—you've learned to fly.

—Kind of.

—have you come to talk to Them?

—How did you know?

The vulture flaps once, as if to shrug.

—when i saw you, i thought, she's come to talk to the big ones.

—Goodbye, Cuyahoga.

—goodbye.

The bird falls back, but the HowFly cruises on. The green dragon is no longer a speck in the distance. It drifts aimlessly, dead ahead, its back to her, its tail swaying leisurely, its wings extended, as tattered as sails left too long at sea, holding it aloft but doing little else. Abby has seen it before, but gliding along its side, she observes it perhaps more closely than anyone has previously survived to report. Beneath the barnacles and dried anemones, she sees the brittle scales, worn away in places to expose the rawhide flesh, or even grayish bone. She counts the creature's ribs, pressed starkly against this un-upholstered skin. She sees a talon that has become painfully ingrown, a weapon curled in upon itself. And as she cruises up to the dragon's face, she sees its snout, whiskered and frilled—the nostrils, which glow orange with each breath—and the eyes. Only the eyes surprise her. The eyes are shut.

—Hello?

And then they're open—violet eyes, electrified with streaks of silver. Twin globes, each three handspans wide. Trained on her.

—HCKXAVUEDQYGPOIWRSBFMJTLZN.

A truly unpronounceable name is not language. It is a roar, a cacophony in which every tone denies the others, every tone asserts itself and itself alone. The dragon cannot form this name as utterance; he can only inscribe it, brand it, in breath or fire or idea. The dissonance shears the air as he sounds out each letter aloud and with his mind simultaneously.

—ZXSAQWCVDEGTRBIYNFOLMJUKHP.

The HowFly rocks in the turbulence of his exhalations. The transmissions throb through Abby's brain. She feels zones of her gray matter lighting up: power surges to neighborhoods in the city of her mind. Neon letters glow searing bright and then explode.

—You wrote my name on the city. You called for me, and I came.

—GLOJDHSZVNXCFBUKAWMYEQRTPI.

The yellow dragon isn't even in sight; she is miles beneath them, down under the clouds. But at the green dragon's cry, she rises. Square-jawed and low-browed, she plows through the air the way a cowfish swims, her teeny limbs cycling like useless fins, her massive leathery wings doing all the work. Those wings: so much stronger than her brother's, scale-less, featherless, with a claw at the top of each, like a bat's thumb. Not lizard, not mammal. What code of transpositions and substitutions, duplications and omissions, wrote her into being? Her unknown glyphs, made flesh, are fearsome strange, the kind of asemic codex that human language dreams about.

—VNGEFKJMIBLQHXYZUCSRDPWOTA.
—UXZAPJGBKOTWFLEDIYMRNQCSVH.

Abby presses the heels of her hands hard into her ears, but the worst of the pressure is inside. The dragons' voices sync then syncopate, vibrations and reverberations merging into a single pulsing rush. Cascading failures black out whole realms of Abby's imagination and thought. It's all too much. Too Much.

—What do you want?!

The green dragon huffs once more, falls silent. The yellow dragon yawns cavernously. Blue flames flicker in the darkness past her uvula, her throat's pilot lights.

Amid the short circuits and showers of sparks that fill her, Abby senses with sudden relief, even ecstasy, that she is no longer alone. This is not the small weight of Scavenger stowing away in her gray matter. The dragons have connected to her, linked the vast machinery of their minds to hers, and as her own thoughts move, she feels theirs move in tandem. Though they are ancient creatures, primordial, byzantine and enormous, they are also incomplete: she sees that now. They do not have language. They do not reproduce. They have no predators; they have no prey. They exist outside of time at the very deepest level. The world is a womb to them, but they have stopped growing, and they have forgotten how to die.

No one else understands Them as she does. No one else understands Her.

—Will you come to my Island with me? Will you make me less alone?

—**LIMOENFUCAKTHJQZRGSYWDVBPX**.

—**EXUCYPMQFVJDGRSOBZTKWIHNLA**.

The dragons' words mean nothing, but Abby feels their truth to her core. Even together, they are alone. The sky is the only place for Them, and it is emptiness. The city will not wake up.

—I don't belong here either. But there must be somewhere in the world we can go. Some place for us. Brother. Sister. Won't you escape with me?

Abby already knows the answer. The dragons bring death to this place because they cannot live without it. They have imprinted on the city, on the voices of its machines; they feed on its electricity and breathe its emissions. They see in the city a creature like themselves, and they tether themselves to it with fire even as it dies. Her kind does not know how to stop loving, even when their love is terrible. Even when it destroys. The only way they will ever leave is if Empire Island rips itself from the Earth and lifts off from the sea, a reverse asteroid dripping with saltwater and heavy with the detritus of four hundred years of human lives, to show them the way. Until then, they will never leave, will never travel a greater distance from the place of their birth.

Their cords don't stretch that far.

—**POWQRITYDSKJLZUHFGEVXABCNM**.

—**YEAMSDRKHPTIVLFCZOBJXGNQWU**.

Abby can go anywhere, do anything. It is within her power. But the dragons are her kin. What would it mean, to wrench herself from this fusion? To be alone again, forever and always? She has always dreamt of impossible things. But even though the city still sleeps, she has finally woken up.

The lullaby overflows from Abby, floods into the dragons: a key, a spell, a pledge.

—*A b c d e f g, h i j k l m n o p, q r s, t u v, w x, y and z* . . .

Her name. Not garbled or jumbled. Not shuffled, truncated, or misremembered. Her name, a simple wisp of a melody, already dissipating up here among the clouds. The dragons still once more.

They are watching. They are waiting. She has answered their call at last.

Abby reaches for the controls.

She steers the HowFly down, from blue sky to blue waves. The sea above, the sea below. No amount of bailing can keep it at bay.

The HowFly noses down into the skin of the sea. Foam rushes against the windscreen, foam and then water, blue and gray and deep gray-green, and still Abby accelerates. Down, down. Beneath the first rush of effervescence, Nereid Bay is opaque and brackish, a Human Nature Preserve wholly submerged. Currents of pink protein solution once flowed here, but now the strange new DNA mixes with all the fluids of man and earth: sewage and seepage and runoff and rain, blood and tears and bathtub drain. Down below, resting on the ocean's floor, Abby can see dim outlines of sunken junk: barrels rusted to lace, rebar, skeletons with concrete boots, an ancient yacht on its side, dreaming.

—*A b c d e f g, h i j k l m n o p, q r s, t u v, w x, y and z* . . .

The windscreen cracks, a single fissure like a bolt across the sky, a stomp on a frozen lake. Abby straps herself into her seat. The HowFly wants to resist, her own body wants to resist, but she wills the throttle down.

The dragons dive into the bay just behind her, almost throw her off course with their tremendous splash. The HowFly bucks in the swell they make. She sees them in the rearview mirror, no longer discernibly yellow and green in the water's murk, just ancient forms in sepia, frilled and taloned, horned and winged, reaching for her.

Demons, angels of the deep. Bubbles pour from their snouts. Can they live underwater? Can they breathe here? She already knows that she cannot.

The windscreen cracks again. *That's God saying we can't be found.*

The HowFly slams into the seabed—foomph!—sending up a cloud of sand. For an instant, the windscreen is a web of cracks, and then there is no windscreen, only the water gushing in, as salty as her blood. Abby cannot see, but she can feel the dragons all around her, swimming, gliding, circling, circling. She thinks back to Hooligan's bird, the one neither of them could fix, its lament for all time: *Fly away, away.* Again, she sings the lullaby to soothe the dragons, make them stay.

—*A b c d e f g, h i j k l m n o p, q r s, t u v, w x, y and z . . .*

She sings it again and again as the air car fills with water, as the water fills her lungs. She sings it to the dragons, to Dunk, to the Lady, to God. A hymn for rats and vultures, for all the scavengers of this world. She sings it so it will be the last transmission she ever sends. She will not last for long, but the dragons will circle her forever if they can.

Her bones will speak.

Her bones will speak.

Her bones will sing her name.

33

THE ASCENT

In the hours after the dragons plunged back into the seas, the surface of the water bubbled like a cauldron, releasing into the air a thick, lingering miasma of yellow smog. The streets became impassably dim, sulfurous caverns forever branching but never leading to plain daylight and fresh air. Crabbed elderly Survivors crept onto their fire escapes to breathe lungfuls of toxicity, examine their withered hands, invisible a mere arm's length from the face. Lost dogs whimpered, truly lost now with the rancid scent muffling their olfactories. Pigeons, spooked, flapped up from the pavement, flurried in hurried circles and collided in midair, their skulls cracking together like Zero-G Snooker balls. A pizza delivery guy, marooned far from home and unable to read the street signs, paused in the intersection to eat a fortifying slice.

In the days after the dragons plunged back into the seas, the smog ebbed and dissipated, its presence a hangover from events hazily remembered. It was difficult, already, to believe that the dragons had tormented us for so long, that we had imagined eternity in the shadow of those wings. It was even more difficult to believe that they were gone for good. Scientists visited the city—new scientists, from new labs, impossibly young scientists who appeared to us as children dressed in lab coats, clear-eyed and pure-hearted and precociously serene, digging the beach with their toylike instruments, sounding echoes to the deep like unanswered prayers.

Here is what the scientists determined:

1. Citydwellers must never swim.
2. Citydwellers must never drink groundwater.
3. Citydwellers must report all prophetic dreams to a data collection center.
4. It is safe to live in the city.

In the weeks after the dragons plunged back into the seas, developers, those eternal optimists, bought up derelict properties, attended auctions for the air rights. It was a seller's market again, despite the soot and unscrubbable yellow scum, the one-eyed park dwellers, the Bird Ladies and Say-Somethings, the gutted husks of buildings that loomed in the middle of every block and the wrecking balls that rolled in noisily to dispatch them.

Without dragons to distract them or a single kingpin in control, the torchies got wise. Their scouts peeked from below manhole covers—stood with telescopes on the few unscorched roofs of Torchtown, ignoring constellations. Rival factions consolidated power, revved chain saws in their streets. Fresh tattoos spelled KEEP OUT and SQUATTERS RITES in blood and ink. The underbelly is always the most vulnerable part of the creature. They knew the walls were coming down. They wanted to be ready.

In the months after the dragons plunged back into the seas, we leveled Torchtown and commenced rebuilding our skyline from the ground up. Reported casualties were few, though we heard gunshots for days after the Outer Walls' demolition, out in the streets past our deadbolts and blackout curtains. Cage-wagons full of feral orphans and grizzled chaw-worn youths rumbled over the bridges, never to return. It filled us with regret but relief also, a monstrous birth we had survived with only minor hemorrhaging. Now, we reminded ourselves, was the time to heal.

And heal we did. How could we not? In the first year after the dragons plunged back into the seas, we broke ground on dozens of new building projects, whimsical and ambitious, daydream spire-domes like the shells of snails who feed at the secret hot vents of the sea, digital clock towers that chimed the names of corporations. Soil experts excavated the park. Shops opened to sell Powdered Zip, Sin Buns, drain cleaner—were joined by new stores selling vintage furs and candied seahorses and gleaming wearable technology from the East. Young girls dressed as if for bed in iridescent slips and silvery anklets. A gilded, many-piped gongflugel rose skyward on creaking ropes; windows opened to receive it. The neighborhoods were vibrant and emerging. The city had character.

It was as good a time as any to come into one's inheritance.

ACKNOWLEDGMENTS

I want to thank my phenomenal agent, Bill Clegg, who went above and beyond with reads, rereads, and reactions at every stage of the manuscript—without his incomparable insights and enthusiasm, my novel would never have found this final form or home. Everyone at the Clegg Agency has been so generous and engaged throughout the entire process: kudos to Chris Clemens, Marion Duvert, Henry Rabinowitz, and Simon Toop.

I'd also like to thank my editor, Lindsay Sagnette, for lending her pitch-perfect sense of pacing, character, and language to this project. It's been a treat to work with the whole team at Hogarth/Crown, especially Rose Fox, Nathan Roberson, Jillian Buckley, the publicity and marketing folks, and Michael Morris.

I owe an enormous debt of gratitude to Stephen Wright, whose visionary novels never cease to amaze and inspire, and in whose invaluable workshop at the 92nd Street Y so many of these chapters took shape. Hooray also for my terrific cohort from that class, especially Carol Prisant, Elena Sigman, Pierre Hauser, Leslie Margolis, Jon Gingerich, Patricia Kruger, and Zak Van Buren.

Much appreciation to Olena Jennings, Ryan Joe, Emily Mintz, Penn Genthner, Valerie Wetlaufer, Stephen Siegel & Nina Stern, Courtney Elizabeth Mauk & Eric Wolff, David Burr Gerrard, Daniel Villarreal, and Meredith Dumyahn for their various and sundry contributions to my world and to the world of this book. Hugs to the Taxier and McConnell families. And shout-outs to everyone in the NYC speculative fiction community, particularly Karen Heuler, Nicholas Kaufmann, and Jim Freund, for giving me the opportunity—and the confidence—to share pieces of this novel at readings when it was still just a work-in-progress.

I am immensely grateful to my parents, Deborah and Dale Smith; without their unyielding love and support I never would have taken on such an ambitious project, let alone finished it. And I consider myself very, very lucky to share my life and work with Eric Taxier (my first reader and partner in all things) and Wolfy (our little hooligan).

ABOUT THE AUTHOR

CHANDLER KLANG SMITH is a graduate of Bennington College and the creative writing MFA program at Columbia University. She lives in New York City.